Love Notes *for* Freddie

ALSO BY EVA RICE

Who's Who in Enid Blyton
The Lost Art of Keeping Secrets
The Misinterpretation of Tara Jupp

Love Notes *for* Freddie

EVA RICE

HERON
BOOKS

First published in Great Britain in 2015 by Heron Books
an imprint of

Quercus Publishing Ltd
Carmelite House
50 Victoria Embankment
London EC4Y 0DZ

An Hachette UK company

A CIP catalogue record for this book is available
from the British Library

HB ISBN 978 1 78206 448 0
ExTPB ISBN 978 1 78206 449 7
EBOOK ISBN 978 1 78206 450 3

This book is a work of fiction. Names, characters,
businesses, organizations, places and events portrayed in it,
are while at times based on historical figures and places,
the product of the author's imagination
or used fictitiously.

10 9 8 7 6 5 4 3 2 1

Typeset in Bembo by CC Book Production

Printed and bound in Great Britain by Clays Ltd, St Ives plc

To Pete

'What a charming boy! I like his hair so much!'

OSCAR WILDE, *The Importance of Being Earnest*

1

Marnie

I suppose I should start by saying that I was under Miss Crewe's spell from the moment she walked into the room, picked up a piece of chalk and scratched an isosceles triangle on to the blackboard. She had that effect on people – made all the more remarkable by her absolute blindness to her own power. She was a Grit, of course, but I didn't know that then. Just as I didn't know that *I* was a Grit until what happened one Saturday afternoon, late in the Easter term of 1969; but I am going too far ahead.

It was the first time Miss Crewe had spoken to me without the rest of the class listening in. All of us went up to her study individually to receive the results of our end-of-term maths exam, taken five days previously. I recall that Rachel went in just before me and returned within minutes, holding up her unfortunate papers, all slashed about with Miss Crewe's red biro. Even from the far side of the room I could see the column of crosses down the page, as though her work had been violated by some crazed lover, unable to leave just one kiss at the end of a letter. A languid, blonde, long-limbed rebel with a talent for painting abstract watercolours between punishments for sloppy prep, Rachel was hardly the sort to give a stuff. She ruled the school in between cigarette breaks.

'Bad luck!' called out Vanessa Simons, who was always sympathetic to beautiful people.

1

Rachel shrugged and floated across the room to her tuck box, from which she pulled out a half-eaten tin of peaches and a silver spoon – somewhat apt, as her family owned half of Hertfordshire. She flopped into the armchair next to the record player and ate.

'You're next,' she said, nodding at me between mouthfuls.

I put down my magazine and stood up, oddly light-headed. For modesty's sake, I pulled the lamb-to-the-slaughter face that seemed to be all the rage that day. Rachel looked at me and grinned, seeing through it.

'You'll be all right, FitzPatrick,' she said sardonically. 'You're the only one of us she hasn't got pinned as a complete imbecile.'

I shook my head in unconvincing objection, swung open the common-room door and walked towards Latimoore Wing, where Miss Crewe had her office, taking the short cut through the library, and – I might add – resisting the urge to skip. There was very little back then that made me happier than talking about maths, and I was quite happy to keep it that way. I knocked on the door of Miss Crewe's room.

'Come in, Marnie,' came the voice from inside.

I remember that I tripped slightly and stumbled into her study, as though I had been listening in at the door and she had opened it suddenly from the other side. I felt myself blushing scarlet – an intense pulse of faint-making heat that I loathed, and in loathing only made worse.

'Sorry,' I said.

I stood in front of her desk and she laughed.

'Sit down,' said she.

'Sorry,' I repeated idiotically.

'Nothing whatever to be sorry for,' observed Miss Crewe, picking up my paper. And her accent – soft, Canadian, cool – floored me as it always did.

She was wearing a tight, orange angora sweater, and her long red hair had been flung up in a careless topknot. No make-up, but no need for make-up. Just that perfect pale skin and those freckles and that big mouth from out of which had come so much that had kept me so happy that term. She was without question the most beautiful woman I knew; I could happily have sat staring at her staring at my papers until the bell rang at the end of the school day.

'Do you want to look at your result?' she asked. She sounded terribly serious. For a second I baulked.

'Did I fail?'

'No. No, quite the opposite. Heavens, no. You didn't fail, Marnie.'

'Oh, good. Thank goodness.'

'You didn't get anything wrong,' said Miss Crewe gently. 'One hundred per cent. No errors at all.'

I gasped – my hand clamped to my mouth to hide my cry of delight. I stared at Miss Crewe, seeing the thrill of my achievement in her eyes. She laughed – a sudden, girlish sound – and I laughed too.

'What do you mean, nothing wrong?' I whispered.

'See for yourself.'

I scanned my eyes down the pages, recalling the pleasure those two and a half hours of peaceful calculation had given me. A pen, full of black ink, forming numbers, symbols and letters on clean pages; infinitely more satisfying to me than any novel, any friendship, any boy.

'This one,' I said, pointing to question five with a shaking finger. 'I thought perhaps I had got this the wrong way round—'

'Ah, yes. A mistake made by every girl in your form,' said Miss Crewe. 'Except you.'

'And the end bit of question ten,' I said. 'I thought you might want to see more of my working out—'

'The fact that you didn't *need* to show any working out was almost worth an extra mark in itself.'

3

I laughed again. These few minutes were the stuff of fantasy for me: this knowing-it-all-ends-well retrospective of my paper with the only other person in the school who liked numbers as much as I did. I wanted to go through every answer on all four pages, to ask Miss Crewe whether she would have reached the same conclusions the same way, to know whether she would have chosen the same winding routes through each sum that I had, but I knew there was no moment for that. There was never any time for what I wanted back then, just little snapshots of happiness that only came from this.

'Mrs Carving says it's the first time in seventeen years that a girl has achieved such a mark in a maths exam at this level,' said Miss Crewe. 'You are to be congratulated, Marnie. I'm very pleased with you.'

I felt tears shooting into my eyes, unstoppable. Blindly, I reached into my regulation grey tunic and fumbled for a handkerchief (only white, please, no lace, no frills, must be clearly labelled, etc.) and blew my nose. Miss Crewe let me run on like this for a bit, blowing and snuffling – all the while saying in a low voice how this boded very well for the rest of my maths A-level course, and how she was looking forward to what the months to come held for me.

'Your parents will be delighted,' she said, smiling.

'Yes, perhaps they will,' I replied, unconvinced. I wished she hadn't mentioned them. Miss Crewe looked surprised.

'Perhaps? There should be no doubt about it.'

'Jukey doesn't really care about academic stuff.'

'Jukey?'

'My mother. We've always called her by her nickname. Her real name is Joanna but she's always been known as Jukey. Everyone calls her Jukey.'

Miss Crewe nodded briskly. I was giving away too much information, as usual.

'Well, you're home in two days for the holidays. I'll write a note telling them how well you've done. They need to be aware of your talent.'

Talent! A word I had until then only associated with the more determined members of the sixth-form drama group and those who had achieved grade eight on the flute by the age of fourteen. Miss Crewe picked up a pen and made a note next to my name.

'My stepfather thinks maths is a man's subject,' I blurted.

'Oh yes?'

'He'd prefer me to be studying the Romantic poets. He says keenness for numbers isn't right in a woman.'

I was dumping Howard right in it, and I didn't care.

'My father thought that dancing was for fools. Didn't stop me wanting to do it,' said Miss Crewe dryly. 'We're not living in the Dark Ages, Marnie.'

I grappled with what she was saying. 'Dancing? Miss Crewe, were you a dancer?'

She shook her head, as though irritated with herself – as though she had spoken someone else's lines without meaning to. 'Used to be,' she said. 'I wanted to be a dancer. Before I was a teacher. When I was young.'

'You're not old,' I cried. I desperately wanted more information, but Miss Crewe had a sudden agitation about her.

She picked up and put down a pile of papers, then coughed. 'The point is that you may as well do what you want to do, because . . . well, because what's the point, if you don't?'

She patted her hair and looked out of the window with sudden distraction, a habit that she normally reserved to pass the time while goons like Caroline Shriver were trying to solve the simplest equations on the blackboard.

'You've two brothers, haven't you, Marnie?' she asked.

'Yes. I've a twin, Caspar. And James is a bit older than us. He's just gone up to Oxford.'

'Are either of them as interested in maths as you are?'

5

'Gosh, no. Caspar's practically incapable of reciting his three times table, but he's the best looking, which probably counts for more than anything.'

Miss Crewe smiled at me. 'Don't kid yourself into presuming that, just because you're good with numbers, you can't have everything else. You *can*, you know, Marnie. Do you understand that?'

'No,' I said. 'I mean – yes.'

She turned back to her list now, frowning with concentration. I sensed my time was up.

'Marnie, please will you send Florence Dunbar in next?'

I nodded.

She looked at me. 'I may see you later,' she went on. 'It's the Lady Richmond Cup tonight, isn't it?'

'Yes, Miss Crewe.'

'You know, Marnie, of all the traditions that I was faced with when I arrived at this school, I think that struck me as the most bizarre. Members of the sixth form racing from one end of the pool to the other, in virtual darkness, holding lit candles and wearing nightdresses . . .'

'My brother says we should charge the locals to watch, and that we'd have all the money needed for the new Science Centre within three minutes of opening the gates.'

'He has a point,' agreed Miss Crewe.

I went red again; I was talking too much.

'Well, good luck to you, Marnie.' Miss Crewe nodded at me.

'Oh, I shan't win. I'm a hopeless swimmer.'

'I didn't mean the swimming. I meant everything else. You've got every chance of succeeding. You've proved to yourself – and to me – that you're capable of great things.'

'Yes, Miss Crewe,' I breathed.

I ran off to find Florence Dunbar, a lacrosse-playing dervish who was grinding her teeth in the common room in grim anticipation of her result, and then raced upstairs to the dorm. I had several hours before we had to meet up at the pool house for the Lady Richmond Cup. I couldn't face telling everyone my mark, and just for a while I wanted my own company, my own thoughts, unaffected by the admiration, jealousy or resentment of those around me. I wanted to dream for a bit, and nothing more.

2

Miss Crewe

I had always loved maths. It was trigonometry that had lit the fire for me, aged nine – the simple brilliance of all angles in a triangle adding up to 180 degrees. That fact remained constant, even if countries changed their names, or Shakespeare was proven to be a fraud. It was the elegance of number that appealed to me, the certainty of a right or wrong answer. The other subjects I had been plagued by at school – English literature with its tiresome emotional drainage system and endlessly flawed heroes, history with its bloodshed, lies and pomposity. These subjects could be scraped through because they had to be – because they were required. After my injury, I turned to maths. For me, it was the logical way out.

When I stopped dancing, my father persuaded me to take my teaching diploma and, despite my reluctance, I had to admit he was right to do so. It was a good way forward for me. I felt – rather as does the drowning man – as though, once I stopped resisting the pull, there was never any other option but to go with it, and once that decision was made, I gave myself up to it entirely. I liked teaching, and I was good at it, but bad at change. I stayed in my first job – a secondary school, called Lord Phillips, in Gloucestershire – for nearly ten years. It was the deputy head who had suggested that I should do something different and try out a private school.

I was offered the post of mathematics teacher at St Libby's on the eve of my thirty-fourth birthday – 4th March, 1962 – and took it lightly, without realizing the extent of my achievement; I later discovered that two hundred people had applied. Perhaps it was my lack of nerves that had got me through the interview with Bethany Slade and the board of governors. I had spent years going to dance auditions, and so sitting still and talking about maths for fifteen minutes was hardly a challenge. No one needed to see me at the barre; no one demanded that I walk into the room again, this time with my shoulders level. What did I say in the interview that persuaded them to take me on? I must have said that maths, to me, was the most fascinating of all disciplines, that I relished the prospect of helping young women to use the subject to help them in their lives when they left school. 'And I don't just mean adding up how much their husbands' spend at Aspreys,' I had said. I think that was the only time I saw Bethany Slade smile.

And so began my time. I walked into St Libby's determined not to be overwhelmed. I had read about the school – everyone knew it was the only educational establishment for girls that came close to Eton. I tried to keep a hold on my disapproval for the private sector, and told myself that it was to be nothing more than somewhere to rest until something better emerged; I was just visiting jail on the Monopoly board. I laugh at myself when I consider this now – how I had not bargained for the all-encompassing nature of what I was taking on, the sheer power that a school like St Libby's held.

And yet, for most of the students, this was as close to independence as they would ever get. When they left the school, they would become someone's wife, someone's mother, and they would be swallowed up, willingly, arms outstretched, because convention is a hard thing to kick against. Perhaps I had been swallowed up too. Perhaps you never know the moment it happens, the moment you lose that urge to be who you thought you could be. Perhaps it happens so slowly, so gently, as to be indistinguishable from wonder, from enchantment – but it happens all the same. It always does. Yet every term that started brought with it fresh hope. I might find the girl who could change the way I felt, who could overrule all of that.

I shared mathematical duties at St Libby's with another woman, Mrs June Carving, who had been at St Libby's for twenty-three years and was the main reason that many of the girls lost their faith in the subject, as she suffered from legendary dizzy spells that the girls took full advantage of. If she called in sick, I was hauled in to take her lessons, which was no real problem as, from the Michaelmas term of 1967, I had been employed as a housemistress to the sixth form and had moved from a small flat in Welwyn Garden City into the sixth-form house, within the grounds of the school. The house had been added to the school the year after I arrived, following the destruction of the old Sports Hall in a fire, which was started half an hour after a netball match against the local state school, West Park, had ended in their heavy defeat. Whether any West Park girl was responsible for what happened was never fully uncovered, but inevitably the St Libby's girls were the ones who came out of it a whole lot better off. A year after the fire, the new and improved Sports Hall was reopened, and with it a new sixth-form block that they named Kelp House after Juliet Kelp, the assistant drama teacher who had discovered the fire and dialled for the emergency services. As a final coda to this story, Miss Kelp ended up marrying the first fireman on the scene, which – as she repeatedly told us – shows you how good things can come from bad. No kidding. As Anne East, St Libby's head of art said, 'I'd have started it myself if I'd known what I could get out of it.'

As housemistress of Kelp, I lived with the girls. In the evenings and during the weekends, I was expected to be there for them whenever they needed me, which was most of the time. If I wasn't searching for someone's lost geography file, I was up a ladder changing a light bulb, sending thirty towels off to laundry, or discreetly removing posters of Keith Richards from the common-room walls before open day. I liked the girls, but it was necessary to keep

10

my distance from them. They all had a story to tell, but if you gave them an inch they took three miles, and I had been at the school for long enough to know that the most successful house staff were those who made the girls feel safe – not those who let them uncover all your secrets. Of course, the effect that this had is just the same as the effect that stepping back has on any relationship: the less they knew about my life, the more they wanted to know. Sometimes I would interrupt them as they stood around drinking their cocoa on Sunday nights, discussing the Holy Trinity of boys, clothes and music, and I would yearn to join in. I never could.

What fascinated most people about Marnie FitzPatrick was not what made her interesting to me. Of course, I knew about her family: her mother and Howard Tempest, her world famous actor of a stepfather. Marnie's twin brother, Caspar, had brought most girls in the sixth to their knees at Founder's Day by showing up wearing a pale yellow suit and dark glasses. But what drew me to Marnie was something quite apart from her family. She was a natural talent – someone who understood maths instinctively. She was one step ahead of me, most of the time, and at least ten ahead of the rest of the class. She had a killer instinct for numbers, and a desire to learn more. As a teacher, to be kept on your toes by your pupils is all you can ask for.

When I first arrived, the girls were drawn to me because my Canadian accent fooled them into considering me American. I remember an early conversation with Rachel Porter that put me very clearly in the picture.

RACHEL: Miss Crewe, you know, half the time, people knock
    on your door just to hear you say, 'Who is it?' from the
    other side. Everyone's in love with your voice.
ME: Don't be silly.
RACHEL: You're American. You ought to know that everyone
    round here is obsessed by the place.

11

ME: Your geography needs work, Rachel. I lived in *Canada* until I was twelve, which even you know is a different country entirely to the United States. They speak French where I grew up.

RACHEL: French! Well, that's just awful—

ME: Since I was eleven years old, I've lived in England most of the time.

RACHEL: Most of the time? Where were you the rest of the time?

ME: Nowhere that would interest you.

RACHEL: Oh, don't say that sort of thing. You may as well pretend you're from Hollywood and be done with it.

I didn't exactly pretend I was from Hollywood, but I took Rachel's advice. I let them think what they wanted to think. Everyone at St Libby's needed to dream. If it helped them to think that I was American and represented everything that they loved about the outside world, then so be it. It wasn't as if I hadn't spent most of my childhood with my head in the clouds too.

Even as a young girl, I always wanted more than anyone around me was capable of giving. From the moment I could walk, I wanted to dance. In Montreal, I used to watch a group of vaudeville dancers that performed to the accompaniment of a comical violin and a bashed-up cello every Saturday morning for two hours while the street market took place. My parents' apartment on the third storey of the market square meant that I could view the dancers from above without being noticed, and I came to know every flick of their fingers, every step they took, and I rehearsed the moves later, in the tight privacy of my bedroom, whispering the tunes they danced to under my breath.

One morning, my mother left me alone and went to visit a friend, and I bolted on to the street. Seeing me unable to keep still, one of the dancers spoke to me.

'*Voulez-vous essayer?*'

'*Je suis seulement a apprendre—*'

'*Allons. Essayer.*'

When I stopped dancing, half an hour later, the crowd started to clap, and that was that. The feeling burned in me from that moment onwards. And it wasn't the applause, the love, the attention, although I understood the power that all that held. It was the escape that it heralded. The open door.

Two years later, we moved to London, and my parents caught me sneaking out of my bedroom window in Chelsea, en route to a marijuana-filled dive in King's Road to watch people dance. I was just twelve years old. The row that my mother and I had that night could have drowned out the noise of the bombs overhead; she kept repeating the line about there being 'a bloody great big war on, in case you hadn't noticed', but that didn't stop me from wanting to get out. I was an invincible little pain in the neck, unafraid. That is the most extraordinary thing. It never occurred to me that I could be killed. Even when – in some cruel twist of fate – the club was bombed a week later, I didn't imagine that it was lucky I wasn't there. At least those inside had lived, had danced! As for my parents, they wouldn't be paying another penny towards something so flighty, so impractical, so *louche*. I would finish my exams in London – and, if I was still fixated on moving my body in ways that defied gravity and logic, then I was on my own.

When the war ended, and I had left school with good grades but no change of heart, I found myself a ballet teacher in the basement of a bombed-out church in Fulham. She must have been well into her sixties by then – a woman called Pat Samuels, who had danced with the Royal Ballet in her youth. An injury to her left knee had stopped a promising career in its tracks, and she had fallen in with the wrong crowd, marrying a man who was later arrested for murder and fraud and ended up in Wormwood Scrubs. Pat wasn't a likeable woman, but she encouraged my quiet rebellion against my parents with proclamations of doom about the industry, her favourite being, 'Every dancer is plagued by three things: their body, their body and their body.'

I would look at her without totally comprehending what she meant, as my body was pretty much on track to take me exactly where I wanted to go, thank you very much, but she was keen to get her message across.

'You take it for granted now,' she said, pulling open a packet of crisps with her teeth. 'Why not? It's not until it fails us that we realize what we had was more precious than everything we're running after in the first place.'

If she hadn't been such a good teacher, I would have turned her in to the police – she was most certainly a thief, and I had a strong hunch that she ran some sort of a hookers' racket when she wasn't bending girls like me into impossible positions at the barre. One afternoon, a girl showed up in the middle of my lesson, covered in blood. Horrified, I clapped a hand to my mouth and stared wide-eyed at Pat, waiting for her to do something.

'Clean yourself up, Hannah, for God's sake,' she said briskly. 'We don't want a mess all over the floor.'

Then she had looked at me.

'Well, come on then,' she said. 'From the top, and keep your shoulders level this time.'

I would have liked to talk to the girls at St Libby's about the past, about working my fingers to the bone, washing up seven days a week so that I could afford to pay for my dance lessons, or about my greatest pleasure in life being the enjoyment I got from books about numbers, but I knew that it was too dangerous. The girls shouldn't know too much or they would push too hard, want too much information, have too much power over me. I realized that keeping my distance meant they behaved in a way I could cope with. They could use me to fire off questions, they could ask for

14

my advice, but nothing that I said to them would ever begin with the words, 'When I was your age . . .' Let them believe that I had always been how I was now. It made it easier for me too.

The girls were convinced that Mr Alexander Hammond, who taught music and history and had been at the school for two years, was in love with me, and they wanted to believe that I felt the same way about him, despite all evidence to the contrary. It wasn't that I didn't like him, but I didn't like him in *that* way. Gosh, I didn't like anyone in that way.

Sometimes the girls came out with things that stuck with me for some time afterwards. I recall one such evening, when Rachel Porter and Araminta Clarke were finishing their prep in my study.

'Tom Mackerson's not writing to Laura Philips any longer, Miss Crewe. He said that he wants to get to know other girls,' Rachel had announced, leaning back on her chair and twiddling her pencil in her fingers.

'I'm sure she'll recover. Take a look at question three again, and see where you've gone wrong—'

'But she won't recover. That's just it. Does anyone? When you love someone that much? She may appear to be all right, but she won't be. She thinks Tom Mackerson is *the one*. How's she supposed to get over it?'

'I think I know what she's suffering from,' offered Araminta.

I put down my pen and sighed.

'What is she suffering from, Araminta?'

'It's the same thing that my sister's had since her fiancé ran off with his second cousin. My aunt calls it *POSH*.'

'Meaning?'

'Permanent Oppressive State of Heartache.'

'Thank you, Araminta. If you paid as much attention to algebraic fractions as you do to recalling idiotic acronyms, the world would be a better place.'

Araminta (an embryonic psychologist whose grandparents owned

15

eight theatres in London's West End) shrugged. 'Sometimes, when you give something a name, it makes it less terrifying,' she said patiently. 'I'm just naming her condition to help her.'

'Be that as it may—'

'You've been hurt, haven't you, Miss Crewe?' Rachel Porter spoke up again. 'That's why you never talk about boys—'

'Boys! Rachel, I'm not sixteen years old!'

'My mother says there's no such thing as men,' said Araminta. 'She says men are just boys with better reflexes. Pass me the protractor, Rachel.'

There was silence after this. Hell – the girl had a point. Araminta looked down at her work and giggled.

Rachel Porter was often like that. She had absolutely no qualms about talking to me as though I was one of the least shockable girls in the house. She knew, with the unreconstructed instinct of the terminally charming, that I would not land her in any trouble, that she was safe with me. Some evenings, she would stand at my door – half dressed for games, her lacrosse stick leaning up against the wall beside her – and just start talking, straight off, as though I knew exactly whom and what she was referring to at all times. She often showed me her artwork, of which – although she didn't admit it – I could tell she was very proud. Like my former dance teacher, Pat Samuels, she had an ability to imbue everything she said with a ring of authenticity as she swept over all topics, from politics (about which she knew nothing) to boys (about which she already knew too much.). She was well known for fixating on older men – the young Etonians that the other girls craved bored her. She had sat next to Marnie FitzPatrick's stepfather at lunch one Founder's Day, and had consequently developed a passionate – and very public – obsession with him.

'How do you sleep at night, FitzPatrick, knowing he's in the same house as you?' I had heard her asking Marnie on more than one occasion.

Marnie would squirm and usually someone would take pity and rescue her, but Rachel's words were still out there, irretrievable.

A few hours after I had seen the girls to give them their results, I found Rachel lurking outside my flat.

'Miss Crewe, do you know where Marnie is?' she asked me, peering into my room.

'Why do you need her?'

'She borrowed my Latin textbook. Mrs Westbrook's doing her nut about it.'

'I think she's in the dorm,' I said.

Rachel nodded and loped off.

'You know, Marnie did very well in her exam,' I called after her.

Rachel stopped and looked back at me.

'What kind of well?'

'Extremely.'

'No surprise there.'

'Just remember to congratulate her,' I added.

She rolled her eyes at me, as only she could.

'See you later,' I called to her departing back. 'Good luck in the Lady Richmond.'

'Sod that!' she said.

I pretended not to hear.

You could read an awful lot into everything at St Libby's – the whole place was awash with nods to those who had kept it going through thick and thin, and I could understand the need to carve names in wood in the chapel to show respect for those who had gone before – but the Lady Richmond Cup? I couldn't agree with Rachel more. I drew the line at that.

In fact, the symbolism of the event wasn't entirely lost on me – girls on the brink of becoming women, trying to keep the flame from a small candle from going out, ploughing their way through deep water, in the semi-darkness. Talk about shoving the metaphor

17

down your throat! The occasion had been initiated on the last Saturday of term in 1913, a year after the sinking of the *Titanic*, upon which the then headmistress had been drowned. The school records state that, *After a fine supper of eggs and ham, it was agreed that the twenty-one girls in Form Five should swim, in their nightclothes and holding candles, to recall the life of Lady Richmond whose life was lost aboard RMS* Titanic.

You had to hand it to the British upper classes – they had a supremely sinister sense of humour.

I needed to get out for a couple of hours. I picked up the papers and checked the theatre times. I knew exactly what I was going to do.

3

Marnie

So here's how it happened: Rachel found me upstairs. The dormitory, during the daytime, was a peculiar place. There were rows of silent, slender, brittle beds, interspersed with little tables covered in photographs of those we had left behind, looking far more glamorous and composed than they ever did when they turned up to collect their daughters from school. Lady Selina Williamson's parents on their wedding day grinned up at everyone who entered the room from the confines of a silver-edged frame. My brother always said that, when you're away at boarding school, you are kept alive by three things: oranges sliced into quarters, cold toast and fantasy. So what did it matter that Selina's father had vanished to Belgium with his secretary, leaving his marriage in tatters? Her parents would always be together in dorm four. At the beginning of the school year, a joke had started: so very regal did the Williamsons look that we had to acknowledge the picture with a bow or curtsy every time we walked into the room, as one does a single magpie. Not doing so would bring bad luck. It was a joke in bad taste, but it had stuck. As I walked in, I had muttered a greeting to them both, then flopped down on to my bed.

I lay there, my eyes closed, breathing in the smell of Dettol and nicotine; the school cleaners chain-smoked as they worked, sloshing green liquid into buckets and over every surface. The smell of smoke

19

clung to our uniforms. I allowed myself to drift off into a very happy daydream – that I had been accepted at Cambridge to study advanced maths. '*You are easily the most talented student I have encountered in all my years here,*' my tutor was telling me. '*You must*—'

I was interrupted by Rachel Porter – she of the peaches and silver spoon – clomping into the room.

'What are you doing up here all on your own?' she asked me. 'No – don't tell me. You're dreaming in numbers, aren't you, FitzPatrick?'

'You didn't curtsy to the Williamsons,' I said automatically.

'The Williamsons can bugger off.'

'It's bad luck,' I protested weakly.

'Oh, don't be such a banana, FitzPatrick. Have you got my Latin book?'

'I gave it to Kate Morrison to give back to you. Didn't she?'

I felt anxious; the cost of any missing books would be added to the bill at the end of term, and that never went down well with Howard and Jukey.

Rachel flopped on to the end of my bed and I sat up quickly. She was defiantly groovy, someone who wore the same school clothes as the rest of us, but made it look as though they had come off the rails of a cool boutique on the King's Road. It was well known that she had only ever wanted to be an artist, and believe me, she would have fitted just fine at Andy Warhol's Factory. She had danced with Mick Jagger at a party and talked all the time about the men she fantasized about – including my stepfather, which made me nervous as I imagined that he wouldn't need much encouragement to stray, were she ever to make her desire known to him. Rachel Porter wrote her own rules and didn't care what any of the rest of us thought about her, and I generally stayed out of her way, but she had a bit of a thing about me, probably influenced by her thumping great crush on Howard. Whenever we were alone, she would tell me how pretty I was – which always

20

threw me a bit – and said that, even though I was always studying numbers, I was actually a Grit in disguise. Ah – the Grits and the Doves; now *that* was a naming craze that had stuck. You were either one or the other, and your Dove-ness or Grit-ness was defined by such things as your behaviour: good (Doves) or bad (Grits); the music groups you liked: the Beatles (Doves) or the Rolling Stones (Grits); and whether you liked *Barbarella* (Grits) more than *Funny Girl* (Doves). You get the picture. Anyway, Rachel Porter was the biggest Grit of the lot and not someone I ever felt especially comfortable around.

'What did you get in your exam, then?' she demanded. 'Miss Crewe said I should come and ask you.'

I thought, If I don't give her any information, she'll go away and leave me alone. On the other hand, Rachel Porter had a magnetic personality, and everyone in the school knew it. So when she talked to you, she drew you in, and you couldn't help wanting to impress her. I laughed but said nothing.

'Your silence speaks volumes,' said Rachel, 'and is cause for celebration.'

She dug her hand into the pocket of her blazer and pulled out a bottle.

'Oh, gosh, Rachel. Don't.'

'Come on,' she said.

I looked at the bottle. I recognized it from home, and had seen my brother, Caspar, with similar bottles. 'Gin?'

'What else?'

'You know I don't drink. Especially not gin.'

'You don't? I always assumed that was just an affectation,' said Rachel. 'Why on earth don't you? It strikes me as a pretty high-minded attitude, FitzPatrick.'

'Why do you need to do it?'

'I don't know.' Suddenly Rachel looked serious. 'Tonight I think I rather hate myself for doing so badly in maths. So my reason for

21

drinking is quite the opposite of yours. You shall be drinking to celebrate, and I to escape.'

'Since when did you care about maths?'

I thought it was a reasonable enough question to someone whose idea of revision had been to watch the new Marlon Brando movie twice.

'Oh, don't misunderstand,' said Rachel. 'I really don't care about the exam itself. But I care about Miss Crewe. I don't know why. There's something about her – you know – something that makes me ashamed of myself for being so utterly hopeless in her subject. It's as if she can see the real me – not like my family, who don't really know who I am at all. Even my sister doesn't know me. She thinks I'm someone quite different to who I actually am. And, with Miss Crewe, I can't shake the feeling that, once upon a time, she was the biggest Grit of them all.'

'You're not hopeless at maths, you just don't work.'

'I think that about you too, FitzPatrick,' she went on, ignoring my remark and unscrewing the lid of the gin. 'You're a Grit in Dove's clothing, you know. I think you're more than they all think you are. There's unseen danger in you.'

'I'm no Grit,' I said.

'You are, and you always have been. Only you're a maths prodigy, and you make no effort with your hair, so that disguises your Gritness. But that's what you are, make no mistake. One day a boy will realize it too.'

'A boy?' I laughed nervously. 'One thing I can tell you for sure is that no boy will *ever* look at me in the way that they look at you.'

'Of course not,' said Rachel patiently. 'That's because they look at me and they think they might be in with a chance of getting what they want. There's huge appeal in that.' She sighed and looked down at her feet.

I pulled on my shoes. Rachel drank straight from the bottle, her eyes closed. Grimacing, she swallowed, grinned and held it out to me.

What it was that made me take it, I can't say. Some reckless certainty, perhaps, that, whatever I did now, I was all right – because I had exceeded even Miss Crewe's expectations, because Rachel Porter was paying me attention, calling me a Grit – I don't know. All I recollect is that suddenly I felt invincible. As I took the gin from her, Rachel could barely hide her astonishment, which spurred me on even further. I gulped quickly – and handed it back. I snorted with laughter.

'Gosh,' I said. 'That's strong stuff.'

'Only the best,' said Rachel, without taking her eyes from my face. 'You ever kissed a boy, FitzPatrick?' she said.

'No,' I said. 'Not really.'

'Well, in my view, you have, or you haven't.'

'What if they've kissed you, but you didn't want to kiss them back, so you just ran off?'

Rachel laughed very loudly. 'Who was he?'

She gave me the bottle again and I whizzed back another slug of gin.

'A friend of my brother's. Oliver Wishall. He came to stay, and said he liked me. He was nice. You know, nice looking and everything. I just didn't want to kiss him. Not then, anyway.'

Rachel sighed thoughtfully. 'What would it take, then? What would it take to get you?'

'I don't like the good-looking ones.' I felt entirely displaced, unsure of where this was going. 'I expect I'll know when it happens. I think he'll be different. I like the ones who are different.'

'I used to think like you,' she said. 'Then I realized that the ones who are different are just as clueless as the rest. I'd cut to the chase and go for the handsome ones, if I were you.'

'They wouldn't talk to me,' I said.

'Possibly not,' she agreed, deadly serious. 'Most boys are too dense to appreciate the potential in someone like you. But you may as well aim high.'

A girl called Polly Maynard came into the dorm looking for a hockey stick. For reasons that the poor girl couldn't understand, Rachel and I found this extremely funny.

'What's wrong with you two?' muttered Polly, nodding quickly at the Williamsons, then lying on the floor and peering under her bed. She stood up and straightened her back. Seeing the bottle of gin that Rachel had made no effort to hide, she froze. 'You'll be killed if anyone knows you've been drinking,' she said. She looked from Rachel to me in confusion – the combination of the two of us in cahoots was clearly difficult to comprehend – and clomped out of the room.

'Why don't we go to the theatre?' said Rachel suddenly. 'We could catch a matinee in town and still be back in time for the Lady Richmond.'

'Don't be daft,' I said.

'I'm not. They're just a bunch of amateurs but it could be fun.'

'What's on?'

'*The Pajama Game.*'

'Don't be silly,' I said.

'What's silly about the theatre? And you whose father is an actor, for crying out loud!'

'Stepfather.'

'All right, *step*father.' She sighed. 'You know I've never forgotten sitting next to him at Founder's Day, FitzPatrick.'

'I know.'

'He was completely –' she fished around for the word – 'hypnotizing.'

'I bet he was. He would have loved you. Howard finds something to love in every single woman he meets. I imagine sitting next to you was a dream for him. Gosh, is it normal to feel this dizzy on this stuff?'

24

Rachel didn't dignify my question with an answer, but went back to her previous theme.

'Well, come on. Are you coming with me to the theatre or not?'

The gin was washing into every part of me now. Why hadn't anyone given me this before? Goodness, it was some anaesthetic.

I took a deep breath. 'All right,' I said. 'I'll come with you.'

Rachel stared at me in surprise, and recomposed herself quickly.

'Come on then. We'll be back in time for the Lady Richmond,' she reassured me again.

'Here's to the sinking of RMS *Titanic* and all who went down with her!' I said.

'Aye aye,' said Rachel, saluting. 'And while we're out, you never know, we might find you someone.'

'What do you mean?'

'A boy. We might find you a boy.'

'I don't want a boy,' I mumbled.

'Yes, you do. Only you don't know it yet. Come on. I'll meet you downstairs, outside Quarry Hall in five minutes.'

Walking out of the school gates felt dangerous to me, the world around me uneven, every blade of grass seeming shocked at our appearance outside the grounds. Rachel linked her arm through mine.

'No one's even going to know we're not at school,' she said.

'But they'll be taking the register and checking everyone after lunch,' I pointed out. 'We'll have to get back soon—'

'Florence Dunbar,' said Rachel firmly.

'What about her?'

'She always covers for me. We have an arrangement.'

I stopped in my tracks and stared at Rachel. 'What do you mean?'

'I mean that I pay her to come up with excuses for me. It's a copper-bottomed system I've had in place since the start of the lower fifth.'

'How does that work?' I asked. We were heading towards the bus stop now. Rachel's long legs necessitated my jogging along beside her to keep up.

'Florence has a five-minute rule. She shows up at the event — netball match, lecture, chapel, whatever. As soon as she realizes that I'm not there, she puts in place a series of excuses that keep me out of trouble.'

'Like last Friday,' I said slowly. 'She told Miss Alderney that you had been excused double games due to an ankle injury. She even handed her a note from Sister Harlowe — I saw it!'

Rachel nodded. 'Oh, she's good,' she said sagely. 'And what makes it nice is that she enjoys it so much. And no one would ever question Florence, would they?'

'You seem terribly confident about it,' I said. 'But I don't think Florence thinks too much of me.'

'No, but she thinks a great deal of *me*, for some unfathomable reason, and what I ask gets done. I just left her a note telling her to include you in her plans.'

I must have looked doubtful because Rachel said, 'All right? Don't worry so much. Come on — if we run, we'll make the bus into town. We can jump out just before the cinema.'

'How many times have you done this?' I asked her.

'Ten, eleven, perhaps,' said Rachel, shrugging. 'Not many. Come on, I'll pay.'

We boarded the bus into town, which made me feel — at that time of day, when we should have been at school — as though we could be shot down in flames at any second. The places that were familiar to me during the holidays looked strange through the lens of a St Libby's girl playing truant; the prim, ordered rows of shops seemed reticent and tentative when set against the blatant drama of what we were doing.

'You're all right,' said Rachel, reading my mind. 'We're hardly in Spanish Harlem.'

'When were you in Spain?'

'Oh, very funny, FitzPatrick.'

The point she was making was sound – that a place like WGC – a town constructed entirely from philanthropic dreams in the 1920s – was a pretty safe bet for anyone; we weren't going to get kidnapped here. If we wanted trouble, we could certainly find it, but it wasn't the sort of place where trouble came looking for you. Down Bridge Road we went, past the Welwyn Department Stores and towards the cinema. The Shredded Wheat factory with its vast silos – a building that held the livelihood of so many people in the town – stretched up ahead of us.

'You ever seen inside?' Rachel asked me, staring at it.

I shook my head.

'Me neither.'

At the next stop, Rachel nodded and nudged me as a boy of about our age, dressed in blue overalls, walked past us to the back of the bus. The driver lurched the bus back into action, and the boy lost his balance for a moment and, in doing so, dropped a bag on to the floor of the bus, out of which spilled several records. He bent down to retrieve them; I noticed there were holes in the soles of his shoes. Stepping out of my seat, I picked up two 45s that had slipped out of their sleeves and handed them to him.

'Thanks,' he muttered.

'I like the Rolling Stones too,' I heard myself saying.

'They're all right,' he said, sitting down on the back seat. He looked out of the window.

'Nice,' said Rachel, snorting with laughter as I lurched back to my seat. 'You see what I mean? You're a Grit.'

'I just helped him pick up his records; it was hardly anything important.'

'That's how everything starts,' said Rachel.

Even high on gin, I wished that she would shut up. Turning

around in my seat, I saw the boy glance over at us, but I don't think that he saw us at all. His eyes were far away.

We were off the bus and almost outside the theatre when we saw her in front of us. She stopped outside and glanced up at the awning. I would have known the back of Miss Crewe's hair any-where – even when it was worn long, not piled on top of her head as was her custom at school. I stopped dead and pulled at Rachel's arm.

'Miss Crewe.'

'Shit,' said Rachel.

We dived into the shadows, waiting to see if she would walk on, but she didn't.

'Must be waiting for someone,' hissed Rachel.

Miss Crewe was wearing a long, grey coat, and she seemed to be alone. Thinking about it, she was one of those people who always seemed to be alone.

'Shouldn't she be at school?' I whispered. 'I thought she would be helping to prepare for the Lady Rich.'

We watched as she stopped, took something out of the bag she always carried – a handkerchief – and blew her nose.

'Still waters run deep,' said Rachel quietly, not taking her eyes from Miss Crewe. Rachel was the sort of person who got away with saying this and even made it sound profound. If I had said it, I would have been mocked into the next week.

'I feel like we're spying,' I said.

'Well, that's because we are,' whispered Rachel.

Miss Crewe pulled her bag back over her shoulder and walked into the building.

'We can't go in there now,' I said. 'She'll see us.'

Rachel tutted with irritation. 'I know,' she said. 'It's too risky, even for me.' She sighed. 'Perhaps we should go back to school.'

I felt detached from my body, a spinning head watching from

above. I had scored top marks in my exam! I could do anything I wanted!

'I've walked out of the school grounds illegally for the first time in my life! We're *not* going back to school now,' I said.

Rachel looked at me with something verging on respect. 'All right,' she said. 'Where to, then?'

'Well, neither of us has ever been inside the factory,' I said.

Rachel didn't reply, but she lit two cigarettes and, handing one to me, took a long drag from the other.

'I don't smoke,' I said.

'You really are horribly middle class, FitzPatrick.'

I took the cigarette.

'Well, come on then,' said Rachel.

We linked arms and sang – songs from years earlier, songs from America that Jukey loved – the Everly Brothers, Elvis, Bob Dylan. Rachel's voice was high and piercing and always fractionally off the note, but she sang with such confidence that it didn't matter. Perhaps that's the answer, I thought, tripping down the road with her. Perhaps the answer to everything in life was simply to do it as if you were great at it – then people would believe you.

'Gosh, it's hot,' said Rachel.

She pulled off her cloak, and then her jumper, and pushed down her socks. Then she pulled a rubber band out of her pocket and scraped her hair off her face and into a bun on top of her head. Without that mass of hair, she became much more ordinary looking, and I liked her more for it. Yet, after today, would Rachel Porter be my friend again? Would I be relegated back down with the other Doves, the other girls who didn't know one end of a cigarette from the other?

I saw the boy from the bus quite suddenly. We were almost outside the factory when he appeared from a side street, cutting in front of us and striding with a purpose in his gait that we were entirely lacking.

29

Rachel nudged me in the ribs.

'Hey!' she said. 'It's him!'

For some reason, I felt as though I had known all along that we would see him again.

'He must work here,' I said.

'Thanks for that, Sherlock,' said Rachel. 'Now. Shall we go and talk to him?'

'No! What would we say? Don't be an . . .'

But Rachel Porter was already off, breaking into a run. I could only watch, part horrified, part thrilled. I think that was how everyone felt when they were around Rachel Porter. She was like Milly-Molly-Mandy on Benzedrine.

'Hey!' she called.

He didn't stop.

'*Hey!*' she called again.

This time he glanced behind him, his eyes wide with surprise.

'Yes?' he said.

'Do you have the time?' asked Rachel.

He frowned, and looked at Rachel's wrist, at the Cartier watch her father had given her for her last birthday.

'No,' he said, 'but you do.'

He walked on again.

'My friend and I just wanted to say that we like your hair,' called Rachel.

He stopped again, and looked at her in confusion, and then he laughed and walked on once more, looking down at his feet.

'Rachel!' I called out desperately. 'Don't—'

'My grandmother used to say that you should never waste the chance to tell someone their hair looks good,' went on Rachel, striding after him. 'So that's why we're telling you.'

He stopped again and looked at Rachel with deep suspicion.

'Who's your grandmother?' he asked. 'Doris Day?'

'I wish,' said Rachel with feeling.

He had stopped outside the factory door now and was riffling through a large set of keys.

'What are you doing?' Rachel asked him.

'I'm working,' he said.

'What do you do?' she persisted. 'Inside the factory, I mean? What do you do here?'

'We make cereal.'

'I know *that*. I meant, what do *you* do.'

He found the key he was looking for and slotted it into the door.

'The electrics,' he said. 'I do the electrics.'

'That must be interesting.'

He made a noise to suggest otherwise.

I had edged a little further forward now, spurred on by the gin, but still I was a mere onlooker.

'I'm Rachel.' She gestured behind her to where I was lurking. 'This is Marnie.'

He bit his lip and looked at me properly for the first time. His face was quite in shadow, and his hair covered his eyes. He clocked our uniform.

'St Libby's?' he said. 'I didn't think they let you out much.'

'They don't,' said Rachel.

'We shouldn't be out at the moment,' I said, and immediately regretted it.

'Ooh!' he said.

I detected the sarcasm and blushed like a fool.

'We ditched school this afternoon because we wanted to go to the theatre,' said Rachel. '*The Pajama Game*.'

'Don't bother,' he said.

'You've seen it?'

He said nothing.

'Do you have a smoke?' asked Rachel.

'Are you drunk?' he asked.

'Not at all,' said Rachel crisply. 'Are we, Marnie? Look, can we come in? Have a look around for a minute?'

'Why?' he asked.

'Oh, I don't know. Just because we'd like to.'

'I have to get on,' he muttered.

'Are you always here?' she persisted. 'Every Saturday, I mean? Can we come back and see you next weekend?'

'I'm here every day except for Sundays,' he said. 'That's the whole idea behind having a job. You clock in, you work, you clock out, you repeat it all over again for forty years or so. Not that I imagine any of that will ever concern you,' he added.

He wasn't amused by Rachel, I realized, surprised. This wasn't flirting – he wanted her out of the way.

'I work,' said Rachel unrepentantly. 'Who are you to judge me, anyway? And Marnie's going to be a famous mathematician one day.' This non sequitur was greeted with a snort of laughter.

'Rachel!' I said desperately.

'We shall come back and find you,' said Rachel, 'and beg you to let us into your factory of secrets.'

'This is not a factory of secrets.'

'Well, how do we know that it's just good old Shredded Wheat biscuits that come out of here? For all we know, you could be running a diamond-smuggling ring in there—'

'Pillows,' he said.

'What?' said Rachel.

'They're called pillows, not biscuits.'

He pushed open the factory door, grinned at us briefly, and shut it behind him. That was that. He was inside, and we were outside.

Rachel collapsed into laughter. The gin was having quite the opposite effect on me – I wanted to break down and cry, punching my fists into the ground for being so idiotic.

'Pillows!' howled Rachel.

'Why did you have to tell him about my maths?' I asked Rachel, as we tripped back over Hunters Bridge.

'Oh, shush, Marnie. As if you're ever going to see him again. Except –' she looked at me carefully – 'except that you've fallen in love with him, of course. Oh, dear God! Was he *different* enough for you?'

'I'm not in love with him!' I said. But even as I spoke, I felt the events of the past five minutes moving swiftly into hallowed territory. Was this what gin did to you? 'He certainly didn't love us,' I said.

'I know,' she agreed. 'Funny, that. I mean – we're girls. He's probably bent.'

No, I thought. He was just better than us, that was all. He was a worker; he was part of the world, not standing on the edge of it, like me.

When we got back to school, I was still dazed from our encounter with the boy from the bus. Like a gambler on a winning streak, I couldn't stop myself. Some sort of Today I Am Invincible streak was overwhelming me, and I didn't want Rachel to walk away from me, back to Florence Dunbar and the rest of the Grits, leaving me alone. I wanted her by my side, making things happen, calling the shots, calling out to boys.

Everyone was running around preparing for the Lady Richmond Cup. We clomped up the stairs to the dorm, which was still deserted. Evidence of the other girls was everywhere – clothes had been removed and swimming costumes put on – I could see piles of uniform and discarded socks scattered on every bed. I didn't want any of this any more. I wasn't ready to break the spell – not yet.

'Shall we have another drink?' I heard myself asking Rachel.

She was too cool to look surprised.

'I thought you would never ask, FitzPatrick,' she said. 'Meet me in the bathroom in two minutes.'

Half an hour later, and Rachel and I were wiped out. The door of dorm four opened and Rachel's younger sister, Tamsin, came into the room.

'Nod to the Williamsons!' I bleated, turning to face Tamsin.

'Who?'

'Forget it,' said Rachel.

Tamsin looked uncomfortable, as well she might. Younger girls were not allowed in Kelp House.

'I just came over to tell you that I've got permission from Miss Elsley to watch the Lady Rich. I can come and see you swimming!'

'Ah. Slight change of plan, darling Tam. I'm not doing it.'

'What do you mean? You have to! It's your year! And it's not that cold!'

'I can't do it. Go on, run along now, darling. We're not feeling well.'

Tamsin looked at me. 'What's wrong?'

'Nothing at all,' I said. I stood up, feeling the floor swaying beneath my feet. I cleared my throat to make my next announcement. 'I'm certainly going to swim!'

'Oh, don't listen to Marnie. She's just overexcited because she's spoken to a boy for the first time,' said Rachel.

'A boy?' said Tamsin.

'We've just come back from town,' said Rachel without contrition.

'What do you mean?' Her sister's eyes widened.

'I mean, we've been *out*. We're not in a fit state to be swimming.'

Tamsin looked too astounded to speak.

I laughed. 'I can't believe what you're saying! You of all people, Rachel Porter! I am in a *perfectly* fit state and I shall swim. Come on, Tamsin, you can cheer me on instead.'

Rachel stood up. I looked at her. She had drunk much more than me, there was high colour in her cheeks and, even in the mess that I was in, I could see that her eyes were rolling around in her head.

Tamsin looked alarmed. 'You don't look well,' she said. 'What happened in town? I don't understand.'

I thought she might cry. The lower years cried quite a lot.

'Shall I get Sister Harlowe?' she asked.

'No!' I heard myself shouting. 'We are swimming. Come on, Porter. Get your costume. We can do it. We're going to *win* this thing.'

Rachel exploded into hysterical laughter.

And that, to be perfectly truthful, is the last thing I can recall from that day with any clarity at all.

4

Miss Crewe

As housemistress of Kelp, I should have known what was going on earlier. As it happened, I was summoned to the sickbay at eight o'clock the next morning. The place smelled of disinfectant and drains.

'I've just woken them, Miss Crewe,' said Sister Harlowe, a woman of few words who had – according to St Libby's folklore – murdered her own brother-in-law.

'I had no idea that this had happened,' I said. 'Why didn't anyone telephone me last night?'

'Couldn't raise you,' said Sister Harlowe smugly. 'I heard from Alexander Hammond that you were at the theatre?'

'I had the afternoon off.'

'Funny thing, to miss the Lady Rich.'

'Is it? I would have considered attending it while not on duty to be far more strange.'

'I've always enjoyed the event,' persisted Sister Harlowe. 'I like tradition.'

Marnie was lying in bed, staring at a poster of a girl in the Brownies uniform accepting a sugar lump in return for immunity to polio. I could see Rachel in the bed opposite, motionless. Marnie sat up, and Sister Harlowe was next to her, brandishing a cardboard kidney-shaped bowl.

'Don't expect there's anything left to come up now,' she said, sticking it under her chin.

'Why am I here?' whispered Marnie.

'Hark! It speaks!' said Sister Harlowe grimly.

'Did I faint?' she asked. 'The Lady Richmond Cup . . .' She turned and saw me. 'Oh, Miss Crewe.'

'Marnie, what on earth happened?'

My first instinct was to run to the child, to comfort her. She looked about twelve years old.

'Mrs Slade will be over here in –' Sister Harlowe glanced at her upside-down nurse's watch – 'fifteen minutes. I think I'll leave the explanations to her. Miss Crewe, I suggest you do the same.'

Rachel sat up suddenly. 'Good morning!' she said, seeing Marnie.

We all turned and looked at her. She gave us a watery smile, and was promptly sick. Sister Harlowe pursed her lips with a little smile.

'I'll need clean sheets,' she said, striding out of the room.

Rachel flopped back down on the bed. 'FitzPatrick,' she said, 'you're the one with the brains. Got any clue how you're going to get us out of this? For some reason, my mind has gone completely blank.'

'Mine too,' Marnie said.

'I know one thing,' said Rachel. 'We wrecked the race.' She looked at me. 'You weren't there, were you, Miss Crewe? Very sensible, I say.'

'How do you know I wasn't there?' I asked her sharply.

Rachel didn't reply, but turned to Marnie with some effort. 'Argh! My head. You nearly drowned.'

'I did?' whispered Marnie. 'I *did*,' she repeated.

'Mr Hammond had to jump in and pull you out. You sank like a stone.'

'*Mr Hammond?* I don't believe you!'

Rachel smiled at her sympathetically. 'Yeah. What lengths we go to for a man's touch. Oh, God! I think I'm going to be sick again—'

I offered her the bowl, but Rachel merely leaned forward and closed her eyes, opened them again and grinned at me.

'I remember the first time I drank too much,' she said. 'You know, it almost put me off forever.'

'What's going to happen to us?' asked Marnie.

'They might chuck me out,' said Rachel. 'I'm not so sure about you, FitzPatrick. I think you'll pull through. I'll take the flack, don't worry.'

'But what was I thinking?' Marnie asked her. 'I think I was the one who got us into all of this. It was *me*, Rachel.'

'To be fair to you, we did laugh a lot. Before it all went wrong.'

'But I—'

The headmistress didn't bother to knock. Rachel actually managed to stand up when she came in, but her eyes could scarcely focus. Marnie looked as though she might black out.

'Girls,' said Mrs Slade, nodding. 'Miss Crewe.'

'Morning,' I said.

'Good morning, Mrs Slade,' said Rachel.

She walked over to the window and opened it wide. 'Fresh air,' she said crisply.

She turned around and faced the girls.

'Miss Porter, Miss FitzPatrick, you know that we don't tolerate alcohol at St Elizabeth's. What possessed the two of you to behave in such an irresponsible and infantile fashion yesterday evening?'

She was genuinely amazed, I thought.

'It was my fault,' said Rachel at once. 'Please, Mrs Slade, if there's one thing you take from this, then let it be that. Marnie – Miss FitzPatrick – had nothing to do with it.'

'Am I to believe that you forced alcohol down her throat, Rachel?'

'Practically. She's never drunk before. She didn't know what she was doing.'

'I *did*!'

I looked at Marnie in surprise.

'I did,' she repeated. 'I knew exactly what I was doing. Rachel didn't force me into anything.'

Rachel rolled her eyes at Marnie.

Mrs Slade folded her arms and shook her head. 'You both could have drowned. Do you have the slightest idea how serious this is? Drinking on any night is ill advised at best. But drinking on the same evening that you are to be in the swimming pool with so many other girls is downright dangerous. Do you realize how long the Lady Richmond Cup has been a part of the fabric of this school? It started in 1913. That's . . . That's –' she stopped briefly – 'fifty-five years. Do you understand that?'

I could hardly bear the miscalculation. Neither, it seemed, could Marnie.

'I think that makes fifty-six years, actually, Mrs Slade,' she said in a small voice.

Rachel stifled a giggle. She was unbelievable.

'I wasn't trying to be funny,' Marnie wailed in her direction.

'I know,' she said. 'That's what makes it even funnier.'

'You two are digging yourselves into a very deep hole indeed,' said Mrs Slade.

'She'd just got her maths results,' said Rachel, flinging an arm towards Marnie. 'She got everything right. No one's ever—'

'I am aware that Miss FitzPatrick's result was exceptional,' snapped Mrs Slade. 'It makes this whole grim situation all the more regrettable. You have let Miss Crewe down in fine style, I must say.'

'Yes, you have, Marnie,' I said. I couldn't help it, even though I hated myself for it.

'Marnie wanted to celebrate,' said Rachel. 'She just didn't know when she'd gone too far. She's not used to alcohol, you see.'

'Oh, and you are, I suppose?' I asked her.

Rachel could be so infuriating. It took all of my self-control not to walk over to where she was standing and shake her. She had walked right into that one.

'Oh, I'm allowed to drink at home,' she said patiently. 'My father practically insists on it when we have guests. Anyway, we lost track of time, and how much we'd knocked back. Oh, Mrs Slade, please don't expel us. At least, don't expel Marnie. She's too clever to throw out. It was a simple mistake, that's all. No harm done.'

'But for the grace of God was there "no harm done", as you put it,' said Mrs Slade. 'There could have been harm done. Very real harm. I am astounded by such reckless behaviour.'

She carried on in this vein for some time. I felt my hip spasm with pain, as it always did when I was uncomfortable. I turned away from the scene, looking out of the window and seeing the protagonists' reflections. How would I direct this scene if it were a dance number? I thought. Marnie and Rachel would start on their beds, then move to the middle of the room, arms stretched out. Two steps forward, hands moving outwards – *ta cha! Ta cha!* – then a raised arm from Mrs Slade – *schooom!* In another universe, it was happening like this. In another universe, everything happened like this . . .

'. . . isn't it, Miss Crewe?' Mrs Slade cut into my routine.

I cleared my throat. 'I'm sorry?'

'I said that it is policy to inform parents of events like this immediately.'

'They should know,' I said. 'Perhaps that's the best idea, Mrs Slade. Leave the parents to find a punishment for the girls. The holidays are nearly here, of course . . .'

I was grasping at straws now. I knew what was coming.

'Miss Crewe's right,' said Rachel. 'It is almost the end of term. Couldn't you just set us a punishment for the holidays – you know, writing lines or learning poems or something – and we'll promise never to do it again? I have most certainly learned my lesson, Mrs Slade. Next term, we'll be good as gold. You won't hear a peep from us.'

'Well, you're certainly right on that front, Miss Porter,' said Mrs

Slade. 'We won't hear a peep from you because neither of you will be coming back to this school next term.'

'What?' wailed Rachel and Marnie in unison.

'It would be quite wrong to dismiss one of you without the other.'

There was silence. Outside I could hear the morning bell signalling that, for every other girl in the school, breakfast was over. For Rachel Porter and Marnie FitzPatrick, much more had come to an end.

'You're both expelled,' said Mrs Slade.

Later that afternoon, the girls were made to pack. I went to find Marnie.

She was in her dormitory, stuffing clothes into her trunk any old how. She looked up when I walked in; her eyes were wet with tears.

'Marnie,' I said, 'why on earth did you do it?'

'I don't know!' She wiped her eyes with the gymslip she was holding. 'I don't know,' she repeated.

'You won't be able to do your A-level,' I said. 'At least not here.'

'I know.'

'You've ruined it for yourself.'

She said nothing, but pressed her washbag into the side of the trunk, then closed the lid. She had to sit down on it to make it shut, which – after considerable shoving – it did. She was deathly pale, almost green. Poor kid, I thought. Silly little child.

'Rachel doesn't mind leaving,' said Marnie. 'She doesn't care. But I do. I don't want to go. I like school.'

A memory of swimming in the sea as a child, my feet sliding over rocks that, despite their thick covering of seaweed, remained sharp, spiky, came to me unbidden. That feeling of stepping out into dark waters, suddenly colder, deeper, more dangerous . . .

'What will you do?' I asked her.

'I don't know. My parents will be furious.' Her face crumpled again.

'Can't you talk to them? You can get them to come in and talk to Mrs Slade. Your stepfather is a powerful man, Marnie.'

I wondered if she was capable of reading between the lines – I had heard distant rumours that, as a young woman, Bethany Slade had had quite an obsession with Howard Tempest.

'He won't care enough to do anything about it,' said Marnie. 'He doesn't really believe in girls being highly educated. I've told you that before.'

'But he must know how good your maths is. You have to talk to him, Marnie. You simply have to.'

Marnie opened the case again and pushed a green and white alarm clock in on top of everything. I watched the second hand tick round, bomb-like.

'Neither of them has any time for anything but themselves,' she said.

There was no ounce of self-pity in her voice. I was used to hearing the other girls talking like this about their lives outside school, but I had never heard anything from Marnie. I changed the subject swiftly.

'If you let Rachel take the blame, then you've a better chance of being let off,' I said.

'I *can't* blame her! It wasn't just her, it was me too. More than her, if anything.'

'But Rachel doesn't mind going, like you said. You do. You can save yourself. Do it for the sake of your maths, if nothing else. Play innocent. Tell Mrs Slade that you were led astray.'

Marnie shook her head frantically. 'I can't,' she said. 'I'm not saying that. It's a lie.'

I should have asked her if she would like me to coach her privately on the weekends – it would have been tricky but we could have found a way. I could have asked her if she would be all right, if she still wanted me to write to her parents to tell them of her potential. But no one had done that for me. When I decided I wanted to dance, I had to do it myself. The sooner the little FitzPatrick girl learned that lesson, the better. I crossed the room and opened the door. My hands were shaking. Life at St Libby's wasn't generally as unpredictable as life in the outside world. I had forgotten how it felt to be shocked.

'Miss Crewe,' said Marnie.

I turned back to her, not wanting her to see how shaken I was.

'Miss Crewe, what was the play like?'

'The play?' I stared at her.

'Rachel and I saw you going into the theatre yesterday.'

'I had a couple of hours off,' I said, hearing the defensiveness in my tone. 'I don't think we need to discuss the merits of what I watched, do we? It's hardly the time.'

'But did you like it?' she persisted. 'Rachel wanted to see it very much. What was is called again?'

I felt annoyed with her questions, but unable not to answer.

'*The Pajama Game*,' I said. My sharp tone made the title even more ridiculous.

'Oh. Isn't that a musical?' asked Marnie.

'Yes.'

'How was the dancing?' She gave me the ghost of a smile.

'The dancing was—' I broke off. 'Marnie, it's not important. The dancing isn't important. Maths A-level is important.'

I opened the door, feeling the need for fresh air.

How could I tell her that the show had been a drug for me? That even though the cast was full of amateurs who couldn't hit the high notes and could never dance in the way that *he* had danced, it was still enough? That every step for those two and a half hours had been in equal parts rapture and agony for me? That through every second of it, I had thought about nothing but the man I had loved, all those years ago, in a country thousands of miles from here, when I had been too young to know anything about heartache until it was too late?

43

5

Marnie

Later that day, I arrived home. Mrs Slade had made a telephone call to my parents after I had finished packing. I had stood in her study, waiting to hear her impart the grim news of my early and permanent homecoming, but fortunately for me, neither of my parents was at home. The call was answered by our sometimes-housekeeper, Mrs George, who was three-quarters deaf. The scene that followed – as Mrs Slade bellowed into the receiver that 'Marnie will be coming home today and please could her parents telephone the school as soon as possible for further information' – would have been comical were I but an innocent bystander. Unhappily, I was neither of these things. I was in deep trouble, and out of St Libby's.

'You'll take a taxi home, the cost of which will be added to your final school bill,' confirmed Mrs Slade, replacing the telephone. 'And this letter will explain everything to your parents.' She looked at me and played her final ace. 'You know, I hate to have to do this to you, Marnie. I really do. You're a talented girl, make no mistake. But you have to understand that there are some things that simply cannot slip through the net and be swept under the carpet. Alcohol is not the answer,' she went on. 'Believe me.'

I swallowed. I would try one more time – if only for Miss Crewe.

'I've never done anything wrong before,' I said. 'Never – and I

44

won't again. I'll just sit inside at my desk and work and work until the last day of the upper sixth. Please. Give me one more chance. I know I've let Miss Crewe down, but I can make it up to her if you let me.'

'It's not always wise to be lured into the web of girls like Miss Porter,' said Mrs Slade. 'This is a valuable lesson, Marnie. Take it home with you and think about it.'

I walked to the door, eyes blinded by hot tears.

North Bridge House, where I had lived since the age of seven, felt shocked at my appearance later that afternoon; I could practically hear a sharp intake of breath from the walls. My twin brother, Caspar, was up a ladder in the hall, removing an old piece of holly from the top of a portrait of Jukey's ancient and revered yellow Labrador, Opium.

'Hold the steps, will you?' he muttered. When my brother stretched up, I noticed that he had bare feet with livid red bramble scratches along his ankles. Caspar was always covered in scratches, but if you knew him well enough then you never asked why.

'I didn't think you'd be back,' he said accusingly and without looking down at me. 'I thought you broke up on Wednesday.'

'I've been kicked out.'

Caspar laughed. 'Come on,' he said, throwing the holly on to the floor. 'You don't expect me to believe that. Keep it still, will you? I've got vertigo.' I gripped the steel frame of the ladder. Caspar carried on talking. 'You know James is back too? We'll all be together tonight — isn't that a delightful prospect? So, come on — what's the real reason you're here? Were you let out early for getting full marks in your latest maths test or something?'

Oh, the irony, I thought miserably.

'I've been expelled,' I said. 'Rachel Porter and I — we've both been asked to leave.'

I twisted a loose ponytail on to my left shoulder.

45

Caspar shot down the ladder and stared at me. 'My God,' he said. 'You're actually serious, aren't you?'

I nodded at him.

'What on earth happened? I can only assume that you're taking the blame for someone else. You shouldn't do that, you know. You don't need to—'

'Oh, I did it all right.'

'Did *what*?'

'I got drunk.' I looked at Caspar for his reaction.

'Don't be ridiculous!'

'Rachel and I went into town on gin, then came back and drank some more, and then we ruined the Lady Richmond Cup.'

'The Lady Richmond Cup?' mused Caspar. 'Remind me. What the fuck is that?'

'You know, that thing where everyone swims in their night-dresses, holding candles to remember Lady Richmond who went down with the *Titanic*.'

'Ah, yes. Wet nightdresses. I knew there was some sort of deviance involved.'

'It's a tradition.' I felt dizzy again, my head pounding. 'I don't think it's sunk in,' I said.

'People only use that ghastly expression when it absolutely *has* sunk in. My God, Marnie. Who on earth is going to tell Jukey?'

'I am,' I said. I held the letter out to him. 'This is from Mrs Slade.'

Caspar gave me a scathing look.

'I must fetch my camera,' he said. 'I hope there's still some film left.'

'You'll do nothing of the sort!'

For four years, Caspar had made a point of photographing and labelling family rows. He claimed that this was a more honest record of our lives, and that relatives in years to come would be charmed and relieved that their petty confrontations were not unique to their day and age. Mostly Caspar and his camera stuck to small things

– some of his best work featured the arguments between me and Jukey over clothes – but on occasion he struck gold with bigger issues, and my expulsion appeared to be fitting the bill.

'I won't interfere too much,' he promised. 'I just have to get Howard's face.'

'You're a horrible person,' I said.

'But the silver lining is that at least you won't have to wear that hideous uniform any longer. I suppose they're hoping to make the lot of you look too ugly to attract any interest at all from the male species.' He stuck a hand out and fingered the material of my school cape. 'Orange and brown! Pure vomit,' he sighed.

I went upstairs to my bedroom, pulled my hair out of its ponytail and lay down on my bed. I wished I knew how they would react. I thought I knew, but then there was never anything certain about Howard and Jukey. How would Simon FitzPatrick have reacted to my expulsion? What would my real father have said? I touched the photograph of him that I kept beside the bed. It had been taken from a magazine and showed him standing next to a model, who was staring up at him with her hair in rollers and a huge smile on her face. Who was this man? I closed my eyes and wished that he were here for me now.

In 1951, when Jukey met my father, Simon FitzPatrick, he was all things to all women. After leaving school, he had spent a year working in his father's shipping insurance offices in Mayfair, but had whiled away most of his time staring out of the window at the women entering the hairdresser's on the opposite side of the street. Later, when interviewed by the *Evening Standard*, he was to remark that it was the glitter in the eyes of these women with their newly styled hair that had planted the seed of possibility in his own mind. He would start a salon himself, and it wouldn't be just for the smartest women in London. It would be for everyone. Eighteen months later, FitzPatrick's was born.

Simon was good looking and amusing, with a trick of making

everyone he spoke to feel as though he had let them in on a big secret, even if they had discussed nothing more than the weather. He worked quickly, making his customers' decisions for them, and delighting them with the results. By the end of his first year, FitzPatrick's of Mayfair needed more staff.

One Monday morning, a young woman called Joanna Davies walked through the door saying she had no experience but felt she was the sort of girl the salon needed. She wasn't wrong. Three weeks later, she had moved in with the man who employed her. Famous for her inability to make solid decisions and to stick by them, Joanna became 'Jukey' because she changed her hairstyle as often as the records change on a jukebox – and, even when I was very little, I had a vague sense that this was something of a euphemism.

Jukey's moon-pale face, peppermint-green eyes and rake-thin legs served her well. She left her middle-class parents and served in the Women's Auxiliary Air Force during the war, and afterwards swanned through the drawing rooms of high society in a cloud of cigarette smoke and blusher, scattering men like skittles. She had always wanted to act, and had considered the hairdressing job to be absolutely temporary. She hadn't accounted for her own talent within the medium of hair – or for the demands the job would make upon her time. If she wasn't being immortalized on celluloid, she was changing the images of those who were, and she found it to be an addictive pastime.

Jukey had a talent for knowing exactly what people wanted to look like that left others in her wake. She made hairdressing an art form, and soon her diary was so full that even the highest-paid models in London had to wait two months for an appointment. Her show-stopping good looks made her the subject of magazine articles, particularly when she and Simon created a scandal by living together but never marrying.

Simon's sudden death – a heart attack when James was eighteen months old, and Caspar and I were still in utero – came out of a clear blue sky – although his friends later admitted that his fifty-a-day cigarette habit and fondness for kicking off every morning with a double whisky might have had something to do with it. Jukey went into shock and withdrew from those around her. Without a marriage, and in the absence of a will, the salon passed into the hands of Simon's brother, Kenton, who had been jealous of his brother's affair with Jukey and who sold it to a competitor of Simon's for a small fortune. Jukey never saw any of this. She became reclusive, unwilling to work any more. She had three children under the age of two and very little money. What was clear to her was that she needed another man – and fast. Enter, stage right, Howard Tempest, the most famous face in theatre, and the man who was to become our stepfather.

Howard had always had a thing for Jukey – which isn't really saying much, as he had a thing for most people – but, unlike her other potential suitors, he wasn't remotely bothered by her entourage; if anything, the novelty of a ready-made family was something to be relished. He gave her sympathy, encouraged her to give up any ideas of working any more, and took her out for dinner at Sheekey's twice a week. His personality – serious about work, serious about himself, but cripplingly insecure and prone to unexpected moments of generosity and humour – contributed to making him the great actor he undoubtedly was, and, being a great actor, he absorbed from people all the time, soaking up everything and storing it for use on stage. He was also a great listener. Howard listened to Jukey talk about Simon, but told her that he had been a fool not to marry her. When he proposed, Jukey accepted with the words, 'Please don't die.' Howard had these words sewn on to a cushion, which he kept in his office – the old railway carriage that sat at the bottom of the garden at North Bridge House, which he had inherited from his parents two years before he met Jukey.

North Bridge House – so called because there used to be a train station at the bottom of the garden, and a little bridge leading passengers out into green and pleasant Hertfordshire beyond – was then and is now a socking great Victorian pile that sits just outside Welwyn Garden City. Never did a building so reflect the man who owned it, for, just when you thought you understood the seriousness of its intent, you would be confounded by something unexpectedly eccentric – the steepest staircase in the county ('Who measures these things?' Caspar was fond of asking), or a first-floor landing with stained-glass windows showing Jesus lecturing a group of mermaids. There were odd little carvings of dolphins over every door frame – Howard's grandmother had been convinced that dolphins could speak to humans and became obsessed by them during the last ten years of her life.

The house smelled strongly of marijuana (Howard's grandfather had smoked every night to 'improve his system' until dropping dead at eighty), old oil lamps, mothballs and slightly damp curtains. Any attempt to obliterate these smells always failed, even Jukey's persistent use of Frances Denney's 'Interlude' – a scent she had shipped over from America when it was launched in the mid 1960s – couldn't quite overcome what had gone before.

The real brilliance of North Bridge House came from the garden – still known as the Sidings from the railway-station days – which had opened to the public twice a year since Howard's parents owned it. The garden was breathtaking, a place that people could visit for just five minutes and talk about for fifty years. It was all Jukey's work. When we moved in, my mother took the bit between her teeth, and promptly called on her father's friend, Sir Geffrey Jellicoe, who came to North Bridge and added ornamental delights, like the pond and the lavender steps, in the mid 1950s, then helped Jukey create a rose garden based on the design he had just finished at Cliveden. Shortly after this, an article appeared in *The Times* about Jukey's horticultural skills, stating that 'every plant and flower at the Sidings is treated like a client at FitzPatrick's of Mayfair at its peak – primped, primed and sprayed to within an inch of its life', which was an amusing enough way of looking at it – though, as Howard pointed out, the flowers didn't tip as well. At any rate, the garden was a little paradise for us children as we grew up, an escape from the tension inside the house. And, with Howard at the helm, there was always tension, make no mistake.

Howard had a difficult personality to live with – one day focusing all his energy and attention on us, the next disappearing for a week and returning distant, bored, bad tempered. None of us children could ever feel *entirely* safe with him – although all of us, especially James, longed to. Once, we played a game Howard taught us – an old routine that he had learned in acting classes, where we had to close our eyes and lean back into each other's waiting arms to gain trust. But when Howard was meant to catch me, he failed to do so. Caspar said he was glancing at himself in the mirror and hadn't realized I was falling. Needless to say, none of this stopped me wanting his attention.

Having grown up next to the town, Howard had more of an attachment to the Garden City than we did, and we liked hearing him talk about it. Much of his fondness for the town was directed at the Welwyn Department Stores, where he spent most of his childhood scoffing cakes at the Parkway Restaurant and bobbing around in the toy department on the weekends. Another favourite childhood jaunt was a bicycle ride down to the old film set on Broadwater Road, followed by a 'quick dip' in the River Lea. Now that he had returned here, living in the house that his parents had lived in before him, Howard liked being the local celebrity, the man people saw shopping 'like a normal person' then nudged each other and asked him for autographs. He felt safe in the town, and saw it as somewhere that existed solely to be of comfort to him, unlike London, which he famously said, 'could hold you in her arms one minute, and screw your best friend the next.'

At the risk of sounding awful, I ought to say that Caspar and I were good-looking children – more so than James – but, because it was always remarked upon, it became something *un*remarkable, something without real meaning or seriousness – and seriousness was all I craved. Caspar, however, took it on and shone lights with it. He got huge kicks from compliments and, once fully charged, learned how to translate that into love – wherever he could. Unfortuntely, Caspar had developed what he called a "substantial crush" on a beautiful, long-haired musician called Nick who had been some years ahead of him at school. Nick showed no outward signs of returning Caspar's love, so my twin brother suffered in silence, talking only occasionally to me about it when he couldn't keep it in any longer. It was ironic that his love was unreciprocated, for our teenage years had not dimmed Caspar's beauty, even though they had a good go at mine. Once I started at St Libby's, aged thirteen, I had a tendency to get spots when I ate too much chocolate, my hair lost its white-blonde halo and dulled to a colour that even Jukey, with her plethora of adjectives for all things hair related, simply labelled 'mouse'. Worst of all, if I ate too much, I put on weight with alarming speed.

'It's still a very good face,' my godmother said to me last summer, tilting my chin up to the light. 'Take comfort, dear thing. No one looks their best when they're sixteen.'

Except for Rachel Porter, I thought as I rubbed a rough flannel over my skin and prepared to go downstairs and face the music.

Jukey, Caspar and James were sitting in the drawing room. The fire had been lit for hours; it pumped out heat far too efficiently – the room was stifling. From the corner, the gramophone crackled with Jupiter's theme from *The Planets*. James had a thing about Holst being 'bracing'. My eyes watered.

Jukey looked up at me.

'Marnie!' she cried. 'Goodness! I must have got the date completely wrong! I thought you weren't back till Wednesday! What a wonderful surprise!'

I extracted myself from her grasp. Her delight at seeing me was going to make me cry again. I looked down at my feet. Jukey didn't approve of tears.

'I'm afraid I've got some bad news,' I said.

I looked at Caspar, who gave a sympathetic nod of encouragement.

'What's happened?' asked Jukey.

'I've been expelled.'

Jukey laughed.

'You what? I'm sorry, Marnie. I don't understand.'

'I've been expelled,' I repeated.

James put his glass down on a table and stared at me, open mouthed.

'What for?'

'Rachel Porter and I got drunk.'

'*Drunk?* But you don't drink! Rachel Porter! But she's – she's Rachel Porter! And you're . . . You were drinking?'

Caspar took out his camera and snapped. James was too stunned to notice.

'But you never drink!' said Jukey. She looked puzzled, as though I must have got the facts completely wrong.

'I know,' I said quietly. 'It was a one-off. But it ended badly. We ruined the Lady Richmond Cup.'

'The thing with the nightdresses and the candles because of the *Titanic*?' James sounded amazed. 'Isn't that the biggest tradition in the school?'

'Yes.'

'How did you ruin it?'

'I don't remember, exactly,' I said. ' I know that I had to be pulled out of the water, and Rachel blocked the path of the girls who were winning—'

'Oh, say no more!' said Caspar in mock horror.

Jukey shook her head. Then she picked up her glass of wine and

53

finished it. She looked quite different now, as though she had got the measure of the situation.

'I predict fireworks when Howard finds out,' said James.

'Thank you, Nostradamus,' said Caspar tartly.

My twin brother strode silently towards the drinks cabinet. Usually he was told to stop when he poured himself whisky; now everyone was too shocked to care. I looked at my mother again. Generally very concerned with her appearance, she looked as though she hadn't given her clothes a moment's thought. She was wearing an outsized skirt that must have belonged to my grandmother, and a white blouse that strained over her bosom. She had put on weight, which she always did when she was anxious or unhappy, which, to be honest, was most of the time.

'Lemon?' offered Caspar, holding out a glass of gin and tonic to me and grinning.

I pushed it away. 'That's not funny.'

'I envy you, being expelled,' said Caspar. 'God knows I've tried enough times. Seems that Marlborough just doesn't want to let me go.'

'Can't think why,' snapped James. 'In any event, I think we should refrain from talking about Marnie until Howard's in the room. He'll have a sensible approach on what to do.'

'Bollocks,' muttered Caspar.

'Wasn't that necklace Granny's?' asked James of Jukey, as though noticing her for the first time.

'Yes,' said Jukey defiantly. 'I think it's wonderful to wear things that once belonged to her. It brings her back to me somehow.'

'I hope not,' shuddered Caspar. He and his propensity for scratches had been disapproved of by our grandmother, who had died two years ago. She had possessed tight purse strings and a nose for trouble – two qualities that did not sit well with my brother and his general flightiness.

Suddenly I wanted to say it, to reassure myself that my exam result had happened, that my time in Miss Crewe's study had actually taken place. I cleared my throat.

'It doesn't mean anything now, but you may as well know this: we had our exam results back,' I said quickly. 'I . . . I did rather well in maths.'

There was a thick pause. The fire spat a hot rock of burning coal on to the hearth, and Jukey – quick as a flash – flicked it smartly back into the grate with the worn leather toe of her shoe. Those shoes were good for something then, I supposed. James rattled the ice in his whisky. One term at Oxford had turned him even more pompous than he had been when he left Eton.

'How did you do in French?' he asked meanly, aiming and firing at my Achilles heel.

'Bugger French. She's on about her maths,' said Caspar with irritation.

Jukey looked at me. There were dark rings around her eyes.

'Reveal all, darling,' she said.

'I got a hundred per cent,' I said. I could feel my face hot and red, feel the rush of excitement in my fingertips. 'I got – well – I got it all right. Everything in the paper. I didn't make any mistakes. None.' I gave a high bark of astonished laughter at hearing the words out loud from my own lips. Then the dizziness returned, and I reached a hand out to steady myself on the arm of the sofa.

James looked grim.

'Good God,' he said, stubbing out a cigarette. 'You've really blown it, haven't you?'

'Little genius!' said Caspar. 'I expect your maths mistress wanted to have you there and then.'

I went puce. 'Don't be disgusting.'

Jukey never seemed to mind Caspar's lurid asides. She reached out and touched my burning cheek.

'Clever little one,' she said. Her voice was unsteady, almost unrecognizable.

I felt tears shooting into my eyes yet again. This was all I wanted – all I had ever wanted: for them to realize that I had done something extraordinary, that I could go on to do more of it, given half the chance, but the moment was extinguished by Howard striding into the room. He stopped dead when he saw us all gathered like something out of Noël Coward and laughed brightly.

'Ha! I didn't expect you to be here, Marnie. End of term already? I thought you broke up later in the week.'

I looked at Jukey.

'What's happened at St Libby's?' he asked fondly, opening the paper and sitting down in his favourite chair. 'Outbreak of scurvy? Fire in the gymnasium? Plague of frogs in the dorm?' He pulled a cigarette out of the silver holder that he carried everywhere, and lit it.

'She's been expelled,' said Caspar calmly.

Howard inhaled, grinning at Caspar.

'Come on,' he said. 'What's the real reason you're here? Don't tell me! Bethany Slade's broken a fingernail on the lacrosse pitch!'

When no one joined in his laughter, he turned around and stared at us.

'You can't expect me to believe you,' he said slowly. 'You haven't been expelled!'

'I'm afraid I have been,' I said.

'She really has,' said Caspar seriously. 'Marnie never jokes about matters like this.' He pulled out his camera and snapped.

'For God's sake, Caspar!' shouted James, Howard, Jukey and I in unison.

'Sorry,' he said, shutting the lens with a satisfied snap. 'You'll thank me for it one day. When you all see the funny side.'

'There is no funny side!' I shouted.

He was enjoying this, I thought. Caspar was one of those odd people who reasoned that life was only worth living if it lurched from blissful high to terrible low; anything in between didn't interest him at all.

'She's been kicked out,' said Jukey, in case Howard needed it spelling out for him any more clearly.

'Kicked out?' echoed Howard, astounded.

'Yes.' I felt myself floating upwards, as though watching the scene unravel from the ceiling.

'She was led astray by the Porter girl,' said Jukey. 'They were both expelled.'

I wasn't often the cause of Howard's jaw dropping.

'What on earth for?' he asked incredulously.

'Drinking,' I said quietly. The scene was happening, the conversation was happening, and yet I couldn't believe it was taking place at all. In that sense, it was reminiscent of those few moments that had taken place between Rachel Porter and me and the boy from the bus.

'But you *never* drink,' said Howard, brow furrowing.

'That's just what I said,' cried Jukey.

'I'd just had a rather good exam result back. I thought I could get away with it.'

Howard inhaled deeply. 'My God,' he said. 'All that money! Do you have the slightest clue what the fees are at that place? Do you? *Do* you?'

'Yes,' I said. 'I'm awfully sorry. It was just a big mistake.'

'Everyone makes mistakes—' began Jukey.

'Mistakes!' interrupted Howard. 'Christ in heaven! What will the Edmonsons say? Charlie pulled terrific strings to get you in the front door!'

'She would have got in anyway – she was too clever not to pass the entrance exam,' pointed out Caspar.

'Entrance exam or not, when it comes to a school like that, girls should be put down at birth.'

Realizing how this sentence sounded when shouted out loud, and ignoring Caspar's hollow laughter, Howard clicked his tongue with exasperation.

'You *silly* girl!' he said. 'Silly, silly girl!'

For a moment, I felt very sorry for my stepfather. As I expected, it was the details of the thing that were bothering him: what he would say to his friends, how much money he had spent on sending me to the best girls' school in the county. For all that his acting career had allowed him to mess around as much as he liked, he needed his perceived offspring to be seen toeing the party line.

'When did all this happen?' he asked with a heavy sigh.

'Why don't you telephone Bethany Slade yourself and ask her?' said Jukey. She poured him a whisky and crossed the room to hand it to him.

Howard looked at her, and for a second his focus shifted. He gulped at the drink, grimaced and placed the glass down next to a framed photograph of him and John Gielgud backstage at the Old Vic.

'I would expect better from you, Marnie. You've let yourself down . . .'

For a moment, I lost him. I didn't need to hear what he was saying, not when I had heard it all already. My thoughts turned, without any effort, to the boy from the bus. Where was he now? Eating with his parents? Sitting in the pub with a girlfriend? Had he thought about us for one moment since we had met him? How would he feel if he could have seen a newsreel of what had happened to Rachel and me after we had left him that day?

'. . . and I didn't think that I would have to say this. But, in fact, I think it's true.'

I stared at Howard. 'What's true?' I muttered.

James shook his head in mock disbelief. I could have hit him.

'I said that at least this has happened now that you're the age you are. There's no real reason for you to have to go back to school at all – to any school. Darling, you're a girl. You simply do not *need* school any longer.'

I got it instantly. The reintroduction of 'darling' signified that

Howard had come to the swift conclusion that there was no need to worry. I was female. It didn't really matter.

'But I *want* to be at school,' I said.

'You should have thought of that before you went off boozing with girls like Rachel Porter,' said James smugly. He had always had a crush on Rachel, who had once spurned his advances at a party. The news of her fall from grace was evidently more than pleasing to him.

'There aren't girls like Rachel Porter,' I said. 'There's only her.'

'Which one is she?' demanded Howard suddenly. 'Not David Porter's girl?'

'Yes,' said James.

Howard's brain was whirring back to the occasion of Founder's Day.

'I sat next to her, didn't I?' he said.

'She's a knockout,' said Jukey. 'Don't pretend you can't remember.'

'I don't remember her face particularly, but I certainly remember what she was talking about. She was quite unlike a schoolgirl. Wiser than her years.'

'Can't be that wise or she'd still have a place in the sixth form,' quipped James.

Howard pulled himself back to the present and fixed his famous oceanic eyes on me.

'Marnie, for goodness' sake, I'm not sure that you're grasping what I'm saying here,' he said. 'You can take a French course – why not go and stay with Madame Pontaine in Paris for a couple of months—?'

'Oh, the great Madame Pontaine!' said Jukey in disgust. 'I won't have Marnie anywhere near her. Not after what she tried to do to the boys.'

James shuddered.

'Don't take offence on my part,' said Caspar. 'I learned more from that lecherous old bird in three weeks than—'

59

'That is *enough*, Caspar!' shouted Howard. He turned to me and flapped his hands up and down in exasperation. 'For God's sake!'

'I'm certain that Queenswood would take her for the sixth form. I know Dora Walton-Jones, who has two daughters there. I could telephone her tomorrow,' said Jukey.

'Dora Walton-Jones is a monster,' said Howard.

'Just because her brother gave you a bad review in 1961,' snapped Jukey. She looked at me. 'Aren't you going to tell Howard what you got in your maths exam?'

'What would be the point?' I asked.

'What did you get?' asked Howard in despair.

'She got everything right,' said Jukey. 'One hundred per cent! She didn't lose a single mark!' Jukey clapped her hands together briskly in syncopation with these last two words to emphasize her point.

Howard looked at James, who stared into his empty glass.

'Hard to justify her leaving school when I failed maths this term,' said Caspar, picking up a handful of salted almonds from a bowl. 'But, of course, I am a *man*!' He squared his shoulders, drained the rest of his whisky and saluted.

'You're missing the point of what Howard's trying to say,' snapped James.

'Marnie's got it all natural, like,' said Caspar. 'It just comes to her. Like other stuff just comes to me.' He didn't elaborate on precisely what this was.

'Maths will always be useful to you in your daily life,' conceded Howard. 'But there's little more you can do with it now. And, in any event, James is right: you should have thought about the consequences of your actions before you decided to get drunk and go swimming.'

Caspar winced. Howard saw this, and did one of his extraordinary and confusing volte-faces.

'Darling Marnie,' he said softly. He actually came over and

60

kneeled down at my feet. 'You're cleverer than everyone else in that school. Why do you need them?'

I heard my voice trembling as it always did when Howard disarmed me like this. 'I want to take maths A-level.'

He stood up again.

'My dear child, even if you hadn't been thrown out of the school, I would *not* suggest that you carried on with maths. What have I always said? Study a language, like your cousin Albertine. Immerse yourself in the Romantic poets. Don't waste your time with any more numbers. It's an odd thing for a girl to like numbers as much as you do – I've always said it.'

'I'm not interested in love,' I said.

'Amen to that,' said Caspar, reaching forward and pulling a cigarette from Howard's case.

'Of course, if you really want to continue with it, you could go to West Park,' said Howard, offering up the services of the local comprehensive school.

It was with these words from my stepfather that the truth of what was happening suddenly became very clear. There would be no Miss Crewe, but not only that: there would be no other school, unless I went to West Park. And that was impossible, wasn't it?

'You'll have to talk to Mrs Slade tomorrow, Howard,' said Jukey. 'Her letter says that she'll see you to discuss the matter further. You need to make her see sense.' She looked at me defiantly. 'Of course, Marnie, you know that Howard has a history with the woman. That's what makes this whole thing so difficult.'

'Well, I know that she admires him as an actor—'

'Oh, please, don't,' said Caspar.

'I turned her down, Joanna. You know I did,' said Howard, exasperated. 'It was years before I met you. She can't have been more than twenty-one. My brother brought her to a family party. She was a very pretty country girl back then.'

'Spare me,' said Jukey grimly.

'No! You asked me!'

'You did, Jukey,' agreed Caspar, picking up his camera again.

'I sat next to her at supper and it was clear that she had only come to meet me. I knew that Philip was keen on her, so I resisted her. After that night, she kept showing up at the stage door, every time with a new excuse. It was some sort of a crush, that's all.'

'A *crush*?'

'Christ! It's not my fault! I don't go around begging women to throw themselves at me. It just happens!'

There was a short silence after the delivery of this astounding line, which had – for all its horrifying lack of irony – foundations in undeniable truth.

'She's a headmistress now!' exploded Jukey. 'What the hell is wrong with the woman?'

'She wasn't headmistress when Marnie first arrived at the school. How was I to know she was going to turn up two years ago—'

'Probably engineered her way to St Libby's to have another crack at you!'

'Oh, give the woman some credit!'

'Did she see you in *Roof*?' demanded Jukey.

'Yes,' said Howard defiantly. 'Yes, she did.'

Another silence. It was commonly acknowledged that anyone who had seen Howard Tempest channel Brick Pollitt in *Cat on a Hot Tin Roof* was wrecked – for weeks afterwards. Men and women had queued every night to watch him sneak out of the stage door. One desperate soul had even sent him a small box containing her menstrual blood as a sign of her devotion to him. Quite what this grim present was supposed to signify, none of us knew, but Howard kept it on the top shelf of his railway carriage in the garden and refused to dispose of it, saying it would be bad luck to do so, as she was probably a witch and they would all be cursed if he threw it away.

'She's always been angry with me for turning her down,' Howard was saying. 'I suppose getting rid of Marnie is the perfect punishment.'

I wanted very much to feel shocked by these revelations, but I couldn't. Nothing about Howard's past ever surprised me.

'I'll speak to Bethany Slade in the morning,' said Howard soothingly. 'See what I can do to persuade her to keep Marnie on. But I can't promise anything. What's the name of the maths teacher? I should really talk to him.'

'It's a woman. Don't you ever listen to what Marnie says? She's called Miss Crewe. Marnie thinks the world of her.'

'Probably some old boot who's been at the school since 1873,' shuddered Howard.

I slipped away through the door. The thought of Howard talking to Miss Crewe about me was almost as horrifying as the idea of Bethany Slade's 'crush'. I went to my bedroom, shut the door and lay down on the floor because my head was spinning too violently to risk falling off the bed. It really was happening. I really was expelled.

And yet, when I lay awake in bed that night, the image that came back to me, over and over again, was not of Howard and Bethany Slade decades before, nor of Jukey's face when she learned of my expulsion, but of the boy from the bus, standing outside the factory, smiling at Rachel Porter and me, calling them 'pillows' of Shredded Wheat, and then shutting the door in our faces.

6

Miss Crewe

Bethany Slade told me she was expecting Marnie's stepfather to come to see her on the afternoon of the day after the girls' expulsion.

'He'll be trying to reverse the decision,' she said. 'I am not budging on this, Julie.'

She knew how I felt, but I tried again: 'It will be a terrible thing for Marnie if she has to confess to any university that she was expelled from school during the sixth form. They won't have her. You've her future in your hands, Bethany.'

'Well, perhaps that's as it should be.'

'You can't mean that! Did you never do anything you regretted? Never step a foot out of line?'

Bethany Slade looked at me.

'I have always been extremely careful, Julie. That's what disappoints me most about these two girls. Both acted with such disregard for everyone and everything. It can't be accepted.'

Howard Tempest had been directed from the entrance of the school to the small waiting room outside the office. He lifted his eyes from the back issue of *Liberate*, the St Libby's school magazine, smiled, and stood up to shake my hand.

'Julie Crewe,' I said. 'Head of maths. I also look after the girls in Kelp House.'

I resisted using my official title of 'housemistress'.

'My God! *You're* Miss Crewe? I was expecting someone quite different.'

I didn't respond to this, so he coughed and tried again.

'I expect you know why I'm here,' he said. 'My stepdaughter's made an ass of herself.'

He was so inescapably famous – that thick, boyish blond hair the colour of rich-tea biscuits, the slant of that elegant nose, the lines around his eyes signifying late nights and good living. My mother had called him 'the most beautiful man to have walked God's earth', which was a statement that I had always felt was stretching things a little bit, but up close, I had to admit, the whole package was compelling enough. I took a deep breath.

'For what it's worth, I don't think she should have done it,' I said.

'Oh, I *know* she shouldn't have,' he said with feeling.

'I meant I don't think she should have been expelled,' I said. 'Marnie's very bright. Her maths result this term is unprecedented.'

'I know, I know. It's the most disastrous turn of events.'

I turned on my heels, unwilling to be drawn into handing out sympathy.

'Do come this way, Mr Tempest,' I said. 'Mrs Slade will see you shortly. Rachel Porter's father is talking to her at the moment.'

'Is she here?' he asked me.

'Who?'

'Rachel. My wife believes she's the one behind all the trouble.'

'I think both girls have taken their share of the blame.'

As we approached the door of Bethany Slade's office, it opened and out stepped Rachel Porter's father; thin as a rake, and even stooping a little as he was, he looked almost a foot taller than Howard, who squared his shoulders instinctively in response. The outline of Rachel's beauty had come entirely from this source. I felt sorry for him, but irritated at the same time. Couldn't he have controlled her

better at home? If she had come to the school knowing her bound-
aries then perhaps this wouldn't have happened.

'You're in next,' he said to Howard without irony.

'Did it work?' asked Howard. 'Is your girl going to be back again
next term?'

'God knows.' David Porter took the glasses off his nose and
rubbed his eyes. 'You know, I sometimes wonder why the hell I
bothered sending her to school in the first place,' he said in a low
voice. 'Waste of time and money.' He looked at me for the answer
to this question. 'What were you like when you were her age?' he
asked suddenly. 'Were you anything like Rachel?'

'I don't know that anyone could be exactly like Rachel,' I said
with as much tact as I could muster.

'Ha,' said David Porter without mirth. 'I suppose what I mean
by that question is, when does this nonsense end? When did *you*
grow up?'

I was saved from answering by Mrs Slade opening the door.

'Mr Tempest,' she said. 'Do come in.'

As he stepped inside, Howard Tempest turned and caught my
eye, just briefly. If he had smiled, I think I would have disliked
him intensely. But his instinct served him well. He shook his head,
and the lightness to his features had entirely shut down. This was
serious stuff, and he wasn't here to flirt with me, or anyone else,
when his stepdaughter's academic future was at stake. He wasn't
that stupid.

I grew up when I was twenty-three, the year that I met Jo. It was
the summer of 1951, my second in New York. I was dizzy with
love for the place, enraptured by the glamour of the little apartment
I shared with my best friend, Eloise de Veer – a shrimp of a girl
with an outlandish sense of humour and the stamina of an ox. We
felt invincible, Eloise and I. We had survived a year in the city – the
noise, the dirt, the cockroaches, the heat, the flies, the shared mattress

on the splintered floor, the breathtaking cold of the winter when our flannels froze stiff in the night, the power cuts, the lack of hot water, the landlady's death from liver failure, her husband's subsequent lecherous advances when we came in late, living from hand to mouth and dancing until our feet bled. I would not have had it any other way, and Eloise, though she complained endlessly and spent a fortune telephoning her kind father in London to ask for more money, felt the same.

Eloise had written *Another day in Paradise* in red chalk on the board in the area of the apartment that we optimistically named the kitchen. She said it was there to remind her, 'Even when the shit hits the fan and we have no money, no work and no friends, that we want to be here more than anything.' For me, having grown up with a mother who favoured my elder sister and disapproved of my desire to dance, there was no need for any reminder at all. I was unusually aware of the brilliance of it all; I had an older-than-my-years sensitivity to quite how much of a good time I was having and, knowing so, was already living partly in mourning for it. I could foresee its demise, yet – like we all do – I went along for the ride all the same.

I met him when I was walking through Central Park. That fact alone sounds invented, untrue, even to me. It was the end of May; the city was bursting out in blossom and dust, sunlight, grit and exhaust fumes. I was wearing thin brown leather sandals and a long yellow and white spotted sundress, sent across the Atlantic in a much-anticipated parcel from England by my Aunt Gina, who liked sewing and lacked daughters.

I walked slowly, my bag with my dance shoes and a copy of Hemingway slung over my shoulder, knowing that Eloise wouldn't be back yet from the audition she had been preparing for all week. I had no auditions, but I had endless optimism and that counted for everything.

Earlier that day, I had danced for a director who said that he thought I had 'great legs and a face that, in the right hands, could melt the wrong hearts.' I asked him whom the wrong hearts belonged to, and he just laughed like it was the biggest joke he'd ever heard. He had even taken me out to lunch; I had a prawn cocktail and a steak, and, after a glass of white wine, he had repeatedly touched one of my 'great legs'. I was used to this sort of thing and, if it meant a free dinner, then that was fine by me, but I made a quick escape soon after. He was a short man – fat, balding, approaching fifty. I felt I was superior to him – as all young girls feel, whether they're pretty or plain as can be, in the presence of much older men who desire them. I certainly didn't think I needed him. Men who admired me were two a penny, but I was yet to jump into bed with any of them and, as is often the case with the sexually naïve, I was an outrageous flirt if given half the chance.

Five minutes after my lunch, just as I was walking into the park, a boy of about eleven years old, riding a bicycle, stopped me and asked me if I was Katherine Hepburn's little sister.

'Sure am,' I replied.

He laughed in delight and looked for a moment as though he was considering following me, so I set off pretty quickly out of his sight and ducked into the Conservatory Garden, opposite Fifth Avenue, where Eloise and I came to read the papers and eat salt beef sandwiches on Sundays.

It was there that I did what any girl in my shoes would have done – I sat down in the sun and threaded a daisy chain, closed my eyes and made a wish: *Make it happen for me. Please.* New York was the only place in the world I wanted to be, and I believed that I was destined to succeed here. That's when I saw him for the first time – the man beside a fountain – and he was dancing.

I don't mean he was dancing so that everyone could see; he was dancing in secret, little half-steps and short flicks of the arm, interspersed with just walking and kicking at the ground a bit, and pushing back the bowler hat he was wearing, tilted at a seventy-degree angle. He had corduroys on, rolled up so that you could see his ankles, and a pullover sweater, despite the heat of the afternoon. Yet it wasn't this that made him unlike anyone else I had seen before. It was the way he moved. In the plainest terms, it was like watching someone who had been dropped into a vat of fairy dust, then plonked back among the ordinary people. For a long moment, I sat and watched him, pretending not to, and then at last, unable to help myself, I took a deep breath, walked over to him, tapped him lightly on the shoulder and spoke.

'You a dancer?'

He turned and looked at me. 'I think so. Is it that obvious?'

I laughed. 'Only to me. I dance too.'

'You a Canadian?' he asked me.

'I used to be. Is it that obvious?'

'Only to me. I can't get enough of the place,' he said. 'They say it's just scenery over there, no action. I don't think that's true.'

I laughed at him, and he looked encouraged.

'Course it's not true,' I said. 'The scenery *is* the action.'

He laughed. 'You heading anywhere?' he asked.

'Not for a while.'

'C'mon on, then. I'll buy you a coffee.'

He was twenty-four, he said. He was in New York studying at the American Theatre Wing for six weeks, under José Limón. He had already had some time with Anna Sokolow.

'No! Really?' I wanted to play it cool, but information like this was too much – the stuff of fantasy.

'Really,' he said. He grinned, enjoying how impressed I was.

'How's it been?' I asked him.

'Like nothing else,' he said. 'And the best thing is, it's all being paid for by the GI Bill.'

'They must really think you're something.'

He looked at me and threw his cigarette to the ground, tapping it dead under his foot.

'Everyone's something. Even you. Just gotta figure out what the hell that something is.'

He paid for my coffee – which I drank, even though I hated the stuff – and I pulled three little packets from my bag that I kept for such emergencies.

'I never go anywhere without sugar,' I said.

'If I was a regular guy, I'd crack some awful line like, "Hey, you don't need sugar. You're sweet enough without it." Ha ha ha.'

I looked at him from under my eyelashes in the way that Eloise had trained me to look at the landlord's son when we wanted another day's grace on our rent.

'But you're not a regular guy?' I asked.

'Yeah. Sure I am.' He cleared his throat. 'You don't need sugar. You're sweet enough without it.'

He grinned at me and pulled out another cigarette.

I spilled most of the sugar – my hand was shaking so much. He picked a pencil out from his pocket to stir his coffee with. After he had used it, he offered it to me. That gesture – his red and white striped pencil, with its chewed end, stirring *my* coffee – felt heavy with significance. Even the movement of his fingers did something to me. My stomach lurched like it used to when I was a kid riding on the handlebars of my cousin's bike across rough fields; there were actual electrical jolts shooting through my fingers, I swear it. What was this? I was half afraid of it – it felt too powerful for me. I was thrown by everything about him; he was nothing like the men that Eloise and I usually mooned over. He looked like no film star I had ever seen; there was an unremarkable ordinariness in his face. But he was doing something to me, and no mistake. Was it possible for me to feel it and not him? I wondered. Was it possible for all this new energy to come just from me?

'And you,' he said, taking the pencil back and putting it into his pocket again. 'Where are you dancing?'

'Oh, everywhere and anywhere,' I said as lightly as I dared. 'Just trying to get work, like all the rest. I've made some contacts. I met a guy this morning – a director.'

'Oh, yeah? Who?'

'Karl Antipov. I just saw him. He liked me,' I said defensively.

Jo snorted. 'Course he fuckin' did. I hope you told him where to stick it.'

'He bought me lunch. He said I had good legs.'

'You don't have to sit through prawn salad with that great ape to be told that. I could tell you that right now for free, and I won't try to jump into bed with you, just for telling you, either.'

I looked at him for a beat too long. I hadn't jumped into bed with *anyone*, but right now I felt like here would be just about the best place to start. He grinned at me. He had done it all before, I knew that much.

'I'm just getting myself out there,' I said carefully. 'You know. Seeing anyone who'll see me.'

'You look like *you* do, anyone will see you. But seeing you's not the point. They've gotta love you. What've you got to make people love you, huh?'

'I don't know. I guess I'm working on that.'

He gulped at his coffee. 'The thing is, baby, you don't have long,' he said. 'We don't have long. Dancers are like dragonflies – in one day, dead in the water the next. So you just have to work, all the time, because if you don't love it, and if you don't want to do it so much that it's like breathing to you, then you might as well stop now.'

The brutality of his phrasing took my breath away.

He looked at me and laughed at my expression. 'Cheer up, baby. You know, for anyone with any sense, work is more fun than fun.'

'Work is more fun than fun,' I repeated.

'Don't forget that,' he said.

'*Je me presse de rire de tout, de peur d'être obligé d'en pleurer.*'

'I was wondering when you were gonna throw some French my way. Y'know that's really why I love Canadian girls.'

Even then, I felt a thrill at the implication that he could – even in the most tenuous sense – love me, and a simultaneous wave of despair that he could love others, too. I should have held on to that line, used it to beat some sense into me in the weeks that followed, but I didn't.

'C'mon then. What does that shit mean?'

'It means, "I force myself to laugh at everything, for fear of being compelled to weep."' I pulled this line out quite a bit; it usually invited some sort of admiration. What was the point in growing up in Montreal if I couldn't use some French now and then?

'I like the way you say that,' he said. 'Bullshit philosophy, but it sounds good.'

I laughed . . .

I glanced out of the window of the upper-fourth classroom where I was preparing for my next lesson. Down in the car park at the back of the main St Libby's building, I saw Howard Tempest striding out of the back door of the school. He had his hands thrust into his pockets; he looked younger than he had any right to. He stopped beside his filthy white Ford Classic, but just as he opened the driver's door and prepared to exit the school grounds, he spotted Rachel Porter, sitting in the car next door, in the passenger seat of her father's Jaguar. Tempest walked over and bent down to talk to her. Rachel wound down the window. It was a still afternoon; their voices travelled up and through the open window of the classroom with no need for me to strain to hear what they were saying.

'Rachel?'

'Oh, hello.'

'How are you?'

'Expelled, I think. I don't know what Daddy's doing here. He dragged me out of bed and made me come with him today, just so he can lecture me all the way home again.'

'You don't sound very contrite.'

'Why should I be? I don't care if they don't want me here any longer. The only thing I regret is that Marnie's been kicked out too. She likes it here.'

'She thinks it was her fault as much as yours.'

At this point Rachel seemed to think that the turn of events merited her getting out of the car. She stood up, stretched and continued the conversation leaning on the car door.

I watched Howard pull a smoke out of a silver case, light it, inhale, glance around to check for witnesses, then pass it to her. She took it, inhaled deeply and handed it back to him.

'Thanks,' she said. 'I needed that.'

From the far side of the car park, I could see David Porter approaching. Rachel only had a matter of seconds in the company of Howard Tempest, but it was all she needed. Dressed in denim shorts, blonde hair falling down her back now that she was free from the restraints of the school system, she looked like Brigitte Bardot – only better. Her modernity felt absolute; she wasn't of this age – she belonged some time in the future, not at the tail end of the 1960s. From where I stood, textbook in my left hand and board rubber in my right, the two of them suddenly looked unmistakably right together. Their glamour seemed positively bonkers in a setting as ordinary as a Hertfordshire school car park on an overcast spring afternoon, her lines of beauty and experience crossing each other and sparking like electric wires. Seconds later, David Porter was back at the car, Howard Tempest had shaken his hand and they were parted again. But I swear I could almost feel the heat that their encounter had given Rachel. I had to go and say goodbye, I thought suddenly. I had to tell her not to give up.

David Porter had just turned the key in the ignition. Rachel was sitting beside him, her arm resting on the open window.

'Rachel!' I said.

'Hello, Miss Crewe. Don't say anything, please. I know what you're thinking.'

'I don't think you do,' I said.

David Porter looked straight ahead; there was a muscle twitching in his jaw.

'I wanted to tell you that you shouldn't see this as the end. You're a bright girl, Rachel. Don't blow it. This doesn't have to be the end of anything.'

'Oh, I know that,' said Rachel.

'We're late,' said David Porter. He revved the engine.

'Daddy, don't be so overdramatic; it's boring.' Rachel turned to me. 'Miss Crewe's only trying to say goodbye, for God's sake.'

'You don't talk to me like that. You don't *talk* to me like that!' He spoke through gritted teeth, turning in his seat and actually pointing his finger at his daughter as though she were five years old. Rachel laughed, but there was fear in her eyes. I could see it. I stood back.

Looking at her there in the car with her father, I couldn't help feeling that I had let her down somehow. Could have done more to save her? I wasn't sure.

'Well, goodbye,' I said. 'Please keep in touch. You know where I am.'

Rachel smiled. 'You're a Grit, Miss Crewe. You know that?'

I had a feeling I had only made matters worse.

It wasn't until two days later that I heard the news from Bethany Slade. Rachel and her father had been in a car crash on their way home – mere minutes after she had spoken to Howard Tempest in the car park outside St Libby's. A van had come out in front of them and swept their car off the road. David Porter had escaped unharmed, but Rachel had been thrown out of the window. She had lost her left arm and had smashed up one side of that exquisite face.

I was appalled. Bethany, to her credit, was shaking when told me.

74

'I never meant for any of this to happen,' she kept saying. Then, minutes later: 'If they had only listened.'

She left me on my own. Once the door had shut behind her, I picked up the telephone and tried to call Alexander Hammond. Finding he was out, I sat down at my table and breathed deeply. Over and over again, I thought about Rachel and how I had spoken to her before she left St Libby's for the last time. I had held them up by at least a minute. It didn't take much to realize that, if I hadn't run down and spoken to Rachel, she would still have her arm and her face. The van wouldn't have hit them.

The girls at the school were stunned, the carnival atmosphere that usually accompanied the end of term, shattered. Rachel might have been expelled, but she was still one of them. In a boarding school, even the girls who never talked to her knew what toothpaste she used, what pyjamas she wore, how her hair looked after a shower. I sensed from one or two of them that there was a slight feeling of justice being done – she had been too pretty, too popular, she had got away with too much for too long.

'I think it will make her into a better person,' was the unforgive-able response from one of the upper sixth, as she pored over the grainy photographs of the crash scene in the local paper. They were deeply shocked. Rachel Porter had been that most necessary thing in any institution: the rebel, the one who hadn't so much torn up the rule book as completely ignored its existence. Without her, the rest of the sixth form was as rudderless as they would have been if Bethany Slade herself had walked out of the school. They needed both ends of the scale to know where they stood.

And so, in the space of a few days, everything changed, and I had lost the two girls that I cared most about. One whose mathematical ability far outstripped my own, and the other whose nightly con-versations, standing outside the door of my flat, suggested that she – more than anyone else in my life – somehow understood that there was more to me than I let on. I took comfort in the same way

I always had: going over every dance that he had taught me, recalling every step, counting in every flick of the wrist, every movement of my head. Timing: everything in dance and life was about timing, counting, adding everything up to make the right answer. *One, two, three, four, five, six, seven, eight!* You lost count, and you lost everything. He used to say that, too. All is number.

Every night for the week that followed, I lay in bed needing to cry, yet quite unable to.

7

Marnie

It was Howard who told me what had happened to Rachel. He came upstairs to my bedroom, where I was sitting listlessly on the end of my bed, reading the last dog-eared pages of an old Barbara Cartland novel. He knocked on my door and pushed it open.

'Hello?' I said, confused. Howard didn't do the top floor of the house – it was the exclusive territory of Caspar and I. Seeing him up here was confusing – it certainly didn't feel right.

'Sorry,' he said, stepping inside.

He had a newspaper under his arm. I remember thinking that he looked pale – almost green.

'What is it?' I asked, immediately alarmed. The book fell to the floor, its opening pages fluttering out from the covers. Howard unfolded the paper, then folded it again.

'Bloody hell, Marnie. I hardly know how to tell you this. It's – it's your friend. Rachel Porter.'

Momentarily, I relaxed. It wasn't Caspar, or Jukey, or James. Rachel had probably been caught out on the town with one of Howard's friends. He wouldn't like that, I thought. No wonder he looked so tense.

'What's she done?' I asked, picking up the book.

Howard stepped back, as though preparing to deliver a line; yet, when he spoke, it was too quickly, as though the words were dangerous in themselves and might cause further harm if they weren't dealt with immediately.

'She's . . . There's been a car crash. Two days ago. Must have been just after she left St Libby's with her father. They had to operate on her immediately. It says here that she's lost her arm.'

'*What?*'

Howard opened the paper and read. Even under these circumstances, he projected properly, as though auditioning. He just couldn't help it.

'Landowner and successful banker, David Porter, fifty-eight, escaped unharmed, but his daughter, Rachel, sixteen, had to be cut from the wreckage and taken to hospital. Later, doctors made the decision to amputate her right arm. She is also suffering from burns.'

He stared down at the photograph of Rachel and her father, evidently taken at some red-hot event in London, months before. Rachel was wearing a pale blue dress and carrying a glass of champagne. Her father was smoking and looking away from the camera, but Rachel was right there – staring at whoever had taken the picture, with all that familiar confidence. And why shouldn't she?

'I don't believe it,' I whispered. 'It can't be true. *Is* it true?'

Howard shrugged and shook his head. 'I'm afraid it must be.'

In that instant, I felt my whole body reacting to the news as though the force of its impact were travelling from my head right down to my toes. I started to shake, uncontrollably, my teeth chattering as though I were freezing cold, but I could feel my face flaming – on fire.

'She's a painter,' I said. 'It's what she wants to do. She's a painter.' I was aware of my own arms waving in front of me in imitation brush strokes. 'It's what she's good at. She can't paint without her arm.'

I felt a crazed desire to laugh.

'Sixteen,' said Howard. 'Who deserves that at sixteen? She's just a baby!'

'I don't know why she even went back to school that day,' I muttered. 'Why didn't she just stay at home?'

'I spoke to her briefly,' said Howard. 'She said that her father had wanted her to come so that he could lecture her in peace.'

Even then, I knew that this wasn't true. Rachel had turned up because there was a chance that she could see Howard.

'And now look what's happened,' I said. 'If he had just let her be . . . He *never* lets her be. He doesn't understand her. She told me that.'

'Does any father understand his daughter?' said Howard bleakly. He stood up and looked out of my bedroom window. 'Do you want a cigarette?'

Generally, I didn't accept this sort of offer from Howard. It represented the side of him that seemed to want to be our friend, rather than a parent, and I didn't want that from him. That afternoon I nodded dumbly. He pulled a cigarette from his case and lit it for me.

'I must call Tamsin.' I accepted the cigarette and stood up, light-headed. 'Rachel's little sister. She's in the lower fifth. I need to call her.' I repeated the words. 'I need to speak to Tamsin.'

Howard looked at me. 'Leave it a week or so,' he said.

'But she adores Rachel! I have to talk to her—'

'She'll be surrounded by people. She won't need anyone else—'

'I *have* to talk to her! I need her telephone number. Where would it be?' I started looking around my room frantically.

'Marnie!' said Howard. 'Stop!'

'Why? I must call Tamsin. I need to find out how Rachel is – from her. I want to know how bad the burns are. I want to see her—'

'You mustn't call her,' said Howard. Something in the tone of his voice brought me up sharp.

'Why?'

'Tamsin Porter telephoned here earlier today,' said Howard. 'Your mother didn't want you to know, but I think it's best that you're told.'

'She's already called? Then I must call her back—'

'No. She was insistent that you didn't telephone. She's very upset. It's not a good idea to speak to her now.'

I breathed in, a sudden realization hitting me with brute force.

'Oh. Oh, I see. She thinks it's my fault,' I said. 'All of this. She blames *me*, doesn't she?'

Howard looked at me. 'She's just a child, Marnie.'

Outside I could hear a blackbird's alarm call from the nest in the box on the ash tree.

'She thinks that if we hadn't been expelled, then Rachel wouldn't have been in the crash,' I said. 'And *I* was the reason we were expelled. She knows that.'

I stared at the end of my cigarette. It had gone out. Howard handed me his lighter, but I couldn't do anything with it. I was oddly and acutely aware of my every sensation, my entire body felt as though it had been lit up, adrenalin poured over my consciousness like petrol on a flame.

'If I hadn't been so drunk, and if I hadn't insisted that we should swim, then none of this would have happened,' I said, seeing the clarity of it all in sharp relief. 'She's absolutely right. It's true, isn't it? She rang to tell me that it was my fault?'

'She was upset,' said Howard. 'I don't think she knew what she was saying, and she's just a kid of . . . What is she? Thirteen?'

'Fifteen,' I said.

'Give her a week to settle down.'

'But why should she settle down,' I asked him, 'when she's right?'

In that moment, the world could have swallowed me up. I felt myself hurtling away from everything that I had ever known, all certainty vanishing. Into my mind came the boy from Shredded Wheat. I closed my eyes.

'Leave it,' said Howard again. He put an arm around me. 'It's all right. Life's not always a straight line from A to B. There are messy turns, and false starts, and times when you can't see any good coming from something. But mark my words, something will turn up.'

I didn't know what he was saying, or what he meant, but I was dimly aware of his desire to make everything better, and I think that it was this, more than anything else, that made me want to cry.

'Try to sleep,' said Howard. 'I'll send your mother up to say goodnight.'

He stood in the doorway as though he needed to say more but didn't know how.

'I won't have you blaming yourself,' he said. But, even as he spoke the words, he was giving me permission to do just that. The *lack* of blame – the absence of anger, of reproach or reprimand – from Howard was almost the most painful thing of all. He knew it was too serious for any of these things. He knew that if he had added to my feelings of guilt, then he might well have pushed me over the edge. As it was, I was standing on the brink of it all, afraid of being alone because it meant asking myself the question over and over again: Why did I make her swim? And would she ever forgive me?

Tamsin was right. It was my fault. If I had not suggested that we carried on drinking when we got back to school, then perhaps she would still have all her limbs, and that *face*, and her future. I wrote to Rachel, without knowing what to say. What I wanted to write was, *Please don't blame me. I never wanted this to happen.* Instead, I asked if she would see me, whereupon Tamsin telephoned me at North Bridge and I had the conversation that confirmed everything I felt.

I picked up the telephone and, for a moment, was confused by the high, clear voice on the end of the line, asking for Marnie.

'Rachel!' I said. I put a hand on to the window ledge to steady myself.

'No,' said the voice. 'It's Tamsin.'

'Oh, Tamsin. Hello. I thought—'

'I know what you thought. I've not got long to talk.'

'How is she? I wrote to her—'

'I know you wrote. That's why I'm calling you now.'

I let the silence hang between us.

'You . . . You think it was my fault, don't you? You think that, if I hadn't suggested that we swim, then none of this would have happened.'

She didn't answer me. I heard the sound of muffled sobbing.

'I understand why you think it,' I said. 'I would, if I were you. I'd say I was sorry, if I thought it would make any difference. If I thought that it would make you feel better.'

'There's nothing that can make any of us feel any better,' said Tamsin.

'I know,' I said. 'Don't think I don't feel it too.'

'But you're all right, aren't you? You didn't lose your arm! She's a painter! That's all she wanted to do . . .'

More crying. I felt my chest tightening. Despite everything, I couldn't help recalling Rachel's words to me about her sister: *She doesn't know me. She thinks I'm someone quite different to who I actually am. My family don't really know who I am at all.*

'I don't want you to contact her again,' said Tamsin. 'Not now.'

'If that's what you want,' I said. There was a pause. 'Is that what Rachel wants?'

'Yes,' said Tamsin. 'She's still confused by everything. She's so weak. She mustn't hear from you.'

'If you change your mind, I'm right here.'

'Goodbye, Marnie.'

The receiver clattered down. My hands were shaking. If Tamsin Porter had me pinned as the one whose fault it was, then who was I to take that away from her? But I hated her for it. More than anything else, I hated her for using the word 'weak' to describe her sister. Rachel was never weak, not before the accident and, I was certain, not now. I went straight to the drinks trolley in the corner of the dining room.

Two weeks after Howard told me about Rachel, I started at West Park Comprehensive. I knew it would be tough, but, after what had happened to Rachel, I yearned for the punishment. I didn't even believe in myself as a mathematician any longer, but at least West Park would keep me out of the way of everyone else. Howard and Jukey were difficult to live with, and, in my view, the local comprehensive was what I deserved. I kept my head down and tried not to make enemies, which was easier said than done. I had come from St Libby's, an establishment hated by the kids at West Park – with some justification. What got me through those first weeks there was the same thing that got me through each night since Rachel's accident. It was him – always him: the boy from the factory. I convinced myself that if I could only see him again then everything would be all right somehow.

Maths at my new school was taught by a woman called Mrs Harris, who resembled – ironically – a distorted version of Miss Crewe. Like Miss Crewe, she had red hair, but hers was thinning and greying, parted ferociously in the middle and pinned into a low bun at the back. She chain smoked, and was suspicious of me from the start; I had arrived at West Park as a criminal and was very probably still one now. Miss Crewe had taught in a way that made sense of the most complex mathematical notions; Mrs Harris seemed to be working as hard as she could to complicate everything. She had her favourites, and they were all boys; the few girls in the class had to fend for themselves.

She seemed particularly taken with a stocky, blond boy called Mark Abbot, who sat next to me and answered everything ten seconds before I could, and with a heavy east-London accent. His family had moved to Welwyn from Brick Lane when he was twelve, and he talked all the time about returning there. He had a round, boyish face full of freckles, and huge feet. Mark spoke loudly, with a mouth full of expletives and robust opinions on everyone and everything. Despite his unprepossessing looks, he was something of a hit with the girls – they considered him amusing and he was the owner of a large collection of Rolling Stones records – but I can't say I was about to fall in love with him. I wasn't in the mood for puns about prime numbers every five minutes, nor for his incessant opinions on Fermat. Having never been at school with boys before, I was utterly thrown by the experience of mixed classes, although for the first few weeks I was too shaken by what had happened to Rachel to care.

But I tolerated it because it was what had to happen. I tolerated it because, if I didn't go to West Park, then Howard would have packed me off to Paris, and that felt like running away. I was an unknown quantity to my fellow pupils; the St Libby's expulsion tag lent me a certain exotic appeal, but then I was a maths girl, which lessened the allure considerably. I lived in fear of anyone finding out about Howard, knowing that I would never live it down. One girl who especially disliked me was a fiery brunette called Tina Scott; she spun a great line in prophetic taunts, usually punctuated with some form of physical attack – a swift kick to my left shin, or perhaps a pinch on my arm. We were sixteen – hardly little girls – which must have made my reaction (usually to choke back tears, push her aside and walk off saying nothing) even more absurd to the inevitable onlookers.

'What you goin' to do when you leave?' Mark Abbot asked me quite suddenly at the end of a maths lesson in the middle of May.

'I don't know yet.'

'Me neither,' he said. 'I don't like the idea of maths turning into anyfin' else. I just like it how it is. Like a game now, ain't it?'

I looked at him in surprise.

He leaned forward and spoke to me in barely more than a whisper.

'You know, sometimes I look around the room and I fink, What must it feel like not to get it?'

'Get what?'

'Maths,' he said. 'What else?'

But, when he grinned at me, he could have meant a million different things. I felt myself turning scarlet.

'What's up wiv you, anyway?' he went on. 'Got your period? You're always miserable, you know.'

'Isn't it extraordinary?' I said, glaring at him. 'In a place as wonderful as this!'

I picked up my folders and walked out of the room.

I didn't talk about Rachel to anyone except Caspar, when he was home for weekends; his black-humoured attitude towards her lost arm was shocking – even by his low standards. We sat at the kitchen table, drinking milky tea and eating shards of parmesan cheese from a huge hunk of the stuff that had arrived from Italy in a parcel from a director friend of Howard's. Jukey never ate cheese, fearing nightmares.

'You can't make jokes about it,' I said to Caspar, horrified, when he had remarked that Rachel had lent a hand to the dangerous-driving campaign.

'I would very much hope that, if the same thing happened to me, people would retain their ability to laugh. Pass me another cracker, will you?'

'What is there to laugh about? She can't paint any longer. The one thing that she lived for is gone.'

'Firstly, from what I know about Rachel Porter, she lived for quite a lot of things. Secondly, she's got a left hand, hasn't she?'

'Well, yes. But she'll have to start again.'

I could sense that seasick feeling coming over me whenever I confronted the reality of Rachel's situation.

'Starting again is a golden ticket.'

'Do you really believe that?' I asked him incredulously.

'Yes,' said Caspar firmly. 'She's not dead.'

'Sometimes I think you're not capable of feeling anything at all.'

'I am.' He looked at me defiantly and put down his biscuit. 'I'm going to see Nick playing.'

'What?'

'I'm going to watch him sing. He's performing in Cambridge at a May Ball next week, and I'm going to be there.'

'Cambridge? May Ball?'

'Yes. Sounds quite horrendous, doesn't it? A load of phoney intellectuals prancing about in black tie they've hired from the high street. Ugh!'

'How are you going to wangle that one? Aren't you supposed to be at school?'

'I shall escape somehow,' he said. 'Haven't quite planned it yet. But I'm going. I have to rescue him.' He shuddered and re-engaged with his cheese.

'Does he know you're planning this? Does he want you there?'

'I don't know.' Caspar doodled a heart on an unopened brown envelope on the hall table. 'It's better not to know. His indifference to the situation would kill me.'

'Don't be caught,' I begged him. 'You *can't* get expelled too.'

'Oh, but it would be worth it, wouldn't it? Just to capture James's face on film.'

What amazed me, more than anything, was how much I missed St Libby's. I had never been the centre of attention at school – at least, not until I got mixed up with Rachel Porter for twenty-four hours – but being thrown to the wolves at West Park certainly highlighted the brilliance of St Libby's. West Park was basically an ugly school, all rectangles, it felt as though it had been made from cardboard. It succeeded in being modern without the thrill of the new; functional without promise. I found that I missed St Libby's for the most obvious things: the hordes of girls trooping through the dining room, piling plates of toast and bowls of bran flakes on to their trays and moaning about unfinished essays. I missed listening to the radio in the evening beside the tennis courts and the peace of the library. I missed the space that St Libby's had provided, and wished, savagely, that I had appreciated it while I had it.

I was shocked by the behaviour of some of the West Park pupils, and even more so by the resigned attitude of the teachers. Bullying was rife, as was bunking out of lessons, swearing at staff and throwing food and books around on the bus to school. The only thing that gave me the remotest scrap of comfort on these dismal journeys was dreaming about the boy from the factory. I thought about him so much that he became a figure steeped in fantasy, and it got to the stage where I found it impossible to imagine that our meeting had taken place at all. In my head, he had become an opaque symbol of hope, of good luck. Whenever the bus drove past the Wheat, I stared out of the window, looking for him, but he was never there. What would Rachel do? I thought, knowing the answer as plainly as if I had asked her myself. She would go back and look for him; she would do something about him. I had taken to hearing Rachel's voice in my head quite a lot, particularly after drinking.

At least try, FitzPatrick, I heard her saying to me. *You've got to try.* So, one Saturday, in the middle of May, I hitched a lift into town with Jukey – who had fixated on a finding a specific red wine for some dinner party – and walked towards the factory again. Would he be there? I didn't know, but I had to find out. On that day, it felt like the only thing that was any good in my life was the memory of seeing a boy who had made my heart jump. I had nothing to lose.

It was a warm afternoon and Welwyn Garden City was shot through with pink and white blossom. The town felt exactly how Ebenezer Howard and his cohorts had wanted it to be – a film-set of a place, where the town and country met together in perfect harmony.

Just knowing that I had made the decision to find the boy had lifted my spirits higher than they had been in weeks. I was doing it for Rachel too, I thought. This wasn't just for me. I crossed Hunters Bridge and looked down towards Bridge Road; the whole world seemed to open up in front of me and, for a moment, the endless pushing inside that I felt from Rachel's accident ceased. The sky was so sure, so boundless; there was a certainty in what I was doing that I hadn't felt for some time.

Yet, when I got round the railway side of the factory, I lost my nerve. I couldn't do it. He wouldn't be here, which would be shattering, or he would be here, which would be even worse! I turned to go, to give up, but stopped. There was another building – not physically attached to the factory itself, but right next to it – and the sound of a record was coming from inside: the Rolling Stones, singing 'Paint It Black' – I would have known that menacing sitar anywhere; Caspar had the thing on all the time on his record player in his bedroom.

I walked up to the building and pushed open the door, but as I stepped forward, I hit my leg on the wall. I glanced down and saw it was bleeding. Gosh, was this a sign? Go no further or you'll hurt even worse? I dabbed it with my handkerchief, stuffed the handkerchief into my pocket, and followed the music deeper inside. It led me to a room, on the door of which someone had pinned a piece of paper that read, *Club Room: Darts 3 p.m.*

I edged inside. I can't say what I noticed about the club room at first – I don't think that I took in the unmanned bar at the back, or the sticky floors, or the dart boards, or the pool table. I certainly didn't see the notices pinned up around the room, nor the red walls, nor the tables and chairs pushed to the sides of the room, awaiting action. That was all resolutely ordinary, nothing but a backdrop. I just noticed him. He was right in the middle of the room, and he was dancing, so he didn't notice me. Let me write that again: *he was dancing.*

88

I remember the way he moved and how absorbed he was; he was so entirely in his own space that I felt not just embarrassed for being there, but *cruel*. I knew I shouldn't be seeing this; I had invaded a private world. My reaction was to stand as still as I could, somehow believing that, if I didn't move, I would blend in with my surroundings and he wouldn't notice me, and for at least thirty seconds this actually worked.

He danced on, and I can't say how he was dancing – at least I couldn't back then. All I knew was that the way he was moving reminded me of the films Jukey liked to watch; to put it in the crude terms that I was capable of accessing at that moment, he danced like he knew how to dance. It appeared he was talking to himself as he did so, his face altering with every step, frowning, then clear, bright, almost ecstatic. It was the expressions that I noticed far more clearly than anything else; later that day, his features evaporated from my head, as they do when you try too hard to conjure someone up, but I would always have known him, had I seen him move. I did notice how skinny he was, and what he was wearing – the same overalls, this time with the legs rolled up to the knees, as though he had been paddling in the sea. That hair, which I had dreamed of since I had first seen him on the bus, was just as it had been – almost black, worn quite long – he tucked it behind his ear.

When he saw me, he stopped moving. The song was nearly at an end, but he ran over to the record player and pulled up the needle. I braced myself – my back rammed against the door. For a wild, terrifying moment, I thought he was going to ask me to dance, and I couldn't dance, I just *couldn't*.

But he didn't.

'You here for the darts?' he asked me, frowning.

'I'm sorry?'

'Darts? It doesn't start till later.'

'Darts? No. No, I'm not here for darts.' I laughed, and sounded ridiculous. He did not.

'Well, do you work here? What . . . ? Are you looking for Mr Anderson? He's not here today.'

'No, I don't work here.'

He tapped his head quickly and deliberately, four times on each side.

'Well?' he asked impatiently. 'What d'you want?'

'I have never been inside the factory before.'

'This isn't the factory. This is the club room. How did you get in? Wasn't there anyone on the door?'

'No,' I said. 'I just walked in. Will someone come after me?'

'I doubt it. We're not in a fucking James Bond film.'

I recalled Rachel's questions about diamond smuggling and laughed weakly. Did he know me? Did he remember me at all?

'I'm clearing up,' he said. 'Just listening to some records. It's not illegal, you know.'

'I know. I think it's good. I like the song. My brother listens to it at home.'

'Right.' He hesitaited, then said, 'I like Brian Jones. His style, you know?'

'My brother says he's the most talented,' I said. 'I'm sorry. I shouldn't have just come in like this.' I looked up at the ceiling. 'This is a nice room,' I said weakly.

'People don't work in here. They come to do other things.'

'Like dance?'

He ignored me and picked up his coat.

'Your leg's bleeding, you know,' he said, nodding at the lower half of my body.

I looked down. There was indeed blood running down my bare shin and meeting my sock.

'Shit,' I muttered. I scrambled in my pocket again for my hand-kerchief and held it around the cut.

'I'm sorry. I shouldn't be here. I don't—'

'Club room's never normally empty on a Saturday afternoon,

but there was something up with the lights. I've been mending them.'

'It didn't look like you were mending lights.'

'I know. That's because I don't mend in the same way as other people.' He took a drag of his cigarette. Looking back on it that afternoon, I concluded that he didn't really want to be talking to me, but I was there, and there was precious little he could do about it.

'Have you worked here long?' I asked.

'I'm training here. I do the electrics,' he said.

'I know,' I said.

He frowned at me. 'Do I know you?'

'No. Not really. At least – I've seen you once. My friend, Rachel, and I, we saw you outside the factory a while back. She talked to you.'

I could hear the nerves in my voice that came with talking about Rachel and that fateful afternoon.

'St Libby's girls?' he remembered.

'Not any more. We were expelled, actually. Just after we met you. Not that you were anything to do with it. Rachel – the girl I was with – she was in a car crash. She – she lost an arm.'

'Fuck.'

I had the usual surge of adrenalin that I experienced while relaying these events – a rush of relief at speaking out loud what I thought about so often, combined with dread of knowing that every time I spoke of it, the story became real again.

'I went to West Park,' he said. 'I left two years ago.'

'Did you like it?'

He laughed in amazement, as though I were mad. 'No,' he said. 'Who likes school? Maybe you do if you go to St Libby's,' he added as an afterthought.

He stepped away from the wall; he was chewing gum like James Dean, but he had none of the swagger, no English boy did

– even Mick Jagger was acting. All the same, he had the face to carry it off.

'I can't believe you were dancing,' I said. 'It's like something from a book,' I added, saying what I should have kept to myself.

He snorted. 'No, it's not. It's just that this is the only place I can do it. There's no space anywhere else. They have darts here in an hour. This is the only time I've got to myself. I know I'm safe in here. At least, I thought I was.'

'Is that what you want to do?' I said. 'Dance?'

'Of course it is.'

'You're following your dream,' I breathed.

'Yeah. And it's really beginning to piss me off.'

'Why?'

He looked at me in irritation.

'There's only so much I can do. I can't teach myself any more.' He sighed and tapped his head again, looking away from me.

'You mean you need a teacher?'

'Why? Are you offering to teach me?' He laughed.

'Well, no. But I think I might know someone who could help you. At least – I could ask.'

What was I saying? I stared at him, feeling the blood rushing to my face. Oh, horrors, I thought, I'm going to pass out. I was terrible with fainting; usually I carried an apple in my pocket to stave off attacks, but in the past few weeks I had forgotten entirely. Now all this, combined with too little to eat . . . I felt myself spinning lightly, heard the buzzing in my ears.

'I'm sorry. I feel a bit funny.'

'You OK?'

'I don't know.'

I steadied myself, leaned down over my knees and took several deep breaths.

'I haven't eaten for a while,' I said. 'It always makes me a bit light-headed.'

92

'You need to eat,' he said. He pulled a squashed doughnut from his pocket and handed it to me. 'Go on,' he said. 'Have it.'

'Are you sure?' I stared down at it.

'It's a doughnut, not the bread of eternal life.'

'What?' I sounded anxious; I didn't know if he was joking.

'Have it,' he said.

I ate half of it in silence, then stopped for long enough for him to ask, with a certain amount of impatience, 'You're not going to eat the rest of that?'

'Do you want it back? You can have it!'

I held it out to him, and he took it back from me and shoved the rest of it into his mouth.

Oh! I thought. We be of one doughnut, ye and I!

He was looking at me, waiting for me to say more about the dance teacher. I had started, so I had to finish.

'I knew this lady – this woman – and . . . well, she . . . she told me she used to dance. She was my teacher at St Libby's.'

'Dance teacher?'

'No. Maths.'

'Maths?'

'Well, yes. Only, she used to dance – when she was younger. She told me once. I don't know what kind of dancing she did, but I know she did it. I know she's good, because she's good at everything she does. She could do it. Teach you, I mean. I think I could ask her for you – if you wanted. She's American. Canadian, I mean – which is the same sort of thing, I always think. At least, it's not according to her, but it's near enough, isn't it?'

He stared at me. There was white sugar round the edges of his lips.

'Are you serious?' he asked me. 'Because if you're not, then forget it.'

I don't think I have ever been more serious about any single suggestion in my entire life, I thought.

'I am!' I said, trying to keep my voice steady. 'I am serious!'

'She's not some old lady or something, is she? She can still move?'

'Oh, no. She's not old. I mean, she's older than me – than us. I haven't seen her since I was slung out of St Libby's, but I can find her. I know where to find her. Easy. Then we could meet her – have a cup of coffee and talk about it.' I threw this last line out in the way that I had heard Howard throw it out to countless theatrical people. It sounded ludicrous.

'Well, thanks, but it's not like I have all the time in the world to meet people for cups of coffee,' he said. He sounded agitated – as though I were out to trick him.

'No. I didn't mean literally coffee. I just mean you should meet her. She may be able to help you.'

'It would have to be next Saturday.'

'Right. Next Saturday.'

He moved faster than I did. In my head, I was screaming at myself that Miss Crewe was unlikely to want to come and meet a strange boy and teach him to dance in the Shredded Wheat factory.

'Where?' he asked.

My mind raced. Even if I managed to speak to Miss Crewe before then, I couldn't possibly take my expelled self along with a strange boy into the grounds of St Libby's. There would be a riot.

'Could we meet back here?' I asked him.

He hesitated. 'Yeah, all right. This the club room, right? The club room,' he repeated. 'We'll meet here. About this time? We'll have to be quick. There's a youth group meeting here at midday and darts later on. I can't be seen to be using the place for myself or I'll be screwed. No one must know.'

'Of course.'

'Just you and her, right?'

'No one else,' I breathed.

'And you don't tell anyone, right?'

'Of course not.'

He tapped his fingers rhythmically over his forehead again, in the same way that I had seen him do several times now. I wanted to say something else, but found I couldn't. I looked down at my awful shoes, and hated myself. I wanted to apologize for my whole get-up, wanted to throw myself down at his feet and ask how the hell I could make myself more desirable to him. It felt that primitive. I had absolutely none of the confidence I so craved.

'What's your name?' he asked me.

'Marnie,' I said. 'And yours?'

'Freddie Friday.'

'That's . . . That's a good name.'

'Yeah,' he said. He smiled briefly, and I caught my breath. 'The alliteration. People like that.'

I couldn't sense whether he was being sarcastic.

He looked up at the clock on the wall. 'I need to get going.'

'Me too.'

'You go first,' he said. 'I have to lock up.'

'Can I . . . ? Can I have a look? I'd like to see where all the machines are.'

He looked as though he didn't believe me, but he nodded. 'All right. If we're quick. Come on, then.'

Once inside the factory itself, I felt humbled by my own assumptions. How could I have grown up knowing something from the outside so well, yet never stepping into its interior? The factory floor was warm – the whole place was warm and immaculately neat: rows of chairs waiting to be filled, stacks of unassembled boxes awaiting that famous product that would travel from here to all those hundreds of breakfast tables. And the smell – that was what hit me more than anything. Not the malty, comforting smell of wheat that I associated so potently with a childhood growing up near the factory – it was so much more than that on the inside. Here, it felt overpowering, alcoholic, invading every corner of space and mingling with another smell – that of fresh cardboard, sweat and industry. Standing there and looking at it close up, it was like being inside the beating body of something, no longer hearing the rhythm softly, but feeling and breathing all the guts and the veins that kept a creature alive.

'Gosh,' I said again. 'It's quite something.'

'You get used to it pretty quick,' he said. I liked the way he said 'pretty', leaving out the *ts*, as everyone did at West Park – yet, on him, it was different.

I didn't know how to thank him again, so I offered him my hand. He shook it.

Then I walked out, back into the real world. All that mattered now was that Miss Crewe showed up next Saturday. I tripped towards the railway with wings on my heels.

8

Miss Crewe

The term after Rachel and Marnie left began badly. Bethany Slade, knowing that I had objected so heavily to their expulsion, seemed to have it in for me. Without Marnie, my sixth-form maths group was a bleak place. Certainly there were a couple of other girls who showed vague promise, but no one had that instinct, that love for the subject that I had seen in her. I wondered how she was getting on at West Park. I would have liked to have telephoned to ask her if she wanted extra help, but I was stifled by the same thing that had always stopped me from stepping outside what I knew: fear that I would be rejected. Perhaps best to let sleeping dogs lie.

Alexander Hammond noticed that I was low, and did his best to cheer me up.

'Raymondo's?' he asked cheerfully.

He tried this every week. About once a month, I accepted him. Poor Alexander – I had used him like a drug, and given nothing to him in return.

Washing my hair under the weak shower-head in my basin later on, I had almost forgotten that I was meeting Alexander in town for dinner. I would make an effort for once, I thought. Not for him, but for me. I would dress up as though I was meeting Jo again.

I had to stand on my bed to view my body in the mirror in my room. My scarred leg always looked particularly bad at the start of the summer, the red and white lines undisguised by the light tan I made sure I acquired as soon as the sun started to shine again. My chest was all right – one of the benefits of not having had children was that it remained suspended in time – but the body I had taken for granted when I was eighteen, when I was a dancer . . . it had gone on the day of the crash. The confidence that I used to have – the dancer's posture, the superiority of knowing that I carried myself like royalty – that had vanished overnight.

I stood down again, pulled on a sweater and stared at my face. I didn't much like staring at my face, for fear of what I might encounter. Partly it was the confusion of it all. Forty-one was fraught with confusion. Sometimes when I looked at myself I saw someone little changed since her thirtieth birthday. Other times, I felt I could have passed for fifty-eight, and counting.

Alexander was smoking outside the pub when I arrived. Despite having made a vague effort with a jacket and clean shoes, he still looked like a giant in a smaller man's mufti. Alexander, more than any other person I knew, seemed as though he would be happiest without the restriction of clothing at all; despite his height and his size, he never stooped. I regretted my straight black trousers, boots and newly washed hair. Looking as though I had made even the slightest effort for him was usually a mistake.

'You look very lovely,' he said. 'Far too good for Raymondo's.'

'Let's go somewhere else, then.'

He looked at me, not without suspicion. 'Where?'

'I don't know.'

'You want to have a walk?'

'All right, yes – that would be nice.'

Alexander was so big that he seemed to forge a path in front of us like Moses as he strode down the road. I almost had to trot to keep up with him. He stopped at a bench in the middle of the park and we sat down.

'What's wrong?' he said. He pulled half a packet of Maltesers from his pocket and offered me one. I shook my head.

'I've been thinking about Rachel,' I said. 'I can't stop thinking about her. That face . . .' I tailed off. It didn't need to be said. He knew what I meant.

'Awful,' said Alexander.

I felt the tears coming, unstoppable. It was the way that Alexander said those two syllables: *Awful*. The same would have been said of me, after the fall that left me unable to dance. Alexander must have been shocked, because it certainly hadn't ever been in the script that I should dissolve into silent hysterics, but he acted quickly. For reasons that I think even he would have struggled to explain, he tore off his jersey, as though I were on fire, and wrapped it around my shoulders, then stood back from the bench, as though protecting me from onlookers.

'It's all right,' he said to my crumpled form. 'Crying's a good thing. Anyone with any sense cries now and then.'

His jersey smelled of him – of cigarettes and the soft, uncompli-cated odour of the Old Spice aftershave that he wore, the adverts for which were entirely at odds with his outsized-bear persona. I breathed in and closed my eyes. He was standing back from me still, patting me gingerly from a distance, as though getting any closer might result in his immediate arrest. I couldn't blame him; I had kept Alexander as far away as it was possible to keep a friend.

'Sometimes I think it's my fault,' I said.

'Well, how could that be?'

'I don't know. Perhaps I should have kept a better eye on her that day. I wasn't even there when they were drinking.'

'Where were you?'

'In town. I went to the theatre.' I looked at him, seeing him only dimly.

'The theatre?'

'It doesn't matter,' I said. 'I'm sorry.' I lurched back into the reality of what I was doing, and pulled a tissue out of my pocket. 'Ignore me,' I added. 'I'm tired.'

'Ignore you?' Alexander looked at me. 'Julie, I don't think that's going to happen, I'm afraid.'

There was a split second of possibility, a fractured little moment when anything could have happened. In a parallel universe, I ran into his arms, made him take me home with him and tear off my clothes. I felt it somewhere, that stirring of desire, the need to be held, but it was impossible to access in its entire, pure form. It was too distant – something blurred, out of focus.

'Do you want to come back to mine? Stay the night?' I heard him asking me. 'Not like that,' he added quickly. 'You could stay in my spare bedroom. If you want some company. I've got some marking to do. We could do it together. Marking, I mean,' he added hastily.

'I should get back to Kelp,' I said, and the moment was lost again, and every door closed and locked.

'At least come back to mine and have some food,' he said. 'We don't have to do Raymondo's. I've got six crumpets, half a pint of milk, a packet of Puffed Wheat and some Philadelphia cream cheese.'

I laughed.

'Stay and eat,' he urged, encouraged. 'Then we can watch something on the box.'

I stood up and blew my nose. 'You're too good for me,' I said.

'That's a stupid thing to say,' said Alexander. He sighed and looked at me, right in the eyes.

'You can't wait around for me,' I said. 'There are a hundred women out there who'd do anything to be out with you. You're such a kind man—'

'Oh, sod that!'

'No. You are, Alexander.'

'Being kind doesn't get you anywhere,' he said. '*He* wasn't kind, was he?'

'Who?'

'The one who did this to you, who made you like you are.'

I had never talked to Alexander about him.

'He did nothing to me,' I said. 'I did it to myself.'

'Well, undo it,' said Alexander. He looked out into the park. 'Cassie Packard asked me to go to the cinema with her last week,' he said.

I widened my eyes.

'You didn't tell me that!'

'Why should I?'

'Are you going to go?'

'Maybe,' he said with an edge of defiance. 'She's nice. She likes me, which is a step in the right direction, if nothing else.'

I swallowed. 'Cassie Packard's handwriting is wrong,' I said.

'Her handwriting? What's that got to do with anything?'

'It's too small, too tidy. She's not the one. You can do better. And what are you going to see, anyway?'

'*The Prime of Miss Jean Brodie.*'

'Yup. That would be right.' I lowered my eyes, hating myself.

'Shall I drive you home?' He didn't sound cold, or cross, but distant, which was worse than both of the others put together.

My flat in Kelp House was dismal at the best of times, but when I woke up the following morning, the place was a tip. Clothes were scattered over the bed and trickled on to the rug at its foot; the remains of the lamb cutlets, mashed potato, peas and mayonnaise I had consumed for dinner the night before sat reproachfully on my desk. Why did mayonnaise turn translucent after a few hours out of the jar? The peas had shrivelled up with the shame of it. I went into my little kitchen – brown and orange tiles with a small, round Formica table – to find a sink full of unwashed mugs. I am the biggest unwashed mug, I thought.

I stepped out of my clothes and stood naked and shivering, despite the heat of the morning, until the bath had run. Then I lay down in the tepid water, closed my eyes and did what I always did in the bath. I thought about New York.

I knew him for six weeks – that was all. I think that, had it been only six days, or six hours, it would just as likely have had the same effect on me. After that first coffee in that noisy little café in Central Park, he had asked if he could see me again.

'Sure,' I said.

'You want to dance next time?'

'Are you serious? With you?'

'Why not? I'd like to see what you can do.'

I hesitated. I wasn't great yet, and I knew it. But he was. If I danced in front of him, then he might just help me – that was what he was trying to say.

'You're serious?'

'Why shouldn't I be?'

I laughed, because I couldn't help it. 'All right!' I said. 'Same time next week.' I looked at him. 'What if you're not there? What if you've got some audition or something and you're not there?'

'You'll have to keep looking for me,' he said. He kissed me quickly on the cheek. 'See you around, Daisy.'

'Daisy? My name's not Daisy.' I'd said it before I remembered the flowers I'd strung into my hair.

'It is now.' He picked up his hat. 'You'll always be Daisy to me.'

How could he say this sort of thing and make it sound straight out of a movie?

'Same place?' I asked again.

'Yeah!' he laughed. 'The Conservatory Garden. Why not?'

'And what's your name?' I asked him.

He hesitated. 'What do you want it to be?'

I wanted the truth, I wanted everything I could find, I wanted to know everything about him. Yet there was another, sharper needle in me that wanted nothing at all. I guess I knew that I needed to stay right away from reality, even then.

'Joe,' I said. 'You're Joe, aren't you?'

'Can I be Joe without the *e*? Just the two letters? I like it better that way.'

'If you want,' I said, grinning.

He nodded at me, as though I had made a more serious decision that I realized. Then, suddenly seeming shy, as though he too had given away more than he wanted to, he glanced down at his feet and walked out. I felt something leap inside me.

The next week it rained. Not just the light drizzly stuff where you can get away with wearing a short summer dress and sandals, but the really strong stuff, the kind that soaks you within moments and makes you feel like you're on a film set. I carried a little umbrella and a small bag with my dance shoes. I had been to three auditions that week, and none of them had called me back, which had unnerved me because every one of the directors had showered me with hyperbole.

'Look at the legs on the girl!'

'She's a dancer, all right!'

'Best face I've seen all year!'

'That hair! I'm in love with red hair, you know.'

But what did it matter if I was never going to get cast in a show? If I was never going to dance on Broadway? And now it was raining. Why should he come if it was raining? He had somewhere to be that would mean more to him than being with me. He will have forgotten, I thought. I was just some girl he had shared a coffee with.

The Conservatory Garden was deserted, except for a smartly dressed elderly couple sheltering under a tree. I had copied him and had turned up the bottoms of my denims, but still they were soaked. I longed to take out my mirror and check to see if the mascara, so carefully applied for me by Eloise, had run all down my face. I had no watch. Was he late?

'Excuse me! Hey, mister!' I called out to the man under the tree. 'Do you have the time, please?'

'It's gone two,' he said.

I nodded. How far beyond two, I didn't know. But I felt certain that he wasn't coming, and my heart sank.

'You waiting for someone, miss?' asked the man's wife.

'I don't know,' I said. Then, unable to stop myself from talking, I added, 'Kind of. Yes. Well, I hardly know him, but he said he'd be here.'

'You hang on,' she said. 'He'll show.'

'How do you know?'

'Because you're beautiful, and Central Park never feels more romantic than it does in the rain. He'd have to be crazy not to be here.'

'I don't know,' I said. I smiled at her. 'Maybe you're right.'

'And you're Canadian, aren't you?'

'Yeah.' I laughed ruefully, recalling Jo's observation of this fact the previous week.

'What part?'

'Montreal.'

The man whistled. 'In my experience of the world, no one stands up a girl from Montreal.'

I haven't altered this exchange over the years. I haven't changed a single word of what was said to me before he appeared to me again. Straight out of a play, it was: a page of simple dialogue that I tore out of the script and kept with me for the next eighteen years. Because what happened next is that I saw him, sauntering towards me as though the sun were shining as bright as it had been the last time. He had a wet newspaper folded under his arm and was wearing the same rolled-up corduroys, the same hat. I closed my eyes and said a silent prayer of thanks. I really and truly thanked God. He hadn't forgotten.

★

I dressed and made a couple of telephone calls to various staff members after my bath; then, in the afternoon, I slept for three hours. When I woke, I felt slightly better and extremely hungry. The sixth form would be having tea after the tennis matches that had been taking place, and would all be gathering over in the dining room. If I hurried, there would probably be a scone or two left. If there was one thing that the St Libby's kitchen knew how to pull off, it was a match tea. I pulled up my hair and stepped into a clean skirt and blouse.

The noise of the school hall at teatime was pure Enid Blyton. Rows of girls with red cheeks and deafening voices sat on long wooden benches, reaching over each other for sandwiches – cucumber, cheese and Marmite – scones and rock-hard pieces of chocolate cake. Mrs Middlemarsh, the head cook, was filling enamel mugs with scalding-hot tea. The lower years piled in sugar lumps and stirred them around until they melted into nothing. Oh, goodness, it got to me. Sometimes the joy of it all, the excess of their youth, was near impossible to resist. It was a closed bubble, and once you were in, you were in. Nothing that was happening in the big world out there was quite as important as what was happening within these walls.

'How did you get on?' I called out to Florence Dunbar, who was much more at home on the sports fields than in the classroom.

'We won seven out of eight matches.' She grinned at me.

'Good show!' I said, pleased.

'We absolutely slaughtered them!' called out Camilla George, who was carrying three racquets and a tube of balls with some difficulty.

I helped myself to a cup of tea and a scone and looked around for the jam.

'How's your weekend been, Miss Crewe?' asked Florence, spreading a thick layer of butter on to a slice of gingerbread.

'Oh, you know. The usual,' I said, with perfect truth.

'I haven't done my maths prep,' she said regretfully. 'I wanted to get it finished before the game, but I didn't have time.' She looked at me. 'Seen Mr Hammond lately, Miss Crewe?' she asked with a salty tone to her voice.

'I know what you're asking me, and that is none of your business, Florence.'

'It's a shame you don't love him.'

Yes, I thought. It is.

'We're just friends,' I said.

'I know. That's why it's a shame.'

'Don't talk like that, Florence. I'm a member of staff.'

I made my way back over to Kelp and debated putting in a telephone call to Alexander. He would be back at school on Monday morning, and I would be facing him in the staffroom. And yet this time was different. He had laid his cards on the table and I had dropped them on the floor and swished them around like a toddler.

It wasn't until Monday morning that the letter reached me. I opened the door of the flat after break and sat down at my desk to go through the post that had arrived an hour earlier: a letter from a grateful parent of one of the middle fourth to whom I had given extra maths lessons over half-term; a warning from the library in Welwyn Garden City that a Ray Bradbury book, due back two weeks ago, was 'accruing fines'; a postcard from my sister on holiday in the Lakes (*Wordsworth's house much smaller than expected*); and another letter with handwriting that could have belonged to any number of girls at St Libby's, past or present – they all had very much the same resolutely private-school calligraphy. They had a lifetime of thank-you letters and invitations to write and receive – mantelpieces from SW3 to the far-flung castles of north-west Scotland would be littered with invitations, postcards, letters of congratulation and condolence, all written in this same script. My own writing was still so Canadian, instantly identifiable as belonging to a foreigner. I tore open the envelope and read.

Dear Miss Crewe,

I hope you don't mind me writing to you. I thought it better to write than to telephone. I have a request for you. I have met an eighteen-year-old boy who is a dancer. He is already good, but he needs a teacher to take him further. I don't know him well, but I think he could be very good.

I was wondering whether you might consider taking him on as a pupil? Or at least talking about it to him? I suggested that, if it was all right with you, we could meet at the Shredded Wheat factory (where he works as a trainee electrician) next Saturday at midday. He can use the club room in the factory to practise for a short while on Saturdays.

If you think you could do this, please could you telephone me? My number at home is at the top of the letter. If you call between seven and eight I could speak to you.

I hope everything is all right at St Libby's. I miss it. I am taking maths A-level at West Park. It is all right. The teachers are not as good as at St Lib's.

With all best wishes,

Marnie (FitzPatrick)

I read the letter through twice, picturing Marnie's face. Would this letter have taken some planning? Would she have written it out in rough first? Where had she met this dancer?

Even after reading the letter through just once, I knew what I was going to do. I would be there at the weekend, not because I believed in myself as a dance teacher, or because I wanted to help an eighteen-year-old boy with impossible dreams place one foot in front of the other in a way that might make him famous. Not because I wanted to prove myself to him, or any other kid. I would do it because I believed in Marnie as a mathematician, and that she, of all people, needed a shove in the right direction. If I went, watching the boy dance was merely an excuse so that I could help her.

9

Marnie

It was difficult, that next week, waiting for a reply from Miss Crewe and being at home after school without Caspar. James rolled up on Tuesday afternoon, and that evening spent twenty minutes reading Jukey and me an essay for which he had been awarded his first A. Jukey liked hearing James read, but I failed to take in a word and drifted off, surfing lightly over James's droning to another world, where I would see Freddie Friday again, and would know what to say to him, how to act.

As James stood in front of me, holding ten sheets of A4 paper crammed with his best imitation professor handwriting, I went over a conversation with Tina Scott in the art room at West Park the day before. All of the lower sixth had been roped into painting the set for the forthcoming production of *The Importance of Being Earnest*. I was no artist. Tina Scott, worst luck, was rather good. She had also been given the plum role of Lady Bracknell, and had started talking all the time in the style of Oscar Wilde and with the accent she had adopted for the role, which was somewhere between Joan Greenwood and Jim Dale. It pained me to admit that, as a comic actress, she had considerable flair. I needed to know more about Freddie, so I put up with it.

'Don't suppose you remember a boy who used to be here?' I asked her.

'My dear girl, I won't unless you tell me his name,' Tina-as-Lady-Bracknell replied.

'Freddie,' I said. 'Freddie Friday?'

Tina laughed loudly and delightedly, as well she might. 'Ah! Now that you mention him, I am reminded at once of such a boy. Miss FitzPatrick, are you taken with him in an amorous fashion?'

I could take being taunted in this ridiculous manner if I was being linked with him in any way whatsoever. I sensed I would make progress if I moved quickly with my questions.

'I bumped into him outside the Wheat,' I said. 'We got talking.'

'Oh, *really*?' Tina got at least eight notes out of the word. 'How delightful. He was always a quite mysterious fellow. I don't believe in mystery in a man, it is too childish for words.' She poked me in the ribs.

'Ow,' I said, pulling away from her.

'Mr Freddie Friday,' went on Tina, warming to her theme and to her role. 'It rolls off the tongue, doesn't it? But he is quite wrong for the likes of you. Alliteration in a name doth not a husband make.'

'I didn't say I wanted to marry him!'

I swirled the yellow paint around my brush, willing her to go on. I lowered my voice. 'What did *you* think of him?'

At the front of the class, Mr Aldridge, the art teacher, was leaning in his brown flannel suit over Carla Brooke's attempt to paint a vase of flowers. Carla was leaning into his chest, pressing her boobs against him – I could see it from here.

'Mr Friday was a nice-looking boy,' mused Tina. 'Rather on the thin side, which suggests vanity or ill health.'

I breathed in, hardly daring to say anything. I wanted her to go on, *go on*.

Tina, clearly torn between loathing giving me what information I wanted and the universal urge to gossip as Lady Bracknell, tutted loudly. 'Everyone always said he was a little peculiar,' she said. 'Not that a little eccentricity is anything to be afraid of.' She squirted red

109

paint into a plastic cup and reverted, quite suddenly, to her usual voice. 'Didn't have much int'rest in the girls – hardly, anyway – not the ones who counted. You know, Karen Norris once made a massive pass at him. She turned up at his house on New Year's Eve, up to her eyeballs in drink. She had this thing about getting him to kiss her. He turned her down. That's just not right. Pass me that green powder, will you?'

'*Really?* He turned down Karen Norris?'

'Yup.'

I looked at her in amazement and passed her the paint. Karen Norris was generally considered to be the pick of the girls at West Park – I would have done anything for her hair – but, as Mark Abbot had said last week before maths, she put it about for absolutely anyone. My opinion of Freddie Friday soared even higher.

'That's the red, you total dope,' said Tina. 'I said green. My God, you've got him bad, haven't you?'

Tina liked these American expressions, which she picked up from the Harold Robbins novels she devoured over her packed lunch.

'Who . . . who were his friends?' I asked, neither confirming nor denying her accusation.

'Hadn't many,' considered Tina. 'He left all of a sudden. Said he would stay for A-levels, but pulled out. He could have stayed; he was clever-ish. I mean, not nerd territory, like you or Marky Abbot, but he was all right. He had to get work. Had to support his nan and grandad. None of us ever saw him again, but that's what I heard. Makes sense, if you think about it.'

I leaned forward. This was as close to a normal conversation as Tina Scott and I had ever had.

'Poor Freddie,' I said, trying to sound as casual as I could.

Tina looked at me. 'You'd be a right pair, you and him,' she said.

I tried not to grin, but I just couldn't help it.

'Look at you,' she said. 'You're pink in the face! You're nuts about him! Oh, FitzPatrick, you do make it so very easy for me!'

110

With that, she took my face in her hands and patted my cheeks, briskly. 'He's not the sort of boy who would go for you,' she said.

'Don't,' I said, pulling away. 'I just think that he had something about him. That's all.'

Tina leaned in close to me. 'My dear, you seem to be displaying signs of triviality,' she said in a whisper.

If it hadn't been for the fact that she frightened me and I never knew if laughing was a good idea, I certainly would have smiled.

Sensing that James was approaching the end of his essay, I pulled my mind back to the present.

'. . . and that is why we will always be the ones asking, and not answering, the questions.'

James looked up from the final page at Jukey and me.

'Wonderful,' said Jukey. She wiped away a tear. 'You've captured the time and place so beautifully.'

'Marnie?' James looked at me challengingly. 'What did you think?'

'Yes,' I said blandly. 'Really good.'

'You weren't listening,' said James in a resigned voice.

'Was too.'

'You were not! At least *admit* that you didn't listen.'

I looked to Jukey for support.

'I shouldn't take it personally, darling,' she said to James. 'Marnie hasn't heard a word anyone has said to her for weeks. Caspar thinks she's in love.' She smiled at me and squeezed my hand.

I pulled away and stared at her in horror. 'Did you read my postcard?'

'I just happened to be walking through the hall when the post arrived. Caspar has the sort of handwriting that simply draws one in,' she said regretfully. 'You know as well as I do, darling. Where he writes, it is simply impossible to look away. The ink he uses is so distinctive, and what he has to say always so interesting.'

I bit my lip. James laughed. I glared at him.

'Well?' he said.

'Well, what?'

'*Are* you?'

'Am I what?'

'In love, of course! Are you in love?'

I wanted to thump him in the face.

'Of *course* I'm not!'

'Oh, leave her alone, James. Poor little Marnie. I suppose it had to happen eventually,' said Jukey.

'Who is he? Come on!' said James.

'I have nothing to say to you. He's nothing, and even if he *was* something, it would mean nothing.'

'Oh, come on, darling. Don't take everything so very seriously,' said Jukey infuriatingly. 'Oh, and speaking of post, there's a letter for you on the hall table.'

'Is it him?' asked James.

But I was out of the room before they could ask me anything else.

I recognized that it was from Miss Crewe straight away – she always used peacock-blue ink. I picked up the envelope and walked outside.

Dear Marnie,

I was so pleased to hear from you, and it was sweet of you to think of me in connection with your dancer. Unfortunately, I don't think I am the woman for the job. I can't dance any longer due to injury and, as you know, I have very little free time at St Libby's. I will, however, meet you on Saturday as you wish, so that I can watch him once and give you some idea of what to do next. To be honest, Marnie, there are lots of great dancers out there. He faces stiff competition.

In the meantime, I can tell you that the school seems very different without you and Rachel. We hear she is gradually improving, but still in a lot of pain.

I do hope that the maths at West Park improves. If you can find another pupil to bounce ideas off, you are halfway there. I would love to hear more about what you are working on. I shall bring you some old papers to look through. You can't give up, Marnie.
Until Saturday,
Julie Crewe

I padded inside again and poured two inches of gin into a glass. Funny how easy it was now, not like it had been that first time with Rachel. Now it was something that I did without the thrill of rebellion, or the excitement of celebration. It had become a survival necessity. Without it, I wasn't entirely sure that I could exist at all.

On Saturday afternoon, Caspar – home from school and bored – dropped me ten minutes' walk from the Wheat. I needed the time to feel the regular thudding of my feet on the ground, needed to talk to myself like a tennis player before a match. It was terribly hot. Forty-five minutes in my bedroom at home, pulling T-shirts and dresses on and off in a fit of self-loathing, had got me nowhere. I was wearing a pale pink blouse that Florence Dunbar had lent me for a party last year and I had never given back; I'd ripped off her nametape in fear that he would see it. I had white shorts on, which stopped just below the knee and were supposed to be flattering, but felt anything but. I had painted mascara carefully on to every eyelash, which I felt made my eyes absurd, but I supposed bigger was better. Around my waist I had tied a cricket jumper of James's, and on my feet I wore school plimsolls. I thought of Rachel and realized that her power had not ever come from her clothes, but from how she wore them. Sometimes I pulled my right arm out of my sleeve and let it hang loose at my side. I don't know why I did it, but every time I did I had to drink afterwards.

When I got to the door of the club room, I could hear the music already. I didn't recognize the tune, but that wasn't saying much; I

113

had limited access to music at home – the record player was always under the watchful supervision of Jukey or Caspar. He's rehearsing for her, I thought in despair. And she's not even going to help, beyond today. He had faith in me – some girl he had only spoken to twice in his whole life – but I was going to let him down. I pushed open the door.

As soon as he saw me, he crossed the room to the record player and stopped the music. He walked towards me, tapping his head again. His hair looked chaotic, run through with sweat. He smiled at me briefly and pulled another T-shirt out of his bag on the floor, changing his top in one quick movement. I looked down at my feet, then back at him, praying that I looked less fired up than I felt. He was so thin, so pale; unclothed, he looked very young. He buried his hand further into his bag and pulled out some doughnuts.

'For you,' he said, holding one out. 'Just in case you feel like fainting again.'

I stared from him to the doughnut.

'Take it,' he said impatiently. 'My cousin works at the bakery. I get them for free.'

'How lovely,' I said stupidly. 'Thank you.' I bit into the doughnut, and the jam oozed out over my lips. He took one too, demolishing it in one bite. How can someone so thin eat like that? I thought.

'Is she coming later?' he asked. He was trying to sound casual but I could hear the underlying anxiety in his voice. 'Because I thought she'd be with you.'

He wiped the sugar off his mouth with his hand. I could have cried. His foot started to tap on the floor again. *Tap tap tap tap* – four times. Then he started off on the other foot. *Tap tap tap tap* – four again. Then back up to his head, as he had done the first time that we had talked. His face was deep with concentration.

'Are you all right?' I asked him cautiously.

'Yeah. Ignore it. It's a tic. You know, a habit. It's nothing. I just find it hard to stop.'

114

'I'm sorry.'

'Don't be.'

I spoke again to cover my shame. 'She said that she didn't dance any more and that she couldn't teach. She said she would watch you today but that there wouldn't be any point in your wasting your time with her.'

'*I got so much time to waste, I don't know where to start*,' he sang.

'Wh-what's that?' I asked.

'Nothing.'

'I think you're so good. I'd do anything to help you,' I said.

'Yeah, well, don't beat yourself up about it.' He turned away from me, his face creased into a frown.

It was then that she chose to make her entrance

'Sorry I'm late,' she said. 'I was shown in by someone outside – he didn't ask any questions, thank goodness. I don't know how undercover all this is.'

'Oh my gosh!' I moved forward, hands stretched out towards her as though she were a mirage.

Miss Crewe was shaking off a thin red jacket that clashed rebelliously with her hair. She was wearing denims and white plimsolls and white socks; I had never seen her in trousers before, and it astonished me almost as much as if she had been half naked. She felt alien to me. Without a blackboard, or her desk, or her little flat at Kelp House, she had become another person entirely. Was she capable of breathing outside that school?

'Hello,' she was saying, stepping towards Freddie and holding out her hand. 'Julie Crewe.'

God in heaven! I thought. She can't expect him to call her by her first name!

He hesitated before taking her hand, suspicion etched on his face.

'Goodness, Marnie,' she said, turning to me again. 'You look quite different.' I didn't want her to elaborate. 'It's your hair,' she said kindly. 'Much longer, isn't it? It suits you.'

'I've put on weight,' I blurted. Not saying it would have made everything far worse.

'Nonsense,' said Miss Crewe briskly. I could have collapsed into her arms with gratitude. I'm not sure that Freddie Friday was even listening.

She put her bag down on the floor – the same bag that she always carried at school – a green wicker basket with fraying handles, oddly out of keeping with the rest of her look, which was always so stylish, so well put together. She balanced her cardigan on the top of the basket, covering up a fat pile of yellow sixth-form maths books with the St Libby's crest in the top left-hand corner of each one. There we are, I thought. There's her anchor.

'I'm sorry,' she said, turning to Freddie. 'Marnie told me you were a dancer, and she told me where to find you, but she didn't tell me your name.'

'Marnie? Who's she?' Freddie looked around in confusion.

'Er . . . that's me,' I bleated.

'You're called Marnie?' he said. He looked astonished for a moment. 'I thought your name was Phoebe,' he said.

'Call me what you like,' I said. I wanted to sound skittish and flippant, but failed. *Phoebe?* I thought in despair. Miss Crewe shot me a quick spritz of sympathy and winked at me. She knows, I thought. She can tell I love him, and we've only been here for thirty seconds.

'I'm Freddie Friday,' he said.

'Good name for a dancer,' remarked Miss Crewe. She looked from him to me and shook her head. 'I told Marnie this, and you should know too: I don't dance myself any longer. I'm not sure what I can do to help you, other than just watch and offer a few words of advice. Which, of course, you can ignore.'

'My dad used to say that any advice – good or bad – is worth listening to,' he said.

'Which is sound advice in itself,' said Miss Crewe. 'Does your father know you dance?'

116

There she was – right in there with the sort of question that I wanted to ask but was incapable of phrasing in a way that didn't sound downright wrong.

'Actually, I don't see my father,' he said.

'Oh.'

'My mother's dead,' he said. 'My father's not around.'

'I'm sorry,' said Miss Crewe. 'Who do you live with?'

'My grandparents. Up Birds Close.'

Miss Crewe looked around the club room.

'So you work here?'

'In there,' he said, signalling towards the main body of the building. 'I do the electrics,' he said. 'It's a big job,' he added, sounding defensive.

'It looks like an impossible job,' said Miss Crewe. 'You must be clever.' She managed to say it without making it sound patronizing.

'It's easy, once you know what you're doing. Electrical work is just learning another language, that's all.'

'Like dancing,' said Miss Crewe.

He nodded at her warily. 'There's only ever a few hours each week that there's no one in here,' he said. 'That's when I can use the space. I've got the keys, you see.'

Everything he said was dripping in symbolism for me. I shook my head to try and regain balance – being this far in his thrall was a distinct handicap. Any rational thought I might have was being sent through a filter of quickened heartbeats and acute self-consciousness.

'We need to make the most of the time, Miss Crewe,' I said quickly. I was anxious for her to see him dance; I felt a ticking clock hanging over us all. There was something about the stillness of the factory that felt threatening, as though real peace were impossible here, in a place usually so noisy; it felt as though, any second now, everything would crank up. I had Caspar's hip flask with me, filled

117

with some cheap whisky James had won at the village fête last summer and had forgotten about and left languishing in the corner of his bedroom. I was craving a drink to steady my nerves. Freddie tapped his head again, four times each side, as usual, and walked towards the record deck.

10

Miss Crewe

Trying not to stare too hard at his oddness, I watched him putting the needle on the record. He was displaying ritualistic behaviour – the tapping of his head, the muttering under his breath; it was plain to me that he was trying to keep control of the situation and not entirely succeeding. To add to the tension, Marnie was nervous – more nervous than him – and why wouldn't she be? She had clearly gone loopy for this boy and, from the moment that I first set eyes on Freddie Friday, it was equally obvious to me why she had fallen for him. He was very arresting – thin as a rake and as romantically pale as new death with all that wavy dark hair and those rather haunted green eyes – nothing like the public-school boys that the St Libby's girls tended to fixate on, with their clean, blond faces, rowers' muscles, confident voices and prowess on the cricket pitch. This one was a curved ball and full of nerves with it.

The record crackled into life: 'Aquarius' from *Hair*, a song that reminded me of Florence Dunbar rather too much, as she had worn that album out with playing it on Saturday evenings in the Kelp common room. Freddie glanced over to me and I nodded and smiled, feeling ludicrous – a mother waiting for her son to play the recorder in a school concert. Please, I thought. Please, for all of our sakes, let him be good. Marnie's eyes didn't leave his face; she couldn't have spelled out the way she felt any more obviously if she had unfurled a flag with a big red heart painted on both sides. Oh, God, Marnie, I thought. Don't do it. Keep the flag rolled as tightly as you can. He closed his eyes, and I felt the music filling him from his toes up, illuminating his sallow cheekbones. I saw the match light up his veins, strike him, and he began to dance.

All right. Let's just make it easy and say that my first thought was great relief: he was a dancer. He was good. All right, he was untrained, and that was very obvious – Jo, at his age, would have left him at the starting gate – but Freddie Friday had something. He used the space in the factory as though he had been told that, if he didn't cover every bit of the floor, he would be fined; he had great rhythm and – as Eloise used to put it – his limbs behaved themselves, despite the clear lack of technicality. Once or twice he missed a step, tried something that didn't work, and I could see his face falling. He was determined, I thought, but easily shattered. Sexy – yes – but at an impossible distance. It was hard to imagine anyone getting close to that body; it was too agitated, too nervy. Marnie plainly had no such problems with *her* imagination. She was looking at him without blinking, completely undone, smiling very slightly, not because she wanted to make him feel better, but because she couldn't keep herself from the joy that he made her feel. It was happening to her, as it had happened to me. My heart sped up in a surge of sympathy. I felt quite faint, but then everything about the scene was discombobulating. My God, the smell in that place was strong! Even at this hour, and not even inside the actual factory itself, there was an alcoholic, wheaty punch in the air, and seeing someone dancing in a building that usually housed manual labourers, such industry, gave everything that was happening a surreal quality.

When the song finished, he didn't come back to where we were. He just stood, his eyes closed, his shoulders hunched, breathing quite apart from us – almost as though he required different air. Where he had been as he danced, I didn't know, but it was somewhere far from here. Marnie looked as though she couldn't quite bear the space between us all, as though she might well collapse if he didn't tell her that he loved her, which he was certainly a long way from doing. Eventually he looked up, walked back over to the record deck and lifted the needle. When he came towards us, his shoulders hunched forward, the freedom of the dance seemed forgotten; he was trapped again, just as I had been every time that I stopped moving.

'He's good, Miss Crewe – isn't he? He's really good?' asked Marnie anxiously. She could see it and she was desperate to know that I could see it too.

I nodded, but that wasn't enough for her. She wanted the whole line from me – she wanted me to be falling on to the club room floor with amazement, to cement her suspicion in truth. But the romance of it all was beyond me – I knew too much about dancers and what they were worth to gush over the boy. If Marnie was waiting for me to declare his genius, she was going to have a long wait. He was still a little breathless. I noticed immediately that his arms, despite being so thin, were a dancer's arms. His face was set – I could see the rigid line of his jaw. A tooth grinder, I thought. Like me, he wouldn't be a good sleeper, and would wake up with headaches. He bit his lip and started that tapping thing again on the side of his head. This time he muttered under his breath as he did it. Was he aware that he was doing it, or was it so much a part of him, such a habit, that he didn't know it any longer? I didn't like it.

'I messed up a bit,' he said. He looked beyond us, towards the door we had come through. I think part of him wanted us to leave him; he didn't want us here.

'A little,' I said. 'But messing up doesn't matter. You're very good.'

He looked down at his hands, then up again, and he couldn't stop the smile on his face from spreading, even though I sensed he would much rather have kept it in check.

'Wasn't my best—'

'How could it be? You're far from your best. Your best is yet to come. But you're a dancer. That's the important thing. You want to dance in a company? How do you see yourself in five years' time? If you were to dream.'

'If I were to dream,' he said, 'I'd be in America. Broadway.' He let out a loud laugh as he said the words, which startled me, and made me realize that he had never confessed this out loud to anyone.

'Do you sing?

'No. I don't sing.'

'That doesn't matter.' I thought about Jo and his anxieties about his voice not being good enough.

'I only ever wanted to dance. Eventually –' he paused and looked carefully at me, as though testing how seriously I was taking him – 'I'd like to choreograph. I want to create my own dance.' He started tapping his head again. *One two three four, one two three four.*

He seemed to realize how far off this dream was, because he dignified its flightiness with a coda. 'I'm way off this now. Way off. It's a stupid dream. I work here. This is what's real.'

'Everyone has to start somewhere,' Marnie said. 'This is a start, isn't it, Miss Crewe?'

Her words reminded me of Jo and Central Park. She was close to exploding into flames – her cheeks were flushed scarlet like those of a teething toddler; her longing for him was so strong that it was sending out little electric jolts into the air. Could he feel them? How could he not? Yet he seemed unmoved, unaware. I glanced at Marnie's legs – strong, brown legs, lightly bruised on one shin – and felt that familiar spike of sadness.

'Will you put the record on again, Marnie?' I said calmly. I looked at Freddie Friday. 'Will you do it all again?' I asked him. 'Just as you did.'

I was sounding too condescending, I thought. It was extremely hard to place this boy in my head; he was eighteen – barely a year older than the upper sixth at St Libby's – and practically a man. Yet his vulnerability was palpable and as a result he seemed much younger than many of the girls in Kelp House. He nodded at me. Marnie was across the room in a flash, delighted to have been given a task. I watched her hands shaking as she started up the record once more, and the needle skidded before she got it under control.

I was shocked at how much the music was invading my senses, and my first response was one of fear. It did to me what it did to everyone – made me a sitting duck for those awful, unstoppable tidal waves of nostalgia. Music was the direct line to trouble, to opening up so much that I kept hidden, and, knowing this, I rarely listened to anything these days. It was safer that way, without the constant threat of intoxication. Marnie, I suspected, had never been touched by music before she had seen Freddie Friday dancing – it was one of the reasons that she had always had such excellent concentration in maths. Now it was doing to her what it had done to me. Stay technical, I thought. Don't let anything else in.

'You choreographed what you're doing yourself?' I asked him.

'Yes.'

'Who are the people you admire? Who are the dancers you love?'

He paused. 'Who do you think?'

I sat back in my chair. 'The way I see it, you're dancing a mix of Gene Kelly and Mick Jagger.'

He tried not to smile, but he couldn't help it. When he did, his whole face altered. I smiled back at him; it was impossible not to. That smile would bring an audience to its knees.

'But it's all you,' I said slowly, realizing it myself as I said it. 'The way that you're moving is all yours.'

For half an hour, I worked with him. I showed him better ways to stretch and prepare his body before he started to dance, I raised his eyes, his arms, listened to him talking about the steps he was unsure of, corrected him when he had invented his own way of doing something that I could tell would lead to problems later on.

123

Marnie sat a little apart from us, watching all the time. At first conscious of her presence, and that she had only ever seen me at school, had only known me next to a blackboard, I soon forgot that she was there – or rather, I forgot that there had been that distance between us. Freddie Friday's need for knowledge was so intense that it shattered and then absorbed everything else around us. My worries – that I wouldn't know what to say to him, that I would find explanation difficult – dropped away, became irrelevant.

'I don't understand,' he said in that low, quiet voice of his, with its break in the middle, and I found myself lifting my own arms to show him, taking small, careful steps in time with the music to make clear what I was saying. My God, he was a fast learner.

'Look,' I said. I picked up his arms and placed them where I wanted them. 'Like that. Not there – that's a habit you have to break. There!' I stood back. 'If you can keep that shape when you turn—'

'Show me,' he said quietly.

This was the point where I should have spun and realized that there was no longer any pain in my hip, that just being with a dancer like Freddie had healed the agony – only it wasn't like that, as life so rarely is. I spun around, a full circle – oh, yes, I managed that – but my legs, shocked and disapproving of my behaviour, were having none of it. Down I went, landing on the floor of the club room with a great thud, crunching my left hip and my leg. It broke me out of the dream – that was for sure. Marnie was next to me in seconds.

'Oh, Miss Crewe! Are you OK? Can you get up?' she asked. I could tell she was loath to touch me.

'Shouldn't have tried that,' I said. I struggled to my feet. Tears waited impatiently under starter's orders. I choked them back. Jesus! My whole body had gone rigid with shock; the pain was excruciating.

'I told you I couldn't dance any more,' I said to Marnie. I tried a laugh, but it sounded like a strangled sob. It wasn't the humiliation of falling – I was quite beyond that with teenage kids, even those as pretty as Freddie Friday and Marnie – but the reality of what had just happened was so hard to take. I had tried to move too much, and my body had refused. It was that simple.

'You should sit down,' said Marnie.

'It's all right,' I said through gritted teeth. 'I shouldn't have tried that turn. I just wanted to show . . .'

My voice trailed off. Freddie Friday was standing a little beyond where I had fallen, and he was doing exactly what I had attempted to do, his eyes half screwed up in concentration.

'The fall is optional,' I said, trying to make a joke of it, and for a moment those words hung in the air. *The fall is optional*. But that didn't make it hurt any less.

Freddie stopped and bent down, catching his breath. Still the record player proclaimed the wonders of the universe in that damn song: '*Harmony and understanding! Sympathy and trust abounding!*' Alexander would be horrified to know I had fallen, I thought. He would be fussing about calling a doctor and getting me a drink of water and should he walk me home? I was relieved that he wasn't there.

Marnie opened her mouth, anxious to fill the silence. 'I've got whisky,' she said. 'It's in my brother's hip flask. It's good for shock, isn't it? Would you like some?'

Is the Pope Catholic? I thought. Of course I wanted some, but drinking whisky in front of Marnie didn't feel right at all.

'Do you carry your brother's hip flask everywhere you go?' asked Freddie.

Marnie went very red. 'No,' she said. 'It was in the side pocket of the bag I'm using. By chance.'

She's lying, I thought in surprise. I hadn't spent this many years with teenage girls not to recognize the signs of untruth. Rachel Porter, I thought. Could it be that Marnie was still bearing the pain of that awful crash? She couldn't be blaming herself for anything?

In any event, Freddie seemed to accept Marnie's explanation, and why wouldn't he? But he started tapping his head again; Marnie turned away quickly and marched over to her bag and pulled out the hip flask, opening it with telltale familiarity and shoving it in my direction. I could tell it embarrassed her to stand *still* with Freddie. She didn't want to watch him filling spaces with the grinding, the tapping, the strange muttering that he seemed to employ as a matter of course. She needed me to step in with something, and I liked her too much not to.

'Thank you,' I said to her.

I felt the whisky warming into my hip. All I wanted to do was lie down on my coat, right there in the Shredded Wheat factory club room, and fall asleep. I could be packed into a paper packet and put into a box and sent off, and that didn't seem like such a bad thing.

'How many biscuits do they send out every day, anyway?' I asked Freddie. I felt dream-ish.

'They call them pillows,' Marnie said in a low voice. She went red. 'People always make that mistake.'

'Yes,' I said. 'Pillow. That's nice. A good word.'

'We've only twenty minutes,' said Marnie, jerking us back to the present. She sounded worried, as well she should be. I was aware, in the way that all long-term teachers have a sixth sense for impending trouble, that none of us should have been using the factory like this. The last thing Freddie Friday needed was a drunk woman of twice his age, collapsed on the club room floor before the darts club arrived.

'Shall we walk back into town?' I suggested, ignoring the ironic guffawing from my left leg. 'I could treat you both to an ice cream at the Stores?'

'I've brought a picnic,' blurted Marnie unexpectedly.

'What do you mean?' said Freddie. He looked confused, as though Marnie was speaking in code.

'My mum sent me out with it,' said Marnie. 'It's in my bag. It weighs half a ton.'

She looked deeply miserable suddenly, as though hearing herself as he would have heard her – ridiculous, childish. Personally, I was highly relieved. I could sit and eat, regain strength and think quickly about what to do. This was just the start, I knew that much immediately. But if Freddie wanted to dance, it would have to move forward soon. If I thought about it too hard, then I would run away. I had to act.

'Cucumber sandwich?' said Marnie, handing me a plump package wrapped in greaseproof paper.

'Thank you, Marnie.'

She opened her mouth to say something and shut it again. She passed a sandwich to the boy, who ate like a savage, as though he had never seen food before.

'Don't they feed you at home?' I asked, grinning at him.

'Not enough,' he said. He looked at Marnie with genuine gratitude. 'Thanks,' he said.

'They feed me too much,' offered Marnie in return. 'Everyone in our house eats all the time – I think out of habit, more than anything else. It's disgusting. Just one long sit-down at the dining table. And when you think of the starving in Africa . . .'

She went very red, and I rescued her. For the next five minutes, Marnie and I talked about St Libby's and what had been happening since she left – keeping everything as superficial as we could. Marnie talked louder than usual, dropping a great deal of St Libby's jargon into the conversation, wrongly thinking that it would make her seem more fascinating to him. In fact, the most interesting thing about Marnie FitzPatrick – her extraordinary mathematical ability – was something I steered clear of. It was more than likely that she didn't want Freddie Friday to know of her ability with numbers. He dived into the next sandwich. I doubted that he wanted to hear me talking about Mrs Slade's decision to introduce Italian to the curriculum the following term. I watched him as closely as I dared.

None of his features, taken individually, should have worked: his skin was too sallow and was interrupted by the occasional spot; his green eyes were too dark to be remarkable and were clouded with suspicion. He had what my mother used to refer to as a Roman nose, which seemed at odds with his distinctly modern hairstyle. But, my God, that dark hair was beautiful – that was the only word for it – and run through with sweat, and his body gave off that singular, menacing, almost hallucinogenic heat that good dancing was capable of producing in greater quantity than any other form of physical activity – even sex.

Instinctively, I felt my whole being edging fractionally closer to him. It was the lure of those dancing bones, the fresh sweat, the terrifying high that came with knowing that the last time I was with a boy on the cusp of something great, it was Jo. As if feeling it, Freddie Friday turned and looked at me, and for a brief moment our eyes met. I dragged mine away and shifted myself back.

'What do you like best in a sandwich?' Marnie was asking me. 'I'll make sure I bring it next time.'

'Marmite,' I said firmly. 'My mother covered everything in Marmite. She used it in all her cooking – during the war, especially.'

That should settle any nonsense, I thought. Marmite and war. There was nothing like reminding kids like this that I had lived through those years. They might have felt the aftershocks, heard the stories, seen the evidence of it in their depleted, injured families, but it was all mere leftovers. I had been there. It was the biggest gulf between their generation and mine, and no amount of poetry would ever make it something that they would understand in its entirety.

And yet I felt pulled towards Freddie Friday. It was an instinct, something beyond control. Whether he felt it too, I couldn't say. But I knew that there was something different about him. I just couldn't yet place what it was.

11

Marnie

We sat in a little circle, the three of us, poor Miss Crewe sitting slightly sideways, at a peculiar angle. Her hip was obviously hurting. Should I have offered her the whisky? I didn't know. I think that she and Freddie believed me when I said that I had found the hip flask, but I had felt a great thump of sadness knowing that it was a lie. I had stored little things in my head on the way to the factory, things to talk about because I feared silence more than anything else. I need not have worried. Miss Crewe kept things interesting. She hesitated for a moment, and then reached into her basket and, to my obvious surprise and Freddie's rather more guarded amazement, she produced a miniature salt shaker and small wooden pepper grinder. I looked at them with curiousity.

'Gosh, Miss Crewe. Do you carry them with you everywhere?'

'Everywhere,' she confirmed. 'At St Libby's they don't believe in seasoning food, as I'm sure you recall. It struck me about two years ago that being in permanent possession of these items might well enliven many a flavourless stew. I was right. When I was younger, I always had sugar with me,' she added with sudden bleakness, making the fact sound like much more than it was. She shook herself, smiled, opened up the sandwich and started to shake salt into it. I didn't dare mention that Jukey over-salted everything and that it would probably be inedible when she had finished with it. 'Now it's force of habit,' she said. 'A superstition. If I don't use these on everything I eat, I feel wrong.'

Miss Crewe spoke for me, she asked the questions I wanted asked, felt none of my reservation – despite Freddie's awkwardness. He wasn't someone to whom conversation seemed to come naturally; he was a far cry from Caspar's friends, with their ready-to-roll repartee and constant fountain of outrageous anecdotes and amusing asides. Caspar could be flung into a room with anyone and get something out of them, put them at ease, make everything all right. Freddie Friday was the opposite; I doubted his ability to sleep at night without making the bed feel awkward. The sense of humour that Tina Scott had spoken of was thus far not present.

'I don't suppose you can dance much at home,' said Miss Crewe.

'Not really. The house is so small, I bang my head on every idea I have.'

'I'm sorry,' she said. 'Goodness. Well – does your grandfather work?'

'He used to work here, at the Wheat.' He glanced up quickly, as though he might find him suspended from the rafters.

'He was a spark too.' He looked at us. 'Electrician,' he translated. 'He's the one who got me the job. Then he had a heart attack and had to stay at home and give it all up.'

'Is he all right?' I asked.

'He can't work any more. That's why I left school. To help out.'

'What was your best subject?' asked Miss Crewe.

'History, I suppose. I like facts over fiction.'

'I see. And who got you thinking you could dance?' persisted Miss Crewe.

Freddie looked right at her. His green eyes were suspicious and puzzled, as though she had asked him to reveal much more than she had.

'I did, of course,' he said. 'I'm on my own. My grandmother's

131

tone deaf. My grandad's a difficult old bastard. He limits how much I use the record player. Not everyone's a fucking von Trapp.'

'Ah,' said Miss Crewe without turning a hair, 'but Captain von Trapp was a difficult old bastard to start with too. He hadn't sung "Edelweiss" for years before Maria came into his life and filled it with music again.'

'There's no Maria in Birds Close,' said Freddie. There was bitterness in his voice.

'Isn't there?' said Miss Crewe. There was faint amusement in hers.

Freddie gave a knowing laugh and bit into his third fig roll. I wanted him to access some sort of ability to talk less frankly, and yet it was this that made him so utterly lovely to me, so foreign. I wished I had Miss Crewe's distance from him; her age and her status lifted her out of the realms of humiliation – even when she fell over, it had seemed somehow glamorous and other-worldly. She was incapable of making a fool of herself, whatever she did, whereas I was incapable of not appearing idiotic, even when I wasn't.

'So, if you could get out of Birds Close, where would you go?' she asked him, grinding more pepper on to her sandwich.

'I told Freddie that perhaps you still knew people in America,' I heard myself saying, before he had a chance to speak. 'Someone from when you used to dance. You know, someone who could see Freddie and perhaps help him . . .'

My voice trailed off. I sounded about three years old. What did I know about *anything*? Freddie was looking down at his hands. He could feel my embarrassment too: it was chilli-hot, so undeniably present.

'I can't go anywhere,' he said. 'Even if I wanted to. I can't leave my grandparents. It would kill them.'

'That's no slouch of a statement,' said Miss Crewe.

'It's true.' He pointed at me. 'You've got a brother, right?'

'Two.'

'Well, lucky you. They won't let you starve. But Barry and Linda

132

have only got me. I've got to cover all three of us, and I won't do that dancing.'

'How do you know? If you make a success of it—' I said.

Freddie laughed suddenly and looked at me. 'Were you born so fucking optimistic?'

I blushed to my roots. 'I just think you're good,' I mumbled. 'And when people are good, they deserve a chance, don't they?'

Freddie was tapping his head again. He needed Miss Crewe to tell him more, to let him know that it was all possibility.

'This is just the start, isn't it?' I said to Miss Crewe.

She hesitated. 'I don't know,' she said. 'It's not that you can't dance . . .' She slapped her hands over her denims briskly, as though trying to wipe her hands clean of some invisible stain. 'It's not that *you* can't dance,' she repeated, 'it's that *I* can't dance. I really don't think I can help.'

'But I bet you still could if you put your mind to it!' I bleated. 'My stepfather's always going on about mind over matter. I think that you could dance again, Miss Crewe. You're not old or anything . . .' I wasn't entirely sure what I was saying now.

Miss Crewe laughed in exactly the same way that Freddie had, moments before, when discussing the lack of Marias in Birds Close.

'I don't know that it would be fair on either of you – you, Freddie, because you need instruction, and you, Marnie, because your hopes are even higher than his. I'm no dance teacher – never was. I learned from other people, but I never taught.'

'You taught maths,' I said. Whisky infected me with a terrific stubbornness. 'Maths is just the same, isn't it? A discipline?'

'Maths is simple by comparison,' said Miss Crewe. 'There's a right and a wrong. You don't require the depth of emotion needed for dancing. That's why you get kids of ten years old passing maths O-level with flying colours.'

'For me, dancing's never been about depth of emotion,' said Freddie suddenly. He wasn't looking at either of us; he was staring into the middle distance again, eyes fixed on the floor across the room. 'Dancing's always been about escaping all of that stuff. It's the only thing I can do that clears my head. Always has been.' He shrugged and picked up the flask of orange squash. I couldn't quite make out what he was feeling – whether he very badly wanted Miss Crewe to say that she would help him, or whether he was hoping to be left alone.

'I used to think like you,' Miss Crewe said.

For a moment or two, none of us said a word. The low hum of the club room lights above us sounded oddly threatening. In half an hour we'll all be gone from here, I thought. Miss Crewe would disappear back to St Libby's, Freddie Friday would return to his grandparents, and I to North Bridge. It was unbearable.

'It seems awfully silly, Miss Crewe,' I said, 'for you to be someone who could help but to think that you can't, when we know you can.'

She looked at me and I could feel exasperation. She had absolutely made up her mind that we would not be meeting again, that much was plain.

I tried one more angle. 'I don't think you've anything to lose,' I said.

Miss Crewe put her salt and pepper back into her basket. 'What about you, Marnie?' she said in that same, gentle voice.

'What do you mean?'

'Your maths,' said Miss Crewe. 'Your A-level. What's happening there?'

I felt myself going red. 'Nothing,' I said. 'They don't teach in the same way. Sometimes I think I may as well pull out . . .'

Miss Crewe said nothing. Freddie took a gulp of orange squash and screwed the lid back on.

'Pull out?' said Miss Crewe.

'Doesn't seem any point,' I said.

'And so they all win,' said Miss Crewe.

'What do you mean?'

'All the people who said that you would never do it, of course. Your stepfather, Bethany Slade . . .'

'Well, maybe they were right,' I said.

'They don't have to be,' said Miss Crewe.

'I can't do it any longer,' I said, feeling close to tears. 'I can't make myself learn. It's more complicated than you can imagine. There are girls at West Park who hate me. I spend most of my time running away. Since Rachel and I were expelled, it's been difficult.'

Now my teeth were chattering together and I felt the colour draining from me, filling me up with waves of heat and shock, as though, in saying the words and telling the story again, I was hearing it for the first time. I am going to faint! I thought in horror. Talking about Rachel like this is going to make me faint! I stood quickly, my legs quivering. I had to get out of there. Freddie Friday couldn't see me doing this – he just couldn't.

'I need some air.' My choked voice sounded high and strange.

'Marnie!' said Miss Crewe. 'Are you all right?'

She went to stand up, but the pain from her fall was clearly so bad that she crashed back down on to her chair. She swore under her breath and made a second attempt, and when I looked back as I left the building she was on her feet and moving towards me.

'Sorry!' I shouted the word back at the two of them, but it sounded desperate – a cry for help.

Outside the building, I stood still to catch my breath, ducking beside one of the silos – huge white columns, full of wheat – that, up close, made me feel even more insignificant, more lost than I had felt inside. All around the factory, life in Welwyn Garden City went on. Nobody would notice if I melted into the ground forever, I thought. It was incredibly hot out there after the relative cool inside, the blue sky untouched by clouds. No breeze, no relief. I tilted my head up, my eyes closed, breathing deeply as though recharging myself with the sunlight, and as I stood there a sudden vision of the pool at St Libby's came into my head.

Days like this in the summer term had been rare, but, when they occurred, we knew how to play them out. We would wait until after prep, then race up to the pool, shedding books and shoes, bare feet racing over the mown grass . . . None of us, in those brief hours, ever wanted to be anywhere else – all we needed was fifty metres of cool, chlorinated water and each other's company. Fifteen, sometimes twenty of us would be up there at a time, all of us dancing on the edge of the cloudless sky – unbeaten. Anxiety had no real blood supply back then. Now it was free, it had the ability to spring up and trip me whenever it chose. It had me hostage.

'Marnie!' Miss Crewe had found me. She was blinking in the sunlight, coming towards me with her green basket hooked over her arm, as though she were walking to the library to invigilate lower-years prep.

'I'm quite all right,' I said to her. 'I just get this sometimes.'

'What is "this"?'

'The feeling that I might faint. I'm always fine after a few minutes. It looks more dramatic than it actually is.'

Miss Crewe placed an arm on my left shoulder. I felt my lip wobbling.

'The drink won't help that,' she said quietly. 'Not really. You might think it will, but it's no good.'

'I'm not drinking.'

'All right,' she said. 'I believe you. I'm just telling you for the future.'

'You've left him inside,' I said. 'Where is he?'

'He's fine,' she said. 'Breathe. Just breathe. He's got to clear up before the darts club arrives.'

I'll be out of here by then, I thought. He won't see me for dust.

She rubbed my back with her hand. I looked down and watched the tears plop rapidly on to the ground. Miss Crewe didn't mention them, but extracted a hankie from her sleeve, embroidered in a corner with a bunch of bluebells. I blotted my eyes.

'Sorry,' I said. I was still looking down. 'I never know when it's going to happen. I just don't know.'

'My sister was always getting like this,' said Miss Crewe. 'You know what works?'

'What?'

'Maths. Simple maths. Distracts the brain from anything else. Come on. Let's give it a go.'

'I don't know . . .'

'Give me the square root of pi.'

'One point seven seven two five.' I sniffed. 'Rounded.'

'Beautiful,' said Miss Crewe, encouraged.

I gave a weak half-laugh.

'Which famous Greek gave us the proof that there are an infinite number of primes?'

'Euclid.'

'Right again. OK. What's four hundred and eight times sixteen.'

I sucked in some air, my brain scrambling. 'Six . . . er . . . Six thousand . . . Wait . . . Six thousand, five hundred and sixteen – no! – five hundred and twenty-eight!' I stood up and looked at Miss Crewe. I bit my lip to restrain the smile. 'Is that right?'

'God knows, Marnie. You've always been quicker than me.'

She pulled a packet of cigarettes out of her bag and offered me one.

'Oh, no, thank you!' I laughed, wishing I didn't sound as shocked as I felt.

Miss Crewe shrugged and lit one for herself.

'I didn't know you smoked,' I said.

'I don't,' she said. 'At least – very rarely. I just carry them for emergencies.'

I hesitated, and then took one with trembling fingers. Miss Crewe held up her lighter.

'He's a good dancer,' she went on. 'Your Freddie Friday.'

'He's not mine,' I said, inhaling gingerly.

'No,' she said. 'But there's a *version* of him that's yours.'

'What's that?'

'The one that's in your head,' said Miss Crewe. 'The version of him that you've created, Marnie. It's partly real and partly what you want him to be. And that's fine.' She rubbed my back again. 'That's as it should be.'

Then she just stood next to me and, despite the mortification of what I had done, her presence was a calming thing – a good thing.

'He reminds me of someone I knew once,' she said.

I looked at her properly.

'Who?'

'Someone I knew a long time ago. In America, when I was a dancer. A boy called Jo. He was good – talented, like Freddie.'

I didn't say anything. That terrifying panicky feeling had quite left me now; already I was struggling to recall it in its full intensity. With the headiness of the nicotine, I felt sleepy, drugged. The anxiety did that to me – I recognized the pattern of things now. It injected me with something afterwards that made me want to lie down and sleep for weeks.

'It's very easy to fall in love with dancers,' went on Miss Crewe. She was talking quickly, as though someone were timing her, drumming their fingers impatiently on a table, waiting for her to get to the point. 'They represent a certain freedom. I don't know. Perhaps it's because they can get away with behaving like children for a living.'

'You mean they have the excuse to do so, because they're not sitting behind a desk in an office, or teaching, or being a grown-up?'

'Yes. When my niece was just one year old, there were two things that came to her instinctively. One of them was the urge to move, to dance, to react to music.'

'What was the other?'

'The desire to fight,' said Miss Crewe.

She straightened her shoulders very suddenly and stood up taller, as though someone had poked her in the back. 'You take my toy – I'll bash you over the head for it. That's just common logic. Survival of the fittest. All that business with Rachel Porter – you know it wasn't your fault. Nothing was. You're not to blame.'

I said nothing. How to tell her that I *was* to blame? How could I tell her that Tamsin Porter thought that, without me, none of it would have happened – and she was right?

Miss Crewe looked at her watch. 'I must go,' she said.

I felt clouds gathering, the heat from the sun growing cold.

'Would you like to walk back to town with me?' she asked. 'How are you getting home?'

'My brother's picking me up,' I said.

'I've never met your brother. Is he like you?'

'No,' I said. I didn't want to talk about Caspar now.

Miss Crewe hesitated.

'Will you come again?' I asked her suddenly. 'For Freddie? Will you come again for him?'

'I'll come again for *you*, Marnie,' said Miss Crewe.

'Thank you.' I paused. 'I wouldn't like him to see North Bridge,' I said quickly. 'He doesn't know anything about . . . any of it. And I don't want him to. Not at all.'

'If you're to be friends, he'll have to know one day,' she said.

I shook my head. I didn't want this conversation. I changed the subject. 'Next weekend?'

There was a long pause.

'Once a week,' she said. She inhaled quickly. 'It's all I can manage. Every Saturday. He'll have to work like mad in between. If he wants, we can meet here again. Here, at the factory.'

Every Saturday! The words hung in the air, a balloon – full of potential.

'Tell him it's then or nothing. If he's serious, he'll have to find a way.'

'Oh, I know he's serious,' I said. 'I *know* it.'

'Will you tell him?' she asked, her voice brisk again.

'I'll tell him,' I breathed.

And there – with another date in place – I had already begun the countdown, was already willing the days away.

'Funny,' she went on. 'I never knew what on earth went on inside the factory. What it even looked like on the inside. All I ever knew was that Shredded Wheat came out of it.'

'And boys who dance,' I said, after a pause.

'And boys who dance,' agreed Miss Crewe.

She looked certain of herself again, and nodded, as though dismissing a class from assembly, as she walked off, the sun burning white light on to her red hair, her long legs with that slight, barely perceptible limp, her basket, her poise. *She would do it for me.* I leaned back and closed my eyes again.

12

Miss Crewe

There was a part of me that felt I had dreamed it all. I had no contact from Marnie during the week that followed, but I went over and over the afternoon in my head, until it became distorted, fused with my half-waking dreams, until the conversation with Marnie outside the factory became something dragonish, and the way that Freddie had danced impossible to recall. In the mornings, when I woke up in Kelp House and hustled the girls down to breakfast, I felt a quiet thrill that I was doing something nobody else could have guessed at. In the evenings, it felt much bigger than this, something outrageous. Who was this boy, anyway? I knew nothing of him, and that was probably for the best. What would Bethany Slade say if she were to know? I talked to Alexander about it, the day before I was due to see them again. I had been wrestling with the idea of telephoning Marnie and pulling out of the whole thing.

'The boy's not meant to be using the room at that time, and I don't think that La Slade would think much of me spending every weekend with a girl she kicked out of the school. I should be at Kelp as much as possible on Saturdays.'

I looked at Alexander, who was sitting opposite me in the staff room, frowning into a library copy of *Don Juan*. Alexander relished the Romantic movement, but his own lack of aesthetic principle would have had Lord Byron spinning in his grave. I had never

141

known anyone to look quite so divorced from their clothes as Alexander.

'You could always tell Bethany what you're up to,' he said.

'No. I know what she'd say. "I highly recommend that you think again about this little venture, Miss Crewe. There are other girls at school who need your help more than Marnie FitzPatrick."'

'But this is about you, isn't it? This is all making *you* feel better. Giving *you* something to live for.'

We were interrupted by Richard Morely, head of sciences, exploding into the room in a cloud of expletives. Two enterprising members of the lower fourth had released a pair of white mice, destined for dissection, into the woods beyond the school grounds.

'Bloody little idiots,' he stormed, pulling open the biscuit cupboard and tearing open a packet of Wagon Wheels. 'Those mice are born and bred in captivity. Idiotic, thinking they can fend for themselves.'

'I'll have one of those, Richard,' said Alexander. Mr Morely threw a biscuit over to him like a Frisbee. Alexander caught it, unwrapped it from the foil and handed me half.

'Marnie's not a white mouse,' he said to me, demolishing the biscuit. His chair creaked as he leaned back.

'I never thought she was.'

'You, on the other hand—'

'Oh, shut up.'

And so it began. That Saturday, as for the three that followed, Freddie was there first, opening up the doors, checking everything was safe, glancing at switches and lists. I was amazed that the club room could be so entirely ours. It felt like the last word in hedonism, our indulgence in dance somehow enhanced by the functional practicality of the room with its clean, swept floor, ghostly bar, scuffed snooker balls and smoky curtains.

Freddie was always edgy – almost ashamed – as though this were a guilty secret, which indeed it was. Marnie, too, was yet to conquer her nerves. She had always been a pretty girl, but at St Libby's had been outshone by firecrackers like Rachel and Araminta, who knew how to work what they had. She suffered from bad skin and greasy hair, but any fool could see beyond that. I found myself crossing my fingers that Freddie Friday could.

Every week, I brought past A-level papers for Marnie to go through. She would start them immediately, despite my concerns that working alongside the dance lesson of a boy she was so drawn to was hardly ideal.

'Marnie, you can't concentrate while he's in the room,' I said.

'But I can't concentrate while he's *not* in the room,' she replied.

I came armed with textbooks or papers I had ordered from the school library on new theories that I thought would interest her. It worried me that West Park didn't seem to know what they had in Marnie. Her confidence in the subject had vanished, her instinct replaced by uncertainty. Where she had flown, she was now walking with a limp, and I knew that what had happened to Rachel Porter was the likely cause of this. I even felt as though Freddie were aware of it – that something was blocking her, making her show up with bottles hidden in the bottom of her bag. She thought she was clever and that we didn't know they were there. I always knew. I was just waiting for the right time to talk to her about it, and I sensed that she wasn't ready yet. There was still too much that frightened her – not least the way that she felt about Freddie, who was still so unknown to her, so foreign. Here was a sixteen-year-old girl on the brink, and wanting him so much that sometimes I felt embarrassed by it myself. He didn't seem to notice. Did he want me? I didn't think so. If he did, then it was misplaced – he didn't mean it. I had a feeling that he didn't yet know what he wanted, that he was unwritten at present. He would know when it happened, but all that mattered to him now was the dancing. I had never seen such dedication, such desire to learn. I pulled out everything I had, every trick and every move. I heard Jo speaking through me.

'What I want from you is to isolate,' I said to Freddie, as Jo had said to me all those years ago. 'I want you to be able to move one part of you and one part alone, to swivel an ankle without moving the rest of your body, and for that to be enough. You can hold an audience just by that, if you get it right.'

He would copy me, his eyes on mine, his hands stretching out, every joint in his body synchronized with mine, then he would snap back afterwards, and we were as disjointed as two people could be, tripping over ourselves to keep on track. I liked that he saw no need to sell himself with a big smile and flashy gestures. Jo had hated that. Yet, when Freddie danced, there was always pain from somewhere, an unspoken fear, a need to escape. It was always there.

The most challenging thing for me was how full my life had become. I was teaching during the week, but in the evenings I was reading about dance again, the books that I had abandoned long ago and, in turn, this brought back Jo larger than ever in my mind, and I couldn't sleep afterwards. Then I would wake early in order to mark Marnie's work. I thought about Freddie all the time; I found myself having to work hard at keeping my mind on anything but Saturdays. Maths lessons with the younger years were particularly troublesome.

'Why isn't this right?' asked Beth French, a punchy little thirteen year old who had reached grade eight on the oboe.

'Come here, Beth. Let me have a look.' I ran my eye over her paper. 'Since when did adjacent angles on a straight line add up to ninety degrees? Think about it, Beth. And I don't know why you used a green pen.'

'You borrowed my blue one at the end of last week and never gave it back,' she said indignantly.

'Sit down, Beth.' I rummaged in my pencil case – an old Bendicks Bittermints box – and handed the blue pen back to her, resisting

144

the urge to click my fingers at the same time. I had always day-dreamed in dance. The dance of the blue pens. Back row, standing up, shoulder rolls, clicking on the offbeat, moving forward, striking the pen through the air . . . I would write to Eloise for him, I thought. I had to get him out.

'Who is she?' asked Freddie, five days later. He flicked on the kettle at the back of the club room and pulled on his sweater.

'Eloise de Veer,' I said. 'You won't know of—'

'I know her,' said Freddie instantly. 'Everyone knows her.'

'Yes, well, she's an old friend. I used to dance with her.'

'You used to dance with her? Why didn't you say so?' He looked at me in bewilderment.

'We haven't danced together for years. But she's coming to London at the end of the summer. I thought that perhaps you should see her.'

Marnie looked at him with those wide blue eyes. She was wearing a pink T-shirt and a dusty white skirt with fringes around the hem that combined with her long hair and sandals to give her a hippie-ish look. You could have placed her in the middle of San Francisco and she would have got along just fine.

'No,' he said quickly. 'I can't see her.'

'What do you mean, you can't?'

'I mean, thank you very much, but I can't do it.'

'But why not?' asked Marnie. 'What's the point in all of this if you're not going to dance for anyone else? I thought that you wanted to get out of here—'

'She comes to London every year, and usually returns to New York with a couple of dancers in her hand luggage.' I laughed suddenly, hearing Eloise say the words to me as I had seen them written in her letter.

'I'm not going to New York in anyone's hand luggage,' said Freddie. 'Even if I wanted to,' he added quietly.

'But, Freddie, just think, this is your chance. Isn't it, Miss Crewe? Isn't it his chance?' Marnie stepped forward and the maths paper she was working on fluttered to the floor. She stooped to retrieve it.

'It can't work,' said Freddie. 'I'm not good enough. I'd make a fool of myself. Don't make me do it.' He started to tap furiously, his jaw going at the same time.

'All right,' I said. 'No one can force you to dance.'

Damn it, I thought. He needed to be handled so carefully. What had made me think that springing Eloise on him was a good idea? He hadn't the confidence yet.

'But you may never get another chance,' insisted Marnie. 'What if this is it?'

'If she likes me, which she won't, I'll have to tell her that I can never go to New York. I can't leave them. If I walk out on this job, he'll never forgive me. If she hates me—'

'How could she hate you?' asked Marnie reasonably.

'I can't do it. All right? Don't you see? I can dance for myself, but that's all. I can't make anything of it. I just do it for myself.'

'But why? When you could be so good?' I asked him.

'Because, even if I was good enough, I couldn't leave them. He'd never forgive me. He doesn't even know I dance now. He'd *kill* me if he knew.'

'Your grandfather?'

He nodded, looking down at the floor and tapping again.

'So they're happy for you to stay stuck here, working at the Wheat until you're too tired to switch the lights on any more? I think that's crazy.' Marnie banged the sheets of work back on to the table. 'What's the point in all of this if you're just going to be stuck here forever?'

'Christ, it's hardly like I'm in Vietnam,' said Freddie. 'This isn't the end of the world.'

'Well, all right, if that's what you tell yourself,' said Marnie. I was

146

surprised at her, and impressed with her persistence. He started tapping again. This time he counted with it – *one, two, three four, one, two, three four* – and he closed his eyes as he did so. I had never seen him this stressed before. He kept tapping. I wanted to hold him, and I wanted to wrench his hand away.

'Come on. Don't work yourself up, Freddie,' I said crisply. 'It isn't worth it. I don't have to contact Eloise yet. It was just a suggestion. I haven't spoken to her for years.'

Freddie was looking at Marnie.

'Just say you might see her,' she begged. 'Say you'll think about it. Don't rule everything out.'

'All right,' he said. 'All right, I'll think about it. I'm scared, though. If I don't ever do this for anyone else, then I can't fail.'

'You can't win, either,' I pointed out.

'No,' said Freddie. 'And I'm grateful, I really am. You know – for everything that you're doing. It's not like you have to do it. You've got better things to do on your weekends.'

'I haven't,' said Marnie.

I said nothing.

Freddie looked at Marnie and laughed.

'You've nothing better to do than hang around here with an unskilled worker like me? You could be anywhere.'

'You're not unskilled.'

'Course I am. Left school with close to nothing—'

'But you can dance! That's a skill. Come on! What are you afraid of?' Marnie's eyes were burning into his. I caught my breath.

'I'm afraid of seeing the world outside. I don't want to know what I could have, but can't. It's better to stay closed off from it.'

'That's what you believe?'

'That's what I *have* to believe.'

'So what's the point?' Marnie folded her arms. 'What's the point, when there are boys of your age dying in Vietnam? What's the point, when no one knows what's going to happen next? When we

147

don't even trust the good guys any more? Is that what you're saying? It's safer just to be shut away, and not even trying?'

The kettle started to whistle and we all jumped.

'When I dance, it makes me happy. That's all. That's all it *needs* to do. Maybe that's enough. If I stop having that, then what replaces it?'

'Nothing that you think is so very different to anything I think,' said Marnie. 'That's all I'm saying.'

'It's the differences between you two that make the common ground mean much more.'

Marnie smiled at me. I could tell that she was trading on the fact that she was the centre of this conversation; I don't think the outcome was of much significance to her. All that mattered was that we were talking about her in some form. I stood up, picturing not just Marnie but all the St Libby's girls that I had known.

'All right,' she said. 'What are the differences?'

'Well, where do I start? Let's see. You're different because you have an idea of what the world looks like outside of Hertfordshire. You can quote Shakespeare, probably even tell me when he was born and died—'

'I couldn't,' Marnie muttered at Freddie. He laughed and put his hand on her shoulder. I watched her freeze at his touch.

'You've held foreign coins in your hand,' I went on. 'You can have a conversation in French, and you'd be able to give Italian a reasonable stab too.'

Marnie looked at me and grinned. '*Sì*,' she said.

'You've got an idea of what the Romans were trying to do when they were kicking around this country. You could tell me how good ice cream tastes in the interval of a show in the West End—'

'Well, that hardly makes me unique, even Freddie's been to the Palladium.'

'Yeah, but we couldn't afford the fucking ice cream. Be quiet, please.' He prodded her in the side this time.

I ploughed on, aware that there was something in the air between them now that hadn't been present even five minutes before. 'You can't cook much, but you know what to order if you're taken out for lunch.'

'Caesar salad.'

'You always write thank-you letters because, if you don't, it's a crime.' I snapped my fingers. 'You can spell Eton!'

Marnie looked at Freddie. 'There's no *a* in the middle,' she said gently.

'Fuck.'

'You can play the piano to grade four—'

'Five, actually.'

'And you've got a handle on how the *Magnificat* sounds in several different cathedrals, because you've sung in the choir for five terms.'

'Four, actually.'

'Don't be awkward, that's not the point.' I held up my hand to indicate that there was more to come. 'You can hold your own on the tennis court, even though it bores you. You relate to dogs rather than cats.'

'Opium!' sighed Marnie, her hand on her heart.

'You can ride a horse. You can type. You know how to talk to the people who work for your parents. You can give me a great line from Proust –' I clicked my fingers, awaiting her response, and she didn't disappoint.

'Ooh! I know!' She cleared her throat and looked right at Freddie. '"Everything great in the world is done by neurotics."'

'What a man!' said Freddie.

'You know what people are shouting to each other during a game of cricket,' I said, not sure how much longer I could do on.

'Howzat?' mumbled Marnie doubtfully.

All three of us exploded into laughter. I hadn't seen Marnie laugh like this before, not even before Rachel's accident, when she was at St Libby's.

149

'Tell me if there was anything in there that I got wrong,' I said. I took a low bow.

'Tennis doesn't bore me,' said Marnie with defiance. 'I like the scoring system.'

'Typical,' said Freddie.

'All right,' I said. 'Now look.'

I rummaged in my basket, and pulled out a pen and an A4 pad of paper. I sketched the rough outline of two circles crossing over to form an oval shape at their centre. In the left-hand circle, I wrote, *Skilled*, and in the right-hand circle, I wrote, *Unskilled*.

'What are you doing?' asked Marnie.

I held the paper up. Marnie gasped at the sight of what I had drawn. She always reacted to maths like this, as though every small sum could give her new answers to the hardest of equations.

'What's that?' said Freddie suspiciously. 'Oh. More maths.'

'Now this is very crude, but it illustrates something,' I said. 'Oh, and Marnie, come on – bonus question for you. When was he born?'

Marnie looked at Freddie. 'Oh. 1951?'

'Not Freddie, you idiot. John Venn: the inventor of the diagram.'

'John Venn! Oh, gosh, Miss Crewe! I can't remember! Mid eighteen-thirties?' She clapped her hands and looked at me expectantly, her face creased with anticipation. 'Am I right?'

'Eighteen thirty-four.'

'*Yes!*' Marnie looked at Freddie with triumph. He snorted with laughter.

'Don't look at me like that,' he said. 'I don't know who the hell you're on about. What are you going to write in the middle bit, anyway? Isn't that the only bit that matters?'

'Yes. I think that you two share one characteristic that can't be denied.'

I picked up the pen again and wrote a word in large capitals in the centre of the diagram.

'STAMINA,' read Marnie slowly. 'Stamina,' she repeated.

'That's right.'

Freddie looked from Marnie to me.

'What do you mean?' They asked me at the same time.

'Stamina. You're both stronger than you know.'

'I can believe that,' said Freddie. He nodded at Marnie, and held her eyes in his. She looked down, as though the light in his eyes was too bright for her.

Marnie picked up the pen and wrote *Doughnuts* next to *Stamina*. It looked absurd.

Later that afternoon, I arrived back at Kelp House and took three painkillers, poured myself a huge glass of red wine – something I never usually drank because it gave my already intense dreams additional dysfunction – then sat down and marked thirty sets of homework. I worked like a woman possessed; I could feel the heat and energy burning on to every page. Swift red ticks and crosses, executed at high speed, my mind calculating and checking every page of work with rare authority. Laughing with Freddie and Marnie had done this to me. I had seen him breaking out of that enclosed, tight little space, not just with choreographed steps, but because he liked being with us. It had made him happy. Usually, I was blurred when I marked large numbers of books, I needed the answer sheet in front of me. Not so today. *Very poor work*, I wrote on the bottom of Agatha Page's appalling work, but then, feeling a sudden rush of elation, I crossed it out and put, *If you're struggling, please come and see me. I can help you, Aggie.*

Three girls had produced surprisingly competent drawings of the front elevation of the sickbay, illustrating angles and measurements with unusual accuracy, almost as though they had actually been paying attention in the lesson. One girl – a dreamy romantic called Anna Knightley, who everyone knew was already secretly engaged to her Harrovian boyfriend – had spent some time adding into her drawing the wisteria that clambered up the outside of the building, and colouring it violet. She may as well have sprayed it with perfume, I thought. What the hell! Let them run on hearts and purple flowers if it helped them!

At six, I switched on the lamp on my desk, hearing the familiar sound of the girls arriving back in the house after a trip to the pictures, shouting to each other, wailing about prep, laughing at idiotic jokes about nothing I understood from where I was sitting. I would continue to plough through this work, and then I would tidy the flat, and after that I would—

There was a knock at the door and I jumped in shock, sending my biro rocketing up the page, disfiguring Emma Gregson's laboured three-page stab at algebra.

That was it, I thought. The girls would be in and out of the room like extras on a film set from now on, trailing over to me, wanting anything and everything: *Can I have a stamp for a letter home? I need coins for the payphone in the hall. I want help with French prep. I'm trying to dump Sebastian-from-Wellington – how do I let him down gently? I had too many Maltesers in the cinema – can you wake me early tomorrow morning, as I need a run? Can I borrow a squirt of toothpaste, as Claire Jackson's used all of mine, even though she denies it? Could I possibly have some milk for tea? Has anyone seen my shampoo? Could I quickly use the iron to press a choir robe into shape for a rehearsal in the chapel tomorrow morning?* I could deal with any of this now. I had the armour of my afternoon in the Shredded Wheat factory. I had had my afternoon with Marnie and Freddie Friday.

'Come in!' I said.

It was Florence Dunbar. She would want to know if I had seen her swimming hat, or whether parents could have permission to take her out for tea after the county tennis tournament next weekend.

'What can I do you for?' I asked her. It was my standard question to any girl who entered the flat in the evening.

'Hello, Miss Crewe. Oh, look at that! Anna Knightley's drawn

152

in the wisteria!' exclaimed Florence in disgust, staring at the book on my desk.

'Yes. I suppose she has.'

'Idiot,' muttered Florence. 'She needs to wise up and stop behaving like Doris Day. I've heard that Charles-from-Harrow's writing to half the sixth form at St Mary's Calne, and I wouldn't blame him. Anna's a wet blanket.'

'That's enough, Florence,' I said sharply. I hoped for poor Anna's sake that what she said was mere hearsay, but I strongly doubted it. One thing I knew from my time at St Libby's was that where there was smoke, there was nearly always fire. 'What do you want?' I asked her.

'It's a bit of a strange thing,' she said, her brow furrowing.

'Oh, yes? What's happened?' I folded my arms, preparing for the absurd. The last time Florence had come to me with a strange happening, it had been the news that Annabel Robertson had removed her vanilla yoghurt from the common room without telling her, ignoring the warning notice she had stuck on the fridge with the word *LOOK!* illustrated with eyes drawn into the Os.

'Well, the thing is this: I've got a message for you, of sorts,' she said.

'A message? Is it from Mr Hammond?' I asked, my voice sounding thick and odd.

'Mr Hammond? Oh, no. It's from someone quite different. Someone called – if I heard correctly – Freddie Friday?'

I looked at Florence, wondering for a moment if I had misheard her.

'I'm . . . I'm sorry?'

Florence took it upon herself to explain.

'I was coming out of the cinema, a bit after the others,' she said. 'I'd left my coat on my chair, so I had to run back inside – got absolutely flayed alive by Miss Rolt last week for leaving my hat at the theatre. Anyway, I was just walking out when this boy came up to me and said did I go to St Libby's? Well, I was quite shocked, as you can imagine, but I said yes, and he said could I give a message to *Julie Crewe*? I couldn't think whom he meant, for a moment; there I was, going through all the girls called Julie in the school – Julie Dixon-Read, Julie Potts, Merls – that's Julie Merlin from the upper fourth,' she added, as if anyone could possibly be unfamiliar with Merls, whose father was an MP and had recently been exposed as not paying enough tax. 'And then I realized it was you he was talking about. I said, "Do you mean Miss Crewe, the maths teacher?" And he said yes. He said you were a dancer too, and I said, "Well, I didn't know about *that*."' She coloured pink. 'He said, can you please say to her, thank you for everything, and that he thinks you're –' she cleared her throat – '*bloody lovely* for helping him, and he's sorry about what he said this morning, and he'll do it.'

I stared at Florence and laughed. 'I beg your pardon?' I said. I could feel heat flooding my face. I gripped my fist around my biro and wondered if Florence could sense my astonishment.

'I'm just telling you like he said it to me,' said Florence defensively. 'And I said to him, "All right, I'll tell her, but what's your name?" And he looked rather put out, as though he didn't need to tell me, so I said, "Look here, it's no use me passing on messages from a nameless boy," and he said he was called Freddie Friday, and off he went.'

'What was he wearing?' I heard myself asking her.

'Can't really recall,' said Florence. 'He was very skinny. Needed feeding up, if you know what I mean. I think he was in old overalls. Yes, he was – with the legs rolled up. Probably works "oop the Wheat", does he?' she asked, gingerly applying what she considered to be a 'workers' accent' to this last phrase.

'Yes,' I said. 'As a matter of fact, he does.'

'He seemed a nervous sort of chap. Kept on tapping his head. I didn't know if he was completely wired up right, if you know what I mean.'

'Yes,' I said. 'I know what you mean.'

There was a brief silence between us.

'Florence,' I said. 'You won't say anything about this to anyone, will you?'

She shrugged. 'No, Miss Crewe,' she said. 'Why should I?'

'He's a friend of Marnie's,' I said, feeling I owed her a little more explanation and, more to the point, unwilling to let her go just yet when she had been the bearer of news like this.

'*Marnie?*' asked Florence in surprise. 'I didn't know that you still kept up with her, Miss Crewe.'

'She wrote to me. He wants to learn to dance, and she told him about me.'

'So you can dance?'

'I used to dance,' I corrected her. 'Long before I came here.'

'Oh, all right. I see.' Florence was one of the few girls in the school who demanded very little in the way of explanation. She accepted an answer and moved on, which made her unique among the girls in Kelp House.

'Thank you,' I said. 'I expect he recognized the uniform and thought it would be quicker to pass the message on rather than write me a thank-you card. I'm sorry about the bad language.'

'Oh, that's all right. You should've heard my father trying to untangle my brother's kite last hols. He fell into the ha-ha at the same time. What he said would have turned the air blue.' She glanced at the clock on my wall. 'I've still got that French prep to finish!' she groaned.

'Off you go,' I said.

Florence looked at me. 'Miss Crewe, if you don't mind me saying, I think you ought to be a bit careful of him,' she said. 'My cousin, Henry, fell hook, line and sinker for a woman twice his age last summer. Mummy says boys of that age are very susceptible to the charms of older women. Good-looking ones like you, I mean. Not any old bag.'

155

'I'm quite certain that there won't be any issues like that, Florence,' I said. Then, without meaning to, I added out loud, 'He couldn't possibly be interested in me!'

'He jolly well could,' said Florence darkly. 'He was all right,' she added. 'Attractive, if you like that sort of thing.'

'Thank you, Florence.'

That night was an adventure in itself. My head throbbed. I felt hot, feverish, possessed. Every time I fell asleep, Freddie Friday came to me in distorted dreams where I was back in New York during the heat of that summer of 1951, but suddenly it wasn't Jo I was with, it was Freddie.

Something that I had kept away from everything and everyone had been awoken in my Saturday afternoons with Freddie. The smell of malt and industry, 'Aquarius' on permanent rotation in my head, the white silos that I had driven past a thousand times but never got close to before, the Shredded Wheat sign and the simplicity of a breakfast cereal that I didn't even like. Being inside that building had felt like stepping on to a stage again.

When Jo and I met for the second time in Central Park, I was absolutely ready for him: a pear, sliced open at the peak of its deliciousness, lying on a blue chintz china plate. But much of that I could only see afterwards. At the time, despite my awareness of my youth and my capabilities, I was turned upside down by his presence, because he was the only man I had ever met whom I felt quite sure I wanted to sleep with, and that fact alone terrified me.

'I thought you might not be here,' he said. 'You know, with the rain and all.'

'I knew you'd come,' I said.

'Oh yeah? How did you know?'

'Because there's nowhere more romantic than Central Park in the rain.'

He laughed. 'Says who?'

'I don't know. Just something I heard.'

I looked at him sideways. It had been a week since I had seen him and part of me had expected to be disappointed by him. I didn't trust my powers of recollection; in the past, I had known myself to turn perfectly ordinary boys into Howard Keel overnight, only to be bitterly let down when they actually appeared in front of me again. I had wanted it so much – that was it. I had wanted to fall in love very badly; I desired the whole package – the yearning, the heartache, the dreaminess of it all. But I wasn't prepared for it to happen for real. I ask you: is *anybody*? Would anyone choose for it to happen outside of their imagination, if they knew what lay ahead?

'So, you're going to dance for me?' he asked. He pulled a cigarette out of his pocket.

'Sure.'

'Go on, then.'

'What? Here?'

'Why not?' He planted his cigarette in the corner of his smiling mouth. 'Give me something. C'mon. Show me what you've been showing those bug-eyed directors all over town.'

I hesitated. We were almost alone now; everyone had run for shelter half an hour ago, even though the rain had more or less stopped. A warm, watery white sun bled through the trees. It wouldn't be long before the park filled up again. He took a long drag of his cigarette and waved it in front of me.

'Go on, Daisy,' he said. 'Dance.'

I danced for him, but I danced something different,; something I had been working on myself that I hadn't tried in any of my auditions, where they usually wanted nothing but the standard stuff – the vaudeville poses, the things that everyone expected from girls. I danced like a boy, like the boys I watched auditioning through dirty windows, with their abandon, their strength. I threw in crazy moves that Eloise and I had practised in our apartment, moves that had comedy and edge and flair, things that I had learned from the movies

157

of my youth. He stood watching me, laughing, his eyes squinting from his cigarette and the sunlight. Then, when I felt close to finishing, he moved forward into the space that I had occupied and took my hands.

'I didn't think you'd dance like that,' he said.

'Like what?' I was panting, the sweat cooling on me.

'It's funny,' he said. 'You dance like me.'

'No!' I looked at him, my eyes on fire. 'You dance like *me*.'

'Show me what you did. That move where you did this,' He copied one of my steps with perfect recollection.

'Ah. Eloise and I, we came up with that together. I like it. Do you like it?'

'Sure, I like it. Why wouldn't anyone like it? Try putting in a shoulder roll. Go on – try it. Show me. C'mon, show me again.'

So we danced on and, after a while, a little crowd gathered around us, and he grew with that, seemed to love having people watching. For me, it was all about him. If I could keep his attention, then nothing else mattered. Who was he, the boy called Jo, with his rolled-up corduroys and that way of dancing that I had never known before? We were thrilled with each other, that was the only way of putting it. When I stopped, I watched him for another five minutes; all he did was stand still and move his arms and fingers – they splayed out, facing upwards, his every finger a singular beat of energy. I wanted to kiss his hands more than any other part of him. They were so beautiful, his hands. And what was remarkable was that the lack of orchestra was part of the romance of the whole thing; there was music enough in the rhythm that came from the little clicks and kicks, the intakes of breath, the sharp, sudden claps, the soft thud of his feet on the ground. We hadn't noticed, but, by the time he stopped, it was raining again, and the sky was blackening. We looked upwards together, and he raced back to where he had left his umbrella, opening it and pulling me under its shelter.

'Coffee,' he said. It was a more a statement than a question. *Coffee*:

I didn't like it, but right then I determined that I would drink it every day for the rest of my life to remember him.

'I have an audition,' I said firmly. I had prepared myself to tell him this. It wasn't true, but Eloise had instructed me to leave him something to want next time. And then, because I knew that he would see through me, and because I was too crazy about him to do anything else, I burst into delighted laughter. He looked up at the sky, smiling and rolling his eyes.

'Oh yeah? Who for this time?' he asked.

'Oh, just some guy. I don't remember.'

'Yeah, well, whoever he is, he doesn't deserve your company this afternoon. Don't go,' he said.

'I *have* to go,' I said weakly.

'No one ever *has* to do anything. You stay the afternoon with me. I'll teach you everything you need to know to get through the next one. I'll get you the next one.'

There was a sudden rumble of thunder, and a screech of police sirens in the distance. I jumped. I still hadn't got used to New York.

'Do you sometimes feel like the end of the world's coming?' he asked me. 'I mean, imagine what they would have thought if they heard thunder or saw a rainbow or a shooting star or—'

'Or understood prime numbers.'

He looked at me, frowning. 'Huh?'

'Prime numbers change everything,' I said. I felt embarrassed.

'They do?'

'Forget it,' I said. 'It's just something I like thinking about. You know – when I'm waiting to be seen.'

'You think through mathematical problems while waiting to audition?'

'Well, the way I see it, who – in any audition, at any time – isn't sitting there counting and calculating? What's the probability of me getting the part? How many other dancers have they seen? Maths is everywhere. It calms me down.'

159

He breathed in sharply through his teeth.

'The brinking, baby. It's everywhere. You know – everything and everyone, on the brink of something. I've heard it said that you only feel it for eighteen months of your life. Everything before that is leading up to it, and everything after is falling away from it again.'

'Is that where we are now? We've got just eighteen months of this?'

'Maybe so. Eighteen months of waiting to fall off the edge of the world. And so we dance because it's the only damn thing that keeps us straight.'

I shivered. 'That's five hundred and forty-seven days, or thereabouts. Not long, when you think of it like that – and could be a couple of days less, if February's in there twice. Depends when you're starting from . . .'

He stopped walking and stared at me.

'You're crazy,' he said. 'But I like it. I like you. I like crazy. And anyway,' he went on, 'you know you should never audition in a storm.'

'Says who?'

'Says me. It's a bad omen, you know? Once I had this friend – sweet girl – who auditioned in a storm, and she lost all her hair by the end of the day. All of it.'

I looked at him suspiciously. I knew he was making it up, but he had a way of talking about the oddest things and making them sound plausible.

'It was the storm that did it? *Really?*'

'Sure was.'

'Well, I don't want to lose my hair.'

'No. Why would you? Not *your* hair. I mean – everyone loves a redhead.'

I knew it was coming, but I had to hear it from him. I had to make him work for me on this score, because it was the only power over him that I would ever have. He would forever hold all the aces from now on, and I think we both knew it.

'Do you . . . Would you . . . have the time to dance with me this afternoon?'

He looked at me sideways, threw away his cigarette and passed me the umbrella so that he could dive into his pocket and pull out another smoke.

'I've got time for nothing else.'

I stopped suddenly. 'You have?'

'I need you this afternoon,' he said. 'I've got ideas – things I want to try out.' He sighed and grinned at me. 'Daisy, do you ever worry that you'll never be able to make things happen the way that you want them to happen?'

I looked at him. 'I see things in my head and I know how I want to move because it's all there in my imagination, but then I know I can't do it myself. Does that make me a dancer, or an idiot, watching?' I asked him.

'Ha!' He laughed, pulled me suddenly towards him and kissed me quickly on the side of my head, like a father kissing a child who has amused his friends. 'That makes you both those things, baby.'

We walked closer.

'Why did we choose it?' I felt convinced that he, of all people, would know the answer.

'It chose us, I'm afraid,' he said. 'We do it because we can't *not* do it. It's a cold, hard fact. You gotta do what you gotta do.'

'And those who were seen dancing were thought to be insane by those who could not hear the music,' I said. 'That's Nietzsche, you know,' I added nonchalantly, hoping to God I was pronouncing the damned name right. I liked my smart lines about dance; it was a medium that lent itself to every kind of romantic hyperbole. Eloise and I were forever writing out lines like this and sticking them on to our bathroom walls.

'And those who were dancing *were* insane. *The end*,' he said flatly.

161

'You've got to learn one thing, and learn it fast,' he went on. 'It's the oldest line in the business.'

'Practice makes perfect?' I said.

'Exactly. Now come *on*, Daisy. You want me for the afternoon; we're going to work.'

The brinking, I thought. It sure was everywhere. He lit his cigarette.

When I awoke in my single bed in Kelp House the next morning, I opened my desk and pulled out the last Christmas card I had receieved from Eloise. It was of Central Park in the snow. I opened it.

My dear Julie,

Happy Christmas to you. How was 1968 for you in good old England? I was only back once, in July. Did you get my message? I'll be back again next year in June, to see dancers for four days. Funny, before I audition anyone, I always think of us in that little apartment, with no money. I walked past the block the other day, and they were renovating the whole building. You won't believe how much this city's changing. Please drop me a line some time. You don't give much away in your cards to me. What I really want to know is have you danced lately? And if so, who with?

   Happy times for you, my friend.

   Love, E x

I folded the card back into the envelope. My hip throbbed with pain. I looked in the mirror at new lines across my forehead. I found a pen and my notepad and began to write. Freddie Friday may have called me lovely, I thought, but I knew that I wasn't. But he *was* going to dance for Eloise. And in dancing for her, there was a good chance that he could heal us both.

13

Marnie

It was the middle of the following week, and I was sitting in the kitchen, peeling apples for a crumble. Whatever he thought of me, at least I had found him a teacher, I thought. Even if he never talked to me again, at least I had done that much. It was just before five when the telephone rang. I picked it up, wary.

'Hello?'

'Marnie? Is that you?'

'Yes? *Freddie?*' Instinctively I spun around to see whether any of my family was lurking in the background. I was quite alone. I wished that I could have hidden the incredulity in my voice.

'How did you get my telephone number?'

'Doesn't matter about that. Will you come over?'

'Where? To your house? *To Birds Close?*'

The name had an almost biblical significance to me.

He laughed in surprise. 'Yes. To Birds Close.'

'*Now?* What's happened?'

'Nothing. I'll tell you when you get here.'

'What number are you?'

'Number four. Except the four has fallen off.'

'So I suppose I should look next door to number three?'

'Well, thank God one of us is doing maths A-level.'

'What?'

163

'It doesn't matter.'

When I put down the telephone, I closed my eyes. Breathe, I told myself. Just breathe. I heard Rachel's voice louder than ever: *If you're going to meet a boy that you like, you have to make a bit of an effort, FitzPatrick. They're too simple to see beyond all that stuff to start with. You have to try.*

For once, he was going to see me looking as all right as it was possible for me to look. I raced upstairs, flinging clothes out of every cupboard until I had found what I was looking for: an item of clothing that some lover of Howard's had left in his dressing room in the days before Jukey. He had refused to throw it away, which had driven Jukey insane until he agreed that it could be used as fancy dress by us children. To be honest, Caspar had spent more of his childhood wearing it than I had, but I had put it on last year on New Year's Eve and it had been the only good thing about that ghastly night. It was a microscopically short minidress in black-and-white cotton – the sort of thing that had made Mary Quant famous and had drawn so many of the St Libby's girls up to the King's Road on their weekend exeats. I put it on over my denims, then kicked them off. Standing in front of the mirror in my bedroom, I pulled my hair out of its band and pushed it away from my eyes. Then I padded quickly down the hall and into Jukey and Howard's bedroom, where I crept into their bathroom and plundered Jukey's make-up bag. Creeping out again, I collided with Caspar, who was striding down the corridor, spinning Howard's car keys around his fingers. He rolled his eyes at me.

'Dressing for dinner?' he said, nodding at me in surprise. 'You'd better return that to my wardrobe when you've finished with it.'

'Ha ha,' I said, pushing past him.

'Where are you going?' he persisted. 'I think that's the first time I've seen your legs bared since 1955.'

I looked at him in agitation.

'It's the boy, isn't it? The dancing boy,' he said, barely suppressing his smile.

'He's just called and invited me to his house,' I said. 'He needs to tell me something.' My eyes lit on the keys in Caspar's hand. 'Give me a lift into town, will you?'

Caspar sighed. 'I knew passing my test was the biggest mistake of my life,' he said. 'All right. As long as you promise to bring him here next time.'

I don't know what I expected to find inside the place that Freddie Friday called his home. In my fevered imagination, Birds Close had become somewhere steeped in legend simply because he lived there. I had imagined the pitiful squalor of a Dickens subplot: his grandmother an old hag with a ghostly voice, and his grandfather a wall-eyed monster who shoved his grandson out to work all hours that God gave, with no care for anything but his own personal reward. But it was nothing like that. My first thought was how utterly ordinary it all was.

He answered the door wearing a faded pair of black denims and a white T-shirt. He had glued down his hair with gel; it made him look younger rather than older.

'I came as quickly as I could,' I said. 'My brother gave me a lift.' I peered into the house. 'Your grandparents are out?'

'Yes. They go into town on a Wednesday. They're not back, thank God.' He looked at me. 'You look different,' he said.

'This is just an old dress of . . . someone's.'

'It's nice.'

'Thanks.' I cleared my throat. 'So this is where you live? I like this street. This is a sweet house.' Oh gosh, I was sounding condescending. Freddie didn't appear to notice.

'We've got twenty minutes,' he said.

'What are we going to do in twenty minutes?'

'Come in. I'll tell you.'

Inside, my dress felt suddenly like a preposterous choice of clothing – I shouldn't have got changed.

165

I found myself in the front room. It was small – tiny compared to North Bridge, in fact – but it was tidy, clean, looked after. A small carriage clock ticked on a mantelpiece uncluttered with the invitations, theatre tickets, keys and ashtrays which littered every surface at North Bridge House. There were two pictures next to each other of Freddie as a young child, smiling with a lack of self-consciousness that I found hard to equate with the boy that I knew. Or *thought* I knew. Suddenly I felt I didn't know him at all. I had a surge of vulnerability and amazement at what I was doing. Every window was shut, which enclosed the space in a fearsome heat, accentuating the powerful aroma of sweet peas coming from a pink-and-white vase beside a tiny television set.

Freddie opened one of the windows, just a fraction, and drew the curtains quickly, as though frightened of the air outside. Then he walked over to a wooden cabinet and opened it up. Quickly, he pulled a record out of its sleeve, picked up the needle of the record player and dropped it on to the circle of black vinyl, as shiny and promising as a new round of liquorice. There was a crackle and then the room was filled with music: 'On the Road Again' by Canned Heat. Apt, I thought, feeling the sweat trickling down my chest and through the cotton of the minidress. I knew this song from the more sophisticated boys at West Park; it had that hippy, American sound favoured by those stuck as far from the west coast of America as they could get.

'They like the idea of me having a girl in my life,' he said. He wasn't looking at me, but out of the window.

'Having a girl? What do you mean?'

'I mean having a girl.'

'You mean, a *girlfriend*?'

He took a breath. 'Something like that. They think I'm queer, so for them to walk in and see me with you . . . You would be doing me a big favour.'

'Queer?' I said. 'What do you mean?'

166

Freddie laughed with frustration. 'Come on. Don't make me spell it out to you. Or did that school protect you from all that stuff?'

'Hardly,' I said, nettled.

'The thing is this: they caught me once. At least, they *think* they did. My grandad – he saw me with another boy.'

I stared at Freddie, my mind scrambling to untie what he was saying. 'Saw you? But—'

'He didn't believe we were just friends, you know? But we were. He was teaching me a dance move. He was just a boy I knew from school. But my grandad didn't believe me. He beat me for it. Knocked me out. Linda found me lying on my bedroom floor, out cold.'

'What? He knocked you out?'

'Look, I'm only telling you this because you seem like you understand what I'm talking about, right? Because you seem like you won't tell or say anything about it. But Barry . . . He swore that, if he got wind of anything like that ever again . . .' He stopped. 'Well, he didn't say what he'd do. But he didn't need to say.'

'He wouldn't.'

'You don't know him. I love him, but he's a primitive. He sees something and he reacts to it, and that's it. He just goes off.'

'How could he do that to you?'

'Because he doesn't want me getting the shit beaten out of me by anyone else. He means well.'

'But how could someone who means well hurt you like that?'

'You'll see when you meet him. I'm all they've got. They don't want me to put a foot wrong.' Freddie Friday stepped back from the window and looked at me. 'I told Barry that I had a girlfriend. He said, "Well, bring her home, then. Let us meet her. I want to see her." So I thought of you. And it would be a great thing you were doing for me, if you could stay for tea tonight and meet them both. You don't have to do anything else. I mean, if you have some other boyfriend at school, don't worry. It's not real, all right?'

He was tapping his head again. Four times on one side, four on the other, like he always did.

'I don't have a boyfriend at school,' I said.

'It's hard to believe that,' he said.

'What do you mean?'

'I mean, with a face like yours.'

I must have lit up, and he must have realized that what he was saying sounded like he was coming on to me, because he then added very quickly, 'Look, you're a beautiful girl. I mean, that's just a fact, you know? Like the sky is blue and Welwyn's not where either of us wants to be. It's not up for debate or anything.'

I thought about Mark Abbot and his apparent interest in me, and for a moment everything seemed to stop for just long enough for me to hold what Freddie Friday had said, and photograph it, and keep it for later.

'But *were* you just friends?' I heard myself asking.

'What?'

'You know! What he saw? *Were* you just friends?'

'Of course we were just friends! Jesus Christ!' he said in a low voice. 'What do you take me for?' he asked. He sounded weary and frightened at the same time, my instinct was to make everything better again.

'I'm sorry,' I said.

'Yeah, well, now you've asked once, you won't need to again.'

'My brother − Caspar − he . . .' I stalled, unsure of how to put it. Because Caspar had been Caspar for as long as I had been me, there had never been even a small element of shock about what he got up to; I had grown up knowing that he was different to other boys. 'He has a sort of strange . . . well, I suppose it might be *love* for another boy. This boy − Nick − he's a musician. Caspar talks about him in a way that makes me feel that he'll never talk about a girl in the same way.'

I looked at him, searching his face for clues that what I was saying made sense to him, that he understood, but he looked quite blank. I am betraying Caspar, I thought with horror. I shouldn't be saying this! 'Please,' I said, 'don't think of him any differently. *Don't*.' I actually held my hands out with the urgency of it. 'I'm sure he'll meet a girl one day and get married and it'll be fine.' I could hear the high strains of anxiety in my voice.

'Don't worry,' said Freddie softly.

We were so close now. I wanted to fall into his arms and never come back. Instead, I swallowed and looked down.

'You can tell them I'm your girlfriend if you want,' I said. 'If they'd like to hear it; if it would help . . .'

He looked restless. 'It *would* help,' he said. 'Thank you.'

I took a step forward, and some kind of instinct made me reach out and hold him. He felt rigid in my arms for a moment, probably too shocked and embarrassed to move. I was amazed at myself, but the feeling of wanting to hold him, of wanting him to know that I was there for him, overpowered all that. We must have stood in that little sitting room like that for some time. I breathed in the smell of him, thrilled by the unfamiliarity of a new person. My God, I didn't go around hugging people! Seeing John Lennon and Yoko Ono naked on the cover of their *Two Virgins* album and lying in bed together at that hotel in Amsterdam had unnerved me; the Monkees sending girls crashing through barriers at concerts had seemed like footage of an alien species. I didn't get all of that until that moment in Birds Close, with Freddie Friday in my arms and Canned Heat playing in the background.

When it finished, he stepped away, quickly pulling up his T-shirt and wiping his eyes; if it had been anyone but him, I would have sworn that he had been crying. As he did so, I saw his stomach for a moment – pale, boyish, delicious.

'They'll be back in ten minutes,' he said. He looked at the clock on the mantelpiece. 'There's time,' he said.

'Time for what?'

He moved quickly, pushing the two dark green velvet chairs, which certainly hadn't been reupholstered since Queen Victoria's day, across the patterned carpet to the wall.

'What are you doing?' I asked him.

He laughed at me and clicked his fingers. 'This is where the magic happens,' he said sardonically.

I loved him when he spoke like that; my stomach flipped upside down with the wanting I had for him. All the time it was there. It was unstoppable, a proper chemical reaction, mathematical in its assurance.

He went over and changed the record. He played a song from *The Pajama Game* – which made me think of Miss Crewe and her outing to the theatre on the afternoon of the Lady Richmond Cup. I could have sat there and watched Freddie Friday dance through the score of the entire show, but I knew that there was not time for that.

It was watching him then that I twigged that *this* was why those small movements of the hands and shoulders worked so brilliantly; there was simply no room in this house for him to rehearse great big routines. Everything was in the detail; the splay of his fingers and the sharp movements of his head were all that he had in the space that he had been given. Also, putting any weight on each step sent the record jumping, which explained the cat-like stealth of his movements. I laughed, and sat back. In a single fluid gesture, he pulled a packet of cigarettes from his back pocket and threw them towards me, freezing his arm in position, pointing at me and clicking his fingers again. I stared hard at him; I couldn't have torn my eyes away. Then he looked away, and I sparked up. For the three minutes that followed, I sat, spellbound, in a dimly lit haze of sweat, sweet peas and nicotine. The pictures of Freddie as a schoolboy grinned out at me. The thin orange-and-brown rayon curtains bleeding light from the sun became the curtains on a stage in the West End. I wasn't even drunk, I realized, though I may as well have been.

When the record finished, he replaced it in its sleeve, swept the curtains and the windows wide open, pushed everything back to where it had been and rolled down the legs of his trousers. He looked at me, holding my cigarette and standing at the back of the room.

Hearing the front door, he turned away from me and called out, in a voice that seemed to hold regret and hope, 'Linda! Barry! I've got a friend here with me. Thought you might like to meet her?'

'Lovely,' said a woman's voice in reply. I was aware, even without seeing the expression on her face, that she was astonished. 'Let us just hang up our things.'

I tried to pull down my skirt. 'Linda and Barry?' I whispered to Freddie, confused. 'I thought you lived with your grandparents?'

'I do. I've always called them by their names.'

'Same as me and my mother.'

'Oh yeah? What's her name?'

'Joanna,' I said cautiously. I didn't want to say 'Jukey' in case he recognized the name and put it together with Howard Tempest.

I felt enormous as soon as Linda walked into the room – Alice in Wonderland, growing wider and taller by the second.

'Pleased to meet you,' she said, holding out a thin arm. Her hands were dry, cold, tiny. Barry stood next to her; he was short and stout, grey hair sticking up on end, and he was hanging on to his wife's arm, his face contorted with pain. It was a few seconds before he realized that there was someone else in the room besides his wife and grandson.

'Who's this?' he croaked. He lowered himself into a chair with some difficulty. Freddie stepped forward to help him, and Barry hung on to his arm as he descended on to the Black Watch tartan rug that covered the seat. Just moments earlier, Freddie had jumped

171

off that same chair, mid-dance. I felt some power knowing this had happened when they didn't. I braced myself.

'This is a friend of mine – Marnie.'

'Marnie? What kind of a name is that? Is it a nickname?' wheezed Barry.

'No.' I raised my voice a little. 'I was named after a singer called Marni Nixon.'

Barry looked at me as though I were making it up.

'Never 'eard of 'er. Funny thing, to be named after a singer no one's ever 'eard of.'

'No,' I conceded. 'She's not well known. Her voice was used in place of the voices of other actresses who couldn't sing. They recorded Marni Nixon first, then played her voice instead of the famous actress miming the words. Have you seen *West Side Story*?'

'No.'

'It's a musical – based on *Romeo and Juliet*?'

'Musical? You're asking the wrong man,' barked Barry.

'The actress in *West Side Story* was Natalie Wood. But she couldn't sing, so Marni Nixon did it for her. My mother added an 'e' on to the end of my name for fun.'

'For fun? And why didn't they just employ someone who could sing and act in the first place?'

'I-I don't know. That's a very good question.'

'Or why didn't they name you Natalie? Eh? Save you the bother of this convoluted story every time you meet someone?'

'Perhaps they just liked the name Marnie?' suggested Freddie.

'Takes all sorts,' said Barry.

I looked at Freddie and saw his mouth twitching. He was going to laugh. He glanced at me and bit his lip. I looked down at my feet. For a second, both of us were trapped, suppressing the urge for hysterics. It was this moment, more than any other with Freddie Friday – the moment that his grandfather poured scorn on my name – that I started liking him as much as I wanted him.

172

'You won't know her family,' managed Freddie at last, and with perfect truth. 'They're not at the Wheat.'

'Where did you meet her, then? Where's she at school?'

'I'm at West Park,' I said.

'What was that? West Park? You have my sincere sympathies,' bellowed Barry. He nodded towards Freddie. 'He hated the place. Couldn't wait to get out of there. Now he's damned near running the electrics up the Wheat single-handed. I taught him everything he knows, of course. Heh-heh!' He waved his hands in a wide circle to illuminate this fact.

I didn't dare look at Freddie.

'Is this the young lady you were telling us about this morning?' asked Linda.

'Yes.'

'Won't you stay for tea, love?'

'Oh, thank you. If that's all right—'

'Course it's all right,' said Barry. 'He needs a girl around him. He never has girls round. It's not right, you know. When I was his age, I were cavalier as they come. Different girl every week. Trick was, you didn't get caught, if you know what I mean. Eighteen, he is! Eighteen's the bloody golden age for a lad like him. All that choice!' His eyes watered at the memory. 'It's all wrong not to be looking.'

He gave a hoarse, loud laugh that turned quickly into a hoarse, loud cough.

'I'm nearly nineteen, Barry.'

I glanced at Linda to see how she was reacting to this, but she appeared not to have heard. She was staring out of the window, her forehead creased with concern – but I felt certain that it wasn't anxiety over what her husband was saying; it was something quite different – something far off, a memory of something that had happened a long time ago. I knew this look from Jukey's face. That sort of anxiety was frozen in time. Then I looked at Freddie and saw the amusement of the last few minutes had been replaced by

173

something else; there was something in his eyes that I recognized as urgency. I felt a surge of adrenalin prickling my fingertips.

Ten minutes later, we sat down around a little table in the kitchen. Linda pulled four cheese-and-pickle sandwiches out of some grease-proof paper and started to slice up hard orange tomatoes.

'If we'd had a warning you were bringing her home, we'd have done something more than just this,' she said. 'Something better.' She smiled at me nervously.

'Oh, yes? What would you have done, eh?' demanded the old man. 'Roast partridge and crème caramel? Oh, yes, we usually eat like we're at the bloody Ritz, in here. Bloody hell, Linda!'

He roared with laughter again and we all joined in, Freddie and I relieved to release the tension. Once more, his grandfather's laughter morphed into a terrible cough – the sort that I had seen Howard adopt on stage to signify impending illness. His eyes watered again and he grabbed the jug of water in front of him, hands padding round the table in search of a glass.

'I'm a sandwich girl,' I said loudly. 'Mrs George always says that making an excellent cheese sandwich is an art, and one that not many are truly proficient in.'

There was a silence.

'I can't say I'm an artist,' said Linda.

'Who's Mrs George?' asked Freddie, as well he might.

'A friend of my stepfather's,' I said firmly, and not without truth.

The old man rolled a cigarette and prattled on. Freddie ate with the same speed as he had when he consumed my sandwiches in the factory.

'She's still in a spin over seeing *him* again in town,' said Barry.

Freddie grinned. 'Not again?' he asked, reaching across me for the salt. I breathed in, hardly registering a word of what they were saying.

'Yes. This is the third week running,' said Linda. 'First time it were the bakery, loading up with iced buns; second time he were coming out of the coffee shop with a girl – must have been his daughter – would have been far too young to be the wife. Third time was this morning. Boots. Boots the chemist, it was.'

'The man lives down the road. It's hardly the first sighting of the risen Christ,' bellowed Barry.

Freddie looked at me. 'Howard Tempest,' he explained. 'The actor. You know?'

Oh, God. This happened all the time. People spoke without realizing it. All I had ever thought, from the moment I met him, was that, if Freddie knew about Howard, it would change things. It always did.

'Went into a spin, she did,' said Barry. 'Absolutely red in the face, she was. He was standing behind her in the queue at Boots, waiting to pay. Plain as day, it were him.'

'What was he buying?' I asked, my voice thick.

'Small bottle of Johnson's baby shampoo, some shaving cream and a packet of aspirin,' said Linda automatically, ticking each item off on her fingers. 'Oh! And some Polos.'

'The mint with the 'ole,' said Barry.

'Whenever I've seen him, he always seems *exactly* like he is on the television. Do you know what I mean, love?' asked Linda, turning to me for support. 'Just so – well – charming, you know? A real star, he is. The sort they don't make any more.'

'I know,' I said.

'I remember when he inherited North Bridge House,' boomed Barry. 'It'd been in his family since it were built, but when he moved back in, everyone sat up.'

'The gardens are wonderful,' said Linda. 'Have you ever seen them? Known as the Sidings on account of the fact that there used to be a railway station at bottom of them. They're open to the public twice a year. Barry and I went once. The tea was a bit disappointing.'

'Was it?' My voice sounded strangled and unnatural.

175

'Yes. You know, dry buns and weak orange squash. Not the sort of thing you'd expect from somewhere like that.'

'Perhaps their cook was away,' I mumbled.

'Who's he married to?' asked Freddie.

'I don't know. You don't ever read much about her. I think she were an actress too, back in the day,' said Linda.

'She was a hairdresser, back in the day,' I said quietly. 'Apparently.'

Linda looked at me and frowned. 'Are you sure, love? Seems very odd, a man like him marrying a hairdresser!'

'Maybe she was a very good hairdresser. Everyone needs their hair cut, don't they?' said Freddie.

'Some of us more than others,' said Barry, nodding at him in disapproval.

'She was his childhood sweetheart, they say,' said Linda, who seemed unable to leave the subject alone.

'Childhood sweetheart, my foot!' shouted Barry. 'Whenever you hear that phrase, it spells trouble. Whoever she is, I pity the poor cow. If you think for one minute that he's just smiling at women and nothing more, then you can think again. Randy sods, actors.'

'Oh, I don't think he's that sort,' said Linda.

'Oh, he is,' said Barry with a conviction that – knowing the truth myself – I could only admire. 'All actors are the same. Remember Dick Welsh when he got the part of bloody Prince Charming in t' panto back in fifty-nine? Went to his head. Started behaving like Lord bloody Byron, and that were only *Cinderella* in the village hall! Pass me the butter, Fred,' he added, catching my eye and nodding at me. 'Judging by the state of this sandwich, my dear, Linda is not going to knock your Mrs George off her perch.'

Freddie slid the butter dish towards him. I felt suddenly too hot.

'I ask you this: why on earth wouldn't you do it, if you were him?' he went on, smoothing a thick layer of butter on top of his bread. 'You've got every woman in the country falling over themselves to be with you. What are you going to do? Turn them all down? Don't be daft!'

'Maybe he loves his wife?' I suggested, and it sounded as foolish as I knew it was.

'Doesn't mean he won't love others too,' said Barry darkly.

'Not everyone thinks like that, Barry,' said Linda.

No, I thought. But Howard does. I gulped at my water; it was tepid and tasted of chlorine.

Barry coughed again, and reached into his pocket for a handkerchief.

'So what does your father do then?' he asked me.

'He's dead,' I said. 'He was a hairdresser.'

'He was?' said Freddie in surprise.

'I'm sorry that he's no longer with us,' said Linda.

'So am I. But I didn't really know him,' I said. 'I was very young. My mother married again.'

I imagined how Caspar would conclude the sentence: *And you'll never guess whom she married? Such a coincidence! We've just been talking about him. Ladies and gentlemen, it's Howarrrrd Tempest!*

'And is it just you? Have you any brothers and sisters?' persisted Linda.

'I have two brothers.'

'Lovely,' said Linda. 'Nice for you and your mother. Three children,' she mused. 'Lovely,' she repeated. 'We had one. A daughter. She died. I expect Fred's told you.'

'Yes. I'm so sorry.' Linda didn't seem to notice that Freddie was tapping again, looking down at his plate. I felt his feet drumming under the table.

'He's all we have. You know, the only family left.'

'Don't,' said Barry. There was a sudden sharpness to his tone. 'Don't put the child off. She's just walked through the door, for God's sake, Linda. First girl Fred's ever brought home. Spare her the bloody sob story. Makes people uncomfortable.'

Then he reached out and grabbed Freddie's hand that was tapping, and wrenched it down so that it was on the table in front of him.

'Thank you,' muttered Freddie. He looked up and spoke in quite a different voice. 'Think we might change the day of the week that we do the main bulbs,' he said. 'It seems that most people would rather start ten minutes late on a Wednesday. So it makes sense. What do you think? I said that, in your day, it was always Wednesdays. They were in favour of swapping back. Of course, the rota would have to be altered, but that's not impossible—'

'Sensible,' said Barry. 'Very sensible thinking.' Anchored to his grandson's words about the factory, Barry relaxed.

I ached for Freddie. I think I just sat there aching with love for him. I knew that, within an hour, I would be walking back to the bus stop and then to North Bridge, and then I wouldn't see him until Saturday. And what if he never returned? What if he disappeared? Was this enough for me to hold on to forever? In that moment, I thought that it was. I could go through the drought of time without him because I had stood with Freddie Friday in my arms for the length of 'On the Road Again'.

He walked me back to the bus stop. When would I see him again? I thought in despair. Sooner rather than later he would need to know about Howard and then everything would change, I knew it. But I had to tell him before he found out. I had to.

'You should come to the party,' I said suddenly.

'What party?'

'My mum and stepfather. They throw a party every year at our house for their friends.' I looked at him warily, trying to gauge his reaction to these brief words. 'They always ask me if I want to bring anyone along.'

'Oh, yeah?'

'Well, I thought that maybe—'

'I'm not much use at parties,' he said.

'No,' I said. 'Well, it was just a suggestion. You know, in case you had nothing else to do. It's next Saturday night.'

He looked at me. 'Where do you live?'

'I'll write it down,' I said. 'You got a pen?'

In the end, I discovered a pencil stub in the pocket of my bag. I found an old receipt for a pound of cherries in my pocket and wrote on the back: *I live at North Bridge House. Howard Tempest is my step-father. Too difficult to tell you before. But please come next weekend. There won't be a dry bun in sight.*

I read it through quickly. I think if I had been given a minute more, I would have crossed out the bit about the dry buns, but the bus was rocketing towards us. I could have sworn at the driver for his wretched punctuality. I folded the paper up and handed it to Freddie Friday.

'Bye,' I said. 'Thanks for asking me in. Thanks for tea and everything.' Then I boarded the bus quickly before he could read what I had written, and question me.

As we drove off, I watched him, waiting for him open the paper. For a wild, uncertain moment, I thought that he would throw it away, discard my address because it didn't matter to him. But just as we set off, he unfolded the receipt. I watched him read what I had written, and then he looked up at the bus, but we were too far away. His face was impossible to read.

14

Miss Crewe

The summer term at St Libby's was some kind of strange Arcadia. It was incredibly warm. When the sun shone on the place, when woollen cardigans and lace-up boots were discarded, when the evenings stretched long and golden, all the austerity and darkness of winter obliterated, it was close to paradise.

One hot Tuesday, I sat in the staffroom during thirds – far be it from anyone at St Libby's to use such an obvious term as 'morning break' – eating a melting chocolate digestive. The sun streamed through the windows, showing up a thin layer of dust on top of the recently unveiled, highly flattering portrait of Bethany Slade, commissioned to mark her tenth year as head. The room smelled of instant coffee and cigarettes. It was no place to be on a morning like this.

I looked outside to the little orchard opposite the entrance of Kelp House. Several of the girls were lying on the grass, sunning themselves before their next class. Against my better judgment, and knowing that several members of staff would not approve, I made a decision that I would never have made even a week earlier. I would take the girls outside for lessons on the little lawn, spreading rugs on the grass.

It was no exaggeration to say that the girls couldn't believe it.

'If only every lesson could be outside,' said Alice Bowles, stretching out long legs under the apple tree and tilting her head up to the sun. 'Thanks, Miss Crewe.'

'That's all right,' I said. I was shocked at how thrilled they were. Just that little act, spurred by my own happiness – the re-emerging of some long-dormant butterfly from a cold cocoon – had given the girls simple joy.

'What page, Miss Crewe?' asked Joan Dixon, flipping open her textbook.

I looked at them all gathered around me, pouring orange juice into mugs and laughing. I saw Alexander walking, carrying his guitar, towards the music school.

'Mr Hammond!' I shouted.

He turned and waved. I beckoned him over. I noticed several of the girls nudging each other.

Alexander loped over to us. 'How are we all, girls?'

'Miss Crewe says that we can have the whole of double maths outside today,' said Emily Gary.

'Does she?' Alexander looked at me, trying hard to hide his surprise.

'Mr Hammond,' I said, 'you've got your guitar. Could you sit with us and play us a few songs?'

I might as well have suggested that he take his clothes off and dance naked in front of us, such was the level of amazement on the faces of the girls.

'Oh, please, yes!' cried Joan Dixon, recovering first. 'It's just the day for it!'

'I don't know,' he said.

'Oh, do!' said Joan again.

He didn't want to do it, I thought. He was trying to pull away from me, and I shouldn't be doing this. Flipping open the case, he pulled out his guitar and strummed a few chords.

'Luckily for you lot, the woodwind group meeting this morning's been cancelled,' he said.

'It must be fate,' said Madeline Andrews. 'Has to be, Mr Hammond. You were *meant* to play the guitar to us this morning.' She batted her eyelashes at him, the little minx.

Alexander, usually proficient in ignoring such behaviour – however difficult it was to do so when presented with a face as good as hers – couldn't resist grinning this time. 'Any requests?' he asked, turning and looking right at me. I tried to read the look, but couldn't.

'Do something we all know,' said Madeline.

'Yes,' I said. 'Something we all know.'

He played 'Norwegian Wood' by the Beatles, a song that he knew I loved, and all the girls sang along, self-conscious at first, then gradually louder and louder, as though the orange juice had been spiked with vodka. We were on borrowed time out there – any second now, Bethany Slade could emerge and scatter us away – but for now it was all perfect. And, for those girls, Alexander might as well have been Paul McCartney – the effect of his singing was no less potent. I was aware of something – a feeling that had left me years ago, a feeling that I hadn't had since I had last seen Jo. I was aware of the happiness of anticipation, of knowing that he was out there, not far from here, and that I would be seeing him again soon. Alexander, long fingers strumming the strings on his guitar, kept looking at me, and he knew. He knew because he always did. And, for the hour that followed, the sun shone, and the girls sang, and sharp pencils remained in their cases until the bell rang, signalling the imminence of lunch, and they vanished like butterflies in the direction of the main school.

I stood, picking up stray maths textbooks that a couple of the girls had forgotten to take with them. One fell open, the names of its previous owners written in a column stretching down the left-hand side of the inside cover. There were seven names there – I had been the member of staff who had introduced this book to the girls. Helen Shard was the first name – *April 1963*. Then followed a list of girls

I had taught, some with a certain degree of success. Kate Bower, Alice Jenkins, Cecily Jones, Marina Edwards . . .

'I've been here too long,' I said, sighing at the names. 'I taught all of this lot.'

Alexander glanced down at the list.

'Cecily Jones has just given birth to her second daughter,' he said. 'I read the announcement in yesterday's *Times*. They've called her Persephone.'

'Good Lord! I'm amazed she can even spell that. She wasn't exactly the sharpest tool in the box.'

'Her husband's a professor of Greek at Oxford.'

He was good like that, Alexander. He liked to keep up with what happened to the girls after they left. He ran a finger down the list.

'I bet you never once took any of that lot outside.'

'No,' I admitted. 'Never.'

'You did a good thing. They won't forget it. This is gold dust for the memory banks. Magic dust. For every hot summer for the rest of their lives, this will come back to them all. Sitting around in the sun, outside Kelp with everything to play for, and singing along to the Beatles with Miss Crewe.'

'I imagine most of them will only remember you,' I said archly.

And that was it, I thought. They each had the so-called clean slate, the chance to make something of their lives. That was what set the pupils apart from the teachers. Not age, nor their clothes, nor their views on rules and which ones were worth breaking. It was the clean slate that they had that none of us could buy back for ourselves. Most of our errors had come to pass already; we were just swimming against a current now, treading water, keeping ourselves inside the walls of this place. We wanted to stay inside, because we knew that what was outside was not what we had expected, after all.

Alexander sighed and looked at me. 'Come over,' he said. 'Later on. If you want to. Even if you just want to talk about him.'

I stepped away.

'Who?' I asked.

'Your dancer. He's the one who's got you out here in the sun, isn't he?' He went on packing away his guitar. He wasn't looking at me any longer.

I hesitated. 'I don't know what you mean,' I said.

He shrugged. 'It's all right,' he said. 'Anyone that gets you out of the classroom has got to have something good going for them.' He pulled a stick of gum out of his pocket, split it in two and gave half to me. 'In fact, there's something I need to tell you too.'

'What's that?'

'I've taken the advice of the masses. I took Cassie out last night.'

'Oh.'

'She's a nice woman.'

'Never said she wasn't. I think it's a good thing.'

'*I* think it's a good thing.'

'Oh.'

'Can you stop saying that?'

I looked at him. 'She's nice,' I said. 'My sixth form think she's wonderful.'

'Yeah,' he sighed. 'She's all that. But you know, she's not you,' he added quietly. He stood up.

'No,' I said. 'She's not me. And that's a good thing.'

'And I'm not him,' he said.

And Freddie wasn't Jo. I had to keep telling myself that. And we weren't in New York, and I wasn't that girl any longer. But since I had met Freddie, everything was illuminated. I'd known Jo for six weeks only, but those six weeks shaped everything that I was, and everything that I became. We got into the habit of meeting in the park every Saturday, and from there we would find somewhere to dance. These places varied considerably – the basement of some seedy bar in Brooklyn, a dive of a rehearsal studio behind the Radio

City Music Hall, the apartment of a friend of his who had enough space across their bedroom floor to throw shapes. When we weren't dancing – and we were dancing most of the time that we were together – we were lying on endless wooden floors, talking to each other. When he danced, he had instant and entire possession of me; I became a bendable doll for him.

He liked the way that I moved my hands – he had a thing about them. One afternoon, I was feeling less than beautiful; my feet hurt and my eyes were red and tired from lack of sleep and yet another failed audition. Every time that I didn't get a part, I feared that he would lose interest in me, yet I feared success even more because it would mean that this perfect arrangement would have to change. If I had the choice of opening in a new show or missing a meeting with Jo, I am fairly certain that I knew which I would choose. I realized that love had won out – that no amount of desire to make it as a dancer could compete with my desire to be with him. That, in itself, was terrifying.

'Daisy, your hands! Your hands kill me. Really, they do.'

And his hands, though never free of the cigarettes that he was so addicted to, killed me too. I understood what he meant. They just killed me.

I never asked him about anything to do with his life outside dance – that was the deal from the start. But I learned small things, scraps of information about his childhood, his first performances in front of an audience, his parents. But it was a jigsaw puzzle that I knew – even then – I had no hope of completing, however much I wanted to.

Eloise got a part in a show, opening in the new year, and, to celebrate, she and I managed to get tickets to *Paint Your Wagon* – a show that everyone was talking about and that we were convinced we could have been cast in, if only we'd been in the right place at the right time. There was plenty of dance in that piece, and we wanted to see what was happening. We had chosen carefully. We didn't get to the theatre much – at least not to a show like this – but Eloise had a friend working backstage, and friends backstage were all you needed if you wanted to get by.

It was a Friday night, so I was tilting forward with anticipation, with knowing that he was just twelve hours away. We took ages getting ready to go out, standing in the bathroom in front of the mirror like a couple of brides on the morning of their wedding, smoothing little tubes of an expensive face cream I had been given during my weekly glide through Bloomingdales on to our foreheads: *Oh, you should try this, miss. You don't want to lose a complexion like yours, and this cream is something else . . . You have no money on you? Take this sample, my dear . . .*

We always wore black, and we usually wore dresses with waists so tiny that Eloise had fainted with heat and lack of breathing space while wearing one at the opening of a new gallery downtown the weekend before.

'I don't want to stay up late,' I said, standing on tiptoe behind Eloise so that I could see in the mirror as I drew a line around my lips in a pink lip pencil I had taken from my mother's cabinet last time I was home. 'I'm meeting Jo tomorrow.'

Eloise sprayed a cloud of Chanel N° 5, from a bottle that she had taken from *her* mother's handbag, on to the soles of her feet and did a little two-step across the bathroom and into the bedroom we shared. That girl can dance, I thought.

'When am I going to meet this man?' she demanded, tipping her chest forward into a black lace brassiere at least three sizes too small for her and swearing under her breath as she tried to fasten it. 'C'mon, help me out, will you?'

I stood behind her, using all my strength to make the two ends meet. For all that she danced and starved and smoked to keep her weight down, Eloise only had to look at a Hershey's bar and she ran to fat.

'I like having him to myself,' I said. I could always be truthful with her – our friendship was played out in front of the brutal backdrop of theatrical auditions, which, if nothing else, gave you a thicker skin than you had before.

'Well, you know what *I* think,' she said.

'Yeah, yeah.'

'I'm just saying. Any man who takes you out, and dances with you, and talks all hours, and wants to be with you, but isn't kissing you – and I mean you! Of all people! – *has* to be married or—'

'He's not married. And he *has* kissed me.'

'Not properly. That peck-on-the-cheek stuff and touching your hands doesn't count.'

'It does too!'

'Not in my book.'

'He's not like everyone else.'

'Oh, shucks,' said Eloise. 'Nor is anyone else.'

But she couldn't dent my happiness. No one could.

When Eloise and I went out, we planned every moment. On the one hand, we liked to walk into the theatre early, so that we could watch everyone. On the other, we liked to walk into the theatre late, so that we could be watched by everyone else. On this occasion, we chose the former, and sat down a good twenty minutes before the show was due to begin. The building hummed with energy. This catwalk of modern Americana before the show was good enough for me – I would have paid the money just to sit there and take it all in, even without seeing the show; this was better than the show! This was New York in 1951: the big dresses, the outrageous shoes, every major perfume clashing in heady abandon in the tight, smoky aisles, every tailor on the Upper East Side represented and worn with confidence and clarity by men who actually cared about what they were wearing. I had arrived, hadn't I? All right, so I hadn't quite got the job – but I was halfway there, wasn't I? The message among these people was plain: *We have money, and we are prepared to spend our money on those who can entertain us. So do it! Give us the best you can!* Eloise and I were nothing more than imposters. But that was good enough. We were here. I wasn't to know that the pin was hovering next to the balloon of my happiness. I couldn't have seen it coming.

I recognized Jo from behind, from the way that he moved down the slope of the aisle and into his seat. We were in the circle, and he was in the expensive seats, down in the stalls. He arrived just before the curtain went up. It was a shock – like seeing a ghost – because in my mind he was always with me, so to see him standing before me felt unnatural, surreal. He dressed with very little concession to the fact that he was seeing the hottest show in town – just a pale blue shirt and a casual jacket that I had seen him carrying over his arm before – but his hair was arranged differently, as though his mother had told him to smarten himself up. And right behind him was the reason. Walking right there, as plain as the day was long, was a girl – an eye-popping girl who looked at least a decade older than I was, with all the sophistication that came with it.

She had red hair, like mine, a huge red mouth to match, and a bright pink dress that left little to the imagination of anyone looking down on her from the dress circle, as we were. I sat mute, my heart hammering until it was up in my mouth.

'You all right?' asked Eloise. 'You haven't heard a word I've said to you.'

'Huh?'

'I was talking about that girl down there. Y'see? The one stopping the crowd, with the red hair? Looks like Brigitte Bardot after a late night? Amazing legs, pink dress?'

'What about her?'

'She's someone, isn't she? I just can't figure it out yet. What do you think? Those are real pearls, sister. My God, I'd sell my baby cousin for that dress—'

'I think she looks like any other broad,' I said.

Eloise looked at me, taking in the expression on my face. She

188

was a smart girl, always a few paces ahead when it came to matters of the heart; she would have fitted right in with Rachel Porter and her set at St Libby's. She was a Grit.

'Christ!' she said with feeling. 'It's *him*, isn't it? She's with him.' She said it again, with an emphatic tilt of her head in his direction: 'She's with *him*.'

'Shush,' I said tersely. 'And yes. That's Jo. But shut up, won't you?'

Eloise stared down at him, squinting her eyes for a better look. 'Well, I don't know what you've got so worked up about – he's not special-looking.'

'I wasn't expecting him to be here.'

'Course you were,' said Eloise sagely. 'Anyone who falls in love expects the object of that love to show up everywhere; that's why you look a million bucks right now. That's the deal, with obsession.'

'Only you don't expect him to show up with someone else.'

'Only you don't expect him to show up with someone else,' she repeated.

'I don't want to stay,' I said, with a sudden surge of panic. 'I don't want to be here with them. I can't sit here, when he's there—'

'She looks old enough to be his mother,' said Eloise with considerable disdain. I loved that about her: she went into attack as soon as she knew that this woman was The Enemy.

'I don't care. I can't sit here—'

But the orchestra had struck up, the lights were dimming, people were putting out cigarettes and shuffling into a position in which they could suspend their heartaches comfortably for the next hour and a half. The seat next to me had been filled by an ancient New York grande dame – grey hair set perfectly, diamonds blinking unashamedly under the lights. I couldn't move now.

'It might be his sister?' said Eloise to me, out of the corner of her mouth in an undertone. 'Or an old friend?' She raised her eyebrows at me. 'Where "old" is the operative word,' she whispered. 'She's got nothing on you.'

I didn't take in a note of the show. During the interval, Eloise stationed herself in a position so that she could watch him while I went outside for air. I didn't want to stay, but I sure as hell didn't want to go. Part of me wanted to bump into him, to force him to introduce me to her. There was another part of me that wanted to pretend that it wasn't happening – that she wasn't there and that it wasn't him, after all.

Afterwards, I lay on my unmade bed, surrounded by the chaos of our preparation – two different dresses, discarded on top of the sheets, bottles of cheap perfume, eyeshadow in crumbs around the shared basin. Eloise flopped down next to me.

'What did he do?' I asked her. 'Was he *with* her? You know, properly with her?' I closed my eyes, bracing myself for her answer, seeing the car coming to hit me, head on, and not knowing how to do anything but wait for the impact.

'Yes,' she said bluntly. 'Although I don't know what was proper about it. You need to get over him. Use him for the dancing, if that's what you need to do. But he's going to break your heart, Julie. I tell you that for free.'

I didn't listen, even though I knew perfectly well that she had never spoken such truth.

The telegram was waiting in the school office. I'd had word to collect it after tea. I took it back to Kelp to open.


```
Will be staying in Covent Gd Hotel first week
July STOP. Telephone me there STOP. Will see
your dancer if I can see you too STOP. Eloise.
```

190

15

Marnie

For the two days after I had supper at Birds Close with Freddie, Barry and Linda, I heard nothing from him, and everything that I had done felt like a mistake. I should never have told him about Howard. All the good, all the brilliance of that evening when I had pretended to be more than his friend, had been ruined by my admission. In my bleakest moments at West Park, I convinced myself that he wouldn't want to see me ever again. Tina Scott dispensed advice that I could have done without.

'Get over him, FitzPatrick,' she said, taking a KitKat from *my* lunch tray and placing it on hers.

'Give that back!' I swiped at it, and both trays fell to the ground with an almighty crash. Oh, gosh. I knew what was coming next. There was a strange, tribal tradition at both West Park and St Libby's where, every time someone dropped something in the dining room, the pupils assembled would shout '*Spill! Spill! Spill!*' and clap with increasing speed until the mess was cleared up. Instantly, Mr Welman, who taught PE and terrorized everyone with talk of cold showers after games, appeared on the scene, silencing the chanters, who went back to their egg and chips.

'Careless, girls,' he said to Tina and me. He was wearing *very* short shorts, a tight blue Aertex shirt and the requisite whistle around his neck. He had a mean face, I thought. Why would anyone employ a teacher with a mean face? I thought of Mr Hammond, with his wide smile and weakness for the Beatles, and felt a wave of longing for St Libby's.

'No use cryin' over spilt milk, eh, Mr Welman?' said Tina.

'It was just an accident,' I said.

'Oh, was it, Miss FitzPatrick? I've had it up to *here* with you two quarrelling all the time like a couple of babies!' shouted Mr Welman. He only ever shouted. I often wondered whether he might be deaf. 'Both of you, back to your desks. NOW.'

'But we've not had our lunch—' protested Tina.

'Well, unless you're prepared to eat your tomato soup off the floor, I suggest you forget about lunch for today.'

Tina gave him one of her superior glares. Then she marched over to the cutlery stand, which also boasted several dirty salt and pepper shakers. Taking one in each hand, she returned to the scene of our crash and sprinkled salt and pepper over the spilt soup. Then she kneeled down, ostentatiously placing a white paper napkin over her lap. She picked up her spoon, scraped some of the soup on to it and ate.

'Actually, sir, it tastes better off the floor,' she said. 'Pass me a bit of bread, FitzPatrick.'

Mr Welman turned purple. He glanced around the dining hall to see whether any other members of staff were around to witness what was happening.

'Think I'll join you,' I said, plonking myself down next to Tina.

'If we're taken ill, we'll have the school for insufficient hygiene measures,' said Tina blithely. I giggled.

'Get up, both of you,' snapped Mr Welman. 'We've visitors in school today. What are they going to think if they walk in and see this?'

'That the tomato soup must be bloody good,' said Tina.

I snorted with laughter and used a napkin to dab my mouth.

'You're meant to be at a play rehearsal this afternoon, aren't you?' Mr Welman said.

Tina looked at him, her face falling. 'I can't miss it,' she said.

'You should have considered that before you put on this little show. You'll come to my office for detention instead. And you,' he said, turning to me. 'What have you got first period after lunch?'

'Maths,' I said.

'Ah, yes. Quite the budding Isaac Newton, aren't you? Well, you can join the class after you've finished a hundred lines for me.' Mr Welman spotted Mark Abbot on the other side of the canteen and called him over. Mark's eyes widened at the sight of Tina and me, slumped on the floor next to our trays.

'Tell Mrs Harris that Marnie FitzPatrick will be late,' he said. 'She seems to think that having a famous father is enough to keep her from trouble.'

Au contraire, I thought.

Mark Abbot gave me a sympathetic look. 'I'll take notes for you,' he said.

Mr Welman gave us a nasty grin, and was gone.

'What a prick,' said Tina to his departing back. She stood up and actually gave me her hand, hauling me to my feet. 'I don't know what the hell you were doing getting expelled from St Libby's. I bet you didn't get this sort of shit there.' She half smiled at me, then seemed to think better of it and walked off, hands in her pockets, leaving me to clear up the mess.

A possible bond with Tina Scott aside, Mark Abbot and my project to get Freddie dancing were the only distractions in my life while I was at West Park. Mark had taken to calling me 'Lovelace' after Ada Lovelace – the mathematician daughter of Lord Byron. On the one hand, it annoyed me. On the other, I recognized that his teasing showed that he cared about me, which, despite everything, I felt grateful for. The next day, we sat alone in the classroom after our lesson, talking each other into break time.

'I know you're thinking about him,' he said. 'I wish you wouldn't.'

'What difference does it make to you?'

'Nothing. Except I know that you're wasted on him, Lovelace.'

'Stop calling me that. And anyway, you don't know him. He doesn't have anything easy.'

'Like the rest of us do?' Mark snorted with textbook derision. 'Listen, I knew him when he came here, and I bet, if Friday was in here now, he couldn't even get through his seven times table without help. You're better than him. You know it. You just can't admit it.'

'Oh, shut up, Mark.' I said. 'You're only making it worse. Life's not all about maths.'

He watched me rummaging for a protractor in my pencil case.

'Oh, come on,' he said. 'Don't tell me you're going over to the Art Side.'

'I might,' I said.

'Don't,' he said. 'All is number, remember?'

'You can't just spout Pythagoras at me and expect me to reject love.'

'Maths is love – just as much as anything else. It's the distant father that we spend all our time trying to please.'

'Oh, what have you been reading now—?'

'It's cold, it doesn't give praise lightly, but when it works, maths is prettier than any bloody sonnet.'

I found myself staring at Mark Abbot and wondering how on earth he came to be the person he was. Maths, for me, had been easy to progress in because I had Miss Crewe and I had St Libby's. He had got to this point on an altogether more difficult horse. But he *was* here, and he knew what he was talking about.

'All right,' I said. I couldn't resist smiling. 'That's good.'

'Lovelace, I think you have to admit, I talk good maths.' He flipped his pencil between his fingers, encouraged. 'You know what pisses me off about every other subject?'

Without waiting for me to reply, he jumped on to Miss Jones's desk at the front of the room. His big dirty brown school shoes with their worn soles crumpled up a stack of blotched lines written out on three sheets of A4 by some brave rebel in the lower school: *I must learn to listen more carefully.* His tie was askew and his shirt untucked, his trousers – hand-me-downs from his terrifying older brother, Dean – were too short and there was a blob of dried Tipp-Ex on the jersey he had tied around his waist.

'What are you doing? You'll be killed if she sees you up there—'

'This!' he said. 'What's this?' He opened both his arms wide in the direction of the blackboard, where a circle and its circumference remained after the first years' maths lesson.

'It's a bloody circle,' I said. 'Get down!'

'And what is the circumference of the bloody circle?'

'Pi times the diameter, sir!' I shouted. He looked absurd up there. 'What are you trying to teach me, Einstein?'

He laughed right back at me. 'And what would it be if Shakespeare hadn't lived? If Plato hadn't set foot on Earth? If we weren't standing here now? What would the circumference be then?'

'Pi times the diameter!'

'Precisely.' He closed his eyes and held the position on the desk for a moment, then took a wobbly bow. 'I rest my case,' he said, jumping down again with a thud and rearranging the scrunched papers. There was a large footprint on the top page.

'Except that isn't a circle on the board,' I said slowly. 'Not really.'

Mark looked at me. 'Don't say what I think you're going to say, Lovelace . . . C'mon—'

'It's a *chalk drawing* of an *approximate* circle on a blackboard.'

He threw his hands up in the air and pulled a stick of chewing gum out of his pocket. Tearing it in two, he handed me one part.

'Shut up, yourself,' he said. 'Just don't run away with the poets and the dancers for too long. They dress themselves up to look interesting, but in actual fact they're just as boring as the rest of us.'

I walked over to the blackboard and picked up the chalk. *SOD OFF*, I wrote in big letters. Mark shrugged.

The door opened and Tina Scott came in, dressed as Lady Bracknell.

'There's a dress rehearsal in here,' she said.

She looked at the board and her face set in disapproval.

'You'd better rub that out before the rest of the cast get in. Everyone's gone right off swearing since we got into this play. There are better ways of expressing yourself, you know.'

When I finished school on Friday, I dumped my bag in the hall and ran outside to meet Caspar. He was waiting on the wall that separated the kitchen garden from the paddock. From here, there was a good view of the road that curled past the house and led towards the shop and on into town. You saw stuff, if you hung around on the wall for long enough. Caspar would know. He was wearing grass-stained cricket whites and had stolen a bowl of dry-roasted peanuts from the pub for us to share, and had a bottle of lemonade and two paper cups. He had binoculars around his neck, like someone out of *Just William*. The summer suited Caspar, who liked lounging around outside, playing bad tennis, reading poetry and watching life go by.

'Just seen the vicar coming out of Mrs Dresdon's house carrying a brand-new television set,' he muttered, not taking his eyes away from the binoculars.

I scrambled up the wall.

'I've heard a new song of Nick's,' he said, without any other greeting. 'I can't get it out of my head.'

It wasn't often that Caspar talked about Nick; he only ever brought him into conversation with me when the pressure of not doing so outweighed the pain of talking.

'What you mean is that you can't get *him* out of your head,' I said archly.

'Perhaps,' he said. 'It's an interesting philosophical point. Do we like them for them, or for the art they create?'

He pulled tobacco and a packet of Rizla papers out of his pocket. '*Five leaves left*,' he read wearily, looking at the words on the packet. 'Oh, what's the point?' He started to roll. 'Should you love someone for the way their mind works and not the way they look? Or they way their fingers move down the neck of a guitar? Is that just as silly? Just as hollow?'

'If they loved us back,' I said, 'would that make us love them less?'

'In my case, I fear so,' said Caspar. 'I have terrible Marxist tendencies. If he gave me any more of himself, I suppose there's every chance I would think him ludicrous for doing so.'

I watched as he finished concocting his cigarette, finally lighting it and inhaling deeply.

'But *anyone* would love you, given half the chance,' I said without sentiment, just truth.

'Well, they'd *all* be fools then.'

'Don't be so dramatic.'

Caspar picked at lichen on the wall. 'You think it's all right, because you know me,' he said quietly. 'It's *not* all right. You know it's not.'

'People will just have to get used to it,' I said.

'Except that people won't,' he said. 'Not ever. Not here, anyway. For me, love is entirely pointless and I shall remain tortured. For you, there is every chance that you could win.'

'I can't,' I said. 'I've blown it.'

'Why?'

I looked pained. 'When I was with him and his grandparents for tea on Wednesday, they started talking about Howard. I was too embarrassed to say anything. They're not like us,' I said.

'Thank God,' said Caspar with feeling.

197

'I had to tell Freddie. I wrote it on a piece of paper and stuffed it into his hand just before I got on the bus home because I was too pathetic to tell him face to face. I invited him to the party at the same time. I will have scared him off. I'm no longer just an ordinary girl to him.'

'Don't flatter yourself,' said Caspar. 'Being in love is the most inconvenient addiction. I really ought to replace it with something more healthy, like LSD.'

I laughed.

'When Nick was at school, all I noticed was the way that he looked. And I couldn't talk to him in the way that I could talk to anyone else. Now I just hear about what he's doing and want to weep.'

'Why? Isn't it good that he's doing what he actually set out to do?'

'Yes,' said Caspar. 'Except that he'll be swallowed up by other people, and no one will really understand what he's trying to do – even if they think they do. Last night, at supper, some idiot who had an older brother in his year mentioned him. "Oh, Drake's been in the recording studio and his record's going to be out later in the year." I had to walk away and take deep breaths. What kind of screw-up does that make me?' He closed his eyes as though the pain were too much. 'Talk to me,' he begged. 'Don't let me think about him for a moment. Tell me about the dancer, for God's sake.' He passed me his cigarette but I declined.

'I dream about him,' I said. 'Every night.'

'Yeah, that will happen.'

'And I can't eat.'

'Yeah, that too.'

'And I feel hot all the time, as though I'm ill. Am I ill? Do you feel like that? Is it normal?'

Caspar shrugged. He said very little to me in the half an hour that followed. It was this that made him irresistible to all people – that ability to listen, to know when someone just needed to talk and not to hear any opinions, any views. He got a great deal out of people through the slightest movements of his head – a brief nod here, a raised eyebrow there. I don't know that I would have stopped talking when Howard came to find us, were it not for Caspar nudging his foot into my leg.

'Shhh,' he whispered under his breath. 'We have company.'

It was unlike our stepfather to venture out to this part of the garden, and he was walking at some speed, sheltering his head from the sun's rays with a copy of the *Stage*; being tanned was not something that Howard thought appropriate for actors. He was wearing a blue shirt and denims, and looked every inch the man that the entire female population wanted him to be.

'Isn't he dreamy?' sighed Caspar ironically.

Howard stood looking up at us on the wall. 'What are you two doing out here, for God's sake? I've been calling for you all over the house.'

'A thousand apologies, o master!' said Caspar.

Howard ignored him.

'There's someone here for you, Marnie.'

'Who?'

'Young man.'

'Young man?'

I looked at Caspar, who, assessing the situation quickly, jumped off the wall and held out his arms to lift me down.

'He's turned up with a broken bicycle and a cut head, wearing the most extraordinary suit and saying you invited him to the party,' went on Howard. 'I told him it's not until tomorrow and he opened the door to leave, but your mother swooped down on him and started wittering on about whisky and warm baths – barking mad, in this heat. It's like something out of Chekhov.'

'In what sense?' asked Caspar innocently.

Howard was fond of bringing Chekhov into the conversation,

but Caspar had a theory that he had never read any of his plays. For the second time in as many moments, Howard ignored him.

'I'm going to my office,' he said, striding on down the garden towards his railway carriage. 'If that boy ends up staying the night, you'd better ask your mother to put him in the blue room.'

'What are you suggesting? That Marnie can't be trusted?' asked Caspar.

'Shut up, Caspar,' I said, horrified.

'It's not Marnie I'm worried about,' muttered Howard.

I ran towards the house, my heart pounding in double time with my feet; all I could grasp was the disaster of him talking to Jukey and what she might say. I skidded through the front door and into the hall and found him standing on his own, looking at the framed programme of Howard's Edinburgh production of *Blithe Spirit* – the legendary fringe show that had found him his first agent. In the picture, Howard was staring in over-emphasized horror at a vast-bosomed woman in a white gown, standing framed by a window. During the run, he had slept with the woman who had played his wife, *and* the woman who had played the ghost, *and* the girl who played the housemaid. For all that Freddie Friday had invaded my thoughts every second of every day since I had first clapped eyes on him, no fantasy had *ever* involved him at home with me, looking at pictures like this. I was horrified.

'Freddie!' I said weakly.

He turned at his name, and I saw it for myself – his head, just above his left eye, was grazed; already a golf-ball–sized lump had risen up.

'What happened?'

Instinctively, I rushed forward, but stopped, as though reaching an invisible electric fence, as I remembered that I had an audience.

'Nothing,' he said, stepping backwards.

'But your head—'

'Oh, yeah. I fell off my bike. Stupid. The tyres slipped. I don't know why . . .' He trailed off, rubbing the back of his head and looking embarrassed, as though he had been caught doing something he wasn't supposed to.

'You said something about a party,' he said to me. 'I thought it was supposed to be tonight, wasn't it? Your party?'

He looked around wildly, as though searching for signs of it – clowns, bowls of peanuts, pineapple and cheese on sticks, balloons. Irrationally, I wanted to laugh.

'It's tomorrow night,' I said. 'It's always on a Saturday.'

'I thought parties were always on Fridays. They're on Fridays at the Wheat.'

'I can't believe you wanted to come,' I said, unable to hide my incredulity.

'I wasn't going to,' he said. 'But then I read your note and—'

'And?' I whispered.

'You should have told me,' he said. 'Why didn't you tell me?'

'I didn't want it to make a difference to anything. I didn't want it to change the way that you think about me. People change when they know about Howard.'

His hand was tapping his head – so lightly, with that same old rhythm – yet, when he took his fingers away, he encountered blood and pulled out a dirty white handkerchief. He was more unhinged than me, I thought. How was it possible that, when he danced, all of this melted away? That he became so certain, so uncompromisingly *himself*? He looked at me and gave me a half-smile.

It had taken some courage to show up here, I thought, in that badly fitting suit, and with a bleeding head; yet still he had the spark of something, the essence of brilliance in his bones, that beat of energy about him, even when standing still. Oh, God, I was stark staring mad about him. My face felt feverish. I wanted a drink, but I was afraid that I would lose him if I stepped away for a moment.

'*Marnie!*'

Oh, God, it was Jukey! I could see her hurrying down the stairs, carrying a damp flannel and her old sewing basket from school – optimistically renamed her first-aid box, as it now contained a small pot of zinc cream, several safety pins, some rusting nail scissors and an old bandage.

'What are you doing with that?' I asked her in horror.

She looked at me as though I were mad. 'This poor boy has arrived on our doorstep in an appalling state, Marnie. Look at him! Just look at him!'

She leaned towards Freddie and inspected the wound. He froze as though he were playing musical statues.

'I've had worse injuries,' he muttered eventually. 'This is nothing—'

'Wonderful hair,' murmured Jukey. I could feel her suppressing the urge to run her fingers through it. She might not cut hair any longer, but nothing would ever stop her from recognizing greatness in that area.

'You need something on that head. *Ice!*' Jukey clapped her hands together as though she had struck gold. 'He needs *ice*! Run to the freezer, Marnie. Get a packet of peas and a tea towel to wrap them in. Come and sit down,' she added to Freddie, guiding him out of the hallway and towards the morning room.

'I really think I should go,' he said. 'I got the wrong day. It was my mistake—'

'Absolutely not!' cried Jukey. 'You could be concussed! This is a head injury, dear boy!'

She was dabbing Freddie's head with a damp flannel when I returned with the peas. 'We must make sure the cut is clean, at least,' she said, 'and you *must* let Caspar look at your bicycle.'

'Oh, I can fix that,' said Freddie, with an unexpected burst of laughter. I suppose the thought that he could provide electricity for the whole of the Shredded Wheat factory but not mend his own bike was too silly not to laugh at.

'Caspar's a whizz with bikes,' said Jukey.

'You need to be if you're permanently in need of a fast getaway,' I muttered.

'I won't . . . er . . . disturb you any longer,' said Freddie.

His voice, now that we were standing inside North Bridge, was noticeably different to ours; I heard him speaking in the way that the other members of my family heard him, and he sounded like the boys we were always told to avoid at St Libby's. In this situation, his lack of private school education couldn't have been spelled out in bolder text.

'He wants to go, Jukey,' I said, wishing to goodness that she would buzz off and leave us alone. Her presence was absolutely stifling me; yet she who picked up blackbirds that had fallen early from their nests, and rescued aging donkeys from execution, would rather explode than let Freddie leave the house without the full extent of her sympathy.

'Of course he can't go! This young man man needs medical attention, a glass of red wine, a decent steak, a hot bath and an early night,' said Jukey, ticking off each of these requirements on long fingers.

'Well, the red wine's out,' came Caspar's voice from the hall. 'I finished the last case at lunchtime.' He walked up to Freddie and held out his hand. Freddie shook it warily. 'I expect you know nothing about me,' Caspar drawled, looking straight into Freddie's eyes, 'which is not something I can say about you.'

'Caspar . . .' I warned.

He looked at me and then back at Freddie, who seemed for a moment like a rabbit caught in the headlights, unsure which way to run.

'I'm the evil twin,' Caspar said.

'*Twin?*' Freddie looked from Caspar to me in confusion. 'I didn't realize you had a twin,' he said to me. He sounded accusatory.

'I'm sorry,' I heard myself saying. 'As you can see, we're not terribly alike.'

'You are,' he said quickly. 'You *are*,' he repeated with some insistence.

I looked at him, puzzled. 'I'm thirty-two minutes older.'

'And when you think of what people are capable of doing in thirty-two minutes, you realize it counts for rather a lot,' said Caspar. He raised his eyebrows at Freddie and looked at him from under long lashes. 'So, what are you doing here?'

'I thought there was a party today,' said Freddie. 'I was wrong.'

'All the best parties happen when they're not supposed to,' said Caspar. 'Your arrival's already far more exciting than anything that could possibly happen tomorrow, isn't it, Marnie? Tomorrow will be nothing but theatrical bores droning on about the good old days. You've come at just the right time.'

Stop, stop, stop! I wanted to shout. Caspar – incapable of moderation, and drawn to irrational behaviour in others – was clearly fascinated by Freddie's arrival. I felt as though I were floating above the scene, watching from the rafters of North Bridge. Here he was, standing in my house – as real as he ever was in the factory – yet now he was surrounded by the loons that I had to put up with every day: Jukey, face creased with concern; Caspar, one part watchful to two parts amused. I looked at Freddie, waiting for him to make his final excuses, to vanish off into the evening air with his broken bicycle and his bleeding head, but it was too late. The spell had been cast.

'Did you say steak?' he asked suddenly.

'Marnie will show you the garden,' said Jukey. 'And Caspar and I will prepare a feast.'

Walking through North Bridge, I was aware of the price of everything, as I always was with Freddie Friday. All I could think of was to get him outside as fast as possible. I willed him not to look at the pictures of Howard and Jukey when they were first married, the photographs of actors and singers laughing as though they had the meaning of life all sewn up, sofas that could have been sold at auction to pay for half the contents of his house in Birds Close. I whizzed him past James's study, overflowing with high ideas, reeking of the cigarette smoke and inward despair of a boy trying to be a man. I had to get him out – I had to get *myself* out. I held my breath, as I often did, walking through the drawing room into the garden; it was a funny thing I had – that I had to get from the kitchen to the kitchen garden without breathing. Once outside, I was safe, my tongue was untied and nothing in that place could get me any longer. When my feet hit the paved stones outside the drawing room, I breathed in.

I took him to the spot below the wall. I knew that Caspar, for all that he was shining his lights on Freddie, would leave us for now. He wouldn't give me long, I reasoned. But long enough.

Be brave, I thought. Be brave. I was so concentrated on him, on getting him where we could be on our own, away from others, that I lost track of the fact that it was his first time inside the walled garden at North Bridge. He stopped and stared.

'Blimey,' he mumbled.

'I love the garden,' I said.

'But not the house?'

'You can tell?'

'You shot me through it in about thirty seconds flat.'

'I'm sorry.'

He gestured at the roses in front of us. 'You're lucky,' he said simply. 'I remember Linda coming back from being here. She said that it was like walking into paradise . . .' He looked at me and stopped talking.

We walked on in silence. I stopped under the lilac tree, the creamy spring flowers of which had already turned brown. Caspar had been lying up here earlier in the day – he had re-employed the tartan travelling rug that had accompanied me to St Libby's and back for so many terms, and had spread it on the grass. A copy of *Women in Love,* spine broken, lay abandoned where he had left it beside another almost-empty packet of Rizlas. *Five Leaves Left,* I thought. Next to them lay his silver Zippo lighter, a blunt HB pencil, worn almost down to a stub, and three perfectly ripe pears, spilling out of a brown paper bag. A peacock butterfly settled on one of the pears, and then flew away again. Only Caspar could create such a romantic little vignette without trying, simply by being himself. If this had been my set-up, we would be knee-deep in maths textbooks, packets of chocolate biscuits and bottles of almost-flat lemonade fused with illegal gin, attracting crowds of drunken wasps.

'Do you want to sit down?' I asked.

Freddie Friday lay down on the rug with his head on one side and closed his eyes. It was a curious position for him to choose; it felt terribly intimate, yet there was still no ounce of flirtation from him, no sign that he had the slightest awareness of the sparks that were almost blinding me. I sat down next to him, awkward and longing for a drink, but for once the need to leave the house had been greater than the need to consume gin. For a good thirty seconds, neither of us said a word, although the questions inside me were still burning, burning.

I didn't want the answers. The answers could slay me.

His tics had slowed down; he had stopped that relentless tapping on his poor, injured head. I longed to reach out and touch him. Carefully, I lay down next to him, on my back, my eyes closed. Oh, God, it was difficult, all of this! It was so hot now, even in the shade of the lilac tree. I could feel the sun prickling my skin. I didn't do heat very well. This didn't happen in the movies, or in Petula Clark records. I bit my lip.

'I just need an hour,' he said. 'I just had to get away. Just for an hour.'

His eyes were still tight closed.

'I think my mother wants you to move in,' I said. Making a joke of Jukey's concern felt like the only thing to do, and yet, as soon as I had spoken the words, they sounded absurd.

'She's nice,' he said. 'Nice to have a mother who worries. Nice to have a mother at all.'

As he said this last sentence, his voice rose up as though he were holding back hysterical laughter, and I saw the expression on his face contort and his shoulders hunch. He stood up, quickly.

'What?' I said, scrambling up next to him with a break of surprised laughter in my own voice. 'What is it?'

When I realized that he was crying, my first reaction was one of absolute disbelief. He was *crying*! Here, in my garden! I had no preparation for this; I had barely been able to digest the fact of him actually talking to me, revealing anything at all, yet now, here he was, *crying* in front of me. At St Libby's, when tears had arisen in someone, which was a rare thing in the first place, we had rescued the situation by holding the one who was crying close to our chests like our mothers would have done. I felt rooted to the spot, unable to cross that invisible line that had always existed between us. He just stood there, rigid and shuddering, fighting the tears, yet completely unable to stop them. He sobbed silently, with clear loathing of himself for doing so, his left hand shielding his face.

'I can't go back,' he said. 'I *can't* go back to them.'

He stepped back three paces from me. Then he took three deep breaths, pulled a handkerchief out of his pocket and blew his nose. This act made me want to cry myself. He stood still – patiently – as though he knew that the moment was passing and he just had to wait until the burst of emotion had gone.

I stepped forward again. He wasn't a girl from the lower fifth, upset because she had been left out of the lacrosse team, or a first year weeping over a bad result in a history test. He was Freddie Friday, and someone quite separate from me; I had never felt it more so than then.

'I'm sorry,' he said.

'Don't . . .' I began.

He walked towards the gate that led into the ponies' field and leaned over the side, looking out towards the woods in the distance. He was biting his bottom lip, and his fingers tapped relentlessly on the wood of the post-and-rail fence. I stood beside him and pulled a packet of cigarettes from my back pocket. I offered one to him, but he refused. Then – not wanting to smoke at all, but feeling that it at least gave me something to do with my hands – I lit one for myself. He just kept on looking out into the field, those green eyes full of something that I couldn't identify with any certainty at all.

'Has something happened?' I asked him eventually. 'Is that why you came here?'

He swallowed and carried on looking straight ahead.

'It's always happening,' he said. 'There's nothing different about this week to last week, or to last year, or the year before that.'

'Do they know that you're dancing? That you're using the factory? Is that why he's angry with you?'

'He's angry with himself,' said Freddie Friday. 'But what's the use in knowing that when *he* won't ever realize it?' He took the cigarette from my fingers, without the slightest awareness of the magnitude of the act. 'I've been there with them since I was twelve. Nothing's ever changed. He won't ever change, and she just sits there and takes it because she doesn't know any better.' He handed me back the cigarette. 'She thinks it's normal to be treated like that. She doesn't expect anything else.' He looked at me steadily. 'He pushed her last night.'

'Pushed her?'

'Pushed her over. He got angry because she'd forgotten to do something – I can't even remember exactly what. They're off on holiday – I think she'd forgotten to buy new film for his camera. She said she was sorry, and he stood up like a giant and walked past her, shouting that she was useless. As he walked past her, he just pushed her. She fell.'

'Is she all right?'

He shrugged. 'When I came into the room to help her, she started saying that I had to understand that he was tired, that he wasn't himself at the moment. I wanted to say, "Oh yeah? And who is he then? Because the only man I've ever known is that one – that one who acts like this all the time." She kept saying, "But you know he loves me really. Deep down, don't you? Like you love him." And she's right, because I do. I do love him, I *do*.' His voice broke again. 'Now they've gone off on the bus, off to Bournemouth for the week, like they always do, and she's saying to everyone that the bruises are because she fell over, and he's saying what a shame it is she won't be able to ride the dodgems with him this year, and it's all a mess.'

'Your head,' I said slowly. 'Was that him too? Did he do that to you?'

He said nothing. What would Miss Crewe do now? I thought. She would know exactly what Freddie Friday needed – she would know what to say and, more importantly, what *not* to say. All I could do was let him talk. I didn't have words to make him feel better.

'Thing is, he's the funniest man I know. And sometimes that counts. Sometimes – when I was just a kid – he'd make me laugh so hard I'd think I might die laughing. It was a proper performance he'd give, wherever we were, whatever we were doing. Didn't care what he said, as long as people laughed. Especially me. His eyes on me all the time, just to check I was laughing – and I would be, always. She should never have married him,' he said, veering back to his grandmother. 'She's a serious person, a soft person. He's snapped her in two because it was easy for him, because – because –' he rolled his eyes up to heaven, searching for the words – 'because he doesn't know his own strength,' he concluded.

'Not many people do,' I said.

He turned to me, his eyes wide, as though coming out of a dream.

'You don't,' he said with feeling. 'You *don't*,' he said again, and it sounded accusatory and urgent and serious and charged through with hope.

209

It was me who did it. I kissed him on the head, where his cut was. It was a light kiss, a kiss for a bruise, but it was loaded with a promise of something quite different, something that I knew very little about, except for the fact that I wanted it very badly. He opened his eyes and laughed – like he had laughed when I had agreed to pretend I was his girlfriend.

'I'm sorry,' I said, but I didn't mean it. I was charged through with something new, a fire inside me that was burning so strong it obliterated the shame of what I had just done. If he was going to reject me, he could. At least I had kissed him. At least I had done that much. My desire for him could have laid me out cold – I was utterly in its thrall. *Not* kissing him would have been far more difficult.

I took his hand in mine, and he let me. I led him silently back into the house, and he let me. I don't recall getting through supper with Caspar and his questions and Jukey and her strange, manic mood, but I suppose we must have. I remember feeling as though it was just the two of us in the room, and that as soon as we were alone again, something would have to happen. It was impossible for it not to. I had never been in North Bridge with a boy I wanted to kiss before, and I saw everything differently, as though from black and white into colour.

Jukey went up to bed straight after supper, claiming that she needed to sleep well before the party. Howard vanished into his railway coach again, holding half a bottle of wine. Caspar retired quickly afterwards.

'The blue room won't know what's hit it,' he murmured, saying goodnight to us.

The blue room was at the furthest end of the house; it was rarely used and felt cold even in the height of summer. I sat on the floor, fiddling with the tassels on the end of the curtains, and Freddie Friday sat against the edge of the bed, looking strange and out of context to me – it was as weird as having Brian Jones himself in the room. Familiar objects – the row of William Morris decorated plates on the wall, the three little milkmaid figurines on the chest of drawers – looked different when he was part of the scenery too. He changed everything in a way that no one else ever had. I heard Rachel Porter's voice mocking me: *Come on, FitzPatrick! Aren't you going to kiss him again?*

To grasp at an inadequate analogy, it was as though I had been looking at a painting that I loved for weeks on end behind a velvet rope, and had now been granted permission to view it close up. Those inches between him and me, the space between us when we had talked at Shredded Wheat, or walked in the garden, had formed the borders of my imagination. Until then, I didn't know how his skin felt against mine, how his eyes flickered in the dark, how it felt when his mouth collided with mine; it had all been in my head – uncorroborated by any true source. Now it was happening, and I wanted him completely. This kissing and talking and lying together didn't feel like it was enough.

'I don't mind if you want to,' I said.

Freddie sat up against the headboard that, only last month, Jukey's friend, Laura Ashley, had reupholstered in blue and white flowers. If someone could have told me that the first person to use it would be the boy from the factory, I would have believed them quite mad. Yet there he was, all perfect, as he always was to me. It felt like he was mine. Didn't this kissing and this closeness make him mine?

'This is all a new thing,' I said to him. I wanted him to know. I didn't want him to think for one moment that this was something that I did for just anyone, something that was ordinary to me.

'For me too.'

'I don't believe you.'

'It is,' he said.

'You've never been in a bed with a girl before?'

Freddie paused. 'No,' he said.

'I don't believe you.'

211

'Funny,' he said. 'Every time you've said anything to *me*, I've believed it right away. Everything. And you've said some pretty strong things to me.'

'Like what?' I looked at him, amazed.

'Like you could find me a dance teacher. I believed you. Like Howard Tempest is your stepfather. I believed you. When you told me that your friend had lost her arm, I believed you. I don't know what it is.'

I turned my face from him, wanting to push away the thought of Rachel Porter.

'Would you believe me if I told you that it was my fault that she lost her arm and ruined her face?' I said. I heard myself sounding strangled and clanging.

'No,' he said. 'I wouldn't believe that. Don't say that.'

It wasn't the moment, but I couldn't have held it back for another time. I had to say it. Freddie Friday held me very still in his arms. I could hear the clicky ticking of the clock Aunt Angela had left by the bedside last Christmas. It had glow-in-the-dark hands that were telling quite the wrong time.

'Everything that I did and said that day led to the accident,' I said. 'Everything.'

'Were you driving the car?'

'No, but—'

'It wasn't your fault,' he said. He looked at me sideways. 'She's why you drink so much?'

I said nothing. I wanted him to stop talking about it, right now, before the spell was broken.

'Have you seen her since it happened?' he asked me.

'I've tried to. Her sister told me to stay away from her. Rachel used to paint,' I said. 'She was good. The sort of girl who could have gone on to do great things.'

'Why shouldn't she still?'

'That's what Caspar said. But I think that's just what you say when this sort of thing happens. You try to pretend that they can get through it – that perhaps they're going to come out the other side even better than they were before. I'm sorry,' I said, 'but I don't believe in that sort of miracle. All the evidence I've ever seen points to the fact that it's just wishful thinking.'

'I believe it,' said Freddie Friday. 'Especially for a girl like Rachel.'

'You don't know her,' I said. 'You only talked to her for half a minute.'

'Yes, but what a half a minute. Can I smoke in here?'

'I'll find an ashtray.' Jukey wouldn't be happy, I thought. She didn't like smoking upstairs, but did I care? Not today.

Freddie sat up and sparked a cigarette. 'She came over to me – a total stranger – and told me that she liked my hair.'

'That was just the sort of thing she used to do.' I watched him inhaling. 'Did you . . . Did you think she was beautiful?'

'I thought she was strange.'

'Strange?'

'Yeah. Sort of in the way that you might think a unicorn is strange. I mean, a St Libby's girl, out in the middle of the day, down by the Wheat's not something you expect to see, so when you do, you're more taken with the rarity of it than anything else.'

'Don't suppose you even noticed me,' I said archly.

'You didn't want to be noticed.'

'I didn't stop thinking about you for one minute,' I said.

Freddie passed me the cigarette. 'You're crazy,' he said.

'Maybe.'

'What Rachel had – you don't lose that sort of courage overnight. She'll come through this. Whatever she does next will be the most important thing she's ever done.'

'How do you know? You don't know her.'

'Because after you've lost something – your mother, your face, your money – you've only got one choice.'

'What's that?'

'Find what makes you happy and head for that open door.' He took the cigarette back from me.

'You make me happy.' I didn't like that I was saying it, because it left me with nothing – no secrets, no hidden agenda. Perhaps that didn't matter any more.

'I'm not the answer,' he muttered. But he stubbed out his smoke and he lay back on the bed beside me, holding me next to him and stroking my hair.

'It's so quiet here,' he said.

'Not always.'

We lay in silence for a while. I didn't hear the quiet he spoke of; in the distance, I could hear foxes barking. Through the open window came the smell of mint and lavender from the kitchen garden down below. The whole world is carrying on as usual, I thought. And yet I was forever changed.

'I've never been in this bed before,' I said. 'The only person who's slept in here in the past ten years is my mother's sister, Aunt Angela. She comes at Christmas and spends most of the time crying. Jukey says she suffers from distemper and depression, but Howard says that's just an excuse for being self-obsessed. Caspar took a photo-graph of her sitting alone at the dining-room table, weeping after dinner on Christmas Day. She's wearing a ripped paper hat and her mascara's run down her face, and Opium's looking up at her with these big, mournful eyes, waiting for her to feed him a roast potato. It's one of Caspar's very best.'

Freddie laughed. 'What time do you get back from West Park usually?' he asked me.

'Six. I stay late to work through old A-level maths papers.'

'On your own?'

'No. There's a boy called Mark Abbot. We generally work together.'

Just bringing Mark's name into conversation with Freddie Friday felt jarring.

214

'I remember him,' said Freddie unexpectedly.

'He never shuts up,' I said, feeling disloyal to Mark, but wanting to make it perfectly plain that he was not someone I had any interest in. 'He calls me Lovelace. It's stupid.'

'Why?'

'After Ada Lovelace, Lord Byron's daughter. She was supposed to be one of the great mathematical minds of the mid eighteen-hundreds.'

'He loves you, then?' concluded Freddie.

'Gosh, no. On the contrary, he finds me extremely trying.'

Freddie raised his eyebrows and grinned at me. Was he jealous? Why *wasn't* he jealous? I was jealous of every girl who got to look at him in the factory during the day – the girls on the switchboard or in the canteen who he felt bonded to by background and bloody stamina . . .

'Come and see me when you've finished doing fractions with Mark Abbot. I get back from the Wheat at six. Come then.'

'You mean it?'

'Of course I mean it.' He looked agitated all of a sudden, as though I was trying to trick him. 'Why wouldn't I mean it?'

'I don't know. It's just that . . . you don't need to think that everything has to be different. If you just want us to carry on being friends still, and nothing else, then that's all right.'

'Shut up,' said Freddie. He looked at me without suspicion, beyond wariness. 'You're too pretty for me,' said Freddie. It sounded strange, the way that the words came out – regretful, not full of hope.

'No, I'm not,' I said.

'You are. Believe me, you are.'

There was a moment of quiet between us and then he said, 'I'm sorry I cried.'

'I don't mind.'

'I do. I didn't come here to cry.'

'What did you come here for?' Then, when he didn't answer, I said, 'So, will you stay for the party tomorrow?'

'Yeah,' he said. 'All right.'

I was shocked; I hadn't imagined that he would stay.

At six in the morning, I returned to my bedroom, my head spinning. I had said nothing to him, except to repeat over and over in my head, *I love you, I love you, I love you.* Somehow *this* had happened! Against all the odds, he had been with me, naked in a bedroom that, in the past, I had only ever associated with Aunt Angela and her tears. Well, now that space was holy to me because he had been there. He was there still. And everything would be all right now, I thought. Because, whatever else happened over the course of the next few hours, weeks, years, he had been naked next to me and had told me I was pretty.

16

Miss Crewe

There was no part of me that imagined the garden party at North Bridge House would be anything like as overwhelming as it was. I hadn't been thinking straight. When I walked in, I wanted to swear. I hadn't had time to wash my hair, usually worn long when not at school, so had twisted it up as though I were about to take a maths lesson. I was wearing a pair of red trousers and a white blouse that had looked right in the mirror of my flat, but here, among the great and the good, looked cheap and unfashionable and wrong. As a final masochistic act, I had also chosen to wear flat shoes in order to avoid sore feet, which had completely disarmed me. For a moment, I stood still, considering leaving immediately, but I was too fascinated to turn around.

Alexander – who had looked utterly wrong before we arrived, in a pale grey jumper with patches on the elbows (too small) and jeans (too short) – now looked exactly *right*. His physicality – the strength of his features alone – turned heads. I could imagine what people were thinking: *Who's he? Some eccentric director, perhaps, or an actor, over from America?* I took a glass of champagne from a tray and edged closer to him, wanting to absorb some of that natural power, that confidence that came from his stature, his comfort in his own skin. At school, I was the last word in glamour, I was the one they pulled out when they needed to impress visiting headmasters, I was

217

top dollar. Here, I was at the bottom. Here, the situation was quite different.

The place was awash with famous faces; they were everywhere. I choked back my astonishment with a slug of champagne. There was Joan Greenwood, talking to Anita Pallenberg!

'Are you all right?' Alexander looked at me, sensing weakness. 'This is quite something, isn't it?'

'I didn't expect *this*,' I said. 'Marnie was very dismissive of it all when she mentioned it to me.'

'Of course,' said Alexander. 'Why should any of this matter to her? She's grown up thinking this is normal.'

'Goodness. This is quite something,' I said.

'Yup,' said Alexander.

I wondered where Freddie was. Marnie had told me that he was here, but so far he appeared to be keeping a low profile. I didn't blame him; this was the sort of occasion that I couldn't imagine him relishing. A waitress in black and white, with heels sinking into the grass and wearing considerably more make-up than me, waved a plate of little sausages in front of us.

'Thank you,' said Alexander, spearing three with a cocktail stick. 'Beautiful garden. Though I'd get rid of that row of copper beeches.'

'You're getting ahead of yourself,' I said. 'This is meant to be one of the most remarkable gardens in Hertfordshire, immune even to your criticism.'

Oh! I couldn't have found fault with that place had I lived to be a hundred years old! All I wanted to do was lie down in the middle of the lawn, with my head on the grass, listening for its beating heart. Was there anywhere in the country more alive than here? The air was as perfumed as the scented erasers so favoured by the lower fourth at St Libby's: roses, mint, cucumber and strawberry all mixed with the heavy smell of fame – the scents that dominated the dressing rooms of every theatre in the West End: Chanel N° 5, patchouli oil. From somewhere, I could hear the strains of a jazz band; under the shade of a little cherry tree a number of golden-haired children clutching toffee apples and drinks with straws had gathered in front of a Punch-and-Judy stand. Three horses in ice-cream-sundae colours – pink roan, palomino and chestnut – stood in the adjoining field under the shade of an ancient oak, indifferent to the scene, flicking away flies in the heat, eyes half closed. I'd trade my life to be a horse at North Bridge House, I thought. Back in the garden, colours exploded along the borders, hurting the eye with their bright, unapologetic beauty, every petal of every flower gaping open, demanding what they needed to keep them alive – sun, bees, heat, rain – *gimme, gimme, gimme!* They were as we all were, I thought: putting on a show and hoping something or someone attractive would give a damn.

Alexander had a habit of voicing exactly what I was thinking. 'So this is how the very rich exist,' he said.

'We should find Marnie,' I said.

'There she is.' Alexander nodded over the heads of the crowd in front of us. I followed his gaze.

We walked over. Marnie was facing the other way and didn't see us until we were right next to her.

'Hello,' I said.

She turned around. 'Miss Crewe!' She looked surprised. I had as good as told her that I would not be coming to the party.

'Oh! And Mr Hammond!'

I heard the relief in her voice. If I was here with him, then that made everything safe.

Alexander was delighted to see her. 'Marnie!' he said. 'St Libby's is much the worse off without you. My God – your parents certainly know how to throw a party, don't they?'

'Caspar and I used to dread it.' She looked at me, her eyes on fire.

I wondered how much she had drunk already. She was swaying slightly.

'Can I talk to you, Miss Crewe?' she said.

'I wish you'd call me Julie—'

'Oh, I can't,' she said. 'I couldn't. It would be too odd.'

'Marnie, have you been drinking?'

'Yes,' she said. 'It's a party, isn't it? Everyone's had a drink . . .'

I said nothing. I felt a great sadness.

Marnie took my arm. 'Miss Crewe,' she said, 'he came here yesterday.'

'Who?'

'Freddie. He thought the party was yesterday. He showed up on the doorstep.'

'So he stayed the night?' I asked her. I hadn't meant to sound so abrupt.

'Yes. He's here. He wanted to stay.' She beamed at me. 'I love him,' she said simply.

'I know.'

'But I don't know that he'll ever love me the same way. He always seems to be holding something back. Oh, you're the only one I can talk to about him, the only one who knows what I mean.' She blushed and shook her head as though angry with herself. 'I'm sorry, Miss Crewe. I shouldn't be saying this to you. I feel an idiot. I think I've drunk too much.' It was the first time that she had confessed such a thing to me, but we were on her territory now – this was her space. 'When Freddie was here last night, I forgot about Rachel,' she said. 'For the first time since it happened, I didn't feel guilty.'

'You mustn't confuse Freddie with the need to escape something else,' I said.

We were interrupted by the arrival of Marnie's mother, wearing a long white dress, her hair half plaited and pulled off her face, then cascading down her back in a white-blonde sheet.

'This is Jukey,' said Marnie. 'My mother,' she added, as if I didn't know.

Jukey Tempest was far more arresting in the flesh than any photograph of her had ever suggested. I had always supposed her to be a silly woman who didn't pay enough attention to her daughter; I hadn't accounted for her charm. She seized both of my hands and crushed them with delight.

'Miss Crewe!' she whispered. 'Should I call you that? Nothing else seems right, somehow. I suppose you do have a first name?'

'I'm trying to get your daughter to call me Julie,' I said.

'I've been trying to get her to call me Mum since she was three,' said Jukey. 'She never listens. But then that's Marnie, isn't it? James was calling me Mummy for years before Marnie came along and changed the record.'

'I didn't do it on purpose. I was only little. You could have stopped me,' said Marnie.

Jukey threw back her head and roared with laughter. '*Stopped* you? Has anyone ever managed to stop you doing what you want to do? Not even an expulsion from St Libby's has stopped you from taking maths A-level. She's a little pocket rocket, this one, Miss Crewe. You know that, don't you? She doesn't even see it herself, half the time!'

'She's always like this,' muttered Marnie to me. She was smiling, but she looked desperately uncomfortable.

'Haven't you got a drink, Miss Crewe?' her mother went on. 'Marnie, you're not looking after her, darling.'

Marnie shot off gratefully in the direction of the cocktails. I had blown it, I thought. Marnie needed to be handled with care – no one could think or act straight when they were as in love as she was. I should know that.

To my surprise, Jukey didn't slink off a moment later to join her. Instead, she nudged me with a smile, squeezed my arm, took a huge slug of red wine and bedded in as though we had known each other for years. It was at once unnerving and extremely comforting to someone like me, who usually kept people at a distance through sheer force of habit.

'Three hundred people this year,' she murmured. 'And most of them carrying double their body weight in ego.' She indicated a well-known singer and a trio of girls clustered around him, hanging on his every word. 'What is it about actors and musicians?' she asked me. 'Why do they always feel they have to shout so damn loud all the time?'

'They're probably deaf,' I reasoned.

Jukey looked at me as though trying to assess whether I was joking – which I wasn't.

'What an afternoon!' I said, feeling that some sort of comment on the setting was necessary. 'My God, what gardens! I've heard about them before, of course, but just to be here on a day like this is *quite* something else.'

'Howard always has a wonderful time at this party,' said Jukey. 'He pretends not to, of course. Although this year – I don't know – he seems a little distracted. Me – I find it a tremendous bore to have to pretend that I'm loving every moment.'

She moved closer to me. She had a low voice; I had to strain to hear. 'I wouldn't say this to anyone else, Miss Crewe, but I have to tell you, the whole scene just depresses me. All it means is that I'm another year older, and still yet to do anything that I actually set out to do.' She laughed, looking shocked at herself. 'Listen to me! I'm sorry. You don't want to hear this. But even a setting as glorious as the gardens at North Bridge House is capable of stirring up the most awful self-pity in a woman like me. I mean, I looked at myself in the mirror this afternoon and I thought, Joanna, you could pass for a hundred and ten. But look at *you*. No wonder Marnie dotes on you. You're just gorgeous.'

I muttered something in response. I felt myself going red.

'You're half my age,' said Jukey. 'What are you – thirty? Thirty-one?'

'Forty-one,' I said.

222

She gave a low whistle. 'I'll have what you're having. Is it the maths that keeps you young?'

'Either that or the lack of children,' I said.

'Ah, yes,' said Jukey. 'Of course, that's it. And no husband too. I do envy you that.'

I blinked at her, and laughed. 'You envy me for not being married?'

'Oh, don't be shocked. Sometimes I think I've got an awful lot wrong,' she said. 'Just before I met Simon FitzPatrick, I had got into the most terrible habit of sleeping with all my male friends. And believe me, there were plenty of them around in those days. I just couldn't seem to *help* it. They all went off, of course,' she said dismissively. 'I had them at their best, so to speak. Then they went and married some very interesting women, most of whom can't quite bring themselves to talk to me for very long. So I get rather lonely at events like this – even when I'm the hostess.'

'You mean you've been to bed with most of the men in this garden?' I said, by way of summarizing the situation.

Jukey looked thoughtful and drew in air through her teeth as she calculated.

'Seventy per cent of them,' she said. 'Or thereabouts.'

I must have looked shocked, because she laughed.

'And my husband's done most of their wives, so I'm afraid we're rather a dull couple at this party. Much nicer to talk to someone like you. Adam Wright, over there –' she waved her hand at a short man of about fifty with thinning black hair, enjoying a conversation with an even shorter man twice his age – 'is just about the best screw in this garden.'

'*Him?*' I said in amazement.

'I know,' said Jukey. 'You wouldn't think it, would you? But it's absolutely true. It's always the less attractive ones that come to life behind closed doors – or open doors, in Adam's case; he never minded about that sort of thing. Ask his wife. Oh, I'm sorry,'

223

she went on, pressing her hand into my arm. 'I forget myself. I shouldn't be saying all this to you. I barely know you, and yet I feel I do. Marnie thinks you're the greatest human being ever to have lived.'

'I'm sure she doesn't,' I said.

She read my mind and lowered her voice again. 'You know, that boy she's so mad about stayed over here last night,' she said into her glass.

'Freddie?' I heard my voice sounding thick and wrong.

'That's the one.' Jukey nodded, looking out to the party, and raised a half-hearted glass to a woman in pink heels.

'What did you think of him?' I asked.

She looked at me and her face lit up. 'Oh, he's a *darling* thing. Came over with a great gash on his forehead, all pale and trembling like an ash leaf under a new moon. He got the party day wrong – at least, that's what he told us. He's here now, somewhere.' She looked around vaguely.

'I'm amazed he had the courage to come here at all,' I said. 'He's not exactly the most sociable boy.'

'Marnie's bats about him. It won't last, of course, will it?' said Jukey. She looked at me, her face suddenly full of melancholy.

'I don't know,' I said. 'Perhaps it will.'

'Still, they say that it's the best thing – to fall, the first time, for someone you can never really have—'

'Why can't she?' I asked.

'My dear,' said Jukey. 'He's *queer*. Surely you knew?'

'I don't know what you mean.'

'I'm not even sure that he knows it himself. But it's true. I've never been wrong on these things – it's the instinct of a hairdresser. Simon used to say that we can uncover truths more efficiently than Scotland Yard. Poor Marnie. I haven't the heart to tell her.'

'What makes you so sure?'

'My son, Caspar,' said Jukey. 'And the way that the boy looks at him, like he knows – oh, I don't know. Perhaps I'm reading too much into everything. Hairdressers do, you know,' she added regretfully.

'He reminds me of someone I knew once,' I said.

'Oh? Who?'

I heard my voice saying, 'He was a dancer too. Someone I met in New York when I was young. It was just a silly thing, you know. Nothing ever really happened between us – it was all in my head, really. But I've never been able to forget him.'

'All in your head,' said Jukey. 'Terrible power the mind has, don't you think? Who was he? Anyone we might know?'

I hesitated. I had never wanted to talk to anyone about Jo more than I did in that moment. Jukey, whom Marnie had portrayed as a difficult, volatile and inherently self-centred woman, clearly had a B-side that radiated warmth, empathy and fun. I was saved by the sudden sighting of her husband.

'Oh, God,' she said. 'I don't know what's wrong with him.'

I followed her eyes to where Howard was walking towards the field, quite alone. It wasn't the stride of a man surveying his kingdom, nor the slow, relaxed strolling of someone at ease with the world around him. He walked with his head down, an air of agitation about him.

'I don't understand,' said Jukey. She looked at me. 'He's not happy. It's like I said. All of a sudden, he's just not happy.'

'Perhaps he feels like you do about the party,' I suggested.

'No. That's not it.' When she turned to me again, she looked shocked by her own realization. 'That's not it,' she said. 'He's thinking of someone else. He doesn't want to be here. He's . . . I think he's in love.'

I laughed out of sheer nerves.

'In love?' I repeated.

'Yes,' she said slowly. 'That's it. The question is, who is she?' She looked at me imploringly, as though I were about to reel off a selection of possible names. 'Who is she?' she asked again. She took another gulp of red wine and grimaced. 'I always said that, when he fell in love, everything would be over. Ah,' she said, gathering herself up again as her eyes lit on Alexander, approaching with Marnie and two cocktails. 'Who on earth is that with Marnie?'

'I came with him,' I said. 'Marnie invited us both. He's at St Libby's too. He teaches history and music.'

'Lethal,' said Jukey in horror.

'We're great friends, nothing more.'

Jukey looked at me. 'My dear Miss Crewe,' she said under her breath. 'Stop thinking about the dancer. *He's* the one you should be sleeping with. Look at that body!'

I would have been more shocked were it not for the invasion of rum and coconut into my body. I was astonished at how, quite suddenly, I didn't care about anything I had cared about when I had walked in: my clothes, what to say, who to talk to. I walked slowly across the lawn towards the jazz band. Ahead of me, a group of women had taken their high-heeled shoes off to dance under the trees, because they could, and because it didn't matter what anyone thought. Not here. It felt as though everything were rehearsed, as though it had all been carefully timed to come off as brilliantly as it did. Of course it wasn't, but it happened with the seamless ease of a play, mid-act, changing direction suddenly and taking the audience to a quite different place. Everyone had drunk too much. The garden appeared to have intensified, increased its powers over us all. Alexander was laughing with an actor I recognized from the front cover of last week's *Radio Times*. Marnie was standing with Freddie and her brother, Caspar, who was ploughing through a pavlova using nothing but his index finger.

The band started to play something from *Guys and Dolls* and I felt myself moving towards them. I must have been swaying, or moving my feet in a way that suggested I wanted to be moving them a great deal more, because the band leader – cool, with

McCartney hair and Lennon glasses – shouted out, 'Are you going to dance, then?'

I don't think that he was expecting me to respond. Perhaps all they ever expected from a crowd of drinkers at five in the afternoon was five seconds of waving hands in the air or a shuffle across the lawn in a badly-formed foxtrot, as several others were doing. But I heard Jo in that music, because it was impossible not to. And in the mathematical equation that made up the way that I felt about him, the desire to dance outstripped the possibility of embarrassment. Rum cocktails + Jo + music = dance. Any other answer was wrong.

I wasn't aware of anyone watching, because there were not many people directly next to the band at this stage. I shook off my shoes and felt the grass, warm under my feet. I closed my eyes and heard, not the sound of chattering actresses and clinking glasses, but the low hum of the city outside the park. I was back in the Conservatory Garden with Jo.

The band, watching me dance to the sound they were making, grew louder. The saxophonist shouted something in appreciation. The steps were coming back to me, because they had never left, and because I danced every night in my sleep. The shoulder rolls, the single hand gestures, the backwards exits that he had so favoured.

Once or twice I made a mistake, lost the rhythm, but I heard myself laughing and carrying on. At the end of the song, a crowd had gathered around me and, when the band started to play again, people were dancing with me, finding each other's hands, moving around me as though I were the centre of the flame and they had to move to keep me burning.

A black girl in a short dress the colour of watermelon moved towards the band. 'Can you do something American?' she slurred. 'Something from where I'm from? I'm homesick, baby.'

'Who do you like?'

'What have you got? Something sharp. Something modern. Something sung by a white boy. I just *love* white boys.'

Someone wolf whistled and she grinned with perfect teeth at her audience.

Without waiting for her to suggest anything further, the group cracked into a song that I recognized from the common room at St Libby's. The Monkees were an American group all right, and two years ago I had heard 'I'm a Believer' and its B-side '(I'm Not Your) Steppin' Stone' playing in the common room at St Libby's at least seventeen times every evening. Being a housemistress had its advantages; I was as familiar with every single played on *Pick of the Pops* as a sixteen year old. Now, hearing the record replicated perfectly in the garden at North Bridge House while I was high on cocktails and cigarettes, I felt myself looking instinctively for someone to dance with. Where was Jo? Suddenly, Freddie was in front of me. I held out my hands to him. 'Dance with me!' I said.

He pulled away, laughing. 'I can't dance here.'

'Why not?' I looked beyond him, at the boy I recognized as Marnie's brother.

'Caspar!' I called. I reached out and took him by the hands.

The boy couldn't really dance, but he made the best of it. The crowd started to cheer; here was the son of the host, prancing around the garden with bare feet, sloshing champagne over my toes, a cigarette dangling from his mouth. I saw Freddie watching him, and I knew then. That's when I knew.

Suddenly, Freddie stepped forward.

'Wait,' he said.

I took his hands again and laughed. 'You're a dancer, aren't you?'

'Yeah,' said Freddie. 'I used to dance to this at home. This was one of my favourites.'

'Really? What did you do?'

'I had a whole sequence for it,' he said. 'Shall I show you?'

'Please.'

Taking the next verse, Freddie jumped into the air and leaped on board the song. He swept his hand through his hair, assuming a face of dramatic seriousness. Then he stepped forward and executed a perfect twist, with hand jives and head shakes added in for extra effect. The effect it had on the crowd was instantaneous.

'Hey, hey! Wait up! We'll all do it!' shouted *Radio Times* Man. He threw his cigarette into a row of pansies and came and stood close to Freddie, watching him moving and imitating him. He was surprisingly good.

'Stop! Can you teach us?' said the girl who had requested the song. 'We should all do it! All of us. In a circle! In a line! *We have to do this!*' She spoke with the crowd-rousing urgency and seriousness of someone who had lost control of rational thought some time ago.

Jukey flung herself opposite Freddie and pushed back her shoulders.

Freddie was laughing, his hand in mine. 'She's my teacher,' he said. 'She taught me everything I know.'

And because everyone was drunk – or high, or famous, or all three – they all took his word for it and cheered. The song finished, but the band promptly started it again.

'All right!' shouted Jukey. 'Now, come on. If it's worth doing, it's worth doing well. You – Freddie Friday – you stand – here – like this –' she pulled him into the middle of the lawn – 'and we'll watch you do it. What is this dance you're doing?'

'A jive,' said Freddie. 'It's a jive.'

'Jive. Right. I thought it was a bloody jive! Easy. So, you show us how, Mr Friday, and then we'll all join in. You'll have to shout out what you're doing so we can all follow. All right?' She was very drunk. She turned to the crowd watching her. 'And you,' she said, wobbling in bare feet and grasping me by the arm, leading me up next to Freddie. 'You can do it too. Where's that man with the wonderful body that you showed up with?'

'Alexander? I don't know.'

'Oh, well. We'll have to start without him. Come on, everyone – watch.'

She sounded completely serious, as though stage-managing an impromptu dance routine for nearly two hundred people in the middle of her lawn on a summer's afternoon was the most normal thing in the world. Perhaps it was, I thought. Perhaps only extraordinary, confusing things ever happen in this house. Certainly everyone present that afternoon had been spiked with magic of some sort. Suddenly, she spotted Howard Tempest emerging from an old railway carriage at the bottom of the garden.

'Wait!' she yelled.

Freddie and I stopped. Everyone stopped. Howard stopped. Jukey raced over to him, grasping both his hands in hers and pulling him into the middle of us.

'You're doing this too,' she said.

'What?' He looked at us in bewilderment. I sensed he was trying to place where he had seen me before; I doubt that he wanted to be reminded of Bethany Slade.

'Dance!' ordered Jukey. 'With me. Now.'

He isn't going to like this, I thought. He wouldn't want to be ordered around in front of everyone.

'I don't dance,' he said.

'All the more reason to do it. Come on. We're following Freddie Friday and Julie Crewe.' She looked at her husband with the sort of intensity that is usually reserved for decisions of great magnitude.

'Fuck it,' said Howard. He kicked off his shoes and pulled off his socks. There was a surge of applause.

Freddie and I danced once through the song on our own. Even then, I knew that my hip would repay me for all of this in the morning, but, in the moment, I couldn't stop. The crowd, led by Marnie's mother and stepfather, clapped and cheered as though we were dancing at the Palladium, and Freddie felt like another boy. There was none of the reticence, none of the fear that I associated with teaching him. He had lost all of that in the joy of an audience,

230

because he knew that people were watching him. I had always wondered whether he had the ability to perform in front of others, or whether he would be too self-conscious, too afraid of failure. Now that question was being answered in front of my eyes. Why wasn't Marnie here? I thought. Where was she?

Everyone had lost their shoes now; there was a tribal atmosphere in the air, enhanced by Jukey, who was stomping around the edges of the circle and nodding her head as though she had gathered all of us there for a ritual that she had planned down to the last minute. I was vaguely aware that people were standing too close to each other, that there would be consequences of dancing like this. There always were. Jukey leaned on my shoulder, sighed and whispered, 'See how seriously Howard's taking it? It's what makes him a great actor. He picks everything up in an instant. He's like bloody litmus paper. It's why I fell in love with him in the first place.'

Those who weren't in love with Howard would certainly have been giving their hearts to Freddie. I had never seen him so free, so delighted – so drunk. The next morning, I realized the significance of him seeing other people dance something that he had choreographed, but at the time, all we could do was laugh. When the song finished for a fourth time, Jukey clapped her hands together.

'This is it,' she said. 'Ladies and gentlemen, and everyone in between –' she shot a glance at Caspar, who raised his glass in her direction – 'this is our opening night. We've rehearsed for weeks. We've broken our backs. We've loved and hated each other. We've worn through the soles of our shoes. We've worked under our choreographer, Mr Freddie Friday, and his most capable assistant, Miss Julie Crewe, for long enough. It is time to set this jive free! For the first time and the last time, I give you . . . the North Bridge Dancers!'

She nodded at the band.

There was a silence, punctuated by giggles, while everyone lined up. Then the band started again, and we were off. I wanted to stay with Freddie, because it was the first time since I had danced with Jo that I had danced happy. Once this was over, I knew that I wouldn't get it back again. I reached out to him, and his hands were warm, and he seemed to sense how much I needed him. There was serious intent in that dance, not just from me, from everyone there. Suddenly, everyone wanted it to look right, no one wanted to be the one to mess it up. People were drunk, but on the cusp of drunken brilliance, which only ever lasted a few minutes and had to be harnessed and harvested while it could be. At the end, we cheered like maniacs, clapping, hugging each other and laughing as though we had opened on Broadway. Howard fell into Jukey's arms.

Alexander – who, while we were dancing, had been engaged in conversation with two boys called Bryan Ferry and Andy Mackay in the kitchen at North Bridge House – drove me home. Had I dreamed what I had seen as I had left North Bridge House? I had run outside to fetch my shoes, and had found Caspar and Freddie at the end of the lawn. They were lying down and didn't see me, although I don't know that it would have made any difference if they had.

'I'm in love with him,' Caspar was saying.

'How do you know?'

'Because I just know.' Caspar inhaled and passed him the cigarette. 'You're not in love with my sister,' he said.

'How do you know?'

Caspar leaned forward and kissed Freddie on the lips. I couldn't watch, but I couldn't not watch. Freddie moved forward, but Caspar moved back and lay down again.

'That's how I know,' he said. 'You'd better not break her heart.'

'Don't . . .' said Freddie. 'I didn't mean to . . . I'm just drunk, that's all.'

'You don't have to explain yourself to me,' said Caspar. 'Christ, no one ever has to explain themselves to me. You're all right, love.'

There was kindness in his voice.

I felt something wrenching me when I looked at Freddie, some-thing that I couldn't place in the right part of my soul. Did I love him? I asked myself for the twentieth time that week. And yet I knew the answer. It wasn't him that I loved, but the blurred mirror image of another.

17

Marnie

The short version of what happened is that I was so drunk that I passed out on my bed and missed the rest of the party. I hated myself for it. I awoke the following morning with a crashing headache and the news that Jukey had bundled Freddie into a car with John Mills, who was going to drop him home on his way back to London.

'If this isn't a lesson for you, then nothing will be,' said Caspar. 'You missed the dancing.'

'What dancing?'

'Your Miss Crewe and Freddie Friday. They danced for everyone, and we all joined in.'

Jukey plopped two aspirin into a glass of water.

'I think it was the best garden party we've ever had,' she said. 'My head—'

'Why didn't anyone try to find me?' I squeaked.

'We did. You couldn't be roused.'

'Roused is a ridiculous word,' I snapped. 'Was Freddie looking for me?'

'Darling Marnie,' he said. 'I'm going to tell you this once and once only, and I want you to repeat after me.'

'What?'

'Freddie Friday is going to break my heart. He should be my friend, nothing more.'

But I couldn't repeat that, because I didn't believe it. How could Caspar know how it felt to be with Freddie? How it had felt when he had cried in my arms? He didn't know the way that he had looked at me, the things he had said. *He had called me beautiful.*

I had missed him dancing because I had drunk too much. Yet still, in my head, it was justified. I was nervous, the cocktails were strong, I wanted to be with Freddie but I didn't know how to be with him at home, with everyone else around. I gave myself excuses because they were what I needed to keep drinking. They were what I needed to ignore the glaring lights that spelled out the fact that I had a serious problem.

I expect that, to everyone else that week, the town was just as it had always been. To me that week, it was a place transformed. There was romance in everything. I could get through every day at West Park because I knew that, at the end of every afternoon, there was Freddie Friday. Nothing beyond this mattered. I smuggled drink into school with me and, ashamed and hating myself, locked myself in a cubicle to consume it. I knew that I wasn't the only drinker in the school; I had heard of others, but I didn't see myself as one of them. I thought I could stop whenever I wanted, that I just needed it now to get me through the next few weeks. I needed to drink to be who I wanted to be when I was with him.

Mark Abbot and I worked together on old maths papers most afternoons, which was the only thing that kept me coming into school in the mornings. The Monday after the party at North Bridge, he had guessed that something had changed. He spun an HB pencil around on his desk and looked at me sideways. I had drunk three inches of whisky twenty minutes before; I felt ill and alive at the same time.

'You've done it, then,' he said. It was a statement of fact more than a question. He was wrong. I hadn't done it, but if he wanted to believe it, then I didn't care. I wanted to believe it myself.

'I don't know what you mean,' I said.

'Yes, you do. You're totally distracted.' He looked at my sheet of calculations. 'And your maths is shit today, it really is.' I glared at him. He looked unrepentant. 'Question nine's wrong.'

'No, it's not.'

'It is. Look again.'

I stared down at the paper. 'All right,' I conceded. 'Where's the rubber?'

'That – I hope with all my heart, Lovelace – is not the first time you've asked that question of a member of the opposite sex in the past forty-eight hours. Much better to be safe than sorry.'

'Oh – ha, ha, ha! Do stop! My sides might split.' I looked down so he couldn't see that I was grinning.

Mark leaned forward and pulled my hair away from my neck. 'Ugh! *Love bites?*' he said in disgust. 'They went out with the fucking ark, Lovelace. Really, you've got to get yourself a better lover. No one does that unless they've got something to prove.'

I wrenched myself away from him. 'They're not what you think,' I said weakly.

'Oh, yeah?'

Erasing the mistakes had made my paper smudge into a grey mess. Outside, several girls in our class were hitching up their skirts and walking towards the school gates. Now, newly initiated into a world where I had kissed Freddie Friday, the planet seemed to be waiting for sex, living for the sparks. How could I have been so immune to it before I had known him?

'Was it him? Was he the lucky man?' persisted Mark.

'Who?'

'Mr Friday, of course.'

I couldn't help myself: 'He stayed until midnight,' I said.

'Midnight, eh? Did he leave his glass slipper behind? He'd have been fucking frantic lookin' for that, I can tell you.'

'I don't care what you say about him, you know. You wouldn't talk like this if you knew what he was really like.'

Mark paused, then leaned forward and looked at me with some urgency. 'Come out with me tonight, then,' he said. 'Just out for somefin' to eat. After this. We can talk maths.'

'No, thanks.'

'How did I know you would say that?' He looked at his watch. 'Right. I've got two months and two weeks until I can ask you out again.'

'How did you come to that conclusion?'

Mark looked bleak. 'Simple,' he said. 'That's the amount of time girls stay infatuated for. After that, they might love the bloke, but they don't necessarily want to *kiss* him much longer. I've calculated the whole bloody pantomime, and I know I'm right.'

'You're always right.'

'Hey – I'm not saying that they don't want to have him, to control him, to make sure that he never steps a foot out of line. But, after two months and two weeks, they're looking again, even if they don't know it themselves. Lovelace – you of all people should have worked this out by now. It's all in the numbers. It's an exact time. Two months—'

'And two weeks. Yes, thank you. I heard the first time.'

'How many hours?' demanded Mark.

'Huh?' I knew what he meant, but I was playing for time.

'How many—'

'This time of year? One thousand, eight hundred and twenty-four. Stop wasting my time.'

He pretended to swoon. 'You see, that's why I can't get you out of my head.'

'Shut up, Mark.'

'What's the word for all this?' he asked me. 'You know – me wanting you and you wanting him? And him wanting someone else up Shredded Wheat, I'll bet. It's a love quadrilateral. That's what it is.'

'He doesn't want anyone up the Wheat,' I said.

'Ooh! Touchy!'

Gosh, Mark could be annoying when he wanted to be.

'You only want me because you know I'll always say no. And stop making out that Freddie's like that. He's *not*. You're just saying that about him because you're afraid of him.'

Mark's brow furrowed. 'Don't spin that psycho-whatsit crap at me, Lovelace. I'm asking you out because I like you, plain and simple.' He looked at me unapologetically. 'You need a good time. You might get off swooning in your bedroom, writing love notes to Freddie and watching him dance round the Wheat on the weekends, but, believe me, that ain't gonna last forever. Then you'll need someone who can really *get* you.' He sighed heavily. 'By that, I mean someone who can equal you up here.' He tapped the side of my head with his forefinger, as Freddie always did to himself, only Mark did it just three times, not four. Superstition, and the fact that I had been drinking, made me tap out the remaining one, then four more on the other side. Mark looked at me curiously. I looked back down at his answers.

'Don't, Mark,' I said quietly. 'Please.' He looked at me, half smiling, but there was pain etched on his face. 'You're my friend, aren't you? Can't you go on being my friend? Isn't that worth more than all this other stuff?'

'Look. I'll be your friend as long as you want me to be your friend. I know it's all I've got at the moment. But what are the odds on us being more than friends some time? That is the question.'

'A hundred to one,' I said.

'I can take those odds,' he said, stuffing his work into his bag. 'You know, you might actually break my heart,' he said thoughtfully. 'I hadn't ever considered that. I suppose it has to happen to everyone at some stage. May as well be now, rather than later on with someone else's wife or something.'

Every day that week, after school, as Freddie had suggested, I turned into Birds Close. Each time that I walked up the path to the front door, I felt a stab of sickness and fear in the pit of my stomach. He wouldn't be there! He would open the door and stare at me without knowing me! He would tell me that he couldn't see me any longer – that the kissing and lying around in each other's arms at North Bridge House had been a terrible mistake! But no, for those five days it was all bliss – Freddie Friday and me, and the turntable in the front room playing the Rolling Stones, and dancing, and endless packets of water biscuits and slices of processed cheese and slightly soft apples, and sitting outside on the step in the early-evening sun after he came back from work. He didn't drink, so I didn't drink in front of him. Some part of me was disgusted with myself and the Great Lie between us, but, once again, I told myself that it was temporary, that it didn't really matter because soon I would stop. Yet every time I tried to stop, something would happen that would set me back again.

It was on Friday evening that everything unravelled again. Caspar had returned from school and James from Oxford. Howard was in London, as he had been for most of the week. To begin with, there was little to suggest that the evening was heading in the direction it took.

After we finished supper, we moved to the library, where James opened a bottle of white wine, proclaiming that it 'needed to be drunk' before the end of the month. I felt like a child holding out a cup for Ribena at a party.

'When's Howard back?' asked James. 'I was hoping to talk to him about his speaking at the Union. I know they want to have him.'

It was a few moments before we three realized that Jukey wasn't replying because she couldn't speak.

'Jukey?' said James in confusion.

She had her face in her hands, and her shoulders were shaking. It was the same pose that Caspar frequently adopted when something

239

amusing had happened and he needed to hide his laughter, yet we knew she was crying.

I stood up, and sent James's glass of wine glass flying across the room, where most of the contents were deposited over Jukey's skirt – a terrible beige linen thing with patches on the sides.

'Oh, God,' she muttered between sobs. 'This was Granny's.'

She looked up at us. It was as though her face had been smudged like a child's drawing – her nose was red, her cheeks blotchy and her brow lined with the pain of stopping the tears.

'Whatever's the matter?' asked Caspar.

'Who is she?' I heard myself asking.

'I don't know,' said Jukey. 'But it seems different this time. It's as though he really *minds* about this one. I can't explain. It just feels different, that's all. Not like the other times. There was always something silly about it before. You know – silly women going a bit crazy over him, and him unable to resist them. This isn't like that.' She took a note out of her pocket. 'I found this,' she said, handing it to me.

I looked at Caspar, who nodded.

Thank you. I can't tell you what you've done for me. I stood, naked, in front of the mirror last week and I told myself that this is just the start of everything.

   R

'Who's R?' I asked.

Jukey shook her head. 'I don't know. How should I know?'

'Judging by the state of the handwriting, she's either eight years old or eighty,' I said.

'He's a bastard,' said Caspar calmly.

'No!' shouted Jukey with shocking force. 'Don't *say* that!'

She ran out of the library and into the drawing room opposite. Caspar, James and I exchanged glances and followed her.

Jukey's hair had escaped from her trademark beehive and was trailing down her back. We usually only ever saw her hair loose if we crept into her room in the night, having had a bad dream. It sliced years off her face, yet at the same time the silver-blonde sheet and her wide, grey-blue eyes gave her a ghostly appearance.

'Has it ever occurred to you that *I* might be to blame for the way that he is? That there is a reason why he behaves as he does?'

I gulped and looked at my brother. Caspar was better at 'scenes' than me. He would have to deal with this.

'Of course there's a reason!' he said. 'He's too self-obsessed to notice how much he's hurting everyone around him!' He was speaking quietly; it was as though Jukey's wrath was shooting down his certainty with every second that passed. We were not used to seeing her like this; it was like finding a new chapter at the end of a book you had read a thousand times.

'I swore that I would never tell you,' said Jukey. 'But, my God, promises are hard work. They weigh you down like lead! They're there with you from the moment you open your eyes in the morning until the moment you fall asleep at night, filling up every bit of space you have. And I'm so tired of it! I'm just so *tired*! Then, if that's not enough, even when you go to sleep, they distort like monsters and slither into your dreams too. Well, I'm sorry, but I can't carry it around any longer. If it all falls apart, so be it.' She slapped both palms down on her thighs.

I heard my breath coming short and shallow. I looked at Caspar again and then to James and back at Jukey. 'What do you mean?' I asked her. 'What is it that you're weighed down by? What is it that he's done?'

Jukey sat down in front of the table that contained four albums of Caspar's photographs. She gripped the tabletop as though at a seance and there was every likelihood that it would wobble and take off.

'Howard is not your stepfather,' she said.

241

Caspar laughed. 'Come on,' he said. 'You can do better than that.'

But there was energy in Jukey now; she had the same contained swell of potential in her that always accompanied Freddie before he danced. Even in those short moments following her announcement, I knew that, whatever she said to us now, she was telling the truth.

'You mean you never really married him?' Caspar asked. Everything was scrambling; his cheeks were scarlet. He was fiddling with the top button of his shirt and he looked twelve years old. Jukey didn't answer him.

'Of course I married him,' she said quietly. 'That's not what I meant.'

'Well, what exactly *do* you mean?' he asked, striding across the room to Jukey. 'Stop talking like the end of an Agatha Christie, for God's sake.'

'He's your father – your real father. He's your *father*,' Jukey repeated. 'Your and Marnie's.'

At that very moment, the clock on the mantelpiece began its lumbering twelve strikes to signify midnight was upon us. Caspar was one step behind her for once, possibly deliberately so. 'You always want us to feel he's our father, but how can we? When he treats you the way that he does, when he doesn't seem to care about—'

'*No!*' Jukey shouted again. She fixed her eyes on the clock. '*I hate that clock!*' Striding across the room, she picked it up and raised it above her head, as though to smash it on the floor.

'Oh, Christ!' said James. 'Don't!' He held out his hand, but Jukey had thrown the clock to her feet. It hit the carpet with a loud thud, and carried on chiming.

Jukey stared at it, her hand clamped to her mouth like a little girl beside a broken toy. She looked up at us. 'Can't even smash the bloody thing,' she said, her lip trembling.

Instinctively, I moved closer to Caspar, needing to feel some of his usual conviction, his fire, but he seemed to have stepped back from where he had been moments before. We just stood there, the four of us, listening to the clock chiming in the carpet with a feeble vibrato. When it finished, Jukey took a deep breath, picked it up and placed it back on the shelf.

'Not a scratch. See?' she said, in a shaking voice. She sat down on the arm of the chair that Mrs George collapsed into when she finished cleaning the silver on Saturday afternoons. 'I'm sorry,' she said quietly.

'You'd better tell us what you're talking about,' said Caspar.

I had never seen him so serious before. I wanted him to run and get his camera, to throw out some jokey aside that would put the last few minutes back where I needed them to be, but that wasn't about to happen. Jukey knew that she had to talk now, that she couldn't wrap up what she had said and hide it again.

'I was having an affair with Howard three months before Simon died.' She looked at us both, and when she spoke again it was with conviction, clarity, absolute steadiness, as though she had stalled over her lines but had now remembered them. 'Howard was the man everyone wanted, and I couldn't believe that he wanted to be with *me* when there were so many others around – actresses, models, European princesses dripping with diamonds and promises. Yet he chose me. I had Simon, with James at home – my baby – but I was also very young and stupid and thought that I could do whatever I wanted. Howard wasn't someone you turned down. I can tell you that for free. *Nobody* would have. James is Simon's son, but you twins – you were Howard's children. You *are* Howard's children.'

'I don't believe you,' said Caspar simply. He pulled out a cigarette but didn't light it. 'I don't believe you,' he repeated. 'How do you know? How can you prove that?'

'Simon was away for six weeks in America when I got pregnant,' said Jukey. She looked at me. 'You don't have to be a brilliant mathematician to do the dates. He came back, and I was already

243

feeling sick. He said that he didn't want to know who I'd . . . who I'd shared a bed with—'

'*Shared a bed?* What is this, 1923?' said Caspar.

'All right. Who I'd *slept* with. He said that he would forgive me as long as I pretended that you were his, and he would too. So I did. In the end, I kept everything so hidden that I started to believe that you were his children. I had to believe it. If anyone had found out about Howard and me, then everything would have caved in. *Everything.*' She looked into the unlit fire.

'And in the end, he didn't even live to see us make it to our first birthday,' said Caspar.

'I know,' said Jukey. Her voice cracked. 'He died of a broken heart, because of me. Because he knew what I had done to him.'

'Don't be so dramatic,' said Caspar. 'He died of a heart attack because he smoked fifty cigarettes a day. There's no such thing as dying of a fucking broken heart. If that were the case, I'd be six feet under by now. Jesus Christ!'

'Does Howard know?' James asked. '*Does Howard know?*' he repeated, louder this time.

'No,' said Jukey. 'He asked me once. Only once, in all the time we've been married. It was the afternoon of your fourth birthday,' said Jukey. 'You'd both been ill, up with temperatures, and Howard had sat up with you both all night, and as a result he fluffed an audition the next day. It was a part he really wanted – a Hollywood film. When he heard that he hadn't got the part, he told me that it didn't matter because he liked you two more than he cared about Los Angeles.'

There was all the power in that word – *like*. Not love – that wouldn't have been how Howard would ever have phrased it. But *like*. There was the salty truth, in that one, powerful little word. *He liked us*.

'Didn't we have the right to know that our father was alive?' asked Caspar.

244

'I promised Simon,' repeated Jukey. 'He made me swear that, whatever happened, I would never tell any of you the truth. Not Howard, or you, or Marnie, or James. And this was the one promise I could actually keep. I could at least stay true to him by keeping that secret safe.' She looked at us both, her teeth chattering together.

'So why are you telling us now?' I asked her. I wanted her to put everything she had said back into a box and post it right out of Hertfordshire. 'Why do you need to tell us *now*? What's happened to change your mind?'

'When I found that note, I suddenly realized that, if anything ever happened to him, then he would die without knowing that you were his. And that seemed a terrible thing. I never let him get to me,' she said. 'Not really. I've always kept him at a distance from me. I was too frightened of being hurt again, and I don't like myself for what I did to Simon. It's my punishment,' she said. 'It felt right that Howard shouldn't be faithful to me. I didn't deserve it.'

'You didn't kill Simon,' I said. But I'd heard my own voice in my mother's. That conviction that I had done something terrible, that the world needed to fall apart because that was the right thing to happen.

'I swore that I'd never cut my hair, that I'd leave it long, as Simon liked it.'

We knew this story – it had always been a part of Jukey's mystical back catalogue of information about the man we had believed to be Dad.

'I'd like to cut it,' she said, much louder and with sudden defiance. 'I'm sick of being weighed down by it.'

'*Cut it, then!*' shouted Caspar.

'I *can't!*' she shouted back. 'I'm too frightened to.' She looked at us. 'It means the end of everything. If I cut my hair, it means . . . it means . . .'

'It means nothing,' I said.

'Fear of something is almost always enough reason to do it,'

245

James said. He gulped, and looked at me. 'Where can we find scissors?'

'Oh, don't!' Jukey managed a laugh of surprise 'Please – that's ridiculous. You can't—'

'James is absolutely right,' said Caspar.

He had taken up James's suggestion and was digging into Jukey's handbag, which was swinging on the door handle as it always did when she was at home, and had pulled out the hairbrush and the pair of scissors that she carried with her everywhere, yet never used – the same scissors that she'd had when she worked for Simon. Caspar held them out to her, not in the way that you should hold them, gripping the blades in your fist so as not to hurt anyone. He held them with the closed blades pointing straight out, in a manner that we would have been reprimanded for as children.

'You always used to say that cutting your own hair was a piece of cake,' said James. He looked at Caspar and then back to Jukey. 'Why don't you prove it to us?'

'If I cut my hair then I've forgotten him,' said Jukey. 'You want me to forget your father—?'

'That's just nonsense,' said Caspar, with a gentleness to his voice. 'Don't you see that, Jukey? It's a superstition, nothing more.'

'It changes everything,' said Jukey. She stared at the scissors as though Caspar were going to attack her with them. He looked straight into her eyes.

'Isn't that a good thing?' he said.

'I haven't cut hair since I worked at the salon,' said Jukey. 'Not even when you were little . . .'

She reached her hand slowly towards the blades and took hold of them. Then, without saying anything else, she stood in front of the mirror over the fireplace, picked up the hairbrush, and began to brush her hair with the long, rhythmic strokes that we'd witnessed when we were babies, as children, and now as three quite different people, standing on the edge of being adults.

Neither James, Caspar nor I dared to move, but even in our static state, I had never felt as close to my brothers as I did in that moment. James, usually the outsider, was suddenly in our tribe, regardless of the fact that he was just our half-brother. Jukey snapped the blades together briskly. Her face set in concentration, she began to cut, the blades slicing through all that hair. We didn't talk, but occasionally she issued an instruction:

'Turn on the lamp by the curtains over there.'

'Pass me a glass of water'

'There's a comb inside my purse – can you get it for me?'

But once she had started, she was fast. And, although she stared into the mirror, I knew that she wasn't seeing us, but the scenes of her past in FitzPatrick's: the chaos of the clients on a Saturday after-noon; the smell of peroxide and shampoo; the swish of the broom across the floor; the jokes from the boys and girls who could hold their heads high because they had actually got a job here – even if it was simply sweeping hair off the floor. And at the forefront of it all was Simon himself, the king of all this, the man she had loved and betrayed.

When she stopped, I think we all realised that something magical had happened. It wasn't simply that the hair was short now – she had cut it in a style that many of the girls at St Libby's had clamoured for – but it was that the anxiety had been lifted away. Her eyes were visible; she had pulled back her fringe. Her forehead, a pale, white place, unknown to me before that evening, was now revealed.

'You look so young,' I said.

Jukey stared at herself in the mirror.

'Simon always used to tell us, "Make them look younger, not more fashionable. Nothing else matters but youth. If you can do both, then wonderful, but youth is the only thing they're chasing, whether they admit it or not."'

I thought about Miss Crewe. Jukey touched her head incredulously.

'I'm next,' I said suddenly. 'I want mine like yours. I want you to cut my hair.'

Jukey bit her bottom lip. 'You're going to forgive me?' she asked. 'You understand why I couldn't say anything?'

I nodded, afraid that if I spoke everything would change again, and I needed this spell to stay with us for a while longer. Perhaps I would feel anger, but not now. Now I stood next to her as someone who understood her.

She picked up the scissors again and held my long hair in her left hand. Then she began to cut.

I closed my eyes and wondered what Freddie would think. The sound of the scissors through my hair was intoxicating – every time the blades came together, it was like being drugged – and I felt my eyes sliding half-shut. There was a gentleness in my mother's hands, and I had an absolute trust in the confidence with which she performed this simple act, an act that, in the past, she had performed on tens of people every day.

'Going anywhere nice on holiday this year?' she murmured.

It was a typical Jukey joke. I reached my hand up to hers, and squeezed her fingers.

'A bad haircut shames two men,' said Jukey. 'Simon used to say that. He taught us to cut as though every single client we had could find themselves on the cover of the papers the next morning, and it was up to us to make sure that they looked beautiful. If they didn't look good, then neither did we.'

'You loved working,' I said.

'Yes. But I loved you more.'

It wasn't until I sat down on my bed at three thirty in the morning that I realized it, and I thought how stupid I had been not to have seen it right away. The writer of the note to Howard was Rachel Porter, using her left hand for the first time in her life. She'd been in love with Howard since we were eleven years old, and finally she had got him. A little voice inside of me wanted to tell her that, considering she had lost an arm and smashed up one side of her face, she had done bloody well. I knew that I wouldn't meet Freddie and Miss Crewe that afternoon. How could I, after all of this? When the only thing that loving people seemed to do was throw events off course and shatter everything that was true and good?

When I pulled back my bedclothes, I found a photograph album. It was one of Caspar's – carefully labelled and full of information on family rows. It was open on a page with just two pictures. The first was of me, my face crumpled in indignant rage, half undressed and standing with my hands raised in a gesture of frustration. Underneath, Caspar had written, *Marnie berated for overflowing bath. Sept 1967.* Directly below it, there was a picture of Howard. He was standing in precisely the same pose, his blue eyes wide, his hands up, and an expression on his face that conveyed both remorse and defiance in equal measures. Caspar had written, *June 1968. Howard attempts to mend shelf in master bedroom. Shelf breaks half an hour later, smashing ornament of dog-dressed-as-clown given to Jukey for birthday by Vivien Leigh.*

I stared at the pictures. There was no need for any further questioning. It wasn't just our faces that were the same – it was our addictions. Mine, to drink and to Freddie Friday, whose dancing had blotted out the despair that had filled me since Rachel's accident. Howard's was to pretending, all the time, to be someone he wasn't. Because the truth was too frightening.

18

Miss Crewe

Freddie Friday didn't look his best when we next met. His skin, despite the hot weather of the past few weeks, was sallow and pale – a distinctly winter complexion in midsummer – and there were big black rings around his eyes. He wore what he always wore, the trousers rolled up, as Jo had worn them. It was this that got me every time I saw him. The trousers, the skinny ankles and scuffed shoes: they were Jo, through and through, and they broke my heart every time.

'You look like you could do with a holiday,' I said.

'No chance of that,' he said.

I quickly started the record player because I didn't want to see him start that obsessive tapping again. If I could get him dancing before he started that, then I had achieved something. The factory felt menacing, as though there were demons in every corner waiting to trip us up. But we had to keep working, for Eloise. I felt her presence beside me now, mocking me for moves that weren't working, shouting out when something came together, just like we used to while we rehearsed in New York. In seeing Freddie dance, she would be seeing me dance again.

We didn't stop for a break for nearly two hours. I was exhausted, every part of me hurting, my poor hips crying out for mercy, yet I was compelled to continue. When he was concentrating, when he was listening, not tapping, when I had his attention and I knew that I had him, it was heady stuff. The record went on again and again, and we went over the same moves, hearing the same lines in the music over and over again. In time, I lost myself; we could have been anywhere. Without Marnie, there was no one to ground us in the club room of the Shredded Wheat factory in Welwyn Garden City, no one to remind either of us that she was how this had started. When Freddie was listening to me, when I was talking to him, he was entirely focused, but when he stopped, the tapping came back too. Where did the time go? Despite the pain and the sweat, I wanted more time with him. It was never enough. The real world waited impatiently outside. I glanced at the clock above the bar. I hated that clock, the smugness of its plain, round surface, that dreadful second hand, counting down the hours until we had to leave. It ran five minutes fast. Freddie slid off his chair, on to the floor of the club room and on to his knees, towards his stack of records as smoothly as if it had been choreographed. Oh, God! For a body that could move like that, I thought. A body that could move like that without thinking, without feeling pain!

'I think we should stop,' I said.

Freddie looked at me and I saw disappointment on his face, like that of a child forced to leave the party early. He paused, his legs underneath him, and folded his arms in front of him and seemed to shiver. He looked unbelievably young. He doesn't want to go, I thought. There was something in the music that he needed to hang on to. He stood up and went over to the record player, and put on one of his new 45s. I knew the song right away.

'"The Boxer"?' I said.

'How d'you know?'

'Florence Dunbar,' I said. 'She bought it last week. She's the girl you met outside the cinema that time. You remember? Big girl. Lacrosse player—'

'All St Libby's girls look the same to me.'

251

'Except Marnie,' I said.

'She's not a St Libby's girl any more.'

I wanted to ask more about her, but he wasn't ready for it, so I helped him out.

'Why do you like this song?' It sounded like a question from an English comprehension, I thought. I sounded my age.

'The words make me feel like I know how it would be to stand on Seventh Avenue in New York City. I don't think you can ask much more from a record,' said Freddie. He sounded bleak. He looked at me and his face was eaten up with curiosity. 'Who is he?' he asked me.

'The singer? Art Garfunkel, isn't it?' I looked at him, frowning. 'I think he's from New Jersey—'

'No,' said Freddie. He laughed. 'I don't mean him. I mean who's the one who you dance for? The one you never talk about. Can't you tell me?'

The song had me in its grip now, that quiet, tremulous voice of Garfunkel was bringing me out in goosebumps.

'Don't, Freddie.'

'Why not?'

'It's of no consequence to anyone but me. There's nothing special about it.'

Freddie looked at me and shrugged.

'Dance it for me, then,' he said. 'Dance what happened. You don't have to talk. You don't have to answer to anybody—'

'Stop talking like Steve McQueen. And I can't dance it. Don't be ridiculous.'

'You can. I think you can.'

I looked at the black rings around his tired eyes. The expressions on his face were known to me now. I could have been blindfolded and asked to dance in the arms of fifty different boys and I would have known Freddie Friday, not just by his footwork, but by everything else that made him who he was: the smell of him, the length of his arms, the way he breathed when he needed time to concentrate. I had the details of the boy now, and it frightened me. I hadn't asked for them.

He pulled me to my feet and held my hands in his. 'Start here,' he said. 'Dance it for me.'

'The music's wrong,' I said.

'The music's never wrong,' he said. 'If the music's wrong then you just have to tell the story a different way. Didn't you say that to me the first time?'

Freddie wasn't going to let me off lightly. He stepped forward, holding up my hands in his. He smiled at me, and I had to look away because the affection stirred memories of Jo and the way that he looked at me when I had amused him, whether or not I had meant to. *Je me presse de rire de tout . . .*

'Where did you meet him?' he asked. He placed his arms around my back, holding me, and my hands moved instinctively to his shoulders. We were slow dancing to that strange, lonely song. I rested my head on his chest. Just give me this for five minutes, I thought. That's enough. No longer. I felt myself tipping off into the unknown.

'Central Park,' I said, swallowing. My voice – which had echoed around the club room when I had been calling instructions at him – now sounded so small, so quiet.

'What happened? Did you love him?'

The directness of the question hit me hard. He moved slowly with me, held me as though he wasn't just eighteen, but as my equal. I think he realized that the only way that I would talk would be if we danced at the same time to that sad, sad song, which wasn't the wrong music at all, but exactly right, with its American melancholy and that sweet, hopeful guitar, which Freddie tapped out gently down my spine. I couldn't look at Freddie, but, moving with him, dancing with him, felt closer than kissing him, and every beat of his heart felt as though it were moving in direct synchrony with mine. *Ba boom. Ba boom.*

'I loved him all right. He didn't love me. At least – not in the same way.'

'You danced together?'

'Every week,' I said. 'For six weeks. It's not really very long, is it? Six weeks. That was three hours a week, for six weeks, plus the time that we spent together when we first met, which couldn't have been more than twenty minutes. So, really, it was only about twenty-two hours that we had in each other's company. Twenty-two hours out of the two thousand and something that I've been around for. It's not much.'

This was how I spoke when I was talking to myself about Jo. I didn't talk like this to anyone else. I heard myself as he heard me, and I sounded mad. We were barely moving now.

'I'm sorry,' I said. 'It's the maths in me. Everything has to be calculated to make sense. And the thing is, it still doesn't make sense. The effect it had on me was out of proportion with the time I spent with him.'

'Six weeks is nearly what we've had,' he observed. 'It's enough for anything. Thirty seconds is enough,' he added.

I knew that if I didn't talk now, then I never would.

'I went out to the theatre one night with Eloise, and I saw him there, watching the show with someone else. Another girl.'

'Who was she?'

'I didn't know. It didn't matter,' I said. 'All that was certain was that he cared more about her than he did about me.'

'You didn't say hello?'

'I chose not to. I chose not to believe it, even though I knew that, for him, it had always been –' I searched around for the word – 'a *light* little thing. Something gentle, sweet, fun. Not something that filled every second of his day, like it did mine. He liked pretty girls; I suppose I might have been one.'

Freddie raised his eyebrows.

'But, for me, it was heavier than anything else in my life. It was more than everything and anything. It consumed me. I was helpless – an addict.'

I stepped back from him, out of his arms, but he pulled me back. I lowered my head and leaned into his chest, like a child.

'He made me a dancer,' I said. 'Not just because he gave me the steps, but because he gave me the emotion that went with the steps.'

The record was ending. I closed my eyes, then looked up and snapped my fingers together. *One. Two. Three. Four.* Freddie joined me, his eyes never leaving mine. Then his hands moved outwards and upwards, and every movement that I made, he copied, seeming to second-guess me, to know what I was going to do. I laughed because his timing was perfect. He was better than perfect.

'Shouldn't we be going?' I said.

'We're all right,' said Freddie. His eyes still on mine. 'Go on. What happened?'

'When I next met him, he said that he had got me an audition with a big player – a director that everyone wanted to work with. He had agreed to see me because Jo had told him that I was good, that he had worked on my dancing with me. Then he told me that we couldn't really see each other any more, at least not in the way that I wanted to. I said, "Hey, that's all right, we were only ever just friends, weren't we?" because that's the truth, you see. That's all we ever were. I wanted him too much and I wanted to *believe* too much.'

I pulled away from Freddie and marched across the room to my bag. I felt as raw and as shaken as though someone had stolen something from me, but he had done nothing but ask. The rest of it was all me.

'I've never told *anyone* this!' I shouted.

Freddie stepped backwards, as though slapped. 'Woah,' he said. 'Don't say any more, then.'

'No!' I shouted. 'I don't want to, so I won't.'

He flipped his record back into its sleeve.

With trembling hands, I picked up my basket. Several textbooks dropped out on to the floor. I leaned down to pick them up. 'But you asked, didn't you? You want to know? Why shouldn't you? That's what should happen, isn't it? You meet people, you get to know them, and then their pieces start to add up. You start fitting the jigsaw together. That goes *there,* because that happened *then.*'

We had been dancing for hours, but even the way that he walked across the room towards me looked choreographed.

'Don't shout at me,' he said. 'I don't like it. He shouts at me. Not you. Not you.'

I stared at him.

'I'm sorry,' I said. 'Freddie, I'm sorry. I'm sorry.'

I ran into his arms and he held me so tightly that, for a moment, I was afraid. He could kill me, I thought wildly. Then his arms became softer, and he looked at me.

'Don't tell me any more,' he said. 'I shouldn't have asked you.'

But that was no good, not now. I couldn't see the way back. Hell, it might as well be Freddie Friday! He had asked, hadn't he?

I stepped away from him, and sat down on the floor. He sat next to me, his legs bent up in front of him, his hands tapping. I don't think that he expected me to go on, but I couldn't stop now.

'The night that Jo told me about the audition, I went out and found the first man who looked at me and jumped into his bed.'

'You did?'

'I did.'

'Who was he?'

'He was a friend, I suppose. A guy I knew in New York. His name was Tommy, and he was keen on dancers. He was a student, but he used to hang around with all of us, pretending he knew what we were talking about. We used to make jokes about him, but he was a nice enough boy. He'd liked me for a while. Eloise said, if I really wanted Jo, then I should stick around and fight for him, but I couldn't do that. I was like a broken thing. The aching in my body started then. And it is an ache, you see? The Permanent Oppressive State of Heartache, as one of my pupils calls it. And she's right.'

I ran my fingers over the raised writing on the front of one of the maths textbooks on the floor.

'I stuck around with Tommy for a while. He was there, and I needed someone.' I felt the next sentence sticking in my throat, needing to be prised away from the secret part of my soul where I had kept it for so many years. 'I . . . I got pregnant. I found out one afternoon in January. I'd been sick for two weeks, didn't understand it. Never thought it could happen to me. I was a stupid little child. I . . . I wanted to dance, I didn't want a baby, but here I was with one growing inside me! It was terrifying. There was no one to turn to. My parents wouldn't have spoken to me. My God, my daddy would have roared at me. I was too scared to tell them. I wanted to lose it, until one morning when I felt it moving, and then it all seemed to . . . to . . . make sense suddenly. It became a real thing. But a day after I first felt her move, everything changed again.'

I held my arms outstretched, reaching for the child I wanted, feeling her there, just a beat away from me. Then I wrenched myself back. I was amazed at my calm, at how easy it was to tell Freddie this. It was easy.

'How did it change?' he asked me. He wasn't looking at me any longer, for fear that it would stop me. He wasn't tapping any longer; I had never known him so still and I found his stillness unnerving. I was used to his movement, to his tics. Without them, he didn't seem entirely him.

'I was on the way to another audition,' I said. 'It was the third round, it was a big thing. If I got it, then it would really *mean* something. I was four months gone, but you'd never have known. I was thin. I mean, really thin – thinner than you – from the Permanent Opressive State of Heartache.' I half-smiled. 'I wanted to go to the audition because there was a part of me that hoped he'd be there. I hadn't thought further than the possibility of seeing him again.' I

257

closed my eyes, feeling tears stinging my eyes. 'I slipped on the steps on the way out of the building where we lived. Silly as that, really. I slipped and fell and I broke both my ankles. I was knocked out. That's where my injuries came from – a stupid little fall that changed everything. I never made it to the audition.'

I heard myself gasping to keep in the tears. I didn't want them; I was ashamed of crying in front of him.

'That was *it*?'

I took a deep breath.

'I was taken to hospital, kept there for four weeks because I got some sort of infection. I felt like I was falling apart, as though this was it. People visited. People talked at me, told me things. Tommy came in every day, but I stopped talking to him and eventually he gave up coming. I had just closed myself down. But it didn't stop me hoping. Every time the door opened, I thought Jo might walk in, but he never did. Eloise tried to get a message to him, she even staked out a theatre waiting for him, but she couldn't find him. I think he must have left New York by then. And, the thing was, I didn't even know his real name! And all I could think was that I had let him down. It was the only thing I had – that audition. When I finally got out of the hospital, I couldn't move in the same way. It was as though I had aged ten years overnight. I packed up my things in a suitcase and came back to England.'

'And the baby?'

'I lost the baby. And every other baby I could have carried. I can't have children, Freddie. Not since that morning. They said the best thing would be to take my womb right out of my body and throw it away, but I didn't let them do that. I wanted to keep it, even though it can't do a damn thing.'

'I'm sorry,' he said.

'Don't be,' I said. 'I'm used to it now. I don't think I would have made a good mother.'

'I think you would have,' he said simply.

258

I knew I would cry if I looked up.

'And Jo? You never saw him again?' he asked me.

'No. At least, not in the flesh.' I looked at him sideways. 'I saw him on television, about a year after I came back to England.'

'On telly? So he made it?'

I smiled at him. 'Oh, yes, he made it. It was only then that I found out his real name. Can you believe it? I only ever knew him as Jo. I suppose I never really wanted to know his real name, because then everything else would have to be real too. But that night, when I saw him on television, I was rooted to the spot. Couldn't move. They announced him, and I had to sit down. I couldn't take my eyes away from the screen. It was him, no question about it.'

'Who was he?'

I took a deep breath. I should have told him before, I thought. But how could I? Where to start? I had barely been able to say Jo's name to myself, let alone to anyone else.

'He became very famous. His choreography – all that stuff he used to do with his hands, all those clever ideas based on his vaudeville days – it went out into the big wide world, and he did what he set out to do. He worked like he always said he would, until he made it. He used to say to me that work is more fun than fun.'

'Who is he? Would . . . would I know of him?'

'You dance like him, now,' I said. 'I've taught you to dance like he taught me.'

'Who is he?'

'Jo's real name is Bob Fosse.'

Then – because it was the first time I had ever said this out loud, and hearing myself speak his name was as shocking to me as it was to Freddie Friday – I threw back my head and laughed.

'Bob Fosse?' repeated Freddie. 'Your Jo? He's *Bob Fosse*?'

'Yes,' I said. 'I was always Daisy to him. He was always Jo to me. Just Jo.'

Freddie pulled my hands into his. 'And that's it? That's the end of it? You're never going to see him again?'

'I don't know. Sometimes I worry that he wouldn't know me. That scares me so much, I think I'd rather just live the rest of my life not knowing whether he would or not. That feels safer. Do you know what I mean? When it's best just to stay closed? To stay safe?'

'Of *course* I know,' he said. He sounded angry. Perhaps he was angry, I thought hazily. I had kept all of this back, not just from him – from everyone.

'I should go,' I said. 'I need to get back.'

He looked straight ahead, but he held out his hand to me. His fingers tightened around mine.

'You could escape,' I said. 'If you let yourself. My God, Freddie Friday. You're better than I was at your age.' I smiled, more at myself, than him. 'You and Marnie,' I said. 'You're both better than me.'

'Well she might be—'

'No, no,' I said. 'It's quite all right. I've realized that, if you're any good as a teacher, your pupils have to become better than you.' I looked at him. 'It's quite a privilege to watch you,' I said.

'Stop it,' he said.

We said nothing more. I felt a strange, protective love for Freddie Friday – not just for his dancing, for everything about him. I loved him for his tapping and his black hair, for the way that he had held me, and cared about me enough to let me talk. And for the way that he let me stop talking.

Outside, the temperature had dropped a little; the wind had picked up. He held my hand as we walked, and I couldn't move away. We could have passed Bethany Slade and I wouldn't have been able to tear myself apart from him.

'Eloise is here for a week at the end of the month,' I said. 'I asked her to see you and she said she would.'

He stopped walking.

'What if I don't make it?' he said. 'What if I go out there and it doesn't happen? It doesn't happen for everyone, does it?'

'If I'd got to that audition without injuring myself,' I said, 'perhaps it would have happened for me. But then I never would have met you. You've got to take your chances while you can. You just *have* to, for goodness' sake. Please. You can't let me down now. I told her you'd dance for her. Please, Freddie.'

'I said I would, so I will,' he said. 'But I can't leave. Even if she likes me. I can't leave. I've told you why. You have to understand.'

I nodded. I would have to worry about that when the time came. For the moment, all I wanted to do was sleep.

'Freddie,' I said. 'You know Marnie has a problem, don't you?'

'The drinking?'

I nodded. He sighed and pulled out a cigarette.

'I don't know what to do about it,' I said. 'It's up to her, isn't it?'

When I left Freddie that afternoon, I ran straight into Alexander. It was pouring with rain and I was unprepared; within moments, I was drenched. My white shirt stuck to my chest, my feet slid about inside my heeled shoes. He was stepping into his car outside the cinema, but when he saw me he straightened his back and called out.

'Want to wait in the car till it stops?' he shouted.

I walked quickly over to his battered red Ford Anglia as a violent crack of thunder sent shoppers skidding into each other in surprise.

'The end of the world is nigh!' muttered Alexander, opening the passenger door. I crashed inside, landing heavily on a week-old copy of the *Sun*.

The rain was hammering down on the roof of the car now. There was Alexander, huge, back in the driving seat. The rain had plastered his thin, wavy hair to his head, giving the illusion of sweat. Inside, the car looked like a crime scene. A nearly finished, squashed duty-free box of Marlboro Reds lay on the dashboard. Several packets of Smiths crisps – salt and vinegar – had been ripped open, consumed and left for dead in the passenger footwell. The ashtray was over-spilling, the glove compartment open, revealing a white bag of bread rolls, a brown grocer's bag of tomatoes, a battered map of Devon, a can of WD-40, a bottle of salad cream, a tin of lighter fluid and a fork.

'Real men treat the interiors of their cars like shit,' he said unrepentantly.

'Ha! Where did you hear that?'

Alexander tried to shut the glove compartment and failed.

'Let's go somewhere,' I said suddenly.

Alexander stopped rummaging and looked surprised. 'Where?' he asked cautiously.

'I don't care,' I said. 'Come on. Let's just get out of here.'

He stared at me and gave a laugh of disbelief. 'What's going on?' he asked. 'Since when have you been one for spontaneous decisions?'

'Since about ten minutes ago,' I said.

He was a huge bear of a man – even more so in that tiny crate of a car; the entire world appeared to have been designed a size and a half too small for him – from the steering wheel to the cassette he was trying to ram in his eight-track.

'Pink Floyd,' he muttered. 'I just got this. You'll like them, if I can just get this thing to work . . .'

I stared at Alexander. 'Will you kiss me?' I said.

He didn't wait for me to ask again, he didn't stop to question whether it was what I really wanted, he gave me no room to think about what I had said and whether I would run over those words again in the morning, filled with regret. He just leaned right over the gear stick, pushed my hair off my face and did exactly as I had asked.

Pulling away again, he stared at me. 'I don't know if I heard you right,' he said. 'I'm just hoping I did.'

'You did.'

He leaned back and closed his eyes for a second. When he opened them again, I was looking at him, searching his face for something, though I didn't know what. I needed some sign from him that this was all right.

'I suppose you're going to say that you don't want this to ruin our friendship,' I said.

'Hardly,' he said. 'You're a bloody useless friend, anyway.'

'What?'

'You've been lonely since you arrived at St Libby's, and I've paid you attention, but you've used me. You've used me up, Julie. You want me to mark books with you, to telephone you, to keep you up to date with everything, to console you when your little favourites get chucked out, then you want me to sympathize when you think you've fallen in love with some dancer—'

'Now *wait*!' I held out my hands and turned around in the seat. The wet leather squeaked indignantly.

'And now you think it's all right to ask me to kiss you? Why's that, then? Been rejected by Roger bloody Nureyev?'

'It's *Rudolf* Nureyev. And don't be so facile.'

'I know it's fucking Rudolf. And don't talk to me like I'm one of your incompetent sixth form. You can walk home.'

He leaned over me and opened the door of the car.

'What's wrong with you?' I managed.

'Nothing,' he said. 'I'm meeting Cassie Packard in an hour.' He delivered this line without triumph. 'And I don't care if you think her handwriting's wrong. She's a nice woman, and she likes me. To be quite honest, I'll take that, thank you very much.'

I slammed the door behind me. When I looked back, Alexander had already driven off.

19

Marnie

When I arrived outside the factory on Saturday, they were both there already, standing outside. I was dismayed – I had banked on being the first one to arrive. I had made up my mind not to tell them anything, because I couldn't; it was still too unreal. I wanted Freddie more than ever, to fall into the bliss of being with him, and yet I knew that it wasn't the answer. The intensity of my need for him felt too strong; it had to be contained somehow, but, at the moment, the only way I knew how to do that was by drinking.

'You've cut your hair!' Miss Crewe said, smiling when she saw me. 'It looks very grown up.'

I reached my hand up distractedly. Freddie had seen my new haircut earlier in the week when I was at his house after school, but I'd forgotten that Miss Crewe hadn't seen it yet. I kept forgetting that it was different, myself.

'We can't get in,' Freddie explained. 'They're doing a check in the factory on all the new packing machines. They'll get rid of all the workers soon – they'll have robots all over the place to read our minds before you can blink. We can't get inside the club room today.'

I looked at Miss Crewe, willing her to say something, to come up with a solution. She was wearing a long, pale blue skirt and a pink T-shirt with faded writing on the front; I couldn't make out what it said. All I could think, as I always thought when I saw her, was that she had got it right, and I had got it wrong. *Every* time.

'Julie says we could go to the park,' said Freddie.

There was another barrier between them and me, I thought. Freddie Friday was calling her Julie. There was nothing on earth that would make me call her anything other than Miss Crewe – even after everything.

She pushed her red hair off her face. 'It's just a thought. I used to rehearse in the park occasionally – back in the Dark Ages.' She smiled briefly. 'We don't have long before he sees Eloise.'

'We won't have any music,' I said.

'You don't always need music.'

We walked into town together. There was an edginess to both Miss Crewe and Freddie Friday, though I could tell that it stemmed from different sources; all three of us, despite everything, were reading from different pages, as Jukey used to say. Freddie rolled up the sleeves of his T shirt so that the entirety of his pale arms was exposed to the sun. When we arrived at the park, he kicked off his shoes and walked with them tucked into the front of the bag that he carried slung over his shoulder.

Miss Crewe stopped, quite suddenly. 'Here,' she said. 'Here will do.'

'Too many people,' said Freddie doubtfully.

'Not enough,' responded Miss Crewe. She looked at me directly, as though Freddie wasn't with us at all, and spoke rapidly: 'I used to dance with Jo in Central Park. Parks are made for dancers.'

She looked slowly at Freddie Friday and raised her eyebrows. He hesitated.

'And those who were seen dancing were thought to be insane by those who could not hear the music,' she said.

He flicked his cigarette to the ground, turned around as if to walk off, and backflipped several times into the space behind him, with the nonchalance of a circus clown. Shit! I thought. I might have even said the word out loud. Why does he have to go and do that? Just when I'm trying to tell myself that it's not worth it, that he'll never love me? Several people stopped what they were doing to look. A little girl clapped and Freddie bowed to her, his hair falling forward over his eyes. She laughed delightedly.

Miss Crewe grinned. 'You don't have to show off!' she shouted to him, but she was laughing too. She straightened her skirt and moved towards him. 'Remember what we did last time?'

'Yeah.'

'Have you had a chance to go through it at home?'

Freddie flicked a glance at me. 'Yeah.'

'All right. Let me see.' She folded her arms and stood back.

Even with the space he had, many of his moves remained small, intricate, detailed. It was just the way that he danced, his natural groove, I suppose, created out of necessity from the tight grip that the little house in Birds Close had imprinted on his limbs. Miss Crewe watched him with intensity, whispering rhythms under her breath, clapping time. In my mind, the song that hadn't left me since my first visit to Birds Close played on and on with that incessant harmonica invading every inch of my being.

'Sorry!' shouted Freddie, shaking his head in exasperation when he missed a step. I wouldn't have noticed – but *she* did.

'Start again!' she called.

I lay back on the grass; just knowing that they were there near me was keeping my heart beating faster than usual. I closed my eyes and my hands reached out, feeling for the heads of daisies.

I felt the solid shape of the hip flask in my pocket. Anything that he felt for me, any gratitude for what I had done, was nothing compared to the way that he felt about her. It was that obvious to me and, for all that it splintered my heart, I was unable to pull myself away from it.

Just as the shadows started to lengthen and the light fade, a boy called Ben Boyd from the year above me at West Park walked past the three of us and shouted stuff. It was the sort of thing that I imagined Freddie would have put up with before, but it threw him completely; he swore and stopped moving, his fingers over his eyes.

'Oh, grow up, you idiot!' I shouted.

Ben Boyd turned and, recognizing me, shouted out, 'Hey! Marnie! Who's bloody Fred Astaire, then? Your *boyfriend*? Does Mark Abbot know you're two-timing him?'

I felt the blood rushing to my face.

'You'd do a lot better with Abbot than *that*!' shouted Ben, waving his arm towards Freddie. 'At least Mark likes women!'

'Mark is NOT my boyfriend!' I yelled. But I was angry because I knew what he was saying about Freddie. I hated him for it. 'Leave me alone!' I shouted. 'You bully!' Anger at the events of last week had added a shrill violence to my words.

Miss Crewe, by this point, had had enough. 'Marnie,' she said sharply, beckoning me over.

Flame faced, I followed her to where Ben was standing, his football kit at his feet. Miss Crewe had never taken kindly to people interrupting her lessons, and I suppose this was just the same thing.

'Grow up and buzz off,' she said to him.

'Who are you? Her mum?' asked Ben.

She said nothing, but held his gaze with hers. He gave an impressive sneer and started to walk away.

When he was a little further from us, he turned around and looked back at us. 'You stupid cow! What's he doing with you, anyway?' he called.

That was it. Freddie shot over to us. Within seconds, Ben Boyd was flat on the ground and Freddie was holding his arms behind his head as he struggled like a woodlouse on his back.

'Freddie!' shouted Miss Crewe. 'Let him go, for God's sake!'

Freddie looked up at her, then back down at Ben. With a shrug, he released his grip.

Ben scrambled to his feet. 'You've ripped my shirt!' he said, staring down at the torn material. Freddie turned to walk away, but Ben stepped forward. 'I said, you've ripped my shirt.'

'Better go home and get sewing, then.'

'Yeah? Why don't you do that for me? That's right up your street, Friday! What the hell are you doing hanging around with women, anyway? I didn't think that was your scene. What about Jack Singer, eh? What the hell would he say about this? Y'know? D'you want me to tell your granddad what you're up to, weekends? Do ya?'

Freddie went for him, but Ben was prepared this time. Ben's right fist got him smack in the stomach; Freddie collapsed to the floor, groaning.

I screamed. 'Freddie!' I rushed towards him, but he was up again, panting, his face white. He pushed away from me and went for Ben again, hauling him down and raising his fist in the air towards his face.

'No!' shouted Miss Crewe. 'For God's sake!' She pulled at Freddie, and he stopped. I could see the swell of pink around Ben's right eye. His lip was bleeding on to his ripped shirt.

'Go!' shouted Freddie. 'Go home!'

'With pleasure.'

We watched Ben Boyd loping off. I wondered if he would say anything to any of the boys in his class, and decided that he wouldn't dare. Mark would have been horrified, I thought.

'He doesn't know what he's saying,' said Freddie. He was shaking.

'You shouldn't have gone for him.'

'Did you hear what he was saying? Did you hear?'

He didn't dance any more that afternoon. His agitation was too great. Far from cooling, it felt as though the temperature in the park had risen with the falling sun. It was humid; the threat of thunder hung behind thin purple-grey clouds. We walked back to the centre of town, hardly speaking. Miss Crewe seemed distracted.

'Are you all right?' I asked her.

'Freddie, you can't behave like that,' she said. 'You just can't.'

'I don't do it all the time. Only when I need to.'

'You didn't need to. Let him say what he wants. When you strike back, you're only making his case stronger.'

'What case? He doesn't have a case! What? Now *you're* saying that stuff about me?'

'I don't even know what you're talking about,' she said. 'But you can't go around laying into people like that.'

Once she had left us, Freddie and I walked towards the bus stop that would take me back to North Bridge House. Every time anyone walked past us, all I could think was that they were seeing us together, that they would imagine that we were more than we were. We walked past a little tea room, clattering with china and dry cakes.

'Want a drink?' he said suddenly. 'A Coca-Cola or something?'

'I'll pay,' I said automatically.

'Certainly not. My grandad would blow a fifty-amp fuse if he thought that I wasn't paying for a girl. Especially you.'

He pushed open the door of the café and we stepped inside.

We sat down at a little table near the window and placed our order. Sitting close to him in public was still a strange thing; the café had become a film set, none of it felt entirely real. Did everyone else in the room look at us and see us together and think what I always thought when I saw a girl and a boy drinking Coke at the same table? That we were lucky? That we were in love? That we would kiss later? Perhaps they thought nothing at all, they didn't see us. I felt hot, feverish, my brain overrunning with frantic questions: Did you know, Freddie Friday, that Howard isn't my stepfather after all? He's my father! Is the boy called Jack that Ben Boyd was shouting about the reason that you want to dance now? Who is he?

'You want some chips?' he asked me.

I nodded, though I didn't want them at all. I wanted him to walk away from the table so that I could have a drink without him seeing.

I wanted to be able to look at him, to talk to him, to have him on my own for just twenty minutes without having to worry about anything else. But I needed strength for that. I felt a sweat breaking out on my forehead.

He stood up to ask for water, and I unscrewed the lid of my hip flask and sloshed half of its contents into my Coke. Gulping it down made my eyes sting. I watched him talking to the woman behind the desk. She took down his request without interest. How old was she? I thought. Forty? Fifty? Didn't she want to reach out and touch his hair? Did you reach that age and instantly eradicate the feelings that kept you running while you were young? Did she look at him and see her son reflected in him? Her grandson? I placed my head between my hands and took three deep breaths. I felt faint with running on doughnuts and adrenalin. He came back to the table, carrying a bottle of vinegar and a shaker of salt. He sat down.

'What are you going to do about the maths thing, then?' he asked me.

'Huh?' I wasn't expecting the question. 'What do you mean?'

'You know. Julie's always saying how clever you are. Once you've got your A-level, you should do something with it. So – what *are* you going to do?'

He actually leaned back and folded his arms in front of him. I had never seen him in that pose before. He reminded me suddenly of Caspar. I didn't want to talk about me, or about maths.

'Nothing,' I said. 'I can't do anything any more. It's too hard.'

'What *did* you want to do, then? When you were a St Libby's girl and had the whole world at your feet?'

I looked down at my hands, feeling foolish. How could I be sitting here, talking about ambition – what I wanted to do with my life beyond all of this – as if it mattered any more?

'What did you want to do?' he asked again. He spoke softly, as though he really needed an answer.

'I wanted to be an architect,' I said.

'Say it again,' he said. 'But this time change the tense. I *want* to be a architect.'

'Don't,' I said. 'It won't work on me.'

Freddie tipped some salt into the middle of the table and drew vague, loopy cloud patterns in it with his long fingers. He knew that I would say it, and I did.

'I want to be an architect.'

He leaned forward. 'Now you can make it happen.'

'Oh, stop talking like that.'

'Like what? That's just how you spoke to me—'

'There's no way it can happen any longer.'

'Well, no. Not if you don't stop drinking and start working.'

I put down my little Coca-Cola cocktail. 'Did she tell you to do this to me?'

'No. Course not.'

'I'm not a drinker.'

'Oh, come on. I saw you adding your little hit of gin or whatever it was—'

'I did *not* add gin!' I said with truth, reaching my hand out for the glass.

Freddie got there before me and picked it up. He gulped the remaining liquid down, not taking his eyes from my face. When he had finished, he replaced the glass on the salty table and looked at me.

'Fuck me,' he said quietly. 'What's that in there? *Sherry?* Coke and *sherry?* You should be arrested for that.'

'I only do it when I need to,' I said.

'Which is most of the time, by the looks of it.'

'Why should it matter to you? It's harder than you imagine, being me. It's not what you think it is at all.'

'How do *you* know what *I* think it's like being *you?*'

'You don't know how I feel about anything,' I said. I felt the heat rising in me. 'I don't want to be here,' I said. 'I've given too much away to you. Caspar warned me about it.'

'You've told me nothing,' he said.

'I prefer it that way,' I said. 'I wish that were true.'

'Are you all right?' he asked me.

'No,' I said.

'What's happened? Something's changed. What is it?'

'My father – that's what's changed,' I said. 'Jukey told Caspar and me that Howard's not our stepfather after all: he's our real dad. Turns out that she was keeping it a secret all these years.'

Freddie stared at me. 'Why didn't you say something about this before? You've known this—'

'She made a promise to Simon FitzPatrick –' I interrupted him; I needed to say it – 'the man she always told us was our father. She thinks that she broke his heart and was responsible for his death because he found out that something had happened between her and Howard.'

He looked into my eyes. Still, the hit from him was so strong, the pull so great, that I couldn't tear myself away.

'It doesn't surprise me,' he said.

'What does that mean?'

'I mean, people do strange things out of guilt. That's why she did it. Don't blame her.'

'What does that mean?'

'I mean – do you love Howard?'

I stared at him. 'He's hopeless and selfish and difficult,' I said.

'But do you love him?'

I choked back tears. All I wanted to do was let Freddie solve everything, but I knew he couldn't.

'Of course I do,' I said.

'Well then,' said Freddie quietly, 'aren't you the lucky one? You've just got yourself a father again.'

I glanced at my watch. Twenty past six. Howard's train was arriving

272

in ten minutes. It would be the first time he'd been home in over a week; he was only coming back because Jukey had told him she had something urgent to talk to him about. From the station, he would take a taxi back to North Bridge, where Jukey would tell him that everything was over, that she couldn't do it any more. I stood up.

'Where are you going?'

Typically, when Howard stepped on to the platform, he was engaged in a conversation with a woman. She was older than him, her eyes fixed on his face as he talked, but he was looking down and away from her, attempting escape. She squeezed his arm as the other passengers filed past them. Howard glanced around and caught sight of me. Waving, he looked relieved, breaking away from his captor with apologies and hurrying towards me.

'Marnie, darling! My God! What's happened to your hair?'

'Do you like it?' Suddenly, Howard's opinion seemed to matter very much.

'It's very sophisticated,' he said.

'You don't like short hair,' I said.

'You could look good with no hair at all. Who cut it?'

I hesitated. 'Jukey.'

Howard's eye widened. 'How did that happen?'

'I asked her to.'

Howard looked at me as though I was trying to trick him. Slipping his arm through mine, we walked down the platform together.

'Has someone sent you to collect me? I booked a taxi,' he said.

'No one sent me,' I admitted. 'I came on my own. I was in town. I thought I'd walk down and meet you.'

'Well, how nice,' said Howard. 'How jolly *nice*. Wouldn't it be a miracle if Gregory could be here on time, for once.' He frowned, his eyes searching for his regular driver.

Howard didn't like taking taxis with anyone but Gregory, who worked part-time at the box office at the theatre in town and liked to gossip. Locating his cab, Howard grinned at Gregory and opened the back door of the car for me.

'How *nice*,' he said for a third time, 'to have you meeting me from the station. Gregory, you remember Marnie, don't you?'

Gregory – tall, fat, hairy – turned back to me and grinned. 'Hello, love.'

'Marnie came to meet me,' said Howard, as though still not quite able to believe it himself.

'Following yer dad into theatre?' Gregory asked me.

'Not exactly,' I said, seeing flashing lights over the word *dad*. Up until then, I wouldn't have noticed – now it was all I heard.

'Marnie's a maths whizz,' said Howard, winking at me. 'Likes her numbers.'

'Useful, in a woman,' said Gregory, starting the car, cranking it into reverse and using one hand to rotate the wheel three hundred and sixty degrees.

'Where have you been?' Howard asked me.

'With the boy you met – Freddie.'

'Ah, him – the one with the bleeding head?'

'Yes, that's him.'

'Is he your *boyfriend* now?' Howard frowned.

'He's something,' I said. 'I just don't know what.'

'You could bring bloody Larry Olivier home and that wouldn't be good enough,' Gregory volunteered.

'No, it would not,' agreed Howard crisply. 'The man's sixty-two years old, for Christ's sake. And, in any case, Marnie's all wised up about men in the theatre. I doubt she'd go near one with a bargepole.'

'Freddie wants to be a dancer,' I pointed out.

Howard looked skeptical. 'My first girlfriend was a dancer. Lovely while they're young, but a terrible bore once they're past twenty-eight. It's the knees, you see. Once they've gone, you're playing second fiddle to the physiotherapist.'

I couldn't talk to Howard in the taxi about what I knew, not with Gregory hanging on our every word. Furthermore, I realized that I didn't want to. For those ten minutes, as we motored back through the still, warm evening, I just wanted to be with Howard, knowing that he was my father. I talked about West Park.

'The drama's better than St Libby's,' I said. 'They're doing *The Importance of Being Ernest*. It's really good. Miss Farrell teaches English and drama and she's brilliant.'

'Is she?' Howard looked surprised. 'Haven't seen a decent production of *Ernest* for years. You think it's worth me coming along? Are you in it?'

He was humouring me, I thought. But, on the other hand, an evening at a school play appealed to Howard, I thought. He liked being the big fish in the small pond. Tina Scott would go into orbit.

'Come along, if you like,' I said.

In those minutes, I hadn't thought anything through, except for wanting to be near to him. Even as we stepped out of the car and he handed Gregory his cash and told him that he would see him the next day, I felt incapable of saying a word, and yet I knew that I had to. He walked up the front steps. Within seconds, he would be inside the house, and the whole charade of supper and drinking too much and not saying enough would be upon us. I had to speak up now.

'Howard!' I said. I could hear the desperation in my voice and wondered whether it was obvious to him too. 'Will you come with me for a minute?'

'Come with you?' Howard looked surprised. 'Where to?'

'I just want to tell you something. I couldn't say it before.'

He stepped back down to where I was standing on my own in the drive. A sudden breeze picked up, blowing a shower of petals from the tulip tree beside the gates.

'Can we go into the garden?' I asked him. 'I don't want Jukey to see us.'

275

'You're being terribly mysterious, Marnie. That dancer hasn't proposed or anything, has he? God in heaven, you're not pregnant, are you?' he added in alarm.

'No. Nothing like that.' I felt myself flushing red. 'I just want to ask you something, that's all.' *That's all!* I thought. How could that be all! I didn't know what I was saying.

We walked down to his railway carriage, me following my instinct, and Howard following me. I could hardly feel my feet. I felt as though I was only partly there, and yet I had never been more aware of what I was going to say – never. Howard opened the door and we stepped inside. I sat down and Howard sat opposite me, as though we were about to set off for Edinburgh on the 10:40 from Euston.

'What is it, then?' he asked me.

'There's something that happened last week,' I began. 'We started to talk to Jukey after supper on Friday. She thinks that you're going to leave her.'

Something in Howard's face suggested to me that he wasn't entirely surprised at what I was saying.

'Well, she's wrong,' he said quietly. 'She's wrong.'

'But it was what she said after that . . .' I stopped.

'What was it?'

Oh God, this is it, I thought. This wasn't Caspar being flippant about things, or Jukey having a breakdown and chopping off her hair. This was Marnie FitzPatrick doing the telling. I was in too far to back out now.

'I don't know how to say it,' I confessed. Some part of me wanted him to say it for me, to understand what I was driving at. He didn't.

'What is it?' he asked.

'She says that you're our father,' I said quickly. 'Mine and Caspar's. We are *your* children.'

I heard myself laugh loudly, such was the absurdity of the line – not just in the context of our family, but in any situation.

276

Howard sighed and put a hand up to his head. He looked at me steadily.

'You knew,' I said quietly. 'You always knew.'

'I guessed,' he said. 'I hoped.'

There was a silence. Howard pushed his hands through his hair. There was a red stain on his cheeks and his hands shook as he reached for a cigarette and placed it back in the case again and on to the table between us.

'You *knew*?'

'I never asked more than once because I was afraid that she might tell me that I was wrong,' he said. He pointed the cigarette case at me as he spoke and there was a frightening seriousness in him that I had only ever seen him employ fully on stage. 'She didn't give me an answer when I asked, and I've never asked again. I've just believed it. Believed it here.' He thumped his fist to his chest.

I sat very still. 'You mean you always hoped that we were yours?'

'Of course I did. But it's been safer this way, for all of you. Like I said,' he went on, pulling out a cigarette for the second time, 'Simon was the better man.' He lit the cigarette this time, and passed it to me. I shook my head. 'He was the better man,' said Howard again.

'But I don't care! You're my *father*!' I leaned forward, my eyes hot with it all, with wanting so much from a man who had always held something back from me.

'And haven't I always been?' demanded Howard. 'Haven't I always been your father? Aren't I always there for you when you need me? All right, I may not say the things you want to hear all the time, but what father does? *Who does?* I thought that it was safer to keep everything as it is. Jukey made a promise to Simon that she wasn't prepared to break. You know she thinks that he died of a broken heart because he knew that she'd—'

'I know,' I said. 'But that's not enough of a reason not to tell us.'

'It is,' said Howard. 'He would have done anything for her. She

277

betrayed him, and *I* betrayed him. But it was impossible for us not to be together. There was something between us that was out of our control.'

'Isn't that what people say when they just need an excuse to behave without thinking?'

'Yes. Probably. But, when Simon died, we came together as two damaged people. But damaged people are survivors, Marnie. We were survivors. But that guilt over Simon bleeds into everything: makes me push away from her because I don't deserve to be close to her; makes her push away from me because she's afraid of it. But I've never loved anyone like her. Never. And I never will.'

It was the first time that I had heard him speak without acting. He just said these lines straight up, without the pose, the posturing, or consideration for the acoustics.

'Will anything change?' I asked him. I wanted it to change, so much. I wanted to know that he and Jukey would be all right.

'When the truth tramples over everything else, of course it has to change,' he said. 'No more secrets.'

'But I don't want you to change,' I said. 'I want you to be just as you always have been.'

'Thank God,' said Howard, 'because I don't know that I could ever do much better than I've done with you all. I know I'm not much good as a father, but you have to believe that I try.'

I wanted to cry, but I knew that, if I started, I wouldn't stop.

An hour later, we walked back to the house. I still hadn't asked him about Rachel; I couldn't. I didn't know how to bring her up, how to ask whether she had written the note.

'That note that Jukey found,' I said finally. 'Who was it from?'

Howard opened the door.

'You should call your friend Rachel Porter,' he said softly. 'She'll tell you everything. She's ready for you now.'

But I didn't know that I was ready for her.

20

Miss Crewe

The evening stretched in front of me, peace dropping slow, as Yeats would have it. All of the girls had been bussed over to Stowe for the evening, for a dance. These events happened just twice in the career of the St Libby's girls and formed a talking point for at least six months before and six months afterwards. They would be arriving here after eleven o'clock, which meant that I had to be awake and on hand to welcome them back to the house. Being awake wasn't likely to be a problem. Alexander's words to me spiralled around and around in my head, until I felt sick with it all.

'Do be vigilant when the girls return,' Bethany Slade had said to me earlier. Since the events with Rachel and Marnie, she took no chances. 'I imagine several of them will have found some way of smuggling drink into the dance. I can't say that I blame them – the boys at Stowe are not known for their intellect, but many have terrifyingly accomplished seduction techniques that they will employ to great advantage on nights like these.'

'I'll keep an eye on them,' I said.

I had watched the girls leaving the house – dolled up to the nines and drenched in their mothers' perfumes – feeling a sense of sadness hidden by a sense of excitement. Let them have their moment with the boys. Let them have something to talk about until the end of term. Usually, I would have had Alexander for company. Now, without him as an ally, St Libby's was a different place entirely.

I switched the television on and off, then opened my desk and pulled out my writing paper. I needed to write to my sister, to whom I owed at least a page and a half of cheerful news. Half an hour later, I had written nothing. I put the paper away again, went to my bathroom and removed every scrap of make-up and pulled my hair off my face into a tight bun. Alexander would be halfway through the film now, Cassie Packard clucking away next to him. Good luck to them, I thought savagely. She would be able to give him babies, if nothing else – a woman who bore such a strong resemblance to a hen had to have plenty of eggs.

The telephone rang. It was Anne Bright, a sweet, inefficient Irish woman from the art department, wanting to know if I had heard the rumour that there was going to be fundraising for a new craft and design block next term.

'I expect Mr Hammond knows all about it,' I said, dropping Alexander in it. 'Why not telephone him?'

'Oh, I've already spoken to him,' said Anne. 'He suggested I call you.'

A couple of hours later, I heard the sound of the girls trooping up the gravel path to the front door of Kelp House. It was at least an hour until they were all in bed. I liked receiving them back into the fold of St Libby's; my spirits briefly lifted. Their excitement over the evening at Stowe was palpable – all of them had a story to tell. Who had danced with whom, who had taken whose address, who had vanished off into the undergrowth only to keep the coaches waiting for twenty minutes at the end of the evening. And these boys they spoke of were almost the same age as Freddie Friday! Anna Knightley – she of the illustrated wisteria on her maths – was beating herself up over the fact that she had betrayed Charles-from-Harrow by spending the evening talking about Bembridge Sailing Club to a boy with the extraordinary name of Edgar Thorax.

'I don't know whether I should just *write* to Charles tomorrow and tell him it's all over,' she wailed to Florence Dunbar, climbing into her nightdress and wiping smudged mascara from her eyes.

'I shouldn't bother,' said Florence. 'Charles is an *arse*, Anna. You do know that, don't you? A bloody good-looking arse, I'll grant you that, but an arse all the same. The experience of realizing that the world doesn't revolve around him alone will do him good.'

'He's not an arse, Florrie! He's really not!' said Anna fervently.

'A sharp shock to his system is exactly what he needs. It'll make him a much nicer person for the next girl.'

Alexander couldn't have put it better, I thought bitterly.

The telephone was ringing when I entered my flat, five minutes later. I checked the clock. Nearly midnight. Alexander never called this late. Late calls were ominous, and yet every single time the telephone rang, even after all this time, I couldn't shake the flare of hope that perhaps it was Jo. Perhaps he had tracked me down. Perhaps it had taken him all this time to realize what he had left behind. I was pathetic, I thought. Permanent Oppresive State of Heartache. I picked up the receiver and cleared my throat.

'Hello? Kelp House?'

'Julie.'

'Freddie? Is that you? Do you know what time it is?'

'Sorry. I know it's late. I knew you wouldn't be asleep.'

'How did you know?'

'Lucky guess,' he said.

'Is there something wrong?' I asked him.

'No. At least – I don't know. Can I see you?'

'Now?' I asked idiotically. I glanced at myself in the little mirror that hung over my desk. Not good.

'Tomorrow morning,' he said. 'I could come to the school, meet you there.'

'Freddie, it's just not possible.'

I heard him sighing. I pictured him pushing back that wonderful hair, tapping his head.

'What do you have to do tomorrow?' he asked me.

'Well, at nine thirty I'm showing prospective parents around the school. I've got chapel at eleven, then at four thirty I'm checking name labels of all lower years' mufti and PE kit.'

'You lost me at nine thirty.'

'They've all been at a dance tonight with the boys from Stowe.'

'Who are they?'

'Boys of about your age,' I said. 'None of whom could possibly dance like you but all of whom possess the sort of self-confidence you would die for.' I heard the sound of him lighting a cigarette. 'You *know* how good you are now, don't you?'

Another silence.

'I need to see you,' he said. 'Please.'

'All right. I can come into town at eleven,' I said. 'I'll meet you at the café below Hunters Bridge, but I won't have long.'

'It won't take long,' he said.

I had no time to change between showing the new parents around the school and scuttling off to meet Freddie. I also suffered from several lapses of concentration – showing them the Wentworth Hall twice, and neglecting to show them the science block altogether. Alexander was coming off the tennis courts when I shot past him on my way into town. He waved, but I pretended not to see him. There would be too much explaining to do later on without encouraging any chat now. Thin, soft rain was falling. The soles of my feet slipped inside my sandals.

Freddie wasn't there when I arrived. I sat down and ordered a cup of tea, stirring in three sugars for strength. Freddie appeared suddenly; he walked in with his head low, seemed to want to dissolve into the scenery. He sat down opposite me. There was ink on his hands and two of his fingers had plasters on them – badly applied.

'Hello,' I said.

He glanced at the menu, his legs jittering under the table.

'Thanks for coming,' he said.

'What do you want?' I asked him.

He looked at me. 'I want to tell you something.'

'Of course,' I said. 'What is it?'

'You asked me once how I started dancing,' he said.

'You never answered. I'd still like to know.'

It didn't matter what he said now. What mattered was this little space in time, these few minutes that I would have done anything to have from Jo. I could give him that much.

'I had a brother,' said Freddie. 'A twin brother, Michael. He died.'

'What?' I picked up my teacup, and put it down again. 'Jesus. How old were you?'

'He was twelve. *We* were twelve.'

'What happened?'

'He was born wrong,' said Freddie. 'Disabled. They said he didn't get enough oxygen when he came out. I must've taken more than my share, or something. We looked very alike. It was hard for people to tell that there was anything wrong with him if we were just sitting together.'

He pleated the tablecloth in front of him and looked down.

'But Michael never walked properly,' he went on. 'Then, by the time he was ten, he didn't walk at all. He had this chair he sat in. He liked his chair. After our twelfth birthday, Mum was told he wouldn't last the winter. He always got worse in the cold. He didn't understand stuff, used to get angry, pushed people away. The only one who could keep him quiet was me. I was called on all the time. "He won't eat – get Fred in here!" "He won't tell us what's hurting – get Fred in here!" I was used, by all of them but him. They couldn't help it. What else could they have done? I was the vessel for them, so that they could understand him. But what we had didn't include anyone else. We were just us.'

Freddie swiped away a tear as though it were a violation of his very being, rubbing it into his cheek. The act of doing so made him look even younger. I said nothing.

'I used to dance for him. That's where it all came from. You know – silly stuff – making things up as I went along, a bit Charlie Chaplin, a bit of Harold Lloyd, clown stuff, then Gene Kelly in *Singin' in the Rain*. We had the record of that one – he *loved* it. Always wanted it, used to wave his arms around for it. "Gotta Dance" was his favourite song. Y'know it? *Gotta dance!*' He sung the lines, giving me ironic jazz hands at the same time.

I didn't know it. I nodded. 'Of course, I know it.'

'Well, that song made Michael happier than anything else in the world. And when he saw Gene dancing under those lamp posts with all the rain, he wanted me to pretend to be him for hours on end. And he wouldn't go anywhere without an umbrella, rain or shine.' He grinned at me. Outside, the rain had started falling with intent now.

'Sensible boy.'

'If ever he was having one of his bad times, we'd put the record on and I would dance, and somehow he'd pull through and everyone would clap and he would be calm again. Then, that November, he got ill. Then he couldn't move any longer. Three months, we had, of him being like that. When he died, everyone said, "Oh, it's a blessing, really. He was in so much pain." But I was his twin brother, so when he died . . . I died too. A bit of me, anyway. The bit that I liked, I suppose.'

I leaned forward and touched my hand to his cheek, and he reached up and squeezed my fingers and closed his eyes again. I could feel how hot he was, inside and out, the damp warmth of anxiety and tears on that winter-pale skin. He felt like a child.

'So the dancing is what remains of him in you,' I said.

'The dancing is what remains of *me* in *him*,' he corrected. 'He died on 4th April,' he said. 'The fourth of the fourth.' Then he tapped his head and counted out the numbers as he did so: 'One, two, three, *four*. One, two three, *four*.' He gave a half-laugh. 'Four and four makes eight,' he added. 'You're a maths teacher; I hardly need to tell you that.' He was almost whispering now.

'That's why you do that? Because he died?'

'It started out as just this thing I did to stop me forgetting him. Because sometimes I get scared that I might forget.' He paused and looked at me. There was resolution there. He knew that it was no good, but he would say it anyway. 'When I met *you*, I thought I might forget. I didn't think I'd ever meet someone like you. I didn't think anyone like you would ever look at me and watch me dancing and give me a chance.'

'That's wrong,' I said. I pulled my hand away. 'You mustn't think like that. You're good enough for a thousand chances.'

I was sounding too romantic, too young, and I knew it. He looked at me, his eyes full of hope.

'You're the only one who thinks that,' he said. 'You and Marnie.'

There. He had said her name. I grasped on to it, like a drowning man clambering on to a raft. Once we were talking about Marnie, we were on safe ground again.

'Marnie thinks you're quite wonderful. You know that.'

'I can't fall in love with her just because she's the right age,' said Freddie. 'Is that what you're trying to do? Make me want her, and no one else?'

'I wasn't suggesting that you should fall in love with her,' I said carefully. 'I know you can't do that.'

He looked at me. 'I'm not good for her,' he said. 'You know I'm not.' He paused. 'I can pretend,' he said, 'but it will never be right. Not completely.'

'Was there ever a time when anyone was right?'

'You want the truth?'

'Yes. May as well. Isn't this an afternoon of truths?'

He opened his mouth to say something, but shook his head.

285

Ten minutes later, I watched him walk away, out of the café and back across the bridge. I needed to thank him, I thought. For nothing else but for saying what he felt. No one around me had ever told me how they felt, apart from my parents voicing their passionate dislike for my dancing. When I stood up, my hip stabbed with pain. I struggled after him, limping until I found my pace.

'Freddie!'

He stopped and turned around.

'It's all right, you know. Everything you've said makes perfect sense to me.'

'I'm glad we met,' he said.

'I wish . . . I wish we'd met before.'

He shook his head. 'I didn't know you before. I don't think I would have *wanted* to.' He paused, then said something that I ran over and over in my head on the way back to school: 'I don't know that I would have liked you so much then. I like you for who you are now, not for the person you were when you were a dancer.'

I like you for who you are now.

When I got back to Kelp House, I felt something lifting from me.

That evening, I picked up the telephone and called Alexander.

'I wanted to say I'm sorry and you're right.'

There was a pause.

'I had no right to talk to you like that,' he said.

'Yes, you did.'

'I made you get out of my car, in the pouring rain.'

'Yes, you did.'

'Can I make it up to you? Do you want to come over? I'll cook you something.'

'I'd like that.'

'I'll come and pick you up. I'll be over in fifteen minutes.'

He arrived in ten.

286

Alexander's house – on the unfashionable side of town – radiated chaos. He parked outside, practically pulling the handbrake off as he did so. We stepped out of the car and stood for a moment in front of his house, where, on one of the green spaces that gave Welwyn its Garden City credentials, two girls and five boys of about thirteen, in West Park uniform, were shrieking in the evening light, chasing each other on bikes. I could hear the satisfying rip of an Aertex shirt succumbing to the perils of kiss chase. The two girls collapsed into giggles on a bench. Alexander didn't say anything to me, except to comment that the house was in a worse state than his car. I couldn't have cared less. He could have taken me into the smartest hotel in the western world, or pulled me over into a hay barn. The electric *authenticity* of him and of what was happening were all that mattered now. I felt the scales lifting from my eyes with biblical magnitude. He was here! He had been here all along, and yet I hadn't seen him!

It was as if we both knew exactly what was going to happen, even though, in the car, we had stuck to the lightest of subjects. We were upstairs within moments, him carrying me in his arms as though I weighed little more than a doll. I was oddly relieved by the disorder in the place – my sister had dark theories on men who were too tidy. There were car magazines stacked up in the hall outside his bedroom, coffee cups, old guitar strings and piles of green history books, belonging to the upper fourth, awaiting marking, and unanswered post covered every surface.

'You live like a slut,' I muttered.

'If I'd known I was going to be bringing you here, I would have done something about it,' he said.

He pushed open the bedroom door, dropped me on the bed and pulled the dark blue-and-white checked curtains with such ferocity that one came off the rail.

'Leave it, for God's sake!' I broke into hysterical laughter.

He flung them on to the floor, pulled off his shirt and lay down next to me.

Something had slowed down, now that we were here and I was lying on his bed. Suddenly this was happening, this was real. And that was the thing about Alexander: he was real. Up so close, his face seemed to change completely; I don't know how to put it, other than to say I could *understand* it better. The pieces of him seemed correctly proportioned. When he was with others – when he was outside this house, this bedroom – everything looked too big: his broken nose, his wide forehead, that unapologetically big mouth, the thinning, curly dark hair, his massive feet – nothing made sense. Up close, everything added up much better.

'You know we don't have to do this,' he said.

'I know. That's why we're going to.'

'I was awful to you,' he said. 'I'm sorry.'

'I deserved it.'

Afterwards, he opened the curtains again, and the windows. We lay still. Everything had led to this point. If I hadn't told Freddie Friday about Jo, I was certain that I wouldn't have ended up here.

'You know I can't have babies,' I said to Alexander. Now that I had told Freddie, it felt a lighter thing – something that didn't have to mean the end of everything.

'Come on! Who's talking about babies?'

'I don't know. Just in case you were worried about what just happened.'

'I'm not worried about anything.' He breathed in and kissed the side of my head.

'I'm not telling you because I'm thinking we're getting married or anything,' I said, realizing how it had sounded.

'I know that.'

'I'm just telling you because I'm sick of not saying things.'

'I know that too.'

I looked at him. 'Is there anything you don't know?'

'Yeah,' he said. 'Firstly, who the hell's going to fix my curtains? And secondly, are you going to stay the night?'

In the end, he drove me to Kelp House. I had to get back, but leaving him was painful. Now that the wall had come down between us, I didn't want to go. It wasn't good enough that I would be seeing him later on.

It wasn't until I lay in my own bed, at three in the morning, that I tested how I felt about Jo again. It was still there – the hurt and the difficulty and the pain – but there was something else running alongside all of these things too – a strange feeling that I struggled to interpret with any degree of accuracy. It was a feeling that, for the first time in eighteen years, I wasn't falling, out of control, tripping over the past.

I was sinking into something that I supposed others would label 'happiness'.

21

Marnie

I didn't want to see her, but I did. I didn't want to ask her anything, and yet I knew that if I didn't, I wouldn't be able to sit still ever again. Now that I knew the truth about Howard, I needed to know why Rachel had written the note. On Wednesday evening, I found her telephone number in an old list at the back of a diary I had compiled during my first term at St Libby's, and I crept into my parents' bedroom and shut the door. I needed peace to speak to her. She answered the phone immediately, which threw me off balance.

'Rachel?'

There was a pause. 'Yes. Who's this?'

My heart was thumping out of my T-shirt.

'FitzPatrick?' she asked slowly.

Her voice was as it had always been – amused, laconic. It would have taken greater imaginative powers than mine to picture her sitting there with one arm, face smashed up. She sounded more powerful than ever.

'Can I come and see you?' I said.

'You're making a pre-emptive strike,' she said. I felt thrown; I hadn't expected this from her at all. 'Come and see me,' she said. 'The White Hart.' And, even down the telephone, I sensed her arch smile.

'Midday, tomorrow,' I said, feeling I needed to try to assert some sort of control again, although my legs were shaking and I had to sit down on the bed.

Afterwards, I ran downstairs, poured the remains of last night's wine into a glass and shot it down in one gulp. Fired up, I told myself that I was doing the right thing. The next morning, I felt none of that confidence – even though I had Mark Abbot covering for me and I had the foresight to change out of my West Park uniform and into my denims. The fact remained that last time I had bunked off from school, it had been with Rachel at St Libby's – and look where that had landed us both.

I took the bus into town, and all I could think about was whether Freddie would ever talk to me again, if I would ever watch him dance again; yet, for the first time since I had met him, it felt as though the answers to these questions were less important than what I was doing now. Was there some part of me that was getting over the tidal wave of those feelings for him? I pushed my hands through my newly cut hair and tuned in to the soft thud of my feet on the pavement.

I had not realized the extent of the damage to Rachel's face; it was a shock – especially after I had been disarmed by talking to her on the telephone. My thoughts had always been focused on her lost arm. I had not prepared myself for the worst part of it all. When I saw her, and she turned to me and smiled, I drew in my breath. She was a distortion of what she had been – as though someone had begun her portrait, then had decided it was no good, so had deliberately made a mess of it. All down her right cheek – across her right eye and all the way down to her chin – were raised, livid scars. Her left arm stretched out towards me; where her right arm should have been there was simply a limp sleeve hanging from her red blouse. I felt myself take a sharp breath inwards; my shock must have been clear to Rachel, the Queen Grit of St Libby's.

'FitzPatrick,' she said. 'You've cut your hair. It looks a hundred times better. Sit down, for God's sake. I'll give you a minute.' She smiled at me, challengingly.

She didn't say what the minute was for, but we both knew. The shock had winded me. There was something in me that had been holding on to some false hope that perhaps it wasn't as bad as Tamsin had said, that she had exaggerated, or that Rachel's injuries – at least those to her face – would somehow disappear with time. Now I knew that this was never going to happen.

'What are you drinking?' she said. 'I could order us gin and tonics.'

On the table next to us, a woman looked at her and, noticing her face, looked away again, quickly. I had never wanted a drink more.

'Perhaps we could get a bottle of red wine,' I muttered.

'Good idea. I'll go.'

'Do you want me to go?'

'It was an arm I lost, not a leg.'

As she made her way across the room to the bar, the woman on the table next to us nodded at me, and then at Rachel's back.

'Terrible,' she said. 'What happened to your friend?'

'None of your business,' I said.

'I'm sorry,' said the woman. 'You're right. I only ask because I have a sister . . .' She shrugged. 'I'm sorry,' she repeated.

'She was in a car crash,' I said.

The woman nodded. 'Same as Diane. Still, at least they've come through it. Diane's worse. Your friend'll be all right. She can walk, she can talk—'

Shut up! I wanted to scream.

'She's strong,' I said instead.

'She looks strong. You take care of her, love. Nice she's got her friends. They can be very isolated when their disfigurement is that bad. I always say it's easy to be injured if you're a man. Brings out the mothering instinct in women, you know?'

I picked the newspaper out of my bag to avoid talking any longer,

292

taking in nothing. Instinctively, I flipped my fingers through my hair, and found that there was no hair to flip. I felt exposed – entirely and utterly laid bare. How to tell Rachel that I knew? Did she *know* that I knew?

One of the bar staff came back to the table with Rachel, carrying a bottle and two large glasses. Outside, it had started to rain again; my thoughts turned to Freddie. I looked down at my hands.

'I wanted to see you before,' I said. 'Tamsin said I shouldn't. She said that it wasn't a good idea.'

'She did? When?'

'Just after the accident.' I looked down as I said the word. 'She said that it was better if I stayed away. She blamed me, you see.'

'*Blamed* you? What the hell for? My father driving us off the road?' She barked with incredulous laughter and, for the first time since the accident, I felt the absurdity of what I had been carrying around for all these weeks.

'I know she thinks that, if it hadn't been for me, then you wouldn't have carried on drinking when we got back to school. It was my fault; it *was* my fault.'

Just saying it out loud to her gave me an extraordinary, unexpected burst of energy. I felt it zipping through my body from my heart, pumping all over as I told her what I had kept inside for all this time since it had happened, since I had met Freddie Friday, since Miss Crewe had danced with him. I breathed in and looked at Rachel again, right in the eyes this time. They were still as beautiful, I realized. They were still as certain as they ever were. I felt tears choking me, so I looked back down at my wine. Don't cry; don't cry. Rachel had had no sympathy for tears before the crash. I imagined she had even less truck with them now.

'I had to come and see you today,' I said. 'My . . . my mother knows.'

Rachel went very still.

'I don't know what you mean,' she said.

'She doesn't know that she knows,' I said. 'What I mean is that she knows there's someone. But she doesn't know it's you.'

'So how are you so sure then?'

'She found a note.'

Rachel watched me fumbling in my pocket for it. Even with her smashed face and no right arm, she had the power to make me feel the same way that she always had: mildly intimidated, desperate to impress. When I produced the note and placed it on the table, she didn't even bother to pick it up.

'Oh, yes,' she said. 'I wrote that. But, you know, my handwriting has improved greatly since then.' She laughed. 'Gosh, FitzPatrick! I have to say, well done on the detective work. I didn't even sign it, did I?' She breathed in suddenly, pressed her hand up to her face and closed her eyes for a second, her mouth set in a line that represented pain.

'What? Are you all right?'

'Yeah.' She opened her eyes again. 'I'm fine.'

'How long has it been going on for? When did it start? Not at St Libby's, surely?'

'I was in hospital for ten days after the crash,' said Rachel. 'I didn't look in the mirror until the day before I was due to leave. Shit! That was *some* moment, I can tell you. At first, they wanted me in for longer. They were talking about trying to mend things, trying out some new methods of restoring the skin on my face – I don't know. Once I'd seen myself, I just said I wanted to go. I could see for myself that nothing was going to change anything much. And you want to know what the strangest thing is, FitzPatrick? When your face changes overnight, you start forgetting how it used to look really quickly. *Really* fast. It's as though there's some sort of a function that clicks into place that makes you feel as though having these scars and no arm is the most normal thing in the world – almost as though this was the real you all along, and all that perfection that was there before, all that beauty, wasn't ever real.'

She was speaking to me, but I sensed she was saying the words out loud for the first time too. The charge of vitality coming from her would have been enough to power the Shredded Wheat factory for a week. I had never heard her more alive.

'What happened with Howard?' I asked her.

'Do you remember, on the day that we went into town, the day of the Lady Richmond, you said to me that the problem with Howard was that he found something to love in every single woman he talks to?'

'Yes.'

'Well, when I started recalling things about that day, for some reason those were the lines that kept coming back to me, over and over again. It was all I could remember for hours after I woke up. *Something to love in every single woman he meets.* You, standing in dorm four and telling me that he thought in a way that made it virtually impossible for him not to look at other women – it was etched on my brain like a mantra. I couldn't shake it off. I didn't *want* to shake it off. It felt like the only thing that made any sense to me, the only fact that I had to hang all of this on. If he thought that, then would he still think that about me?'

'I don't understand.'

'A week after I got home, I wrote to him.'

'You wrote to Howard? At North Bridge?'

'I used the typewriter – one finger, one key at a time.' She mimed the action on the table, pulling the face of an idiot as she did so. 'Took a while, but I suppose I'll have to get the hang of it, so there was no harm in starting early. I asked him if he would meet me.'

'But what possible reason could you have given?'

'I lied,' said Rachel simply. 'I wrote to him under Daddy's name, and asked him to meet me and talk over a private matter that could not be discussed on paper. I figured that he would probably be both intrigued and worried enough not to refuse me.'

'And he showed up?'

'He showed up.'

'Where did you meet?'

'The Dorchester Hotel.'

'In *London*?'

'In London. *Unbelievable*, isn't it?' That familiar Rachel sarcasm was back in her voice. 'It's perfectly possible to board a train and travel fifty minutes to the capital – even with one arm!'

'I didn't mean it like that.'

'I booked a table for two. When he showed up, there I was.' She poured another glass of wine, hovering the bottle over my glass and raising her eyebrows to ask me whether I wanted more too.

'Yes,' I said quickly.

'He was strong, when he saw me. Not like anyone else has been. He didn't try not to talk about it, nor did he weep over me and say what a shame and all that crap. He was just honest. That was all.'

I sensed the woman on the table next to us listening in. Rachel lowered her voice.

'We sat and drank jasmine tea. I said that I had pretended to be my father because I had been afraid that he wouldn't have come had he known it was just me. I said that I needed to know if it was true – if what you had said about him was true – if he found something to love in every woman he talked to – even someone who looked as I looked now.'

'What did he say?'

'That's between me and him.' She looked defensive suddenly – bordering on afraid – as though telling me anything more was going to break the spell that Howard had cast.

'You know I only turned up at school with Daddy the day after we were expelled because I thought that *he* would be there, that there was a chance of seeing him. And I did see him! I stood and talked to him in the car park.'

That made sense, I thought.

'He was the last person I spoke to, aside from Daddy, before it happened. And really, I couldn't have asked for anything more, could I? I had my moment in the sun with him, at St Libby's.' She looked at me. 'Aren't I tragic?'

'No,' I said with truth. Rachel could never be tragic, not as the beauty that she was, nor as she was now. She was still calling the shots, holding the cards, making things happen. That was inherent in her, unchangeable.

'He was with me for four hours,' she said. 'I travelled back from London with him on the train. He sat next to me. There were three boys who wouldn't stop staring at me. It's a strange thing, being stared at because you're a freak rather than someone they want to jump.'

'You're not a freak—'

'Howard protected me from them.'

She spoke simply now, as though the facts were plain and clear and should need no further explanation.

'I asked him to tell me that it would all be all right. I asked him to tell me honestly if he still saw something in me that he wanted, or whether it had gone forever.'

I wanted to scream at her, to tell her that Howard hadn't won three Olivier awards for no reason, that he was an astounding actor who could convince at the drop of a hat, whatever the situation required. Yet I knew that, in this case, he would have had no need for any of his method skills. It was obvious to me, and it would have been just as clear to him, that whatever Rachel had back then, she had more of now.

'Did you – did something happen? Something else? Should there be a reason for Jukey to feel like she does?'

'I don't know how she feels.'

'She feels as though this is different. She thinks that she's lost him this time. *Really* lost him. She thinks that he's in love.'

'We just talked, and then went home. He's not in love with me.'

'What's wrong with him, then?'

'He's never really had her, has he?'

'Her?'

'Your mother.'

She edged fractionally closer to me and bit her lip. Again her face clouded with pain, and she winced as though touching her fingers to a flame.

'I've had time to go over everything that he said to me that day, over and over again, and he's confirmed everything that I ever thought or believed about boys.'

'Howard's hardly a—'

'What was that line that Araminta used to say? "Men are just boys with better reflexes." I think that's true.' Rachel took a gulp of her wine. 'He's more of a boy than anyone else I know. But you have to realize why he behaves like he does. It's always been about your mother.'

'You're making excuses for him. He hasn't stopped looking at other women from the moment they were married.'

'That's because *he never really had her in the first place*. Not completely. He knows it. So he's always protected himself by pretending that it doesn't matter to him – only it does.'

'So now I suppose you want me to believe that nothing happened between you and him? That you sat in the Dorchester talking for hours and then went home in different directions.'

'Absolutely nothing happened,' said Rachel. 'It didn't need to.'

I held her gaze for a moment. When she was speaking, I almost forgot about her disfigurement, but now the realization of how profound her injuries were hit me again. I shook my head. 'I thought your accident was all my fault,' I said again. 'I thought that I was to blame, that you would never forgive me—'

'Tamsin should never have told you that,' said Rachel, running her fingers down the stem of the wine glass. 'There's nothing to forgive. She should never have frightened someone as easily swayed as you.'

'What do you mean?'

'I mean that you've always believed what people say about you. You've never had any faith in yourself, so you take what you can from what others believe. If you were told it was your fault, I imagine you believed, from that moment on, that it was your fault.'

I reached for my glass and gulped down the rest of the wine.

'You wouldn't have been able to drink like that before,' she observed.

'I drink all the time,' I muttered. I looked at her and said it again. 'I drink *all* the time.'

Again that hit of energy that came from saying it, from *admitting* it.

Rachel held my hand in hers across the table.

'It was never your fault. Only a silly little girl like Tamsin could say that.' She shrugged. 'Her big sister had let her down by proving that she was human enough to be in a car crash and lose limbs – I didn't rise out of the smashed-up vehicle like some comic-book heroine, without a scratch, which must have been a big shock to her. But she's much better now.' She paused. 'I've started painting again.'

I stared at her. 'You have?'

'Yeah. Sometimes I feel like I might never stop.'

I stood up, suddenly knowing that I had to go now, or I might be dragged back into the world of Rachel Porter forever, because her pull – on me, on Howard, on her sister, on anyone in her presence – was still too hard to resist.

'Go easy on the man,' said Rachel. She raised her glass to her lips. 'They know not what they do, FitzPatrick.'

'Jukey says that he's utterly distracted. That he's different, that he can't concentrate on anything – even flirting with other women.'

'You know why that is, don't you?'

'Because of you,' I said.

'No,' she said, 'you idiot. It's because he found out that you and Caspar are his.'

'What?' I was confused. I'd only told Howard a few days ago – that couldn't explain his behaviour for weeks past. Was Rachel saying he'd found out before? I recalled his lack of surprise when I broke the news in his train carriage, but I thought he'd just worked it out for himself. 'How . . . ?' I asked. 'Jukey said that she'd never told him.'

'I told him,' said Rachel.

'You? What? How did you know?'

'You don't live with someone at boarding school for years on end and not know them well enough to spot their real father in a line-up. You're so like him it's ridiculous. I said it that afternoon in the Dorchester.'

'How did you say it?'

'I just said, "When is everyone going to stop pretending that Marnie and Caspar aren't your children?"'

I blinked at her. 'And what did he say?'

'He didn't say anything. He didn't need to. But if you want to know why he's been like he has – there's the reason. He's been thinking about nothing but that.'

'I told him too,' I said. 'I only just found out, but I told him that we knew.'

'It's a good thing,' said Rachel quietly. 'You see that, don't you? That it's a good thing?'

Rachel had what she had always had: sixth sense, an instinct for truth, and a way of seeing things that set her apart. What I felt for her now was no longer clouded by guilt, or anxiety – she didn't trade in that sort of thing, and it made no sense for me to, either.

'Maths,' she said finally, as I gathered my things to leave. 'You still doing maths?'

'I'm trying,' I said. 'It hasn't been easy.'

300

'It's what you're good at,' said Rachel. 'Silly not to make the most of it.'

I wanted to agree with her, but my mind was too full to listen any more. Maths was far from me now, something I struggled to keep up with, where before I had danced to its music.

It was on the way home that I heard the news. Two girls were leaving a phone box together, sobbing.

'Can't believe it!' one was saying. 'Only twenty-seven! What'll the rest of the group do?'

'He was never my favourite,' said her friend. 'But he was so good looking.'

I pulled on her sleeve.

'Excuse me,' I said. 'What's happened? Who are you talking about.'

'Brian Jones is dead,' she said.

'He can't be.'

'Drowned in his own swimming pool,' she said numbly. 'Happened last night. I just can't believe it.'

She pulled a tissue out from her sleeve and blew her nose.

'Freddie!' I said out loud.

'What?' said the girl, frowning at me. 'Who's Freddie?'

But I was already off. I knew that I had to get to him. He would already know, I could sense it, and he would need me. I took off down the street, running, running to Birds Close, not knowing whether he would be there, only convinced that he needed me. Brian Jones was dead, and Freddie loved him. It was what Rachel would have done, I thought. She would have gone to him, she would have been strong for him.

I raced up the path to number four. The curtains were half shut, as usual, but I could see Freddie sitting on the floor. I went forward to knock on the window so that he could let me in, but I stopped. There was someone else with him. Linda? I thought. But she couldn't sit next to him like that. As I drew closer, I could see that, next to Freddie, was another boy, and he had his arm around Freddie in a gesture of comfort. He knew, I thought. He knew about Brian, but someone else had got to him first. Intuition told me that this boy must be Jack Singer, whom Ben Boyd had shouted about. I stood outside, catching my breath, then losing it again, as I watched them. I could have been there for no more than five seconds before some instinct made Freddie turn around and he saw me at the window. Jumping up, he ran to the door.

'Marnie!' His face was white. 'Are you all right? What are you doing here?'

'I came to tell you the news,' I said.

'I've heard,' he said.

His eyes were searching mine for signs that I had seen him with Jack. I wanted to shout at him that I knew what he was doing, that I had seen him in the arms of someone else, but I couldn't. I couldn't have done that if I had stood there all night; I couldn't bear to embarrass him and, more than that, I couldn't bear to let him go. Once I acknowledged what I knew to be true, I would have lost him.

'Who told you?' I asked.

'A friend. He's still here.'

'Can I come in?'

Freddie nodded and opened the door.

Jack Singer was standing up, holding Freddie's copy of *Beggars Banquet*.

'Hello,' he said. He stretched out his hand, and I shook it. 'You've heard the news.'

'I can't believe it,' I said, and the shock of what I knew to be true of Freddie could be hidden in the shock of the news about Brian Jones. I sat down on Linda's chair. The hour with Rachel Porter felt as though it had happened a week ago.

'Did you like the Stones?' I asked Jack.

'Still do. They'll keep going,' he said.

'It feels like the end of something,' Freddie said. 'Until this afternoon, I couldn't imagine 1970. Now I can, but I don't like it.'

'You sound like a little kid,' I said. I sounded accusatory, angry even.

Freddie picked up the photograph of himself as a child. 'I'm not a kid,' he said.

'Everything feels too modern,' said Jack. He had a smarter voice than Freddie, nearer to the boys we had known at St Libby's. He was confident, unafraid of me being in the room. I half suspected that he knew I had seen them together.

'As if we haven't quite finished with the sixties yet, but it's finishing with us first,' I said. I felt numb

'Yes,' he said. 'It's uneven, like it's muddy. It's as though everyone's waiting for the water to clear, but no one can see anything at the moment, so they're all just guessing at everything, stabbing around in the dark. Do you know what I mean?' He paused. 'The Stones are still playing this weekend,' he said. 'Saturday. In Hyde Park. They're doing it as a tribute to Brian.'

'Do you want to go?' I asked Freddie.

He glanced at Jack, who looked away. They were going together, I thought. It was all planned. Freddie looked down at his hands, then up at me. He was trapped by this, unable to deny or confirm what I knew what happening. Something broke inside me; perhaps the stamina Miss Crewe had spoken of couldn't take it any longer. I stood up and walked to the door. The room was suffocating me; I had to get out.

'Is this what you do to all your friends, Freddie?' I said. 'Make them love you so hard that it hurts? But then I asked for it, didn't I?'

Freddie stepped forward and, for a brief, hilarious moment, I thought he was about to dance.

'Don't,' he said. 'You can come too—'

303

'No!' I shouted it and, shocked by myself, I breathed in and felt strength coming back to me.

There was a silence. Jack looked out of the window. He looked younger than I did, a frightened boy pretending to be a man, pretending that he had it all taken care of, when, of course, the future was frightening and uncertain. *Uneven.*

'I don't think I should come here for a while,' I said. 'I don't think it's right.'

'It *is* right. You're always right—'

'I'm not! This isn't. It *isn't.*'

Now that I had said it, I felt an odd strength.

'But I'm seeing Eloise de Veer next week—'

'Miss Crewe will be there,' I said. 'I can't do this any more, Freddie. It's just too hard.'

I don't know how I got home, but I suppose I did. I did just the same as Freddie had done: I pulled out the Rolling Stones' last record from the shelf above my bed and stared down at the photograph. Just over ten years older than me, and already dead. Next year would be 1970 and, by the time I was only a little older than Miss Crewe, the century would be over. It was happening too quickly. They were sending men up to walk on the moon. The Shredded Wheat factory was investing in more and more machines, so what would happen to those who worked there – the girls with stamina, who had no choice? The whole world was a crazy place, tearing along, out of control.

I had lost him, I thought in despair. I had lost him, and the saddest thing of all was that I had never even had him in the first place.

22

Miss Crewe

Freddie and I stood on the platform, saying nothing. The train to London would take forty minutes, and then we would travel by underground to the dance studio in Covent Garden where we would meet Eloise. I had bought new shoes, which were hurting my feet, and a long black dress, which was digging into my back, but the discomfort was a decent enough distraction from the situation. The hour had come and, as usual, one was never really ready for it.

'It's not right without her,' said Freddie for the fourth time. 'Without her, I can't do it.'

I wanted Marnie there too. He had told me what had happened, how she had seen him with Jack on the day that Brian Jones had died. I'd tried to telephone her, but her brother had told me that she had gone away to stay with an aunt. Whether or not that was true, I didn't know. But I had to get him through today. I had to prove to her that something had been worth the pain.

'Don't be superstitious,' I said to Freddie. 'Not today. It's the downfall of many a perfectly good dancer. And *don't* eat that,' I said, swiping a Twix bar out of his hands. 'Sugar will send you over the edge, and we're not ready for that yet.'

He glared at me. 'Why am I doing this?'

'What choice have you?' I shouted over the noise of the

approaching train. I pulled a face at him, and stuffed the finger of chocolate into my own mouth.

I was as nervous as him about seeing her, but for completely different reasons. She had been my one connection to Jo, the only person who had seen him through my eyes. She had gone on to do what we always wanted to do, and, for the first time since I was nineteen years old, I realized that she had wanted it more. There was never anything else for her – no maths, no heartache. It was all dance for her. Neither of us could have denied that I was the better dancer at the time, but she was the one who had worked at it, and she had become better than me. It was Jo who said that work was more fun than fun. Eloise lived by that maxim.

Far from seeming gauche and out of place as I had feared he may, Freddie seemed to light up when we arrived in London. He walked like he knew where he was going, which was ironic as his map reading was appalling.

He was struck dumb by the sight of a record shop with a huge window display of the Stones, and ducked inside to take a look. A man dressed entirely in white asked him whether he could buy three copies of *Electric Ladyland* by Jimi Hendrix.

'Oh, I don't work here,' explained Freddie.

'You look like you do,' said the stranger accusingly.

Freddie looked at me and beamed.

I had been to London regularly enough since I had started working at St Libby's, but I felt jolted by the West End, out of place on familiar territory, like a guest showing up at the wedding of an old friend and realizing that they have nothing in common with the bride any longer. Streets I had known as a fifteen-year-old girl had been bombarded by a decade of manic change; the Beatles' style oozed out of every shop, familiar landmarks felt shaken by youth and its carelessness. I took the map from Freddie and marched him towards Dean Street. He put his arm through mine, which made me want to cry.

'Marnie doesn't want to talk to me,' he said.

'She does,' I said. 'Only it's too difficult.'

'I miss her.'

'She was in love with you. Come on, Freddie. Leave her to get over it.'

'She should be here,' he said. 'If it wasn't for her—'

'I know,' I said. We stopped outside the front door. I pushed his hair off his face, like his mother. 'Do it for her,' I said.

'I can't leave,' he said automatically. He reached up to his head and started tapping.

'Don't,' I said gently. 'Michael's with you whether or not you're tapping. You don't need to do that any longer.'

'I suppose you're going to say something corny like I should just forget everything and dance.'

'And those who were seen dancing were thought to be insane by those who could not hear the music,' I said quietly.

Freddie pulled me briefly into his arms. 'Thanks,' he said, 'not just for today – for the whole thing. Coming to the Wheat. Believing in some part of me that I didn't believe in myself.'

'Shut up,' I said gently. My voice cracked.

We were led down three flights of stairs. Towards the bottom, Freddie stumbled and almost fell.

'I can't do it,' he said to me in a low voice, urgent with panic. 'I can't go in—'

But it was too late for that now. A door opened and suddenly Eloise was standing in front of us. She was dressed in tight red trousers that she would no doubt refer to as *pants*, and an even tighter pink and white sweater. She looked a million and one dollars, and knew it. My black dress felt ridiculous. I wish I'd listened to Alexander and worn denims and a T-shirt.

Eloise looked at me and folded her arms in front of her. 'Now listen, baby. If you're here about that grey blouse with the flowers that I borrowed off you in 1951, you can have it back next week.'

'I need it for a party,' I said, grinning back at her.

'Whose?' she demanded.

'Some guy I met. You'd love him. He's a director.'

'A director! Not another one. You know, the last time she spun me that line it turned out that she'd been prancing around Central Park with fuckin' Bob Fosse.' She looked at Freddie. 'Come in, baby. Wow — the hair!' She stepped forward and actually ran her hand, with her red polished nails and her New York manicure, over Freddie's head as though he were an animal at a fair. I couldn't blame her. It's what anyone would do if they had the nerve, and nerve was something that Eloise had never lacked.

'Ignore her, Freddie,' I said. 'She never knew how to behave.'

Eloise grinned. Freddie looked wary, as though this were a test that he was already halfway towards failing.

'Sit down, Julie Crewe,' she said. 'You're my last one of the morning. I wanted to have time to take you out to lunch. Why are you dressed in black, like you're going to a funeral?'

I could hardly watch when Freddie danced for her. He was nervous, he missed several steps and he had to start the end section again, but it didn't matter. Watching him through fresh eyes with Eloise, I realized that there was never going to be any doubt. He had always been full of potential, from the moment I had seen him in the Wheat with Marnie, all those weeks ago. When we had danced at North Bridge House, he had started to understand how good he was himself. Now, he was something else entirely.

'Well, he's a star,' said Eloise in an undertone.

'You think so?'

She turned to me. 'He's dancing like Bob. He's dancing like you. You taught him, didn't you?'

'He already knew what he was doing. I just helped him out.'

'You always were too modest. I didn't like that about you then, and I don't like it about you now.'

Freddie was taking off his sweater on the other side of the room.

'Very pretty,' said Eloise. 'You had him?' she asked casually.

'Certainly not,' I said quickly.

'You're not his type, right?'

'Something like that.'

'Good. Much easier for me if I know I'm not in with a hope. Hey, what's with all this?' whispered Eloise to me, tapping her own head in imitation of Freddie.

'He has a tic,' I said.

'Interesting. You say he works in a factory?'

'He does the electrics at the Shredded Wheat factory. It's a huge place. Local landmark. He used part of the building to dance.'

'He does the fuckin' electrics? At *Shredded Wheat?* What does that mean? And he dances there in his free time? And he can dance like *that?* Julie, you couldn't make it up.'

'Will you see him again?' I asked her, but what I was really asking was, will *I* see him again?

Eloise put her hand over mine. 'You could have brought me a one-legged dog with rabies and no rhythm and I would have seen him again for you.' Eloise chucked out compliments with ferocity rather than love. 'But, as it happens, you've brought me . . . What's his name again? Freddie Friday? Well!' She laughed out loud, clapping her hands in delight. 'Even the name works. I want to take him with me, and I don't want to change a thing. Even that funny head-tapping thing. I like it. It can stay.'

And, as she spoke, I felt him slipping away from me, as though I were already watching him from another room, able to see him, but not quite able to touch him any more.

'Who will look after him?' I heard myself asking faintly.

Eloise's assistant was staring at Freddie's legs as he leaned into his bag looking for a change of shoes. I pictured Marnie, and felt a wave of relief that she wasn't here to witness the scene.

'Darling,' said Eloise. 'That boy will have to learn to look after himself.'

23

Marnie

It was the night of the West Park play. I sat towards the back of the hall next to Howard and watched Tina Scott bring the house down. All the energy that she had channelled into goading me at the start of term, to horse-kicking the teachers who annoyed her, had merely been a substitute for this. She was so far and away the best Lady Bracknell Howard had ever seen that he kept glancing down at the piece of paper containing the cast list, and frowning, as though her name might be altering between scenes.

Afterwards, I pushed my way to the piano room behind the hall and found Tina, stripped down to her bra and knickers and wearing a wig, the wrinkles and lines painted on her face giving absurd contrast to a body at the peak of her teenage ripeness.

'I came to say you were good,' I said.

'Oh, thanks, FitzPatrick,' she said. 'Thanks for coming. I didn't think you'd show up.'

'I had to see it,' I said. 'Had to see you.'

Tina pulled off her wig and shook out her hair like a wild thing.

'Wow, this thing's hot.' She looked at me looking at her and her face softened. 'I really mean it when I say thanks for coming. I've given you a hard time.'

'Really?' I said innocently.

She laughed without mirth. 'I've been a twit. I'm sorry.'

'It pains me to tell you, but it's the best school play I've seen,' I said. 'Better than anything we did at St Lib's.'

I hadn't seen Tina delighted before. She offered me a Quality Street from a tin on the table, and I noticed that her bra was grey and fraying at the edges. I had never given much thought to her lack of funds, because she had always made up for them through sheer force of personality.

'Where's Marky Abbot?' she asked. 'Was he watching with you? You and him seem thick as thieves at the moment.'

'Oh, I don't know. I don't think theatre is Mark's thing.'

'Please tell me you're not still in love with Freddie Friday?'

I shrugged. 'I had a friend at St Libby's who told me that the first time your heart breaks you don't think you'll ever recover. It's the Permanent Oppressive State of Heartache. I'm still waiting,' I said.

Tina sighed and squirted a line of Oil of Ulay on a tissue and swiped it across her face, smudging her make-up. A girl I didn't recognize, from much lower down the school, sidled up to us.

'Jus' wanted to say you were amazing,' she said.

'Thank you!' Tina smiled at her.

'C'n I have your autograph? My mum says you'll be famous one day and I should get it now . . .'

'Of course,' said Tina expansively.

She scribbled her name on the back of the cast list using her eye pencil. The girl thanked her and scuttled off, and Tina laughed at my expression.

'First time for everything,' she said.

'It won't be the last time you do that,' I said, truthfully.

'Look,' said Tina, 'school's got to be as good as you make it, right? I mean, this place isn't St Libby's, but we've got Miss Farrell, and she's made it all right for me this term. And that's all you can do at a place like this, ain't it? You find the thing, or the person that makes it all right, and you stick to them for your dear fucking life.

311

And, you want my opinion, FitzPatrick – which you never do, but you're getting it anyway – I think the one who makes it all right for you is Marky.'

'I know he likes me,' I said. 'But it's not the same as how it felt with Freddie.'

'Why *should* it be the same? What? Are you going to spend your whole life chasing after dancers? You'd better get over that. Get on with the maths. That's what you're good at.'

She shivered suddenly, and then burped.

''Scuse me,' she said. 'Someone brought in some cider. S'gone right to my head.'

'Cider?' I looked around, eyes searching for it.

'You don't need to drink,' she said, her eyes meeting mine. 'It don't suit you.' She pulled her school blouse on and started doing up the buttons. 'My dad's a drinker, actually,' she said.

'H-he is?'

'Yeah.' Tina looked into the mirror and pointed to a small red mark above her left eye. 'This is what you get if your dad's a drinker – scars. They're fucking dull, I tell you. They take up time. They distract you from the good things, make you behave stupid, tell lies for them. They take up space in your head, and you don't want that, FitzPatrick.' She looked at her face in the mirror. 'Really, you don't,' she whispered to her reflection.

'I didn't know about your dad,' I said. I felt shocked. I wasn't sure that I wanted to hear this from Tina.

'Why should you? I'm not about to go shouting about it all over the school. No one would care, anyway. And why should they? S'my problem if he hits me. His problem if he drinks. Marky Abbot's mum put him into care, first ten years of his life. Do you hear him talkin' about it?'

I shook my head.

'You've never really spoken to him about much, have you?'

'We talk about maths.'

312

'Well, maybe that's the best thing you can do. I mean, whatever gets you through the night, you know what I mean? At least, that's what *I* say.'

She cleared her throat and morphed into her Lady Bracknell again. 'I've said too much; it is most unbecoming.' She pulled an anorak around her shoulders. 'I must thank you for your kind words of support, my dear girl, and go and find my sister.'

'Tina Scott,' I said, my voice unsteady, '*my* dad's outside. He sat at the back with me. He thought you were good. I don't suppose you want to come along and say hello?'

She looked incredulous. 'Fuckin' 'ell! Your dad?' She pulled her blouse straight and squinted down at herself in the mirror. 'Too right I'd like to say hello. Give me a minute, will you?'

Get on with the maths. That's what you're good at. Rachel Porter had said almost exactly the same thing to me. I had tried to, but all the time there had been the distraction of him, and the all-consuming nature of first love.

When I arrived back at North Bridge, after Howard had suggested to Tina that she meet his great friend, Michael Whitehall, for a drink, I tipped every bottle that I had hidden in the house down the drain in the upstairs bathroom. As I was ridding myself of the final dregs of gin, Caspar appeared with his camera.

'Go away,' I said. 'This isn't for one of your albums.'

'No,' he agreed. 'It's for you, and you only. I'm going to stick the picture on the back of your door, to remind you that you did this. There's no turning back now, you know that, don't you?'

'And for you, too.' I said. 'No more dreaming of Nick.'

Caspar laughed. 'Oh, come on. I can't promise that.'

Returning to my bedroom, I flipped open my maths file, reading the notes that Mark had copied for me when Tina and I had dropped our trays and eaten tomato soup off the floor. Mark's handwriting was appalling, but his spelling was spot on, and there

313

was a joy in the way he wrote that I noticed for the first time that evening.

In all mathematics, it is worth remembering that sometimes the most obvious answers take longer to reach than we expect.

I picked up my pen, and started to write.

24

Miss Crewe

Something changed. I started to like myself again. I could feel it happening, gradually at first, then closer and closer, like a home-coming. I could see the future, not only the past, and I wasn't going to let that go again. I knew that Freddie Friday was good enough to go to New York, and I felt a quiet certainty that, once he was there, he would be embraced. There was something in the air over there that would fill the lungs of Freddie Friday with a purer kind of oxygen. He was ready to go. Marnie would take time to get over him, I thought – perhaps years. And yet, and yet . . . I felt certain that she was stronger than I had been at her age, despite the drinking and the uncertainty.

I was packing the last of my bags to leave for the summer break when I heard the sound of the doorbell ringing. I wished that I could shake off the unbelievable tiredness of the last few weeks. Every morning it got harder to open my eyes; it was as though I had been drugged. Now that Kelp had emptied for the holidays, it could be anyone – a cleaner who had lost her keys, a teacher needing to leave some books in my flat. It wasn't. It was Marnie. It had been raining; everything about her was soaked through. Briefly, I noted how odd it was to see her back at school, how her whole physicality had changed in the past few months, not just her haircut.

'Marnie! What are you doing here?'

'I had to come.'

She was looking older, much tougher, less the ingénue and more the wary, streetwise young woman that had always been lurking inside her. She was a Grit, I thought. Rachel Porter had always been right about that. Marnie had changed beyond measure in the short time that we had been with Freddie Friday. All of us had.

'Freddie's grandfather,' she said. 'He's dead.'

'Oh, God.'

'I hadn't spoken to Freddie since the day Brian Jones died. But I couldn't do it any longer. I couldn't just pretend nothing had ever happened. I telephoned him and he picked up the phone thinking I was the undertaker.'

'Christ,' I whispered. 'Freddie—'

'What's he going to do?' She was looking at me for answers, but I knew nothing.

'Where is he?'

'At home. We can't go there—'

'We need to take a taxi into Welwyn. Come in. I'll order it now.'

Marnie shivered, hovering by the front door in the flat. Her arms were bare and she was wearing thin, dirty white shoes through which the rain had soaked. I thought of Gene Kelly, and of Freddie's brother.

'Put this on,' I said, pulling a jersey out of my wardrobe for her.

'I don't think we should go,' she said again. 'He won't want us there.'

But I knew what I knew: he would always want us there, whether he said so or not.

'We'll push a note through his door,' I muttered.

I had imagined that the curtains would be closed, that we would drop the letter through the letter box and walk away, but when we arrived, Freddie was standing looking out of the window; it was a scene out of a play, the end of something that didn't turn out as happily as the audience had expected. When he saw us, he came to

316

the door and opened it. I could sense that Marnie wanted to step forward, to hold him. Who am I kidding? I did too. Neither of us moved. Freddie looked up and into my eyes.

'He's gone,' he said. 'I didn't get to say goodbye.'

His face crumpled. None of us needed to say anything, all we had to do was this. Just to exist for a few minutes, beside each other, the three of us, in a little group that represented something so much more than any of us knew how to explain rationally.

'I never wanted him to go,' said Freddie, leading us inside the house. He kept repeating it, over and over. He was tapping all the time. Michael was right there with him now, I thought.

'You know, I can't go now,' he said. 'I can *never* go. I can't leave her.'

I nodded, saying nothing. This single event, the death of an old man, shouldn't be enough to stop Freddie from breaking out. And yet I felt that it would be. All that fear that he had swiped away, all the potential that I had seen would be cramped by the power of guilt.

'You can't see anything straight now,' I said to him. 'Don't dismiss everything in this second, on this day. Just give it time. Don't think about it for now.'

'But it's all I ever thought about!' said Freddie. 'Every waking second! I didn't think about anything but getting out! If I had just listened to him a bit more, if I had given something back to him . . .'

After what he did to you? I wanted to shout. After all the times he broke you, then left you to stick yourself back together again? I said nothing.

'He wasn't well – he was an old man,' Freddie went on.

Marnie put her head between her hands.

'He worried about me,' said Freddie in a terse whisper. 'He just wanted me to stay still, but I never could. He . . . he hit me last night. It was so stupid. It was just something I said that he didn't like.'

317

'What did you say?'

Freddie touched a bruise on his eye; I hadn't noticed it before, hidden under the shadow of his hair.

'He asked me if I was going to marry you. I said to him that I wasn't. I said that I couldn't do that to you. He wanted to know why, so I told him.' He thumped his hand against his leg. 'I'm *sick* of it,' he said. 'And he knew I was sick of it.'

He looked at his face in the mirror, at the eye that was black now, that would turn blue and green, and then yellow, and then fade to nothing, so that no one would ever know what was underneath his skin.

'I don't want to lose the bruise,' he said, as though reading what I was thinking. 'I don't want it to go. When it goes, then he's really gone. He's gone . . .'

He started to tap again. He was swimming on his own, out there against the tide, and no one could rescue him. Not now, possibly not ever again. Everything that we had done to lift him away from all of this was closing in on him again.

We heard Linda's footsteps in the room upstairs.

'We should go,' I said.

'No,' said Freddie. 'Please.' He looked at us. 'Come up, won't you? Come and say hello to her. Tell her you're sorry or something.'

I didn't know whether he was simply afraid of being left alone, or whether there was truth in what he was saying. I nodded. Marnie and I followed him up the stairs, every step creaking.

She was sitting on the edge of her bed, wearing a blue-and-white dress, belted neatly, and a soft cloth hat in pale pink. She looked up when she saw us, without surprise, as though she had expected us to be there. So she was the woman that he lived with, that he wanted to protect, I thought. She looked like a doll, ready to be wrapped and put away for another day. I don't think I had ever seen someone so tiny.

'My wedding dress,' she said to us, nodding down at her outfit. 'This is what I wore when we married. It took him weeks to pay back what he borrowed for me to be able to wear this.'

'It's beautiful,' said Marnie. She crossed the room and knelt down in front of the old woman so that their eyes were almost level, and she took Linda's hands in hers. 'We're very sorry,' she said.

'He was difficult,' said Linda. 'But I was used to him, you see? He . . . he made sense to me. I wouldn't have been much without him. I was just a normal girl. Nothing very special. He was like a rocket! Just came into the room and everyone knew about it, didn't they, Fred?'

Freddie nodded.

She took the hat off and looked down at it, bending the folds in her thin little hands. Then she looked up, and held my eyes.

'I never liked it, you know,' she said. 'This hat.'

'You didn't?'

'No. Not a bit. I just wore it because *he* liked it.'

Marnie laughed softly. 'I wonder how often all of us wear things for other people, not ourselves.' She looked at me, then back at Linda. 'I think it's pretty.'

'You shall have it, then,' said Linda, holding it out to her. 'Go on. Take it. I don't want to see it again.'

'I can't—'

'Please,' she said.

Marnie took the hat and looked at it.

'Try it on,' said Linda, nodding.

Marnie looked uncomfortable, but placed the hat on her head and gave us a brief, embarrassed smile.

'Even looks silly on you,' said Linda.

Marnie peered at herself in the small mirror on top of the chest of drawers. 'Yes,' she agreed. 'It does, rather.'

'Why did you cut your hair, girl?'

'I wanted a change,' said Marnie.

'Change!' said Linda in disgust. 'All people talk about it change. There's this odd certainty in some folk that it's always a good thing. I liked things the way they were.'

'Did you?' Freddie asked her softly. 'Did you?'

Marnie looked at me, and I knew that we had to go.

Freddie walked halfway down the road with us, and then he turned back.

'She's proud of you,' I said to him. 'Sometimes you have to allow someone to let you go.'

I wasn't just talking about Linda, but about all of us: Marnie and Freddie and me, all holding on too tightly to something that we never properly understood at all.

25

Marnie

It wasn't easy to let go of him, but I knew that if I didn't then I would never move on, and I *wanted* to move on now; I could see my way out, where before all I had seen was him, and his hair and his eyes, the way that he moved when he danced. Now there was more than all of that. He asked me to go with him to the airport, and although my heart felt as though it might split in two, I said that I would go. What kind of a friend would I have been if I'd refused? Because that's what we were, Freddie Friday and me: *Friends*. Linda had taken him out for tea. Imagine – the first time that they had set foot outside together for food. She had told him that he had to go, and that she would be all right. But she asked me to drop in and see her one in a while. I said that I would visit her every week. I knew that we would do nothing but talk about Freddie, but there was comfort in that.

'I'll be back soon,' he said to me. 'You know I will.'

And I nodded, even though I knew that he wouldn't.

'I looked it up for you,' said Freddie suddenly. 'Stamina – I looked up where the word comes from.'

'What?'

'You know – that time with Miss Crewe and the Venn diagram with *Stamina* in the middle.'

'Oh, yes.'

321

'Well, it's from Latin. It's all connected to the Fates and their scissors.'

'It is?'

'Yeah. I wrote it down.'

He handed me a piece of paper. 'Just in case.'

'That's nice,' I said. 'I wouldn't have known.' I put the piece of paper into my pocket and felt it in my fingers.

When I got back from the airport, I took the bus into town and opened up the paper.

Stamina – from the Latin word Stamen, meaning thread. Derived from the threads spun by the Fates determining the length and course of our lives.

Funny, I had never seen his handwriting before. It was small, neat, ordered, careful – not like him at all. I turned the paper over and read the two words that he had written on the other side: *Gotta Dance*. He had drawn a heart next to these words, with an arrow through it, and I knew that meant he was sorry.

Crying on the bus was idiotic, but I couldn't stop. As we came into town, I looked over to the familiar sight of the factory, and next to it, round the station side, was that other place, where he had danced. It was colder outside than it had been all summer and, inside the factory, I knew that the new machines would soon be growling and pumping and packing, and no one in there would ever know that, for a short time in the summer term of 1969, the club room at the Wheat had been the most precious place on earth for me.

Freddie always danced, because he couldn't not dance, because it was part of his make-up, along with the fact that, even though he had loved me as best he could, I was a girl, so he could never hold me as close as I would have wanted him to. I stood, looking out from Hunters Bridge, watching people leaving the factory and walking home from work, some in groups of three or four, some quite alone. The sky beyond was big and white, but beyond that, what was there for me? For he had gone.

'Hey! Lovelace!'

Mark Abbot had his hands in the pockets of his denim jacket. I hadn't seen him out of school uniform before.

He nodded at me. 'I thought I might find you here.'

'I miss him.'

'I know you do. That's why I'm here. Come on.'

'How did you knew where I would be?'

'Simple maths,' he said. 'The pressure on one object pushing another in a certain direction. It's just good old force, Lovelace, nothing more.' Mark paused. 'All is number.'

'I don't think he's ever coming back,' I said. 'Once he's gone, he's gone.'

Mark put his arm around my shoulders, and I let him. I walked beside him, leaving the factory and the big white-grey sky behind us.

EPILOGUE

Miss Crewe

People have all kinds of theories about how the pregnancy was possible. They say that the woman throws out her eggs in a last-ditch attempt to reproduce. Some people say that, after what I'd been told, and all those years, it was a miracle. I say it was helping Freddie Friday, and letting go of Jo and of the past, and stepping forward instead of backwards for the first time in eighteen years. Alexander wanted to get married, but I said that we didn't have to do that. It wasn't that I didn't want to be with him forever; it was that I'd only just started liking my name again: Julie Crewe, dance teacher.

We called our daughter Rachel, because Marnie insisted that without Rachel Porter none of it would have happened. I always liked the name. It sounded strong to me.

Afterword

This story is partly set in the Shredded Wheat Factory, in Welwyn Garden City. The Shredded Wheat factory closed in 2005. The grade two listed building, with its huge silos, remains. At present, it stands derelict. While I have made every effort to stay true to the building, the town and its surroundings, I have taken the odd liberty. I should also mention that several real-life people enter these pages, in a purely fictitious state.

Bob Fosse was one of the world's greatest choreographers and dancers, and influenced everyone he came into contact with. He is considered to have been a huge influence on Michael Jackson's dancing style and choice of clothes — this is particularly apparent in relation to Fosse's role as the snake in *The Little Prince*. Throughout his life, he had always suffered from ill health — not helped by his love of cigarettes, drink and drugs. He died of a heart attack in September 1987, aged sixty.

Nick Drake never had any real success in his lifetime. He died on 25th November, 1974, aged twenty-six. His album *Five Leaves Left* is regularly voted one of the best of all time.

Acknowledgements

A big thank you to the following people who know a great deal more than me about all the important stuff: Susan Watt and all at Heron and Quercus, Elizabeth Sheinkman, Erin Calderwood (maths), Arthur Rollings (who worked at the Wheat and gave me hours of his time discussing how it used to be), Sandra Lee (who wrote down her memories of growing up in WGC), Donald Rice (who read early drafts and pretended not to be confused), Penelope Price (who deserves a medal for her copy-editing), Claire Conrad (legend) and the Janklow Gang and of course, my family.